SANDUSKY BURNING
by
BRYAN W. CONWAY

Sandusky Burning
Copyright © 2020 Bryan W. Conway.
All Rights Reserved.
ISBN: 979-8-9852648-7-6

In memory of Bonnie and Larry Conway

Prologue
Tuesday, June 23

Todd 1

1:05 a.m.

That damned railroad crossing got me again! Nobody was around, and on most nights, I could sneak across, maneuvering my Accord around the crossing arms. But when I pulled up, the red lights were flashing and the warning bells were clanging, so I stopped and shifted into park. Also, the train horn blasts were very loud when I rolled up, so I figured the train was getting close.

It had been raining on and off for hours but currently just drizzling lightly. I set the windshield-wiper cadence to swipe the window every five or six seconds, just to remove the accumulating mist.

One of the only advantages of working the late shift at the amusement park was that most of the city was asleep when I left. Usually there was no traffic; it was just the damned train that got me if my timing was bad.

I took out my cell and began scrolling as the train approached. Looking down at the screen, I was reminded that my park security uniform was wrinkled and stained, with big sweat rings under my arms. Being a heavier guy was tough when it came to wearing a black uniform in the summer. For most of my shift that night, I had been wearing a clear plastic rain poncho, which seemed to seal in the heat.

Another long horn blast. Then I heard sounds that were unfamiliar. Scraping noises with periodic cracking sounds. I scanned the tracks and didn't see anything unusual. I rolled down the passenger window a few inches to hear a little better.

The train engine whooshed by, causing my car to vibrate. The scraping and cracking noises got louder. I switched my phone to the camera app and started recording a video, capturing the freight cars passing by with a blur. The last car of the train was a few hundred feet away.

There were weird little white and yellow lights blinking behind the last car. I squinted and realized it wasn't actually lights, it was sparks. Freakin' sparks were spraying off the tracks!

The screeching noises became almost deafening. The last train cars were approaching the streetlights, and I finally saw what was making the noises and sparks. I gasped and dropped my phone, scrambling to find it among the empty fast-food bags and pop bottles.

A large gray camper was being dragged behind the train! Holy shit! It was one of those giant park models, more like a residential trailer than a portable camper. It was in tatters, sliding along on its side, sparks shooting out from where the siding was in contact with the tracks. It actually bounced along violently, sometimes as high as a foot off the ground, elevating and then being pulled back down by chains with a crash. It was like a giant, badly designed rectangular metal kite being whipped about.

How the fuck does an RV get chained to a freight train? Was this some sort of prank? Were there people inside?

The train kept rolling west. I watched as the sparks continued to fly, and then it was out of sight. I scanned the tracks and saw that small pieces of debris were scattered about. I stopped the video, switched to the phone app, and dialed 911.

Chapter 1
Tuesday, June 16

Brady 1

1:15 p.m.

In a rare moment when the wireless signal had a strong connection, there was a knock at the camper door. I sighed, reluctant to step away from my laptop, which had a five-bar signal for the first time that day.

I had been working from the kitchen table with just a pair of black gym shorts on, adhering to my summertime home-office dress code. One of the benefits of working remotely. I glanced at the clock at the bottom-right corner of my laptop screen: 1315 hours.

My habit of programming our household digital clocks to display military time always drove Marcy nuts. I figured it was useful for the kids to understand it. Not necessarily for the purpose of joining the military, but if they had a civilian job working with the military as I did. A lot of federal government work environments used military time.

It wasn't rocket science. People who struggled with understanding that 1315 hours equaled 1:15 p.m. were probably not deep thinkers.

The weather was sunny and warm, in the mid-seventies. Not quite warm enough to use the air conditioning, I had the windows and doors open and my shirt off. The interior of the RV was always a few degrees warmer than the outdoors in the summer, even with the large oak tree on our lot blocking portions of the sunlight throughout the afternoon.

Both exterior doors were on the right side of the RV, facing north. The front door was near the main cabin, with the back door allowing outside access to the small bathroom.

Maneuvering around the narrow kitchen table, I made my way to the main cabin at the front of the RV. I reached into the small closet on the right side of the room and found a yellow dry-fit T-shirt from a half-marathon I had run a few years ago. I went to the screen door and found Chuck standing on the bottom-front doorstep, leaning against the metal railing by the door.

Chuck was one of the more social employees at the campground. I guessed him to be in his late forties, a guy with a Harley-Davidson vibe, long brown hair kept in a ponytail beneath a black Harley baseball cap, bearded and tattooed. He was shorter than me, maybe five foot nine, and heavier by fifty pounds.

It wasn't that the other campground employees were necessarily antisocial, but there was a degree of indifference that manifested itself with working there. The pay was low, the hours long, and the work was often unpleasant. Emptying fire pits, cleaning restrooms, cleaning the shower houses, cleaning the cabins, picking up litter, etc.

Chuck was always in a pleasant mood, having a wave and a smile for everyone. He owned a Harley motorcycle of some sort, and there were mornings when he really enjoyed revving it loudly for five to ten minutes before taking off somewhere.

"Hey, dude," he said smiling, adjusting his sunglasses.

I disliked the overly familiar manner some used in a purely employee-customer relationship. The waiter who called me *champ*. The auto mechanic who called me *chief*. The campground employee who called me *dude*. It was a weird, passive-aggressive alpha-male play that never resonated with me.

"Hey," I said, putting on a pair of black flip-flops and stepping out to shake his hand. We shook, and I walked down onto the grass.

"Have a seat," I said, motioning toward the patio table, which was surrounded by six chairs. We went over and sat down.

The furniture was starting to show some wear. Originally our main patio furniture from our back deck at the house, we replaced it and brought the old set to the campground. The cream-color paint on the wrought iron was yellowing. The cloth backing on several of the chairs was wearing thin.

I had un-winterized my camper over a month earlier. It was a thirty-four-foot tow-behind RV, two years old, and fairly well loaded. While we called what we did "camping," it wasn't the variety of camping I had experienced in a tent growing up. The RV had indoor plumbing, electricity, central air, television, a refrigerator, a freezer, and a microwave. It was an efficiency apartment on wheels.

Buying it was my wife Marcy's idea. We had season passes for the nearby amusement park, Gravity Junction, which was about an hour away from our home in the suburbs of Cleveland. It was one of the most popular parks in the country, with dozens of nationally ranked rides that drew in visitors from across the region.

Instead of driving back and forth all summer, why not just camp ten minutes from the front gate? Neither of us had any experience with owning a camper, but how hard could it be?

We went to a local RV show, found a camper, and financed it. Next, we bought a black Chevy Silverado truck with the appropriate towing capacity to haul it.

The first summer, we went to several camping destinations in the region, and the process of transporting the RV was often stressful and frustrating. Hauling six thousand pounds on the highway was harrowing at times, especially when big eighteen-wheelers would come blowing by and the backdraft would seem to jerk the camper over into the next lane.

Maneuvering the RV onto a campsite was challenging and would take multiple tries to situate it properly within reach of the utility hookups. Backing up while towing an RV was counterintuitive; to back it up to the right you turned the steering wheel to the right, and vice versa. It took some getting used to.

The rental fee at a campsite included all the necessary utilities. There was a power box for electricity, a water faucet that connected to the camper with a hose, and sewage ports.

Most RVs had a propane gas system to power some appliances and provide backup power when an electrical hookup was unavailable. A set of two propane tanks were fastened to the front of the RV, concealed under a black, rounded, rectangular plastic hood.

Campgrounds typically offered cable for free. Not everyone utilized it, as some of the more expensive RVs rolled up and raised a satellite dish when they parked. Because there is no way you would want to camp for a few days without having five hundred channels available for viewing.

At some point over the past few decades, human beings became unable to exist without the smallest of conveniences. *God forbid you were forced to read a book or engage with your kids at a campground for a few days.*

I wasn't one to lecture on engagement. I was a typical technology-addicted parent who spent too much time staring at my cell phone in the presence of my kids. In some ways, it served to preserve my sanity by receiving communication from sources other than my spouse or children.

"Hot out today. Got anything to drink?" Chuck asked. He grabbed the bottom of his shirt and used it to wipe his face, revealing the pink-and-white skin of his large, hairy belly.

"Sure, what do you want?"

"Got a beer?"

"I do," I said as I walked over to the outdoor fridge. There was an exterior kitchen area along the right side of the camper that had a sink, cupboards, a propane-powered griddle, and a mini-fridge. It was accessible via a sliding panel that could be locked.

Reaching into the fridge, I grabbed a single can and put it on the counter. I perceived a judging look from him and reached in and grabbed another for myself. Although I was on the clock, it mattered little since my supervisor was sixty miles away.

I walked over and handed a can to him. We opened them with loud popping noises and drank long swigs, with perspiration dripping from our cans.

A yellow work cart passed by heading north, driven by a big black man in a campground uniform. Yellow hat, yellow polo, black shorts. The work cart was essentially a mini truck, with a bench seat in the front and a small truck bed in the back. It was towing a series of yellow open-top passenger cars, with open sides for entering and exiting. Each had the capacity for four passengers.

The first three cars had families in them; the next three were empty. It wound up and down the streets across the campground throughout the day. The kids seemed to love this. I didn't mind riding along. I got to just sit there with them and enjoy the ride instead of doing any number of camping chores or trying to corral the kids.

"So whatcha got goin' on today, Brady?" he asked as he

leaned back, with the two front legs of the chair coming off the ground a few inches.

"Working," I answered.

"Really, you can do a full day's work out here in your camper?"

"Yeah, as long as I have an internet connection, I can work from anywhere in the world. Which reminds me, can someone take a look at the Wi-Fi? It seems unstable at times, and my connection keeps getting dropped," I said.

"I think Travis needs to buy better routers or something. More campers are here, so it is stressin' the server," he said. "So, what is it you do? I think when we chatted last season you mentioned government work."

"Right, I still work for the government. In Cleveland," I said.

"So, you're some sorta government agent?" he asked, laughing. I laughed too.

"Nah, nothing that interesting. I just work on financial projects."

That interested him; he sat up a little straighter. "So, you have a clearance?" he replied. That question should have set off an alarm.

"Sure, all employees do," I said, hoping I could leave it at that. He nodded.

I worked at the Payroll Accounting and Finance (PAF) Agency, which serviced all defense financial transactions. I managed financial-systems projects and thus needed a security clearance. Revealing my clearance was something I had been directed over and over again not to disclose. *A security clearance was not something to be advertised*.

I had a top-secret clearance, not because I worked on ultra-sensitive government projects, but because I had access to restricted business and personal information. Working for a defense agency, I had a significant amount of information stored on everyone in the armed forces, defense civilians, contractors, and retirees, as well as acquisition data.

Holding a top-secret clearance in that context was much different than the public's perception of what that type of clearance permitted. A top-secret clearance allowed access to sensitive information which could pose a "grave threat" to national security. The "grave threat" label was laughable in my line of work.

Action movies about the CIA and FBI lead everyone to believe that having a clearance provided access to information on covert operations. In reality, it was all "need-to-know" information. If I didn't need to know that there was a particular CIA operative in Budapest engaging in counterespionage, then I wouldn't have access to that type of information, even though I had the right clearance.

"I suppose I know what you do for a living, Chuck. What do you do in the off-season?" I asked, eager to change the subject.

"Actually, I'm a union carpenter, but I'm on workers comp and not able to do that work at all right now. I fell off a ladder a few years ago and it fucked my back up. I need to have surgery. So, I do this under the table. I mostly ride around on that all day, so I don't aggravate my back," he said, motioning toward his golf cart.

A lot of the campers had golf carts to get around. I empathized with those like Chuck who had mobility issues, but that wasn't the case for most. They buzzed around on them because being forced to walk twenty to thirty yards from your camper to the pool or the clubhouse was too strenuous. Many invested substantial money into them, adding custom paint jobs and stereo systems.

Chuck's golf cart was one of those premium ones, light gray with orange flames blazing across the sides, and constantly playing music loudly. His musical tastes were consistently Hank Williams Jr., Lynyrd Skynyrd, Bad Company, and Bob Seger. Country, classic rock, and southern rock.

"Sorry to hear about your back," I said.

He shrugged. Chuck stared down at his beer can for a moment. Patting his shirt pocket, he found his pack of cigarettes. Pulling out the pack, he jerked his wrist several times until one popped free. He found his lighter in his pocket, lit it, and took a long drag. Leaning over, he held out the pack.

"No, thanks."

"Don't smoke?"

"No."

"Never have?"

"Not really. I smoked a few as a teen, that's about it."

"Smart. This is a waste of money," he said bitterly, as though someone was forcing him to smoke against his will. He coughed slightly as he exhaled.

"My parents both smoked, so I grew up in a cloud of secondhand smoke. I never enjoyed that," I said.

"I'm surprised, most kids end up smokin' when they grow up if their parents smoked. I was stealin' smokes from my old man all the time as a teen," he said. Chuck regarded the camper next door to me, exhaling a long puff of smoke.

It was a large, white, fifth-wheel model, probably thirty-eight feet long. A clean-cut guy in his thirties with Kentucky plates on his truck stayed there on weekends with his two young boys. We had nodded at each other a few times but never had a conversation.

"I was around smoke constantly until I left home at eighteen and joined the army. Up until that point, we all thought I had asthma; I could never run long distances without losing my breath and wheezing. When I got away from home and quit breathing all of that secondhand smoke, my asthma went away. It turns out my lungs were fine. I haven't had a problem catching my breath since," I said. *Particulars about my anti-smoking journey that you don't give a shit about.*

"Army, huh? Thank you for your service. I have flat feet. Otherwise, I was gonna join the marines," he said. I nodded.

I wasn't the type to self-aggrandize based on my modest military service, but I always disliked the "I almost joined" bullshit. It was a binary status, either you served or you didn't. You don't get credit for an *almost*. And I would have bet money there was nothing wrong with Chuck's feet.

"Did you finish that race?" Chuck asked, motioning with his cigarette hand toward my shirt. It was from a half-marathon I had completed several years earlier.

"Yeah," I replied, wondering what sort of follow-up was coming from a guy who didn't look like he could run 13.1 yards, let alone miles.

"Good for you! I only run if someone is chasing me!" he said with a laugh. I gave the dad joke a halfhearted courtesy laugh.

After sneaking a quick look at his big stomach, I couldn't help but feel that he should definitely consider running, regardless of whether or not he was being chased. Hell, at least walking part of the day instead of carting himself around on that ridiculous golf cart would be helpful. Then again, maybe his flat feet continued to plague him.

The back injury he mentioned could have been a factor. I experienced a brief moment of guilt about judging him without fully knowing his situation.

"Is the family comin' up?" Chuck asked.

I flinched a little before I caught myself. He noticed. I forced a fake smile. "Sure, soon," I said.

"So, why are you up by yourself?" Chuck asked bluntly.

I felt my face flush a little. I took a swig of my beer and wiped my mouth. *Drop by for the free beer, stay to inflict an interrogation.* "I'm working on an important project and needed a little uninterrupted time," I finally said.

"And look at me, over here interruptin' you! Do people interrupt you during the day when you are workin' from home when you are in Cleveland? Your kids are home for the summer, right?" he asked coolly, taking a toke from his cigarette and then a drink of beer.

I slouched back a little, realized I was slouching, and straightened my back. "They are. I do get interrupted by the kids during the summer when I work from home. I also have to work later into the evenings on this project, so I just don't have time to take care of the kids."

"Right, that is all on your wife now," he said, grinning widely.

I tried to match it but was falling short of mustering an actual grin. It felt like a grimace. I hid it with my beer as I took a drink, finishing the last swig. Chuck crushed his can lightly and placed it on the table in front of him. "Another?" I asked, wondering if my lack of sincerity was obvious.

"Sure, Brady! I'm on break," he laughed, winking at me.

Chuck's career at the campground appeared to be one long, continuous break.

I got up and walked to the fridge, retrieving two more cans. "What do you have goin' on the rest of the day?" I asked, hoping to permanently change the subject from my domestic situation.

"I have to take a look at all of the fire pits and shovel some out. A few trees need to be trimmed over on the south side. The usual shit." He popped open his can and took a swig. "Here's to drinking on the job!" he said loudly, leaning across and clicking his can against mine. He belched softly. I nodded and took a drink.

"The boss doesn't care, I take it?" I asked, gesturing toward my beer before taking a drink. He shook his head.

"Nah, day drinkin' is one of the fringe benefits! How are things on your lot here? Everything good?" he asked, looking around as if noticing my campsite for the first time.

"Sure, everything is fine."

"Need some firewood?"

"I think I have enough for tonight. I may drop by the office and buy a bundle."

"Don't bother. I will drop some off later when I make rounds. We cut down a few trees the other day."

"You don't have to do that, Chuck."

"No problem, I insist," he said, laughing. "Are you plannin' on being here through the weekend?"

"Yeah, I should be."

"So, you said your family is joinin' you?"

I paused a few seconds. *Why do you care?* "I'm not sure yet," I replied. The kids were potentially coming up. But I didn't feel the need to elaborate.

"Great! Until then, it is just us bachelors holdin' it down!"

"I didn't realize you were a bachelor. I thought you had some female company in your RV over there," I said.

Chuck laughed and shook his head. "Technically I am, no ring on this finger!" he said, holding up his left hand. "Sharon and I just hang out. I don't have time for no girlfriend."

I wondered if Sharon knew that. I recalled seeing the heavy woman with graying black hair going in and out of his camper at site 57, which was one street over and about five sites north of mine. He owned a StarCraft model with an aluminum-paneled exterior, about thirty feet long. It had definitely seen better days. I estimated by the antiquated aerodynamics of its design that it was built in the 1980s, as the modern ones were less angular and more rounded.

"If you are around later, I will drop by. I may be pullin' a double; the campground is short-staffed." He chugged the rest of his beer and put it down by the other empty.

"Great. I plan on working late, but maybe I can break free for a beer," I said. *Unless I was able to avoid it.*

"I may have a few friends out one night soon, probably in the next few days. We build a fire over at lot 21 after dark. I'll let you know; you can drop by and socialize. You live like a hermit over here!" he said as he stood up.

"Great!" I said, realizing I kept saying "great" over and over and how awkward it sounded. We shook hands, and he waddled over to his golf cart, settling in behind the wheel. He smiled, nodded at me, and took off.

I took a final swig off my can and tossed it in the garbage. Glancing at my watch, I noted it was 1410 hours. I had a few hours of work I should reasonably do, but drinking had sapped me of some of my motivation. Grabbing two more beers from the fridge, I brought them inside.

Chuck 1

2:35 p.m.

I t took every bit of self-control I had not to belch in his face as I left. *Uptight jerkoff.* I needed to play a game of cash poker with him. His face didn't hide a damn thing.

He had been stayin' at his camper alone for weeks. Last summer he was mostly up on weekends with his family. Family vacationers were a waste of time for Randy's side business interests. Solo male campers had potential. Brady had gone from the *family* category to *solo,* so he was worth keepin' an eye on.

Loopin' around Starling Street toward the office, I knew it would be easy to avoid Travis for the rest of the day since he was back supervisin' work at the tent sites. Asshole kept naggin' me about the fire pits and the trees, but why am I always the one doin' the hard labor? About time Patrick got his feet wet and did something besides ridin' around in a work cart chattin' up the female campers.

I drove to Cabin F at the southwest corner of the campground and let myself in. The cabins were all the same, fake wood siding painted light brown with dark-gray shingles on the roof. They were prefabbed and cheaply built but were in decent shape. Two bedrooms, furnished, and not a bad place to hide out and kill time, if I could stash my golf cart around back before anybody saw it. Definitely a lot better than the dump of an RV I lived in.

I lit a cigarette. These were nonsmokin' cabins, but fuck 'em.

The location of the cabins made them perfect for Randy to set up the side jobs. They were away from the seasonal campers, and the sites around the cabins were transient sites, so it wasn't unusual to see strangers comin' and goin'. The seasonals were nosy as hell; a lot of 'em just sat in lawn chairs all day watchin' other people.

I had been ignorin' my text messages while drinkin' with Brady but took a look as I sat on the couch, kickin' my feet up on the coffee table. My burner phone had a few. Viktor. Randy. My regular cell had texts, too, a bunch from Travis, the usual shit, "where are you?", "I need this or that done", "blah blah blah." A few from Sharon too. *Nag alert.*

I checked the time, and it was 2:40 p.m. It was unusual to get a text from Viktor before dinnertime.

Call me, ASAP.

Everything was hot with this guy; it was probably some cultural mix-up again. Dude had been in the States for months, and he still got confused by basic shit. I could hear that terrible Romanian accent in my head when I read his broken English texts.

I thought I heard Randy's motorcycle across the grounds. He had it ratcheted up to blast everyone's eardrums, a lot louder than mine. I wasn't complainin', it was a warnin' he was around.

Another message came in, Travis again. *Jesus.* I flicked my ash into the sink and ran the water. I peeked out the door before leavin', walkin' around back to my golf cart.

Patrick 1

4:00 p.m.

Calling it a security booth was a joke. At the beginning of the season, they had someone in the booth all day, but that happened less and less as the summer wore on.

The seasonal people were allowed access to the campground in late April to start setting up for the season. During the off season, the entrance was blocked by picnic tables that Travis would stack with a forklift.

Sure, you could still get in if you wanted to badly enough, but who wanted to rob any of these RVs? There was almost nothing of value. It was just a bunch of winterized RVs sitting empty from November through April. It was Ohio, so half of that time they were buried in snow. What could you possibly steal that would make it worth unstacking heavy picnic tables? Nothing.

It was only June, and they already stopped manning the booth full time. On Fridays, there was someone there to direct incoming weekend campers to the office, but by Sunday, nobody was around.

Security was random. Service was random. People who worked there didn't care about any of that after a week on the job. *Nobody Cares* should be the slogan sewn on the front pocket of our stupid yellow work shirts.

Sometimes security was needed. Campers routinely got wasted and raised hell past 11 p.m., well after the posted "quiet hours" began at 10 p.m., and nobody on staff did anything about it. People shooting off fireworks at 1 a.m., revving their motorbikes, or generally just being loud.

Travis didn't care. A lot of his employees were also campers, so why bother complaining? Who was going to break up the disturbance? Chuck? Right, he was most likely one of the drunks causing the disturbance.

I played it a lot straighter my first year on the job. Since I was the only Latino guy, I walked a straight line. I introduced myself as

Patrick, although my real name is Patricio. Patrick was better for relating to Anglos and applying for jobs than Patricio.

When I turned in applications with the name "Patrick Correa", I actually got interviews. I sounded white on the phone. When I showed up brown, I had disappointed a few employers, but also gotten the job a few times with a good interview.

My dad barely spoke English, but my mom was lily white, so I was able to communicate good in either world. If I was at a day-labor site, I could banter with the Hispanic guys. If I was working around Anglos, I could speak without a Spanish accent. It was about picking the right culture for the right situation.

I had black friends who did that all the time. They were perfectly capable of sounding educated but chose not to if there was an advantage to speaking broken English. I have heard college-educated blacks do it. They want to be "down," so they pretended to regress. Seemed like some phony shit, but I did it, so I couldn't judge.

I passed by Chuck on my work cart as we drove by the basketball courts. He motioned with his cigarette hand for me to pull over, a weird waving motion he did without looking directly at me. I backed up until I was alongside him. This area of the campground was quiet; only a few lots were occupied.

"Hey, Chuck," I said. Chuck ignored me, looking off to the side and taking a drag on his cigarette.

"Where have you been, dude?" he asked angrily.

"At security. I'm heading back to see what Travis needs in the back."

"Tell Travis I'm checkin' on the electrical box at site 66."

"Who called that in? There hasn't been no one camping there," I said.

He glared at me. "From the last time someone was there. I'm followin' up," he said, blowing out a puff of smoke.

He drove off, and I kept heading toward the back. I could see Travis from a distance. He was wearing his usual black T-shirt and black shorts, black shoes, black socks, and a black hat. His long, black hair spilled everywhere over his big, round back and shoulders. He was an all-around big guy, offensive lineman big—if an offensive lineman had let himself go for a few years. But just a high-school-caliber lineman, he wasn't that tall. I pulled up to him as he stood by a fallen tree, staring down at his cell phone.

Travis 1

4:30 p.m.

Still no response from that waste of air Chuck. I could have guessed at which of the multiple hiding spots he was at, but I didn't have time to play hide-and-go-seek with him.

If it were up to me, I would fire his ass. I could have done it a dozen times for cause. But I was told to keep him by Randy. I didn't want to think about what would happen if I fired him without Randy's approval.

I walked over to Patrick as he pulled up on the work cart. I had a few trees taken down, and the wood needed to be moved over to the north end, near the trail to be stacked. It was an exercise in futility, as campers would help themselves to all of the wood within a few days. Half the shit would be behind Chuck's camper at some point, no doubt.

"Hey, Patrick, would you mind stacking this along the trail?" I asked. He nodded and pulled up closer to the pile.

"Who is on security?" Patrick asked.

"Nobody. I will man it for a while," I said. The security booth was generally a waste of resources. I was always juggling between having a security presence and better utilizing my people. "Have you seen Chuck?"

"Yeah, just passed him, he is on his way to 66 to take a look at the electrical box," Patrick said as he started stacking the wood in the back of his cart.

Patrick didn't look very strong. He was about five-foot-nine with an average build, but he never had a problem with work that involved heavy lifting. I was trying to recall how old he was from his application but couldn't. He had a shaved head and some preteen-looking facial hair, peach fuzz above his lip and on his chin. I thought he was around thirty, but it was hard to tell with Mexicans.

"66? Something is wrong with 66?" I asked, irritated. Patrick shrugged. "I have about fifty things I need addressed out here today, and Chuck is out making shit up to avoid real work. Unbeliev-able."

By unbelievable, I meant totally believable.

Mike 1

6:45 p.m.

was standing at the sink in my RV when I saw the flamboyant golf cart pulling up. Big bad flames along the side; he must be a rebel.

I had actually heard the music first and then saw the pudgy, long-haired white guy with the cigarette in his mouth pull up to 66. Was that Grand Funk Railroad? What year was it, 1974? Better than boy-band music, for sure.

The guy began fiddling around with the electrical box. It appeared that he wasn't really doing anything. It was like he was messing with it because he thought someone may be watching him, and he wanted to be able to claim he fixed a problem.

Odd. But not entirely surprising. If you spend enough time at these campgrounds, you began to understand the labor dynamics.

Campgrounds were only open for part of the year up north. Therefore, you got temporary seasonal help. Teens, immigrants, and general slackers who needed some sort of income but didn't care to work *too* hard at earning it. The kids who were home from college would have been good hires, but they all chose to work at Gravity Junction, since the pay was better.

It was easier for shady people to work at the campground because managers didn't bother with expensive criminal background checks. Otherwise, half of the clowns on the payroll would have been disqualified. That was disturbing, given these campgrounds were marketed as "family-friendly" places.

I had been staying in Ohio at the Sandusky Shores campground for a few weeks and had been making all kinds of observations. I called it being observant; others may call it being nosy.

Twenty years in the army will make you an observant person. My outstanding observational capabilities were one of the many talents that advanced me from a private to a sergeant first class very rapidly. But then I hit a wall.

Sergeant first class wasn't a bad rank. It was a career rank, but it wasn't spectacular.

I stalled at E-7 because I had squandered several critical years of upward mobility floundering in a state of stagnation. I should have been seeking more rigorous leadership opportunities and competing for developmental schools to make myself promotable. But those were the years that things fell apart with my wife, Kelly. The hard-drinking years, the years when things got blurry. I was lucky to keep my career together satisfactorily enough to make it to retirement, let alone worrying about climbing the career ladder.

So many regrets. Maintaining my sanity each day required that I just focus on what went well for me and hope the negatives would eventually fade away. *But they never seemed to.*

I was born on a military base in Italy but was primarily raised in the US south. There were times throughout my army career when I played up the whole "black country boy from Georgia" persona, but in reality, while I was southern, I was not *country*.

I spent my childhood in the suburbs of Atlanta and had a similar upbringing to most suburban kids throughout the country, southern, black, or otherwise. Maybe we did hunt and fish more than kids in other regions, but then we returned to our middle-class neighborhoods with houses on quarter-acre lots in the small town of Smyrna.

If it was to my advantage, I could pour on the southern. I could drop *y'alls* with the best of them, chew tobacco, and knew the lyrics to most country songs. Most of my black friends preferred rhythm-and-blues or rap, but I had always favored country. I could blame that on having a white father from the south.

My dialect was fluid. If I was around northerners, I could strip my accent down to nothing, which was what northern accents were, the absence of an accent. If I was around blacks, I could adjust to a more urban way of speaking. Know your audience.

Growing up, I always knew I would be a soldier. My dad was a soldier, and so that was what I wanted to be. I didn't have a lot of other options following high school, having been a fairly poor student. I knew I was joining the army and didn't try particularly hard. The army didn't care if I got a C in English or math, as long as I had a high school diploma. I didn't seriously entertain the thought of attending college, and I never applied.

My father was pleased with my decision to enlist; my mother, less so. She took me aside several times before I left and reminded me I could live at home and go to a junior college for a few semesters and establish a good GPA. Then, I could transfer to the University of Georgia or Georgia Tech. But my dad would have hit the roof if I backed out of my enlistment contract.

He was a legit country boy who escaped poverty in rural Georgia by joining the army. Growing up in a household of six siblings with an alcoholic father who couldn't hold a job, there was never enough to eat. The first time he saw a doctor or dentist was in the army. He would need those medical benefits throughout his enlistment for a wide range of issues, ranging from having pieces of shrapnel extracted from his back in Vietnam to having a compound leg fracture set following a skydiving accident in Alabama.

My childhood was so much easier by comparison. There was the stress of moving a few times when I was very young, while my dad was wrapping up his military career, but we never had to worry where our next meal was coming from.

My father was a hard man, and he had to be. In the 1970s, when he married my mother; mixed couples had a rough time. Especially in the south.

I was an only child. My parents had me in their late thirties, when, by some miracle, I was conceived despite the fact that my mom was told she could never have kids after being injured in a car accident as a teenager. I was only five years old when my dad retired and moved back to Georgia, so I had little recollection of my army brat days.

I had it better than most dark kids in the south, entirely because of my dad. I was generally allowed to fight my own battles, but if an adult was mistreating me, there was a visit from Sergeant Clemmons. And it wouldn't be pleasant. The stone-faced combat veteran got his point across by any means necessary, and even the most racist of rednecks thought twice about attracting his attention.

One of the greatest lessons he taught me was that flaws are individual traits, not cultural norms. He would not accept excuses from me merely because my skin happened to be darker. He had high expectations of me as a *human being.*

There were some rough moments growing up, and many of those involved being mistreated for being black. But I never allowed myself to believe I was a victim. I was raised to have morals and character, and that allowed me to persist through the tough times in my childhood.

My mom was also an army brat. Her dad retired in the Midwest, where she met my dad at Fort Riley, Kansas. Although she never went to college, she came across as educated, intelligent, and well-spoken. She worked clerical civilian jobs at the various bases where my dad was stationed throughout the years.

Although she knew my enlistment was inevitable, she broke down and cried when we said our goodbyes at the Greyhound station in downtown Atlanta. It was only a short bus ride from Atlanta to Columbus, where I would then be transported to nearby Fort Benning for basic training.

There was a fair amount of racism in the army, but it was much less prevalent than in general society. Affirmative action was firmly rooted in the military by the time I joined, so promotions and other preferences were afforded to minorities across the board.

Basic training was the great equalizer. Boys were mixed together from different races, regions, subcultures, and economic backgrounds. We discovered we weren't all that much different in most respects.

During my first ten years in the army, everything came easily to me. I was physically fit, highly teachable, easy to get along with, and did what was asked of me. I volunteered for every school I could and found my way to the Airborne, Ranger, and Pathfinder schools.

I was even a drill sergeant for a few years. I didn't fit the stereotype of a drill sergeant, as I wasn't brash, loud, or aggressive. That made me stand out in a positive way. Sure, there were times when the job required that I rant and scream a bit, but comparatively, I was level-headed. And the drill sergeant hat was pretty cool; there were times I wished I had saved mine for laughs.

I met a nice girl named Kelly while stationed at Fort Carson,

Colorado, and we got married. We had two kids, a son, Mike Jr., and a daughter, Sadie. Life was good.

I was in the right place at the right time with the right skills when the 9/11 attacks happened in 2001. As a staff sergeant with all kinds of credentials, I found myself in Iraq with my Ranger unit.

I did a few tours there and a few more in Afghanistan. It was tough on the family, but we made it through.

I survived combat with only a few scratches. The closest call was while traveling in a Humvee in Fallujah in a convoy directly behind a truck that ran over an improvised explosive device. A soldier in that vehicle died, and another lost his legs. It would have been me rolling over that bomb if our vehicles happened to be sequenced differently that morning.

After all these schools and deployments, my Class A dress uniform was pretty damn colorful, with a lot of patches and ribbons. I had the right resumé to keep advancing. I was sergeant major material, maybe Pentagon material.

Everything began to unravel after my daughter died. It was sudden and unexpected. It was especially devastating because it was my fault.

My resilience was what got me through life during the challenging times, and in a moment, it disappeared. I couldn't be there for Kelly. I couldn't be there for Mike Jr. I wasn't there for myself. I faded away and never really returned.

It was only the momentum of my early years in the army that allowed me to remain in the service far beyond my usefulness. I rotated out of the forward infantry units and received main post assignments. During my final enlistment contract, I was basically just a supply sergeant. I received mercy waivers from sympathetic commanders for PT tests and rifle marksmanship requalification.

I lived on post in the barracks with the junior enlisted. Although I was given the courtesy of having my own room, beyond that, I was essentially another private.

Except I was outdrinking the lower enlisted. I was a solitary drunk, and so when I was into the bottle, I remained in my room. People suspected I had a problem, but there was no real evidence

I had a problem. As long as I was subtle about bringing the full bottles in and getting rid of the empties while staying off the radar of my leadership, no one was going to confront me about it.

I was a moderate drinker before my daughter died. Going out and tying one on with the boys would happen here and there, but I was never a daily drinker. I devolved into being a daily drinker. It took all my willpower not to drink while in uniform, but the moment I was on my own time, the alcohol began to flow. It was the only way to numb my despair.

My career ended where it began, at Fort Benning. With my twenty-year service date approaching, the first sergeant called me into his office and laid out my options: retire immediately or the process would be set into motion to discharge me for failing to meet basic standards.

On my last day, I loaded up everything I owned into the back of my little green Chevy S-10. It had a lockable bed cover so no one would be tempted to steal my worthless possessions. After twenty years of service, I wasn't leaving with much more than I had arrived with as a teenager.

I left the fort and drove north on I-85 without a destination in mind. I had a modest military pension coming, but no savings and no civilian skills that would earn me more than minimum wage. At thirty-nine years old, and with potentially another thirty-nine plus years to live, I was without use or purpose.

I drove through Atlanta and continued north. My parents were both dead. I had no siblings. I hadn't communicated with my childhood friends in decades. What would be the point of returning "home"?

I had also lost touch with my army buddies. At one time, my army friends were my family. Now I didn't even know where to find them. Not that I was going to try.

When I pulled off for gas near the Tennessee border, I passed by a little dealership with used cars and RVs for sale. Intrigued, I drove over and took a look at the RVs.

The salesman came over and chatted me up. He was a good ole boy and condescending at first. I was just a dumb black, driving a junky little truck that he could take advantage of. His respect level increased when I mentioned I was active-duty army. I was still in the military, *technically*. I was able to take my unused leave in advance of being discharged, so I was on "terminal leave."

As far as anyone knew, I was still fully employed by Uncle Sam. The salesman ran a credit check, and I was able to get a line of credit for ten thousand dollars. A beat-up twenty-seven-foot aluminum Airstream RV was soon mine.

The dealership had a supply store, and I bought most of the RV supplies the salesman recommended, while their service department installed a hitch kit on my truck. A short time later, I was towing it out of the lot.

I found a campground along the highway a few hours north, paid the lot fee for a week, and set up. There was a Walmart nearby, and I picked up groceries and the general supplies I would need. Blankets, pillows, linens, a lawn chair, tools, and a toolbox. I also bought a cheap mountain bike and a bike rack that fastened to the back of the RV.

There was a county liquor store down the street from Walmart. I bought a bottle of vodka, a bottle of whiskey, a two-liter of tonic water, a two-liter of Coke, plastic cups, and a bag of ice.

On my way back, I stopped at the campground office and bought a bundle of firewood. I made myself a turkey, cheese, and mayonnaise sandwich on white bread, with Doritos and a pickle on the side. I also made myself a very stiff Jack and Coke to wash down my first dinner as a camper.

I assessed my financial situation. My current expenses were the RV payment, truck and RV insurance, campsite fees, fuel, food, and drink. This was balanced against my last active-duty paycheck and future pension payments. I owned the truck, and the camper payment would go away in five years. This was sustainable indefinitely.

My pension checks would be automatically deposited into my bank account, so I didn't need a permanent address to receive funds. I could be totally transient and still get paid regularly.

This was the kind of freedom and anonymity I needed years earlier when my life had gone sideways. I had found escape in the bottle when I lost my family, but now I was capable of being physically secluded in my own world whenever I wanted to be.

As tough and resilient as I was perceived to be, as established by all the military patches and medals I earned throughout my career, I lacked emotional resilience. I had folded after the first major serving of personal adversity in my life. Sitting beside my first campfire as a retiree, none of that mattered. The army was out of my life. My ex-wife, son, and deceased daughter were out of my life. I only remained in my life because I couldn't physically walk away from *myself*.

Five years had passed since I was discharged from the army. Driving the same truck and living in the same RV, I had traveled a lot of miles and picked up a lot of camping experience along the way. I had stayed at hundreds of campgrounds, migrating back and forth to different regions of the country according to the season.

The Midwest in the early spring had the best camping. I loved the trees. It was amazing how they all transformed so quickly from skeletal at the end of winter to completely green by late spring. The weather was great, and the bugs, snakes, and rodents were generally out in much smaller numbers than in the south.

I camped across Pennsylvania, Ohio, Michigan, Indiana, Illinois, and Wisconsin in May and stayed around that region until late September. Then I would move slowly southward, sometimes heading a little westward. I wanted to head to the West Coast at some point and camp along the ocean in California and the Pacific Northwest, but I hadn't made it there yet.

People were generally nice and tolerant at the campgrounds. A middle-aged black man camping by himself definitely concerned some people. A lone male traveler of any race was always a little unsettling. Although I received a few glares from time to time, most of my fellow campers seemed fine coexisting with me.

Colorado was occasionally on my mind. That was where Kelly and Mike Jr. likely were. Her parents were still there, assuming they were still alive. But I could never work up the courage to reengage.

I had the same general daily routine. Each morning, I woke up with some degree of a hangover, depending on how deep into the bottle I was the night prior. I would have breakfast according to what my stomach could handle and usually ate outside in my lawn chair. If there was a chill in the air, I built a fire.

Sometimes I would walk or ride my bike to the campground clubhouse and get a newspaper. My cell was a basic flip phone without data, and I didn't own a computer, so I got my news the old-fashioned way. Aside from the newspaper, I also listened to local radio here and there. After breakfast, I would spend an hour or two maintaining the camper.

I took a short nap each day to help recover from my hangover. If things were real bad, I would sweeten my morning coffee with a few splashes of whiskey to take the edge off.

Lunch and dinner were random. I might explore the area and find a diner or cheap Mexican cantina to eat at. Otherwise, I would make a sandwich or cook a burger on the grill. At dusk, I would build a fire and have a few drinks. Some nights I remembered going off to bed, other nights I didn't.

These five years hadn't changed me too much physically. I probably gained ten pounds. My fitness level had decreased, but maybe some of the walking and cycling kept me from slipping too far.

I stepped away from my RV window and walked to my small bathroom. After I splashed water onto my face, I took a look at myself in the mirror. I had aged a bit in the past five years. Most of my dark hair was still present, cut short enough to be within military regulations. My hairline had crept back, and gray was starting to appear at my temples.

My brown eyes seemed to have faded a shade, but that was probably just my imagination. I had crow's feet, small black bags under my eyes, and the skin from underneath my chin was a little too loose. No one had ever accused me of being handsome, but I had always been considered average looking, at worst.

I went back and gazed out the window again. Being in the military for so many years made me feel as though I could read people. A new soldier would arrive at the unit, and after observing him for a short time, I could get a feel for who he was. Sure, I was wrong occasionally, but for the most part, I was effective at sizing people up.

Looking at this fat Harley guy fiddling around with the electrical box at lot 66, I was able to conclude a few things. He was a scammer. He was lazy. He was shifty. He didn't know what he was doing. What could he possibly tell by staring at an electrical box? He was flicking the breaker switches back and forth, but since nothing was plugged in, how was that helpful? The guy was just killing time.

He turned around and caught me staring at him. I had the irrational urge to duck but didn't. He faked a smile and waved. I faked a smile and waved back.

At least I thought I smiled. Since I rarely smiled, I was never sure what the expression on my face was when I tried to feign friendliness. My expression was generally one of a soldier in formation, entirely neutral.

I figured I needed to go outside and talk to him before he showed up at my camper door. There were liquor bottles on the kitchen table that I didn't want this guy to see.

I had also been cleaning my Beretta M9 and had it laying out on a cloth by the bottles. Campground policies usually forbade firearms, and I didn't need a hassle over it with this guy. I walked out the door and met him as he arrived.

"I'm Chuck," he said as he walked up, extending his hand.

"Mike," I responded, shaking it.

"Wow, this thing is a beauty! What year is it?" he asked, stepping back as he glanced up and down the Airstream.

"1974."

"Been out here a few weeks, huh?" he asked. His hand twitched to his shirt pocket where his smokes were, but he didn't go for the pack.

"Yeah, a few weeks," I said.

"Where are you from?" Chuck asked. "I see you got Georgia plates on your S-10."

"From Atlanta."

"Here by yourself?"

"All by myself."

"So, what brings you to Sandusky Shores?"

"I have some family in the area," I said. I wasn't sure why I lied, other than as a push-back to being prodded with questions by this stranger.

"Really, where at?" Chuck asked.

I paused and surveyed the street. A giant motorhome rolled slowly north, towing a white Land Rover behind it. Of course, it was driven by an older guy with white hair. People who owned extravagant toys had money to burn, and those with money to burn were generally not youthful.

"More toward Cleveland," I said.

"So, why would you stay in Sandusky, an hour away?" Chuck asked, smiling. He squinted a little as he sized up my campsite again.

"I didn't have any interest in camping in Cleveland, with the Cuyahoga River burning and all. It didn't seem safe," I said without cracking a smile. He stared at me with a blank look on his face for a few seconds then started laughing.

"Ha ha, right. That happened in the late 1960s. I think they got that under control," he said.

"I'm not taking any chances. Anyway, this area is nice. It has a resort town feel to it, near Gravity Junction and the islands," I stated. He touched his cigarette pocket again.

"Why don't you just have one?" I asked.

"One what?"

"A cigarette. You keep touching your pocket there. I don't mind," I said, folding my arms. I had smoked at various times during my military career but had kicked the habit years ago.

"Nah, I'm good."

"I used to like a smoke when I drank back in the day too," I said.

"Except I'm not drinking," he said with a smile.

"That wasn't you over at lot 31 drinking a few hours ago?" I asked.

"You caught me, a little bit of a liquid lunch," he said, raising his hands up in an *I surrender* pose and laughing nervously.

"No harm in that," I said, showing off my fake smile again. "What is it you are looking at over there at 66, some sort of electrical issue?"

"Yeah. The camper from last week said the fuse kept popping," Chuck said as he walked back toward his golf cart.

"Let me know if you need a hand. I know a little about electrical," I said.

"I'm good, but thanks," he said as he turned the key. He waved without looking at me, speeding off north toward the dumpster.

It seemed like a good time for a drink. Who was I to judge the guy for having a few beers at lunch? It was petty but getting interrogated about my personal business annoyed me. I went back into my RV.

I wasn't intentionally surveilling lot 31, but I had a direct view of it if I stood in the right corner of my lot. The guy in 31 didn't look like he belonged in the company of a guy like Chuck. He was too clean-cut; there was a definite square look to him.

His camper was newer and well kept. But why no wife or kids at a seasonal lot? He didn't have the look of some solo dirtbag loitering at a campground. Then again, I could reasonably be mistaken for a solo dirtbag loitering at a campground.

Across the street, the camper door at site 51 opened, and a man stepped out, holding a big, colorful energy drink can. I had been under the assumption he was there by himself until I saw a woman walking out of his dump of an RV with a basket of laundry a week ago. They looked like the type of people who lived at a campground by necessity rather than for recreation. She appeared to be malnourished, skin and bones, with reddish-brown hair and freckles, wearing black yoga pants, a white tank top, and flip-flops.

The guy had thick, dark hair, cut into something resembling the Beatles' early mop-top cuts, but a little longer. He usually wore a backward baseball cap, mirrored tea shade sunglasses, shoddy clothes, and tennis shoes. He always appeared like he just woke up.

The few times we crossed paths, his eyes had the distant look of someone who got high regularly. I saw him chatting with Chuck here and there; maybe there was a drug dealer/user relationship. I overheard he was a construction worker and hoped he wasn't operating heavy machinery while under the influence.

As I thought about it, site 15 also had a solo camper as well.

The site across from the shower house and down a few lots. The guy generally wore a Gravity Junction uniform and had a foreign look to him. Some sort of Eastern European vibe. He reminded me of some of the guys I encountered while deployed to Bosnia. Super pale and gangly. He constantly had a cigarette dangling from his mouth.

I heard Gravity Junction recruited internationally, so I guessed this guy got a visa to work for the summer and was getting a big helping of Americana at the amusement park. The tacky, overweight, loud, often drunk parkgoers probably left a lasting impression on these foreign workers.

I heard a thundering in the distance and recognized the motorcycle of the Euro guy from site 15. I thought it was a Yamaha Virago, one of the bigger models. My commanding officer rode a similar bike at my last unit.

You could hear it from across the campground, but like most bikers, I guess he didn't mind the attention. He drove it down Starling a little too fast, and as he passed the gazebo structure in front of site 12, a woman's shrill voice boomed, yelling at him to slow down.

The owner of that voice was a short, round, thirty-something-year-old, wearing flip-flops, a bikini top, and cutoff shorts that revealed way too much pale skin. Her dark-brown hair was pulled back in a ponytail, wearing dark sunglasses with white rims, her makeup-less, pockmarked face contorted into a snarl. It wasn't the first time she cracked down on him, along with several other bikers and car drivers. I figured she corrected violators at a rate of one or two per day. The campground's unofficial audio speed bump.

There was usually a small crowd gathered by that gazebo. I assumed its construction was a collective effort, where several families pitched in and built it on the cement pad at site 12. It was a decent-sized wooden structure, a square that was ten feet wide on each side.

The back part was open, with bar tops built on the other three sides. There were various decorations, including large Ohio State and Notre Dame flags and several signs:

If you wanted to stay sober, why'd you come over?
Home is where we park it!
Today's soup: whiskey with ice croutons.
Happy camper!
If you are looking for a sign that you should have a glass of
wine, this is it!

Tiki torch sconces were built into each corner post, and track lights ran along the outside just beneath the roof, so it was fairly well lit at night. So were most of the occupants. There were usually drinkers sitting on barstools placed along the bar, morning, noon, and night.

The Euro guy pulled into the lot and got off his bike. There wasn't a helmet law in Ohio, so his only safety equipment was a pair of wraparound sunglasses. His camper was small compared to most seasonals, maybe twenty feet long, a white StarCraft model from the 1990s. It was curious that he lived at the campground, being a foreign worker and all. I assumed room and board was part of the amusement park compensation package.

He lit a cigarette as he walked up to the front door. Long, gaunt face, dark hair thinning in the front with a narrow widow's peak. Wrinkles around his eyes and mouth, but probably only in his early thirties, prematurely aging from vodka and cigs. He turned and glared at the woman who yelled at him and went in his camper.

Viktor 1

7:00 p.m.

"Shut up, big-mouthed tramp," I mumbled to myself. I did not speed. Well, I did not know for sure, sometimes the miles and kilometers mixed me up. But if I did, I did not speed badly. Three times she has screamed at me, this woman. She needed a punch to shut that mouth.

The idiots at lots 10 to 13 always watched me. Watched everyone who passed by. There was no RV at 12, they built a stupid wooden *chiosc* where they all sit on their big asses all day and drink beer. And let their kids run wild and ride bikes in traffic. One day, one of these little shits was going to *be* a speed bump. They sit there with sour looks on their faces when I go by like I'm the only one on a motorbike in this campground.

I unlocked my camper and went in. It was hot and smelled of *beție* ... booze, dirty laundry, a full wastewater tank, and two-days-old pizza. I heard something moving back in the bunk area. I still had mice and bugs. Until I did something, they were not going away, but I had no time. A mouse chewed some of my blankets and shit in little piles in the bedroom.

A bottle of Stolichnaya was where I left it on the kitchen counter. I looked for a cup, found a used red plastic one in the sink, and rinsed it. The water pooled in the sink because the gray water tank needed to be *golit* ... emptied.

I poured a shot and drank it quickly. I poured another. The smell was too bad, and it was too hot inside the RV, so I walked outside with the cup. Before I would bring the bottle out, but Chuck told me to be careful about drinking vodka straight from the bottle outside. It may upset my fat neighbors.

I sat in the lawn chair I found by the dumpster. A good lawn chair, it was a little dirty and the bottom sagged. I would rinse it when I had time.

I leaned back and looked down at the stupid uniform I wore. A blue polo with the Gravity Junction logo and a name tag: *Viktor,*

Romania.

Nobody at the park cared about Romania. Nobody asked about Romania. People from Colombia and Argentina got other *Spaniolă* speakers to talk to them. Even the *Rusi* and *Polonezi* got interest. Not Viktor, no one knew what to think of Romania. No American could find it on the map.

One tourist asked me what language they speak in Romania. *Chinese, you dumb shit.* America is supposed to be educated, yet they know nothing.

The rest of the uniform was khaki pants, black socks, black sneakers. I went back inside and changed, putting on a pair of gym shorts and a white Gravity Junction T-shirt I found in the laundry pile. Stupid cartoon dog by the logo. I threw the uniform in the pile. It had no stains, so I would wear it again.

I was told I was lucky to be at the campground and not in the Gravity Junction employee wing at Cloverleaf. Rodents and cock- roaches worse than *București*. No one will complain because they are foreign. What are they going to do, go home? Are you going to walk from Sandusky to Columbia or Croatia? *Good luck.*

Gravity Junction, the biggest park company in the country, puts foreign workers in the ghetto by the dirty trailer park and dirty campground. Some of these workers never see anything but the stupid park and ghetto for the season. This is America to them.

I drank again, and the heat from vodka in my stomach began to calm me. Spending ten hours in the park did nothing but annoy. Spending ten minutes in the park would annoy. Stupid adults, stu- pid kids, stupid questions asked. Stupid bosses, stupid coworkers. *All stupid.*

Then I come back to this stupid campground. Fat, lazy people riding everywhere on motor carts. Get your big butt off the cart and walk.

I looked at my watch; it was 1915 hours. Forty-five minutes until the meeting. I had to be at the Taj on time, or Mr. Randy would have a goat. There was no excuse for being late. I was just two sites away.

Calling the trailer the "Taj" was stupid. It had to be a name made up by Chuck. The RV was good, but to *comparație* it to the

Taj Mahal was the usual American *aroganţă*.

Mr. Randy was the American dream guy. By a campfire at the Taj late one night, he told me his story, how he started from nothing and built businesses and bought land. His key to it all was knowing the tourist *cultură* and to *pârghie* … leverage that to find new *oportunităţi*.

The business he was known for by the locals was his bowling alley. Fat people throwing balls down the lanes and drinking pitchers of bad beer. Everywhere in the US, they loved watery beer. Bud, Coors, Miller. All the same. Blue Moon my ass. Squeezing oranges in the beer? What I would give for a Timisoreana. I should have brought some. Maybe Elena would send some. But with what? She had no money; that is why I took the job in America, to make money.

But no foreign worker left Sandusky with money. Everything costs too much. Everything in the park had criminally high prices, and yet the fat tourists all pack in, paying four dollars for a bottled water and twelve dollars for a burger and fries. A cheap T-shirt made in China was twenty-five dollars. So much stupidity.

I would leave Sandusky with money. I had to listen to Mr. Randy and do as he asked. The money I would make from his work would be a lot more than the money made at the park.

Randy 1

7:35 p.m.

Walking out the back door of Glory Bowl, a text came through on my phone. I was wearing my typical biker wear of boots, jeans, a white T-shirt, and a black leather vest.

I could afford to dress better, a lot better. The boots and vest were expensive, but only another biker would know that. I saw no point in trying to dress like a businessman, since that would add nothing to my business's bottom line.

The bowling alley was doing good business for a Tuesday night. It was a little early in the season, so the full tourist surge wasn't happening yet. Being busy meant there were a few more dollars for Sam to skim off the top.

Sam was a reliable guy, but there was no question he skimmed money. I underpaid him, so from that angle, if you included the skimmings, maybe he got paid what he deserved. I knew what I was getting when I hired Sam, and most of his value to me was from things you didn't put on a resume.

Sam was a menacing guy, even as he pushed forty. He was six-foot-four and close to 280 pounds. About fifty pounds of that was flab, but he still had big arms and shoulders from when he played high school football. He was too slow to make it beyond high school ball and too dumb to go to college without an athletic scholarship, so when the marine recruiter took interest in him, he went that route.

Sam's dad died when he was a kid, an overweight factory worker who suffered a heart attack in his forties after a twelve-hour shift racking fenders. I doubted Sam cried a tear about it, since his old man tended to beat the shit out of him on a regular basis. That left Sam without a father figure, as poor of a father as he was, so the marines seemed to be a solid option for a kid with few prospects.

Sam's mom bowled in a league at Glory, and I got updates on

Sam from time to time. He seemed to be doing good as a marine.

The next thing I knew, he was back home. I walked into the bowling alley one day, and there he was, sitting at the bar, watching a football game.

The bowling alley had never been what people would consider a nice place. It was a dump when I bought it, and I hadn't done much with it since. I replaced the roof and renovated the women's bathroom with insurance money after it flooded, but beyond that, I spent just enough money on the business to get by. I replaced the bowling shoes and balls when they were unusable and not a minute sooner.

I did invest in my office, which was originally two storage rooms on the second floor. Walls were knocked out and a big window with one-way glass installed so I could view the lanes. I had the remaining walls soundproofed. Later, I had a full bathroom and a small bedroom constructed. Sometimes I would let friends crash there if they drank too much or if I decided it was safer for me to stay at the alley instead of returning home.

The alley had twenty lanes, a small arcade, and a bar area with a few old TVs mounted above. Most modern lanes installed fancy digital systems with color monitors to track scores with the bowlers' names, but mine were at least twenty years old and were black and white. People come there to throw a bowling ball down a lane and drink; they didn't need all those bells and whistles. Besides, I owned the only alley in Sandusky, so good luck taking your business elsewhere.

That afternoon, when I saw Sam sulking at the bar, I did a double take. He should have been at Camp Pendleton in California. He was trimmer and had a military buzz cut, but beyond that, he was the same Sam I knew before he enlisted.

"Hey, Sam! Home on leave?" I asked, sitting next to him at the bar. "Genie, the next one is on me."

"Uh, thanks Mr. Gorey," Sam said sheepishly, taking a drink from his clear plastic cup and setting it down next to the empty pitcher.

"When you going back?" I asked.

Sam paused, looking down at his hands. "Never," he mumbled.

I sat up a little straighter. "What happened, kid?" I asked, motioning for Genie to bring me a drink. She brought me a bourbon on the rocks.

Genie had been a decent-looking gal when I hired her back when she was a teen, but decades of drinking and smoking had not treated her well. She was still my main bartender, as reliable as they came, and honest, as far as I could tell.

"I was discharged," he said softly.

"Discharged?" I said in disbelief. "You signed up for four years."

"I know. I was accused of stealing," he said, taking a big swig that finished off the cup. Genie had taken the pitcher and was refilling it at the tap.

"Stealing what? From who?" I asked.

"At Walmart. I found a credit card in the barracks parking lot. I have been broke; nobody ever sends me no money," Sam said sadly.

"How much did you steal?" I asked, annoyed.

"I bought a bunch of groceries, fishing poles, a cooler, a Hoyt bow, a few other things. They never asked for ID. I left the store with it all and thought I was good. The guy who lost the credit card reported it, and they traced the charges. They saw me on the store camera and busted me."

"Dear Lord, Sam, you got a dishonorable discharge for that? How fucking dumb are you?" I asked angrily.

"I was always so broke. And the credit card companies pay the customer back. I don't understand why they came down on me so hard."

I let that bit of stupidity go unanswered. From what I understood, military-on-military crime was a sin that would be punished severely. I learned later he also spent thirty days in the stockade.

"You had food, you had a place to live, you had a job. You had a purpose. *You had respect.* You needed a fishing pole and a bow to make your life complete? Are you kidding me?" I asked, raising my voice.

There was a flash of anger in his eyes, then it went away. He took another drink.

"What are you going to do now?"

"I don't know. Mom is real angry. I don't think I can stay at her place for long."

His eyes were glassy, like he was ready to cry, but the tears never came. I took pity on him and offered him a job at the alley. He was a flawed man who would soon become a desperate man if he didn't catch a break. Sam would see me as the guy who pulled him out of a bad situation, and that would make him feel a degree of loyalty.

There were a few empty storage rooms above the alley down the hall from my office. He cleaned one out, set up a cot, moved in there, and never moved out. There was a second-floor bathroom that was seldom used that we added a shower to.

Since that time, Sam had justified my faith in him. He did what I asked unquestioningly, most of the time. He didn't mention my name during the times he found himself being questioned by the cops. Sure, he lost his temper and went too far from time to time, but that was his nature.

I continued along the back of the alley and hopped on my bike. It was a new maroon Harley CVO Limited, a top-of-the-line motorcycle.

I always parked around back because I didn't want to advertise my presence on site. There were ten other spots for employee vehicles and other random vehicles I tended to acquire here and there.

My latest ones were a blue 2012 Ford Explorer and a gray 2007 Chevy Express van, which I had taken instead of cash from guys who owed me a lot of money. Cash was king, but I accepted goods and services if a customer was flat broke.

I started my bike up with a roar, rode across the parking lot, and made my way toward the campground. As I drove out onto Columbus Street, I questioned the wisdom of using the campground for some of my side operations. I could just as easily set up headquarters at the Cloverleaf Apartments outside of the campground for six or seven hundred dollars a month per unit. But this was Sandusky, and it was a seasonal economy. No one was around in the winter, it was too damned cold, so paying rent on unused apartments was a waste of money. A seasonal RV could be left at the campground year round and was much more cost efficient.

The seasonal nature of the area used to be a big economic disadvantage until a few local businesses had the vision to build indoor waterparks. It kept people coming to the area all winter, but that type of tourist was generally locked down where they were staying. A lot of the summer tourists who came to Gravity Junction stayed on the grounds at the park hotel, an offsite hotel, or at the campground. But those were mostly just a place to sleep and shower. Most of the time they were elsewhere. *We operated in the elsewhere.*

Waterpark tourists stayed at the waterpark. They ate, drank, played, and slept on site. Most of these parks had a colored wristband system to show who was authorized to stay there on a particular day. Having my employees do business there on the regular was too risky.

I passed Cloverleaf after I turned onto Nickle Lane. Cloverleaf was the international melting pot of a village that Gravity Junction plopped right next to a grimy trailer park and a dilapidated campground. Did anyone in human resources think this through? No, and I was glad for it.

Once inside the campground, I rode slowly up Starling, being extra careful at the gazebo. There was a woman who always screeched at speeding bikers and drivers. I saw her sitting on a stool out at the outdoor bar area and smiled at her. She ignored me, staring at her cell phone. She lost interest when she recognized I was going the speed limit and wouldn't get a chance to scream at me.

An older white couple was pulling a little black girl in a red Radio Flyer wagon near the shower house. Grandma and Grandpa camping with their granddaughter. Things sure had changed since back in the day. It used to be that seeing mixed families was a rarity, but they had become commonplace. The integration breakthrough had been made possible by rebellious young white girls.

Some from the older generation were never going to accept

blacks as equals. But what happens when your daughter brings home a black child from the hospital? Sure, there were a few stubborn old sticks-in-the-mud who would disown the daughter, but the rest adjusted. Who is going to reject a cute little baby with his own blood flowing in the baby's veins? Suddenly the black kid is part of the family, which made it hard as hell to maintain their racial biases.

The Taj camper was at the end of the street, backing up to the fence that separated the campground from the trailer park. A destination camper, it was designed to be parked semi-permanently rather than towed to different locations. It was more of a residential trailer than an RV. At forty-six feet long, it was much longer than most trailers.

It wasn't just an ordinary stock RV. I spent a decent amount of money having it customized. There was a layer of reinforced steel across the entire exterior, including the roof and floor. It was supposed to be able to withstand high-caliber firearm rounds, and the floor could absorb a small detonation if an explosive was planted underneath.

The windows were also reinforced and close to being bulletproof. They could be breached with a significant amount of gunfire, but they would hold for a while. I had enemies and would have been vulnerable in a regular RV. The extra protection also provided a degree of soundproofing.

I decided to turn the trailer into a bunker when it became obvious I couldn't rely on campground security. If somebody wanted to come on site and shoot up my trailer, nobody would be there to stop them. I had considered putting people in the booth with professional skills, but that would be expensive and a bad fit for an easygoing family recreation spot.

Directly behind the Taj, on the other side of the chain-link fence, was Trailer Alpha. That was where my IT operation was headquartered.

It was a plain, gray doublewide with a small deck built out back. On top of the deck was a small table and two lonely lawn chairs that had never been used. There was also a medium-sized shed on the north side of the backyard with gray siding that matched the trailer.

The grass needed cutting; I would have to get someone over there. That was a detail Chuck should have been taking care of. The less attention that place attracted, the better.

As I rolled up, I saw that Viktor was sitting on a chair on the porch deck of the Taj, drinking from a red cup. He looked greasy and worn out, like he was fighting a summer cold or something. I parked my bike, walking up to the deck. Viktor stood up and shook my hand. He had a sour smell to him like he was sweating out alcohol.

He was about the same height as me, but I had a good hundred pounds on him. Unfortunately, most of it was in my gut and ass. Sitting in a chair in the bowling alley all day, eating bowling-alley food, and sitting on that motorcycle throughout the summer took its toll. I had a financial interest in a gym on Milan Road but rarely set foot in it.

"You smoke cigars?" I asked.

"I do," he replied. I unlocked the camper and went inside. If you didn't know you were in a camper, you would think you were in a nice, furnished apartment. Full kitchen, full dining room, large bedrooms at either end, two bathrooms.

I opened the cupboard to the left of the sink and pulled out a cigar box. I was not wasting a Cuban on this guy, so I pulled out a couple of Macanudos instead of my favorite Montecristo Platinums. I opened a drawer, grabbed the cutter, and went back out.

I fixed up my cigar and handed the cutter over to him. I pulled out my lighter and lit my cigar.

Viktor didn't know what the fuck he was doing with his. He was spinning it around like he didn't know which end to light. I thought about helping him but decided against it. He figured it on his own after a minute.

I lit his cigar and sat back, watching him. He took a deep puff, gasped, and coughed. The cigar went out. I leaned across and lit it again. More gasping, more puffing. His face became even more pale, which I didn't think was possible. But he was a trooper and kept at it.

We sat in silence for a few minutes. Sometimes I didn't have the small talk in me.

"Hey fellas!" came Chuck's booming, raspy voice. It startled me a little. He had come up from the east on foot, a rare bit of walking for him. Viktor stood up. I remained seated.

"Got an extra one of those?" Chuck asked, motioning toward my cigar.

"You know where to find them," I replied. Chuck entered the RV. I could hear him open the cupboard and mill around. He came out with a Montecristo in his palm. Just as I figured, he chose one of the more expensive ones.

"Put that back and get a Macanudo like the rest of us," I said, annoyed.

Viktor was coughing softly, just holding his cigar in his right hand. We sat in silence for maybe ten more minutes. Me and Chuck finished ours. Viktor left his half-smoked cigar in the ashtray.

I stood up and motioned them both inside. Chuck closed the door behind us, locking the handle and then the two bolt locks above it. I motioned toward the kitchen drawers. Chuck nodded and pulled out a handheld device that looked like a walkie-talkie. Except it wasn't, it was an RF bug detector.

Chuck flipped it on and started waving it around the RV, as I had seen him do many times. Last summer, I had Sam pick up a cheap wireless bug set online, and he planted a few in the RV. I wanted to see if the detector worked or not.

Sure enough, Chuck came in, started sweeping, and the thing went off. Chuck's face went pale; I thought he was going to throw up. He found both of them. I let him sweat for a while before I told him they were mine. I was afraid if I didn't, he would have a heart attack.

Once Chuck cleared the camper, he went to work wanding us. I took it from him and wanded him. After I was done, I flicked the detector off and put it down on the small kitchen table.

Chuck opened the fridge and motioned toward us. I nodded. Viktor shook his head. He took out two Great Lakes Brewery Dortmunder Golds, opened them, and passed me one. Sam would have poured me a Woodford Reserve bourbon, but I let it go and accepted the beer.

"Okay. Viktor, so has everyone adjusted to their new work duties?" I asked.

"Everyone? Who is everyone?" he asked. I stared at him for a moment.

"The Romanian National Water Polo Team. Who the fuck you think?" I asked coldly.

"Oh yeah, everyone is good. They all know their jobs and … and do them good," he stammered.

"No complaints so far. Well, except for Thomas Polk. Sam and me will go over that later. Ok, Viktor, and we are talking how many again?" I asked, already knowing the answer.

"Six girls, three men," he replied.

"How much attention have they raised?" Chuck asked.

"I do not understand," Viktor replied.

"Will havin' that many Romanians together seem odd to the other workers?" Chuck asked, taking a swig from his beer. "Don't they spread their recruitin' around to different countries?"

"No. Gravity Junction has many workers from the same country sometimes. It makes recruiting easier, and there will be less homesickness."

"Okay. They are all staying at Cloverleaf?" I asked.

"*Da* … yes. We have them set up in basement-level apartments, as you asked. The girls are in two apartments and the men in the other. The fourth apartment is empty," he said. He was sweating a little, taking a long pull from his drink.

"I have Sam checking in from time to time, but I need you there too. There may be communication gaps that could use some translating. Stop by tomorrow. Make sure they are keeping the place clean. No drugs. No outside guests. The only people who are entering that wing besides them are people I authorize to be there. Understood?" I asked.

Viktor nodded. He took a drink, tilting his head back, finishing it.

The train horn could be heard faintly outside. That meant it was around 8:30 p.m.; I felt the vibration as it approached.

There was a rumbling within the trailer that gradually built. It wasn't powerful enough to knock my beer bottle over, but I grabbed it off the table anyway. The train passing by always killed whatever conversation was happening. The rumbling decreased, and then it was down to a slight vibration again. The train horn sounded from farther away.

"Do you have anything stronger than this?" Viktor said, pointing at my bottle of beer. "Do people get drunk off of that?"

I glared at him for a moment, then pointed to the cupboard by the fridge. He got up, studied the liquor selection, and pulled out a bottle of Absolut. He brought it to the table and poured it into his red cup.

"Rocks are in the freezer," I said.

"Rocks?" he asked, puzzled.

"Ice," I said impatiently.

"No, thank you," he replied, lifting the cup in a sort of saluting motion and taking a long swig.

I took a final swig of my beer, stood up, walked over, and tossed the bottle in the sink. I peered out the windows through Venetian blinds to see if anyone was around. I saw the guy at 31 walking up the street carrying a bag of garbage, heading toward the dumpster.

"What do we know about the stiff at 31?" I asked, sitting back down.

Chuck cleared his throat. "Interestin' you should ask, Randy. I mentioned before he works for the government; we talked a little last season. I had a chat with him at lunch, and it turns out he works as a federal. Bragged about havin' a security clearance. He is workin' from his camper on a laptop," Chuck said.

"Any dealings with him last year beyond a conversation or two?" I asked.

"Not really. He was always kind of a familiar face. His family was around all the time last year, comin' and goin' from the campground to the park. He has been up here for weeks now. I haven't seen his family at all. I think he is having domestic troubles."

"Really?" I asked.

"Yeah. Last year he never came up alone, except to maybe open and close the camper for the season. Now he lives here solo," Chuck said, finishing his beer.

"So, somebody is most definitely having marital problems," I said, shaking my head in mock sadness.

Chuck laughed. Viktor didn't laugh at first but decided to when Chuck did. It was an odd, almost mechanical sound.

"Does he drink?" I asked.

"Yeah, had a few beers with me. He was on the clock at the time."

"Shit, you are an expert on that, Chuck. Take a closer look at him," I said.

"Sure, should I use Data?"

"Yeah. I'm thinking I see some opportunities here. Get with Data," I said.

"Will do," Chuck replied, getting two more beers from the fridge.

Brady 2

9:15 p.m.

I was returning to my camper from the dumpster, which was located about forty yards north of my site. Campground employees came by on work carts a few times per day to collect garbage bags left out by the street, but since it was evening, I walked it there myself.

The dumpster was within sight of the fishing pond. The campground had dug the pond and stocked it with different fish species, including catfish, bluegill, and perch. It was "catch and release," so they were supposed to be thrown back. Unfortunately, a lot of the campers let their kids fish there alone, and when they caught a fish, they were unable to remove it from the hook properly. Occasionally a kid would rip the hook out through the side of the fish's head and throw it back as if it could somehow recover from that type of trauma and live to be caught another day.

The most unusual part of the campground layout was its vicinity to the train tracks. They ran just north of the pond, coming so close to it that a train passenger could probably cast a line from the caboose. There was a fence around the pond, but otherwise, there was nothing between the campground and the tracks. If my kids were younger, I would have been concerned about one of them toddling out onto the tracks.

Instead of returning to the camper on Starling, I decided to loop around and walk down Sparrow. The seasonal campers were to my right, with the transients to my left. The campground's transient sites seemed to be at about a quarter capacity. At the height of summer, all of the sites would be booked.

I cut through the back of lot 51 and entered onto my site at 31. The people at 51 weren't out; otherwise, it would have been bad etiquette to cut through. I went in and washed my hands in the kitchen sink. My red plastic cup was on the kitchen table, still half full of frozen margarita, sweating water rings onto the surface. I made it from a mix earlier and then added a few ounces of Cuervo so that it would have more impact. *It did, indeed.*

I turned on the stereo, pushed a button to broadcast it to the outside speakers, and walked out with my drink. I grabbed a few pieces from the small stack of firewood stored beneath the camper and arranged them in the pit.

I sat down and selected a music app on my phone. I was able to connect to the stereo via Bluetooth. After selecting a 1990s alt-rock station, I adjusted the volume so it couldn't be heard beyond my lot.

I opened the compartment at the front-right side of the camper and found a box of synthetic fire-starting material, taking out a brick of the crumbly brown substance and breaking it in half. I found a lighter, and within a few seconds, the fire began to take off.

I grabbed my drink and pulled a chair closer to the pit. The weather was still fair, in the low sixties, the perfect temperature for an evening fire. I guessed it would drop into the low fifties overnight.

A giant motorhome with Illinois plates cruised by. That vehicle cost about half as much as my house in Medina. Campgrounds were the ultimate in socioeconomic integration. There were huge, lavish motorhomes that cost more than a hundred thousand dollars. These were parked a few rows down from people camping in thirty-dollar tents. Regardless of where they camped, everyone mixed together in the common areas like the pools, basketball courts, horseshoe pits, and playground. For the most part, everyone got along.

The view from my camper on the north side of the campground varied, depending on the volume of campers at the time. Directly in front of our seasonal lot was a row of campsites that were full hookups, the cement pads set out at angles so the RVs could be towed efficiently into the lot and then connected to water, electricity, plumbing, and cable. Each site featured a tree, a patch of grass, a patio, a paver stone fire pit, and a picnic table.

These types of sites comprised the next five or six rows. An equal number of rows east of that were sites without utilities, for either popup campers or tents. This section of the campground was delineated from the other by a yellow cinderblock shower house, identical to the one a site over from my RV.

There was an elevated dirt trail along the northern part of the campground that ran east-west through a narrow range of woods. It began near the fishing hole, ran east about a quarter mile along the shore, then ran south along the basketball courts, ending beside the east shower house. It was adjacent to a swampy bog with a greenish film covering almost all of it, littered with lily pads, cattails, and dead trees. To the north of that was Lake Erie.

About fifteen yards off the coast was the train bridge. It was over a half-mile long, running parallel to Columbus Road and then hooking north to go out above the water, reconnecting with land at the west side of the campground by the fishing pond. The tracks were elevated enough to allow small boats to pass beneath.

The urban legend associated with the costly iron bridge was that it resulted from a pissing contest between the previous landowner and the railroad company. The landowner fought and won an eminent domain battle with the city, which forbade them from bisecting his land with the train tracks. They responded by building a train bridge over the water and across his lake access, reconnecting to the railroad's land near the spot that would later become the fishing pond, greatly diminishing his land value. He was unable to develop the land into a marina as he intended and sold the land at a loss.

The northeast shore beyond the trail curved north, ran east for a few yards, and then straight south, forming a small peninsula. This area east of the north-south trail leg contained a paintball course, an archery range, and a grassy field for playing games and staging outdoor concerts. Worn wooden picnic tables were scattered throughout the field.

The area south of the trail tended to flood, so there was a sump pump expelling the excess water through a PVC pipe running beneath the trail and dumping into the boggy area. Halfway down the trail was a weathered wooden gazebo that the trail ran beneath.

There was a geographic segregation of the different socioeconomic camper statuses. The west side was the "haves" and the east was the "have-lesses."

Even though my family had been camping at Sandusky Shores for a full season and we were permanent seasonal campers, we remained outsiders. There was a barrier to acceptance we unintentionally built ourselves, based upon the way we conducted ourselves when we camped.

We didn't stay up all night drinking. We would have a few drinks while sitting out by the campfire at night, but pulling an all-nighter with our kids running around screaming into the early hours of the morning never appealed to us. I recognize that statement as thinly veiled virtue signaling, but that didn't negate the truth of it.

We accounted for our kids at all times. We didn't allow them to disappear in an environment filled with migratory strangers from around the country for hours at a time.

The people over at lot 18 had a four-year-old and a six-year-old who were generally on their own. We would see them at different places around the campground without parental supervision. Someone could take them and be hours away before anyone noticed they were missing.

Also, we were clearly white-collar people. My wife and I worked in offices and from home; we didn't do manual labor for a living. We both possessed advanced degrees, so the "getting to know you" conversations tended to reveal the gulf between us.

No particular difference between us and the seasonal campground culture was insurmountable. But the sum of all the minor differences contributed to the totality of us being *significantly different*.

I'm sure we could have made friends if we tried, but we didn't. We lined up family events all day that took us away from the campground. We were there because of the campground's vicinity to Gravity Junction. The camper served more as a hotel room to shower and sleep and less as a hangout spot.

There was a part of me that yearned to fit in, because it was a place where my family would have fit in back in my childhood. My parents were extroverted, socially oriented people, who always made friends easily. When we vacationed, we would effortlessly mix with other groups and have fun hanging out together. Neither

Marcy nor I had that skill set.

There was also nostalgia for the minor degree of lawlessness that was pervasive in the pre-digital era. At Sandusky Shores, kids didn't always wear helmets. Sometimes a truck would pass by with a half-dozen kids in the truck bed, traveling to the pool. A thirteen-year-old would zip by behind the wheel of a golf cart. Packs of kids ran around without shoes on.

It was my childhood in the 1970s and 1980s. It was drastically different than the ultra-cautious, overthinking, virtue-signaling, hand sanitizer–saturated, enfold-your-child-in-bubble-wrap environment where our kids were being raised. So, while I didn't let my kids participate in it (beyond occasionally allowing them to cycle helmet free), I enjoyed watching it happening around me at the campground.

I heard the train horn and felt the beginnings of the rumbling that would eventually be so loud, it would be difficult to hold a conversation. This was almost a dealbreaker the first time we heard it.

The kids and I got used to the trains pretty quickly, and they didn't disturb our sleep after a few days. Marcy was another story. She never got used to it and complained about the trains incessantly.

I sat back in the chair and took another long drink of my margarita as a blast from the train horn filled the air. As I reached the bottom of the cup, I could taste the added tequila that settled there. I could feel its boozy tendrils slithering through my mind and welcomed the numbness and detachment.

I poured myself another margarita. I tossed another log onto the fire. The train had passed and was rolling off into the distance, the lights a soft glow as it disappeared.

I wished I could say I missed Marcy. If anyone asked if I missed her, I would certainly lie and say I did. But I didn't. For the first time in years, I could breathe. I could exist without the constant anxiety she imposed upon me.

We concocted a story about me temporarily relocating because of a critical work project requiring my full attention. Marcy's parents knew the truth, and everyone else most likely suspected I moved out because of marital issues. Luckily, no one had called us out on it yet.

I was only buying short-term peace by relocating there. If the current living situation continued, the marriage would come to an end. Marcy had proven herself to be an excellent manipulator and game player, and I was sure that I would end up losing on multiple levels when the relationship officially fell apart.

At best, I would be awarded partial custody of the kids at a rate substantially less than 50 percent. I would take a big financial hit. Visitation and custody arrangements would be constant battles, and as the male in the relationship, I expected to lose most of them.

Marcy and I had been in a relationship for six years and married for four years before our first child Jason's birth. During that time, we had a solid relationship. I don't know if it would be considered a model relationship, but I felt we were pretty happy. We possessed similar values. We got along. We had fun together.

When Jason arrived, he was diagnosed with having a primary immunodeficiency disorder. There were issues with his B and T cell counts. It was a very stressful, scary time, having a baby who spent his first month in a plastic box in the neonatal intensive care unit. This stressful period of our lives triggered a personality change in Marcy that she never recovered from.

She became radically overprotective and extremely germophobic. I was on board with this and willing to do whatever was necessary to protect Jason. We brought him home, and he fought off one infection after another.

The months went by, and miraculously his body began creating more white blood cells and attacking bacteria and viruses more effectively. He became indistinguishable from a "normal" baby after the first year.

Sure, there were minor side effects of his condition, and we were very overprotective of him. Overall, he was a normal kid. But in Marcy's mind, he was still at risk and required an excessive amount of precaution in everything he did.

I figured her personality switch would wear off because it was exhausting for her as well. But it never did wear off. She was driven by anxiety and obsession with Jason. I never felt it was to the extent where it was harming him, but I could see that a Munchausen by proxy type of mindset wouldn't be a stretch if she slipped a few degrees mentally.

We decided to have another kid. I thought the pragmatism of raising our first child and the continued healthiness of Jason would alleviate her anxiety, but it actually worsened.

Katie was born with a severe nut allergy. If she ingested almost any type of nut, she would go into anaphylactic shock. The risks associated with Jason's immune system paled in comparison. Marcy's overbearing ways worsened.

The reality of the danger of Katie's allergies was not enough for Marcy; she would spend hours scouring the internet for allergy articles and forwarding the horror stories to me. Children dead or in comas from peanut exposure. Allergy bullying by kids who intentionally exposed an allergic classmate to peanut butter.

By having Katie, we essentially doubled down on the anxiety. Marcy was on a full anxiety jihad at all times. I worked extremely hard to accommodate it, but everything I did was wrong. Furthermore, everything I did for myself was considered selfish. Fitness was self-indulgence. I had to push my exercise to either early in the morning or late at night. There was zero support.

Everything I enjoyed before having kids slowly faded from my life. I quit attending sporting events. Then I quit watching sports on TV. I lost friends. I communicated less with my parents.

I truly related to life in prison. *Minus the conjugal visits.* I lived to eat and go to sleep. I got my "hour in the yard" at the gym a few times a week. The rest of my life was a continuous grind of work and chores. I looked forward to the day ending the moment I awoke.

After years of this, my soul was being crushed. It all came to a head with an epic argument and my relocation to the campground. I was scheduled to work remotely the following day, and I packed everything I needed and left for Sandusky. It was the equivalent of sleeping on a buddy's couch. I didn't have a buddy with a vacant couch, but I had an RV.

It wasn't a permanent solution. Could I really spend an entire summer there? What happened when the place closed for the season?

Data 1

11:15 p.m.

There was no better time than the present. Minutes after hanging up with Chuck, I dressed and put together a game plan. I was practically salivating at the thought of spending time at Trailer Alpha.

I dressed in a pair of black cargo shorts, a yellow campground polo, a black-and-yellow campground baseball cap, black socks, and a black belt.

Staring at my reflection in the mirror, I frowned at what I saw. Generic glasses with ugly black frames and ridiculously thick lenses. I needed a haircut, which was evident even with the hat on. Strands of greasy black hair hung out on the sides and at the back.

Some idiot in undergrad called me a poor man's Michael Moore, and I hated that comparison, essentially because it was fairly accurate. I had a chin or two less than Moore, but I was also a lot younger. In due time, I'm sure we would be indistinguishable, and that was unfortunate. But not so unfortunate that I was motivated to take measures to avoid that fate.

Physical fitness was an elusive condition I had never achieved. I never even made a reasonable attempt at it, other than the humiliation of being forced to participate in physical education at school. The painful memories of being teased in gym class made me wince and appreciate the distances of time and geography from my gloomy upbringing in Anaheim, California.

Sandusky was Podunk and bland compared to California cities, but it provided a wonderful degree of anonymity to me. No one knew me or my past, and for that, I was grateful. I was just some dumpy little nobody that no one paid any attention to.

Moving out to the Midwest to live in Sandusky with my grandma was a dreadful prospect at first. My brief glory in Silicon Valley had shown me how amazing life could be as a founding partner of a rising software company. One minute I was in a basement with a few friends creating software, and the next I was part of an initial public offering that made me a great deal of money.

My amazing tech skills helped launch some great software products. Somewhere along the startup journey, the other nerds began calling me "Data," after the android in the *Star Trek* series. I took it as a compliment, although it could have been a dig at my lack of emotions. I brought the nickname with me to Sandusky, since I always hated my real name, Henry.

Just as I was wrapping my head around my new economic status with the tech startup, it crumbled. The majority partner cut corners, did some deceptive advertising, and misled the Securities and Exchange Commission. Meanwhile, I had stolen patented software information and hacked several of our competitors to steal trade secrets. We got caught. We lost our company. We lost our money. We went to prison.

Mine was a short sentence at a minimum-security facility in Mendota, California. I was granted an early release for good behavior and sentenced to house arrest. My lawyer negotiated to have my house arrest served at my grandma's in Ohio because I had nowhere to go in California, since my parents had disowned me.

Relocating across the country to a trailer park in the frozen Midwest sounded awful. And it was at first. *But nowhere near as awful as prison.*

So, I went from living in my parents' basement to an upscale downtown studio apartment to prison to a 1970s-era trailer in the Midwest over the course of four years. It was still difficult to wrap my head around it all.

The trailer itself was in decent shape, about one thousand square feet, two bedrooms, and one bathroom. It was situated on a tiny parcel of land, with neighboring trailers so close you could hear their toilets flush and smell what they were cooking for dinner. Grandma tried to keep it tidy, but it needed a refresh. I wished I possessed home-renovation skills, but I didn't.

Luckily, I never acquired the expensive tastes that many of my fellow IPO-enriched techies had during my short stay at the top of the tech world, and I found the simplicity of this lifestyle agreed with me. I heard stories about how Grandma was an overbearing and nosy person when Mother was young, but she had slowed down as she aged and now slept so much that her trailer was almost a bachelor pad for me, albeit a bachelor pad without any female company other than Grandma.

My house arrest ended, and I was put on probation. While I was no longer confined to the trailer legally, I had nowhere else to go. I would remain there until I figured out the next step.

Grandma had a car, a little blue 1980s-model Buick Skylark. The paint had faded, and it had some rust here and there, but it still ran, and I was able to use it every once in a while to run errands. Otherwise, everywhere I needed to go was within walking or biking distance. At least in the summer.

I had arrived in late October and spent the winter and the icy early spring indoors with Grandma. It was fine at first, but by April I was climbing the walls. I was not looking forward to the end of summer when the campground job ended. I would have to find a new job to maintain my sanity.

The lack of technology in Grandma's trailer was maddening. As ordered by the United States District Court for the Northern District of California and enforced by my local probation officer, my living and working environments were to be 100 percent technology free. Of course, Randy provided me with a fully functioning cell phone that my probation officer didn't know about.

I was allowed to have a stripped-down cell phone without any data capabilities, and that was it. There wasn't a PC in Grandma's trailer, which was causing me to suffocate. There wasn't even cable or satellite TV, just a few channels received through a rusty antenna mounted on top of the trailer.

I found my sandals by the door and slipped them on. I grabbed my backpack and walked out, locking the door behind me.

It was a clear night out with no moon, very dark. The lack of city lights always made the nights unusually dark, unlike Los Angeles or Anaheim.

I walked behind the trailer to the shed and grabbed my bike, a rusty ten-speed that was probably salvaged by Grandpa while digging through junk on garbage day decades ago. Grandpa thought discarded junk was like buried treasure and was always bringing it home, if only to stack it on top of his other useless junk. Grandma mentioned that nothing he salvaged had ever earned him a red cent. I was trying to recall how long ago he died; it had to be at least twenty years ago. Grandma was still living off his railroad pension.

Mounting the bike, I headed south toward Trailer Alpha. At this hour, there wasn't much traffic, just a car or two passing by. I should have grabbed my helmet, but the last time I showed up for work at the campground wearing it, I was ridiculed mercilessly. I would need to stop by the campground after finishing this part of the job and didn't want to get caught wearing a helmet. The average campground worker didn't see the need for a helmet because there was so little to protect within their skulls.

Then again, there would only be one or two people working by the time I arrived. The security booth should be empty; it typically was. I turned into the gravel driveway of Trailer Alpha.

I dismounted my bike and walked it up to the front door. I found the keys and let myself in, which took a moment since there were multiple bolt locks. The door was heavy, made of reinforced steel. I wheeled my bike in and locked the door behind me.

Once inside, I was happy to see the place was in the same condition I left it, nice and neat. One time Chuck let himself in and had some sort of one-man party, leaving fast-food wrappers, plastic cups, cigarette butts, and ashes everywhere. I complained to Randy, and he added the security cameras to better control who was coming and going. There was a lot of expensive equipment and sensitive data in the trailer, and no one should be in there partying.

Adding the cameras was beneficial for security but ruined my unfettered use of the trailer. If Randy noticed me there for long periods of time, he wanted to know what I was doing. I suspected there was another tech guy he consulted with, but I wasn't sure. Sometimes he seemed tech ignorant, and other times he seemed to know exactly what was happening.

The sliding glass door at the back of Trailer Alpha had a large piece of reinforced steel covering it. A dark-brown curtain had been closed and left in place before sealing it off, so it appeared to be a normal, functioning sliding glass door from the outside. The window above the kitchen sink facing the Taj was bulletproof.

I went to the door on the west side of the trailer and unlocked it. There had originally been an open hallway along the south side, but a reinforced door was added by the kitchen wall. I walked in and turned on the light. It resembled a legit security control room at a corporate building. There were over a dozen monitors mounted along the western wall. A series of laptops were set up in front of the monitor bank.

The area that was once a full bathroom and spare bedroom was now just one room. There was still a sink and toilet to the right, but it wasn't enclosed, as the walls were removed to allow more space. Across from that were three safes, four feet tall by two feet wide. I was told that two contained weapons and ammo. I only saw the contents of the one closest to the north wall because it was used to hold data-storage devices and documents.

I was given the combination to all of them and told that if "the shit went down," I was to extract a weapon and use it to defend the trailer. When I mentioned I had no weapons experience, Sam promised to take me out to the range and get me up to speed. That hadn't happened yet.

All the windows had been fitted with thick, dark shades that were pulled down. Metal plates had been fastened over the window, with the exterior of the plates painted white. From the outside, it appeared to be an ordinary window. Randy had assured me that the steel plates could stop bullets. I didn't ask why anyone would want to shoot bullets at it.

Setting my backpack down, I went over to the monitors, turning on each one of them. Different live camera angles filled the screens. The front door of Trailer Alpha, the exterior of the campground office, a view from the campground security booth, two cabin exteriors, two cabin bedroom interiors, one clubhouse interior, three from within the bowling alley, two from the bowling alley exterior, and two from Randy's boat.

I shook the mouse attached to the center laptop, and its screen illuminated. I placed my pointer finger on a pad that was connected via the USB slot. After I was authenticated, I entered the password.

I launched the Dark Web browser and went to work. I was blessed with an amazing memory. I never needed to write down passwords or URLs; I just remembered them. My memory was not photographic, but pretty damn close.

I found the site I needed, typed in the requested access information, and a search box appeared. I typed in "Brady Sullivan, Medina, Ohio" and pressed *send*.

Chapter 2
Wednesday, June 17

Chuck 2

1:25 a.m.

Well, look at ole Michael Moore pedalin' up the drive. Dear Lord, and he didn't have no helmet on this time. Seems like he would wear it at this hour, seein' how dark it was.

I don't think he saw me as I sat in my golf cart down by the pool. Some people called me a loudmouth, but I could be real quiet if I wanted to.

Good for Data, gettin' his Sullivan research done right away. Randy would like that. He liked people who moved fast when he told them to move.

I looked down into my red drinkin' cup and saw it was close to empty. Pulling it up close near my eyeball, I figured there was another swig in there. Should have gotten a refill before I left the Taj.

I needed some music. Figured I could play it real soft while I sat here and gathered my thoughts. I turned the stereo on. Credence Clearwater Revival came on, not bad.

I was off work but decided to stay out a bit longer. I didn't want to go back to the camper totally wrecked and have the old lady lay into me. But I didn't want to stop drinkin' either.

I had work at eight in the mornin', but what did I care? I could just show up and keep a low profile for a few hours, maybe find an empty cabin and take a little nap. I drank my last bit of vodka and tossed the cup into the grass. Let Data or Patrick pick it up in the morning, some busy work for 'em.

I got out of the golf cart and looked around, makin' sure no one was there. I took a piss off to the side, splashin' the chain-link pool fence.

Data workin' early wouldn't be a big deal to him. He wasn't drinkin' that night or any night; he was just gonna be a little tired, but not hung over.

I decided to take a spin around the hood. I didn't put the headlights on. That would normally be unsafe, but it didn't matter that late; there wasn't no traffic. I was careful not to go up Sparrow, in case Sharon was out waitin' for me.

I went down a few streets to Dove, headin' north. Most of the campfires were out, with a few still smolderin', but a few people were sittin' out. It was a nice night for it. People were bein' quiet, which was good.

Damn, I was thirsty! I remembered Viktor drank vodka and so I looped a left along the trail and headed west to Starling. Damn Russkie should have some vodka on hand. It would be the cheap shit, but whatever.

Sharon would likely see me as I crept past Sparrow if she was out. I turned off the stereo and squinted to see if I could see her cigarette cherry when my golf cart clipped the fire pit at 24 with a screech. It jolted me, and the cigarette in my hand flipped down and into my lap. I jerked and patted at it, flicking it off me and onto the ground.

I stopped and got out. The cigarette was only half gone, so I relit it. There wasn't a fire in the pit, and the crash wasn't loud, just a scrapin' noise from the bricks grindin' the fender. I would take care of it tomorrow. Or some other day.

I rolled past Viktor's RV, and it looked dead. I kept driving until I saw the shower house between 33 and 32, then pulled over in front of it. None of the gazebo crew was out.

I walked back toward Viktor's. Every step was gettin' to my aches and pains. Damn back, damn hips. I felt myself waddlin' and hated it. Sittin' in that cart was makin' me fat. Not bein' able to walk a lot because of my injury was makin' me fat. Eatin' and drinkin' so much all summer was makin' me fat.

As I was walkin' past 31, I stopped. The fire pit in front of Sullivan's still had some embers smokin'. I paused for a minute, lookin' for movement. The RV was quiet. His truck was there, so he was inside. I focused on the outdoor kitchen at the back of the RV. The slide panel was still up. I looked around carefully and walked toward it.

Brady had more beer in the fridge earlier that day when he gave me a couple. Hopefully, there were a few more left.

I walked around the patio table and stood in front of the

fridge. I scanned the lots around me again. No movement in 50 directly behind me. I stood real still and listened. Nothin' but crickets.

I opened the fridge, and the light inside came on. There was a half-dozen cans of beer and a pitcher of green somethin'. It was one of those pitchers mounted on a blender he pulled off and put in the fridge. Since the liquid was green, probably a margarita.

I figured if I drank a little he wouldn't notice. 'Specially if he was buzzed when he put the pitcher in there. I took a long pull off it. Yup, margarita, and pretty damned tasty. It was really cold, the top layer still slush. I took another small sip and grabbed a few beers, putting 'em down in my pockets.

I closed the fridge and gasped as I saw a black face starin' back at me from where the open door just was. Mike was standin' there. I let out a grunt and damn near fell over. I felt my heart skip, and my lungs wouldn't work for a second. A pain shot along my chest and arm on the left side.

Mike didn't move. He was standing there holding a big, unlit black flashlight like he wanted to beat me with it. His face was blank.

I thought about sayin' somethin', but nothin' came to mind. I didn't want to wake Sullivan up and have to explain I was stealin' from his fridge. I stared Mike in the eye for a spell. Neither of us moved.

Finally, I nodded at him. He didn't nod back. I turned around and started walkin' back to my golf cart. I got in and sat for a minute. It took a long time for my heart to stop hammerin'. I thought better of goin' to Viktor's. It was almost time to face the music at home. But first I was gonna cruise around and drink Sullivan's beers.

Mike 2

2:30 a.m.

The train lights lit the northern part of the campsite as it approached, and I felt the familiar vibration of it as it headed west. There were times I was enjoying the quiet and was ambushed by the train's intrusion. But after a few weeks, it wasn't as disruptive as it had been when I first arrived.

I figured out that there was a cadence to the trains. One would pass by about every ninety minutes. If it was on the half hour, it was heading east, on the hour, west. You could almost set your watch by it.

My heart was still beating rapidly from my encounter with Chuck. *Scumbag.*

I was sitting out in the dark when he drove by on Dove. I didn't think he saw me when he passed by, since my fire was out. Instead of keeping my fire going, I had let it die and put on a black Atlanta Falcons sweatshirt. While I was inside the camper retrieving my sweatshirt, I poured another drink. I wouldn't be able to fall asleep anytime soon, so why not have one more?

Chuck was slinking along on his cart as quietly as possible. No headlights, no music, just driving up Crane in stealth mode. I saw him turn toward Starling.

There was a functioning bathroom in my camper, but I occasionally opted to use the shower house facility. Why not let someone else clean up instead of having to clean my own bathroom? I decided to go use it and maybe get a better look at where Chuck was going. I went into my camper to grab my flashlight.

Stepping outside again, it took a minute for my eyes to readjust to the darkness. I liked to have my big Maglite when I was out and about at night, in case I needed to see my way in the dark, or alternatively, to defend myself if necessary. Not that the campground was a dangerous place, as far as I could tell.

A friend who was a military policeman told me that they regularly used their flashlights on unruly drunk soldiers who would not listen to reason. A thump on the head with the solid metal flashlight would certainly make an impression.

I glanced over at 51 and paused for a moment. The shaggy-haired guy was sleeping in a lawn chair. His white hat was on backward, and he was still wearing sunglasses. There was a bottle of liquor at his feet, maybe Jim Beam.

His one-man party ended with him passed out and dead to the world. He had been drinking from a red cup earlier but must have just ditched that formality and started hitting directly from the bottle.

As I walked out of the shower house after relieving myself, I saw the golf cart roll up. Chuck parked it alongside the building. He didn't notice me, since I was on the other side of a stockade fence that shielded the shower house from lot 49.

I walked up Sparrow to see where he was going and caught sight of him standing in front of 31. I cut across lot 50 to take a closer look.

He opened the fridge, and the interior light revealed he was drinking something from a pitcher. I heard the clatter as he grabbed beer cans and stuffed them into his pockets. A feeling approaching anger came over me.

Who was this guy, a campground employee, to steal beer from a camper's RV in the middle of the night? Someone needed to fire his ass and tow his trailer out of here. Then he needed to have his ass kicked. Before I could think better of it, I found myself walking over and standing alongside the open fridge.

I honestly didn't know what I was going to do when he closed the door. A part of me wanted to grab him and drag him over to the door of 31 and knock on it, telling the owner what Chuck had done. But there was always the chance he was friends with the guy at 31 and it was okay for him to help himself to the fridge. After all, they were drinking together earlier. So, I restrained myself.

When Chuck closed the fridge, we just stared at one another. I gave him my blank drill sergeant look. The one that projected to others that behind the calm was a swirling tornado of anger and violence that was about to be unleashed.

Chuck was pale and sweaty and appeared to be more than a

little scared. His eyes were so glassy that I was surprised he could see anything. He had been doing some serious drinking out on the golf cart. I remembered hearing a screeching sound earlier and wondered if he struck something.

After he walked away, I instantly regretted the confrontation. *Why would I do that?* As the only brother in this zip code, it was a bad idea to go creeping around these campsites in the middle of the night. I was going to have to face that clown at some point during the course of staying at the campground. This was going to make for some awkwardness.

Then again, I liked the fact that he knew someone was on to him. He was on notice. A guy who pulls that sort of trivial bullshit would likely be into more serious shittiness.

I walked back toward my camper with my heart still racing. It was late, but I was wide awake, so another drink was in order.

Chris 1

3:30 a.m.

I had passed out for a short while. The last thing I remembered was hearing a scraping noise, like rock on metal. I had meant to stand up to investigate, but then lowered my head and was out. I had no idea how long.

My eyes suddenly flipped open, and just like that, I was jittery again. *Too damned jittery.* No way in fuck I was falling back asleep. *No way.*

I felt my face, and my glasses were missing. Sitting up, they tumbled down from my chest to my lap. I started laughing. Folding them up, I put them on the top of the mini-fridge.

My head was itching, and when I went to scratch it, I realized I was wearing a baseball cap. I took it off and ran my fingers through my hair, which was a mess of tangles and sweat. I tossed the hat aside.

I needed a vape. Glancing over to the right, I saw it was lying in the grass. I tried to take a hit, but it was empty, so I set it by my glasses.

My fire had gone out a while ago, and I was out of wood. There was plenty of firewood laying around at the back of the campground, but I didn't opt to pilfer any.

Candy passed out a while ago. She hated the hard stuff and just smoked a little weed. That was usually a sleeping pill for her, and tonight I was thankful for it. I had enough going on in my mind without dealing with her shit.

My lack of adult supervision allowed me to get into more serious shit. The shit I wasn't supposed to be smoking anymore. *Shhhhh ...*

I leaned forward and looked down. There was a half-full bottle of bourbon by my chair! I forgot all about it. I took a big chug straight from the bottle, but I barely even tasted it. That was an awesome side effect. Whatever I did after smoking up a tin didn't stick; I could have drunk the whole bottle of Jim Beam and still walked a straight line. Too bad I couldn't *think* in a straight line. *Was it straight-line mental depreciation?*

There was no damned moon; that had to mean something. *To moon something.*

A cricket chirped. It sounded like it was almost under my chair. It chirped again, and I knew that it wasn't under my chair; it was a few feet over.

Usually dogs were barking this late. Why wasn't a dog barking? *Where was the dog?* I didn't have a dog.

I took another drink of Beam. I ran the fingers of my left hand, my non-bottle hand, through my hair again. It was getting long.

I needed a fire, something to focus on besides the stillness and the darkness. *And the quietness of dogs not barking.* I leaned my head back to howl but thought better of it.

This made me laugh, and I actually laughed out loud, a raspy sort of croak. I couldn't remember the last time I laughed.

I swung my head around to the door to see if Candy was there staring at me, but she wasn't. Probably still snoring in the back of the RV.

Looking through my backyard across 30, I saw a glimpse of a golf cart going by. No headlights. If there was one headlight, it was probably Jacob Dylan. But it wasn't. Must be Chuck. Maybe he was heading home to be a wallflower for the rest of the night.

I got up and walked across the lots to Starling. Chuck drove north and took a right. Was he heading home? Was "heading home" even correct, were these RV's "home"? At least for the summer, they were, for guys like Chuck and me.

I walked back to my lot and out onto Sparrow. He passed the street and was heading east. What the fuck was he out doing this late? I decided to take a walk. *Take a walk on the wild side.*

I thought about the train bridge. The crazy bridge that flared out onto the lake and then joined the shore near the pond. I always had the urge to walk out and take a look. I wanted to do it now. Just hang out and watch for the train and see if I could get off the tracks in time. *Or not.*

I heard a camper door slam to the right. It was the black guy with the shiny metal RV. The Airstream. *His air dream.*

Mr. Lone Ranger. The tall dark stranger. He was walking from the shower house. Our eyes met. I nodded. He nodded. He kept walking. Grand-fucking Central Station out there tonight. I heard the racket from the train passing. The trains always ran on time at *Sandusky Grandusky Central Station.*

I walked up Sparrow until I was in front of the office. The office was really dark. I beheld the sky. It was dark too. The side door opened, and the four-eyed employee who looked just like Michael Moore walked out, wearing a backpack and pushing a ten-speed. He didn't see me.

"Hey, Michael!" I yelled, way too loud. He jumped, and his ten-speed fell over. This made me jump too, and I almost dropped my bottle. He stumbled, and his backpack slipped off one of his shoulders, spilling papers. Then he fell to one knee.

"Sorry man, shit," I said as I walked over.

The guy seemed startled for a minute, then pissed. "No. I got it," he said, standing up and picking up the papers.

"Let me help," I said, bending over to pick them up. I reached with my right hand, but it was holding the bottle of bourbon, and I spilled some on the ground, as well as on him, his papers, and his backpack. *Alcohol abuse.* I started laughing.

"No!" he said harshly, causing me to lock up for a minute.

"Sorry, Michael," I said, standing back up.

"My name isn't fucking Michael," he hissed with an angry look on his face. He shoved the papers back into his backpack. *Back into his backpack.* Was that why they called it a backpack?

"Sorry, dude," I muttered, watching him. "What the fuck you doing out here in the office so late? Is the snack bar open?"

He glared at me for a moment as he picked his bike up. He attempted to pedal off, nearly fell, caught himself with his right leg, and then steadied himself.

"You drunk?" I asked. I started laughing. The guy who was sky-high and brandishing a bottle of bourbon was asking the tough questions.

He ignored me and pedaled off. As he approached the guard booth, I saw movement inside. Someone was actually guarding the campground. I started walking in that direction. As the *guy-who-*

hated-being-called-Michael passed the booth, a hand shot out.

"High five!" a voice yelled. The hand connected with his elbow, and he veered off to the right, hopping over the speed bump and swiping the storage garage that had the rental pedal carts and the community lawn mowers. He fell again, his backpack opened again, papers came out again. I walked over but didn't bother to help. The lyrics to the Beatles song about needing help came to mind and I started humming it.

Patrick came walking out of the guard booth, laughing his ass off. This guy was a piece of work. Peace sells. Peace works. Peaceful twerks.

"Help! He needs somebody!" I started singing.

Patrick just stared at me blankly. Who names a Mexican kid Patrick? I guess his parents were trying to whiten him up or something. We had shared a pipe a time or two. I guess he wasn't bad. With his shaved head, tattoos, and constant glare, I never felt comfortable with him.

"What happened, Data?" Patrick laughed. "Let me help you, bro."

Michael jerked back. Not Michael, *Data*. The dude from *Star Trek. Was he an android?*

Data was furious now. "Stay the fuck away," he said in a squeaky voice. *Away, away, away.* The last word Data said seemed to echo, but it wasn't that loud, and we weren't in a canyon, so it was in my mind. He once again picked his papers up and stuffed them in his backpack.

When he pulled his bike up again, he struggled to straighten out his handlebars. They were bent and pointing to the left, even though his front wheel was straight.

"Let me get those bars bent back," I said as I walked over. He lifted his arm in a "stay away" motion. I stopped again.

"Hey, Chris, can I get a hit of that?" Patrick asked, pointing to the bottle. I forgot it was in my hand. *Mr. Hand, you dick!* I did a soft Jeff Spicoli laugh.

Before I could answer, he had my bottle and took a huge gulp from it. He handed it back.

"Whoa!" Patrick shouted. He took a pair of sunglasses out of his pocket and put them on. "Wow, that was the missing ingredient, boy!"

I started laughing. "The secret sauce!"

We laughed together. Data had bent the handlebars of his antique bike back the best he could and was pedaling off again.

"Well, this place looks pretty fucking secure, wouldn't you say, Chris?" Patrick asked, folding his arms and leaning back as if admiring his work.

"I would say so. Myself. You got this security thing down to a science. Why do they call him Data?" I asked, taking a drink from the bottle.

"Don't know. You seen Chuck?" he asked.

"He was scooting around a little while ago."

"I ain't seen him in a while. I will be in the security booth if he needs me. Securin' shit," Patrick said and stumbled back toward the booth. I lifted my arm in a wave.

I started walking back to my place when I saw some white things fluttering on the ground by the fence. Some of Data's papers had blown over there.

I heard the train horn. I had missed my chance to dance with the train out on the bridge. A minute later, I felt it roaring by with its lights shining on the trees and the RVs. I started singing the song "Night Train" as I swayed back and forth like Axl Rose. Then I moved on to "Train Kept a-Rollin'" by Aerosmith. But that was a cover of a song by some other band ...

I lost my train of thought. I turned around to say that out loud but realized I was alone, so I just laughed to myself.

Walking over, I started picking the papers up. I would give them to Data tomorrow. After stuffing them in my back pocket, I started walking back toward my camper.

Tomorrow. It already was tomorrow. I had to work in a few hours. The gloom of my life set in and macheted its way through the good vibes I was feeling. Every day that same urge to escape my life. The grand escape, not just carrying on my life in a new geographic location and fucking it up again.

After a few minutes, I realized I wasn't walking in the right direction. I was in the playground area, standing in front of the deflated jumping pillow. It was this crazy yellow-and-red monster inflatable pillow the kids bounced on like maniacs. I bounced on it drunk once but got yelled at because I had my shoes on. *Lighten up, dude.* I shuffled around the pillow, looking for a way to inflate it, but couldn't figure it out.

The big pile of deflated rubber looked comfortable, and I decided to sit on it. I would never get the chance to hang out on it during the day, so this was my time. *Fuck these kids, it belonged to me.* And my sandals were on! After setting my bottle down, I leaned back and raised my two middle fingers up toward the office building.

I took another big swig of Beam and walked into the middle of it. I made sure the cap was on my bottle and sat down. Then laid down. Crickets. *Where was the moon?*

Brady 3

6:45 a.m.

Running was the last thing I wanted to do. But I hadn't exercised in a while, and the weather was fair, so I felt I had to. My head throbbed a little from the drinks. In some respects, it was the new normal. I couldn't remember the last time I hadn't had at least a few drinks in the evening, and some sort of hangover the following morning.

My cell phone was my alarm, although I rarely needed it. Unless I needed to get up unusually early, my eyes generally just popped open around wakeup time. I didn't need the snooze function either. Once awake, I didn't drift back to sleep.

I had my phone plugged in and sitting on top of my gun safe. It was a small, black safe with a keypad and a fingerprint reader. One swipe of my pointer finger, and it popped open. I was never a big weapons guy, but I was a self-defense guy. I had a Glock 23 with a full magazine in it and another full mag lying next to it.

I sat up and tried to get a read on my hangover. It wasn't severe enough to derail my run. There was always a troublesome voice in my head urging me to evade exercise, but I seldom gave in to it because I was too unforgiving of my own laziness.

This hangover was a three or four on a scale of ten. I envisioned one of those scales in the doctor's office for patients to describe pain, with cartoon faces displaying emotions ranging from *happy* to *oh shit, I'm dying*. They should make one of those charts with drinking cartoons. The range could be from *buzzed* to *blacked-out*, with *tipsy*, *impaired*, and *shitfaced* cartoons along the spectrum. I was probably in the *tipsy* category the night before.

That morning, I wanted to get in a four-mile run. I had set my running clothes out the night before to reduce the chances that I would weasel out. I put on a pair of black running shorts, a gray Warrior Dash dry-fit shirt, a pair of black dry-fit socks, and a pair of gray Saucony running shoes. I grabbed a water bottle from the fridge and drank half of it in one swig.

I slid my cell phone into a black cloth running case and fastened it to my arm. I stepped out of the camper and locked it behind me, putting the key in my pocket.

The heart-rate indicator on my watch, a Garmin fitness tracker, reflected a higher-than-normal reading. Drinking alcohol always caused that, as my heart churned harder to metabolize the poison in my system.

I walked to the back of my lot to stretch and paused. The outdoor kitchen area door was open. *Alcohol-induced carelessness.* I went over and pulled it closed.

I walked out to the street and pushed a button on the right side of the watch. Scrolling through the exercise categories, I selected "Run." It searched for a GPS signal for a moment, then the red indicator changed to green. I took a deep breath, pushed the start button, and took off.

I started off running north on Starling. The campground was quiet. A bit of sun was showing through the clouds. The train horn sounded off in the distance.

I glanced at my watch, which was displaying the duration of the run and my pace. I was averaging about an 8:20 per mile pace. Not bad. A few years ago, I was in the low sevens, but that was before my family life siphoned away most of my training time.

The train barreled by as I ran up to the trail, heading east. I wondered how I slept through the continuous train traffic by the campground, but I actually seemed to sleep better in Sandusky than I did in Medina.

The view from the trail was scenic, with glimpses of sunlight shining through the trees and the cattails waving in the breeze along the surface of the water to the north. I emerged at the east end and ran back to the shoreline area. I approached the tent sites, which showed no signs of life. A dog started barking from somewhere.

Rounding back on Seagull Drive, I passed alongside the kids' area. I cut through between the deflated jumping pillow and activities station, to the east of the swimming pool, entering the south side of the campground.

There was an empty bottle of Jim Beam beside the pillow. I

considered stopping to throw it away, but I didn't want to interrupt my run. I figured the campground staff should see it and would realize they needed to crack down on some of the partying.

I ran back along the east side that had a series of cabins backing up to a tall stockade fence separating the campground from an auto dealership. In front of the cabins were several rows of campsites with full hookups, followed by rows of smaller cabins. The cabins were at about half capacity, judging by the cars parked in front. The west side had another series of seasonal sites, with some larger cabins along the stockade fence running parallel with Nickle Drive.

I circled back and passed by the security booth. An older worker with a blue US Navy baseball hat was standing there and waved. I waved back.

That route was about three-quarters of a mile. I considered just doing a few more loops within the campground and calling it quits, but then I took a left at the security booth and ran out toward the trailer park. The freedom to improvise was part of the allure of running.

I exited the campground and took a right up East Shoreway Drive. There were trailers in varying states of upkeep on either side. Most of them had a tree or two on the small lots. Overall, the area was unremarkable.

Occasionally a car passed by, but for the most part, it was quiet. The sidewalks were oddly narrow and full of deep cracks. A dog barked, and I saw a pit bull mix chained to a front porch. If that chain broke, I would have been in deep shit; it seemed very angry.

I'd had a half-dozen scary encounters during runs, with dogs who were not properly restrained by their negligent owners. Although I had never been bitten, I had been pursued, which definitely escalates your heart rate.

Palmer ended at West Shoreway Drive, where I took a left and headed south. This took me out of the trailer park, and it ran along the western parking lot of the Cloverleaf Apartments. They resembled a run-down housing project, grimy and beaten up. The lot was full of junky, rusted-out cars. Weeds grew through cracks in the pavement.

Just past the apartments was the entrance to Eagle Creek, a gated community. There was a black wrought-iron gate that lifted to allow vehicle access when activated by a keycard. Beside the main gate was a gate for pedestrians to use. There wasn't an actual security booth.

I had run past there multiple times and had always wanted to take a look at the houses within. The area was quiet, so I jogged over to the smaller gate. I pushed the gate lightly, and it didn't move. I turned and started jogging back to the street when a vehicle approached the gate from the inside. The gate slowly rose, and a dark-gray Land Rover rolled through and took a right onto West Shoreway.

The gate had reached its apex as the vehicle turned, and I doubted the driver could see the gate as it slowly lowered. Running over, I ducked beneath the opening. It closed behind me a few seconds later. I felt like I was Indiana Jones, narrowly escaping a cavern in the jungle as it collapsed behind him.

I don't know what I was thinking. I wasn't sure if I could exit through a pedestrian gate or would need a keycard. If trapped, I would have to wait for another vehicle to exit and slip out.

I ran along Eagle Creek Drive heading west and came across Crosstree Lane, taking a right and heading north. The houses were amazing. Maybe five thousand square feet, sided with lake stone, pillared, and well built. There was a canal running through each block, a watery alley, with boat garages and docks at the back of each house. Boaters could travel down the canal into a channel connecting to Lake Erie. I could only imagine how much these houses were worth.

Maybe that was the Holy Grail of luxury in northwest Ohio, living in a cul-de-sac in a gated community that featured boat garages. I was sure these were summer residences, as it wouldn't be appealing to live on a frozen canal in January. But that was what summer homes in Florida or North Carolina were for.

I ran up the street until it dead-ended in a cul-de-sac. I didn't want to push my luck and remain in the neighborhood too long, so I decided to exit instead of exploring the other streets. At the far west end, there was another gate that exited near some condos and an indoor water park owned by Gravity Junction.

I was fairly certain that most people here would identify me to be a stranger, as I assumed the neighbors all knew each other. It would be an awkward conversation if someone called security or the police. All I needed was to have Marcy bail me out of jail and lose my government security clearance for trespassing.

I ran the circle of the cul-de-sac and headed back. About halfway up the street, I heard a motorcycle fire up. I glanced to my left and saw a middle-aged guy roll slowly out of his garage, revving his bike loudly as he slowly drifted down the driveway.

The guy was in his late fifties with that Harley-Davidson biker look, but perhaps a degree more polished. His hair was totally gray, wearing wayfarer sunglasses, jeans, and a black T-shirt with a black leather vest. He had somewhat of a gut protruding over what I assumed was a Harley belt buckle.

I knew nothing about motorcycles, but that bike seemed expensive. I glanced again quickly and thought I recognized him. Or maybe his bike. I wasn't sure.

As I passed him, I tried to take a closer look without blatantly staring at him. I wished I had worn my sunglasses so it wouldn't be obvious.

He didn't look like he belonged in this neighborhood. It wasn't that he was unkempt looking, but he appeared more legit Harley, not the lawyer or doctor who decides to be a rebel and buys a Harley during the course of some midlife crisis. He looked like a blue-collar guy who had built a business, made some money, and clawed his way into the upper class.

Then I remembered where I saw him. He owned an RV in the northwest corner of the campground, the one Chuck and the creepy Euro guy frequented. Along with a few other creepy guys. Guys who were not seasonal campers. Not that I recognized everyone who camped at Sandusky Shores.

So, he had a mansion and a camper. Not quite Elmer J. Fudd with his "mansion and a yacht," but impressive. Within a mile of each other. *Okay.*

Was the camper some sort of rental property? It didn't make sense to have your house and RV located so close to each other. I wasn't entirely sure that he owned the RV. I wished I had checked his mailbox for a name as I ran past his house, but it was too late.

I ran back to Heron and turned left to return to the east gate. The motorcycle growled loudly as he approached me. He passed me slowly, without looking in my direction. I glanced at his vanity plate: *GLORYB*. "Glory be"? Was he a holy roller? He didn't fit the image of an avid churchgoer, but some of them defied stereotypes.

As he approached the gate, he stopped in front of the console and swiped a card. The gate began to rise. However, the guy just sat there.

I passed alongside him, and he looked over at me and smiled. He gestured his hand in a sweeping motion as if to say, "after you." I smiled as best I could, hesitated a moment, and ran past him and beyond the gate. He revved his engine a few times and followed, rolling slowly down the street. I turned right and ran about a hundred yards, turning into the parking lot of a bowling alley.

Glory Bowl. That was the name of the alley. Such a blatant off-color reference, and yet there it was, on a big neon sign in front. It had to be a play on "glory hole." I tried to envision youth bowling leagues with the place emblazoned on their shirts. I nearly laughed out loud when I imagined what the graphic on the shirts would be.

I figured I would do a loop in the parking lot. I glanced behind and saw the motorcycle guy had pulled in right behind me. I felt my tension rise as I reached the sidewalk in front of the alley and slowed a little. Was he tailing me because I was running through his gated neighborhood?

His vanity plate suddenly made sense. *GLORYB*. *Glory Bowl*. The bowling alley was his. It was my bad luck to run into the parking lot that was the Harley guy's destination. If I had just run up to Columbus Road, I would have been free of him.

He rolled up rather close to me as I approached the building but turned right and traveled behind it. Circling the parking lot, I ran back to the street.

The motorcycle engine revved again loudly, and then there was silence. I continued running back toward the camper, reminding myself to check the run stats later to see how high my heart rate had climbed during that particular segment of the run.

As I ran back in the direction of the campground, I could not get the motorcycle guy out of my mind. He had a lot of things going on in this small geographic area. I glanced over as I ran past the Cloverleaf Apartments. Did he have a stake in this too? I thought it would be worth looking into online property records on the county recorder website to see what names were on these properties.

Chuck 3
8:35 a.m.

My damned walkie-talkie shrieked, startlin' me and sendin' a pain up my left shoulder. That pain seemed to happen a few times every day. *Christ.*

The pain went away, and Data's voice crackled through the speaker. "Chuck, we have a problem over here at the jumping pillow. Can you get over here?"

"Yeah," I said, placing the walkie-talkie back on the dashboard. The battery was nearly dead; I would need to charge it. I forgot to bring it back to the office last night.

My head was poundin'. Completely poundin'. I felt queasy.

I dropped by the office when it opened and tried to eat a piece of bacon and toast from the breakfast buffet, only to hurl it up in the garbage can outside of the pool. An old couple walkin' by didn't seem to appreciate that. There was always a set of fuckin' eyes where you didn't need 'em.

I was in the far northeast corner and headed west, roundin' the northeast shower house and goin' south on Hawk. I was afraid somebody had vandalized the jumping pillow. Some dirtbag from the tent area had too much to drink a few summers ago and slashed it up with a pocketknife. Replacin' that thing was expensive.

Headin' west on Seagull Drive, I was careful to drive in the grass to the right of the speedbump. I hit one earlier and nearly threw up; it set my head to poundin' even worse.

I didn't remember comin' home the night before. Well, not the night before, it was earlier that mornin'. I woke up all sprawled out in a lawn chair in front of my camper. My back was killin' me from sleepin' awkward. There was a pile of puke over by the grill I had to clean up, retchin' as I did. Sharon would have gave me some shit if I just left it.

Startin' work early was always a bitch, but this was killin' me. The sun was out and bright as hell. Hangovers needed cloudy days, with rain or snow keepin' you indoors. Not cloudless and sunny. If

I hadn't had my sunglasses to protect me, I would likely have died.

After I half-ass cleaned up my puke, I limped over to my golf cart and found more puke on the hood and wheel well on the driver's side. At least I had the sense not to puke inside. There was also a big scratch alongside the fender. I looked closely, and there was some brownish gravel in the scratch, so it was most likely from the bricks of a fire pit. Much better to hit that than a car or RV.

I drove over to the east shower house, went in the bathroom, gathered a stack of paper towels, ran some water on them, and managed to clean the golf cart up without pukin' again. Luckily, there were no campers around. I entered the building again and washed my face with cold water. That made me feel a little better.

I was still feelin' drunk and dizzy as I pulled up to the playground area. It wasn't supposed to be open until 9 a.m., but both swinging gates were open. It was my job to lock them when it closed at 10 p.m., but I forgot to.

A few golf carts and work carts were parked on the fringes by the chain-link fence, and a small crowd of people gathered by the edge of the jumping pillow. One was Data. The others were campers.

I tried to play off how rough I was feelin' as I walked up. I thought about a cigarette, checked the inside of the golf cart, and didn't find any. Maybe that was for the best; sometimes they made me nauseous after a rough night.

Data waved as I walked up. The black guy in the Airstream at 65 was there too. A sudden drunken memory hit me hard, and I think I flinched. Somethin' about gettin' caught diggin' into someone's camper fridge last night. I couldn't quite grab the full memory. *Jesus Christ*.

The other two bystanders were the elderly couple who had seen me throwin' up in the garbage can earlier. I put on somethin' I thought was a smile but doubted it looked real.

"Hey, folks," I managed to croak.

"Hey, Chuck," Data said nervously.

"Somethin' wrong with the pillow?"

"Uh, yeah, there is somebody passed out here. Why wasn't the playground gate locked?"

"Who?" I asked, ignorin' his question. I would blame it on Patrick if Travis pressed me.

"Um, Chris from 51," Data said softly, almost whisperin'. I walked closer to the edge and saw a figure lyin' there on the deflated pillow. I recognized the greasy black hair. He was missin' his shirt, just a pale figure lyin' on his side.

"I found him earlier when I was cutting through here on a walk," Mike said, takin' a step closer. He was wearing an Atlanta Braves baseball hat, a red Under Armour T-shirt, black gym shorts, and gray runnin' shoes with white socks.

"Is he alive?" I asked in a whisper, feelin' that pain in my left arm again. I was havin' trouble catchin' my breath.

"Yeah, I checked his vitals. I put him in the rescue position. Someone better call an ambulance," Mike said. His voice was a little too loud for my liking. I could feel it in my head.

The elderly couple were millin' about over by the swing set, so maybe they weren't able to hear that. Them being old and all.

"Rescue position?" I asked, not knowin' what the fuck that meant.

"You turn him on his side, so if he vomits, he won't choke on it and die. It looks like he did a fair bit of vomiting earlier, but he is breathing, so there's that," Mike said, foldin' his arms. "They don't teach you any first-aid skills working at a campground? What if you have to pull some drowning kid from the pool or the lake?"

"Fuck no, I ain't no paramedic. Let's see if we can get him up," I said, walkin' gingerly toward the figure.

He appeared to be sleepin' soundly. Then I saw a few small piles of light brown vomit next to him. Some of it was on his gym shorts and the side of his face. The sight of the vomit stopped me in my tracks. Then the smell of it hit me. I backed up a few feet, got caught up in the pillow fabric, and fell back flat on my ass.

I stood up, not takin' the hand Data was tryin' to offer. I shuffled quickly over to the side to a garbage can along the fence and barely made it there as I threw up into it. About two feet over on the other side of the fence, a middle-aged black guy with flowery swim trunks and a white tank top was walkin' a small little dog with a red bow in its hair, frownin' at me. The dog started yippin'.

"Another one of those and you'll have a vomit hat trick," the old man who had seen me pukin' earlier said. I didn't look at him. I wiped my mouth with the inside of my elbow and walked slowly back.

"Did you radio Travis?" I asked.

"No, he isn't due in until lunch," Data said.

"Yeah, but somethin' like this usually … never mind, no police or ambulance involved, he don't need to be here. I can mention it later," I said. "Let's try to move him."

But I didn't move forward. I couldn't hang with the puke; it would send me to the garbage can again. Data looked at Mike, and he nodded.

"Hey folks, if there is nothin' else you need, we got this," I said, directin' it at the elderly couple. The black guy with the Yorkie, or whatever the fuck kind of dog it was, lingered by the fence. He shook his head and kept walkin', pullin' the dog along.

The elderly couple didn't move at first but then turned and started walkin' toward the office. Good thing those two were probably tech ignorant and likely wouldn't be leavin' a campground review on Yelp.

Travis was always goin' on about reviews left on Yelp. Compliments were never brought up, but the complaints were thrown in my face. The music was too loud at night, dogs barking, kids running wild, broken beer bottles, *blah blah blah*. A complaint about employees pukin' wouldn't go over good. About as good as a post about a junkie passed out at the playground.

Mike and Data walked over to Chris. Mike situated himself by his head, Data by his feet. Mike slowly rolled him onto his back. They counted to three and picked him up, with Mike grabbin' under his armpits, careful to avoid touchin' puke. They slowly walked him off the pillow and over beneath a tree, where they leaned him back against it.

Chris 2

8:40 a.m.

There I was, being escorted out of the tower. Not guided or led, physically escorted by two security guards, semi-frog-marched, with each grasping an elbow. A third had a cardboard box with my personal items.

This walk of shame was not a complete surprise. The shift had begun like any other. I arrived for work at Cleveland Hopkins Airport right on time, like I almost always did. Never early, generally on time, occasionally late.

This was seldom appreciated by the person I was relieving, but sometimes I just flaked out. I had been written up a few times, but hey, I was a federal employee. What could they do to me?

My gig as an air-traffic controller was a good one. I had the aptitude for it, as I first discovered as a senior in high school when I took the Armed Services Vocational Aptitude Battery (ASVAB) test, a standardized military test to see what sort of job I qualified for in the air force. I figured I would get a decent job, maybe as an aircraft mechanic or a computer programmer or something.

My ASVAB score came back really high. Not jet-pilot high, but air-traffic-control or foreign-linguist high. Learning a foreign language sounded like a drag, so I went with air-traffic controller.

My first four years in the air force, I managed to be drug free. I had cleaned up prior to going to basic and was able to stay off them.

While stationed at Hickam Air Force Base in Hawaii, I met an airman in the barracks who was getting his private pilot's license. It sounded interesting, so I enrolled and began working toward getting mine. The classroom stuff was easy, and the hours behind the yoke were amazing. I couldn't imagine a better place to learn piloting than the Hawaiian Islands. From that point on, I was able to continue logging hours at the various places I was stationed, although buying my own aircraft was way beyond my financial capabilities.

It was during my fourth year that I stumbled. I was stationed at a Royal Air Force base in England, outside of Suffolk. I had a weekend pass and went to the mainland with a few buddies. We bought rail passes and explored.

After making a few stops, we ended up in Amsterdam, and that was when my drug habit came roaring back. It started with a little weed and got worse. Whatever I found that I could smoke, I smoked. By the end of the weekend, I was totally baked and incoherent, and it took an effort for my buddies to pry me out of our hotel and get me back on the train. I didn't remember the journey home.

I never fully recovered from that relapse. My last two years, I played cat and mouse with the drug testing program, never getting busted. But my work performance degraded. After I was caught sleeping in the tower one night, I was told that if I reenlisted, it wouldn't be as an air-traffic controller.

I had been struggling with depression since I could remember, and that was the root cause of my drug problems. Numbing myself had been necessary just to get through the day in high school. I was able to stay clean in the air force because I was involved in a dynamic and positive profession, but after a while, it became the new normal, *and the normal became boring.*

About three months from being discharged, I received an inquiry from the FAA about applying to civilian jobs. Apparently, my track record still appeared okay from the outside. The sleeping incident was handled in house and didn't make it to my permanent record. I spoke with my supervisor, and he agreed to give me a recommendation. He wanted me gone. I was a liability, and he wanted me to be someone else's problem.

I interviewed with the FAA in Tampa Bay and was offered a job a few weeks later. I was given a few airport choices and decided on Cleveland Hopkins Airport, to be closer to my family in Michigan.

This job prospect returned me to sobriety. I quit smoking as soon as I was offered the job, knowing a drug test was imminent. I made it through the remainder of my enlistment, received an honorable discharge, and packed my shit for Cleveland.

The opportunity was a good one. It was at a high pay level, so

I was making a lot more than I had as a staff sergeant in the air force. I bought a cheap Nissan at a used-car lot in Panama City, loaded it up, and left the air force base and my military career for good. I drove up north to Ohio and found an apartment in Brook Park, the city where the airport was located.

After additional training, I began my career as a civilian air-traffic controller. I performed well and earned the respect of my peers. I had gone clean trying to get the job and remained clean. That wasn't too hard because I didn't have any bad influences.

I had a few friends at work, and all of them were straight. We'd get together for a few drinks or to catch a sporting event, but nobody was into drugs.

That changed when I made the mistake of taking a week off and visiting my parents in Jackson, Michigan, my hometown. It was only about a three-hour drive from Cleveland. While hanging out at a local bar in Jackson, I ran into an old high school buddy.

The next thing I knew, I was sitting in his truck, smoking it up. That was pretty much what I did the rest of the week. When it was time to leave on Sunday, I called into work and stayed an extra day to get more high time in.

When I returned to work, there was an incident on my shift. It wasn't even my fault. A coworker working an adjacent position made an error, and two planes passed too close to each other under his direction. The FAA policy was for all close calls to be followed by drug tests. So, although I didn't make a mistake, I was called in before the end of my shift and forced to give a urine sample on the spot. It came back hot.

A week later, I did a drug retest. Two days after that, I was escorted off the airport premises. I was officially suspended with pay, pending a hearing, but the union could offer little help. I wasn't some government paper-pusher; I was tasked with guiding dozens of airplanes filled with thousands of people safely to the ground each shift. I lost the hearing and a few appeals, and a month later I was terminated.

I picked up odd jobs, managing to keep my apartment for a year, but getting my car repoed. I met Candy at the bar around the corner from the apartment, a blue-collar dive bar with a pool table, a jukebox, and cheap drinks.

We hit it off, and I moved in with her at her dumpy apartment for a few months before a stoner friend of mine told me about a job opportunity his cousin had hooked him up with in Sandusky.

Gravity Junction was building a huge sports complex a few miles down from the park, which would feature several outdoor fields that could be used for soccer, baseball, and lacrosse. They urgently needed laborers from the spring through the fall.

I was working as a cook and dishwasher at Candy's bar and making minimum wage. The construction gig paid double that. My friend acquired a junky RV and set it up at the Sandusky Shores Campground.

Unfortunately, my stoner friend ran into some bad luck. He got pulled over outside of Toledo carrying a huge stash of weed and pills. He had enough contraband to get charged as a dealer and was locked up until his trial in the fall.

So, I inherited the trailer we were going to share. Candy had a conflict with her boss at the bar, quit her job, and moved in with me. That was lucky, because I still didn't have a set of wheels, so I could use her car to get me to work. And since she was a bartender, if she worked the night shift, there would never be a conflict. It turned out she didn't have any interest in getting another job, so there wouldn't be any conflict whatsoever. *My luck was just amazing.*

The work at the sports complex was all manual. I wasn't opposed to working hard, but some of those twelve-hour days were brutal. The most demoralizing reality of my situation was that I could see Griffing Sandusky Airport from my jobsite, so every day I had a reminder of what I used to be. The opportunities I squandered were very clear, as I watched the small planes come and go all day while I shoveled dirt or walked around with a trash bag, cleaning up the worksite throughout the day.

In a different world, I would be working there as an air-traffic controller or piloting some rich guy's G6 to Put-In-Bay Island for a weekend trip. Instead, I was a hundred yards up the street with a shovel, digging a trench to lay drainage pipes for the new sports park.

I reflected on working in a trench being dug alongside the road. The backhoes did most of the work, trenching the earth out and placing it to the side in piles. The laborers like me were needed to then go in and do more detailed digging.

I pictured myself shoveling a large scoop of dirt to the side, taking a dirty rag out of my pocket, and wiping my brow. I sat down with my back along the side of the hole and closed my eyes briefly. Someone was yelling something at me, maybe a coworker telling me to get back to work, but I was so tired.

Something nudged me. My eyes were still closed, but I felt something hard against my back. I managed to open my eyes just a little. Leaning over me, I saw the black guy from across the street in the shiny camper.

I wasn't in the trench; I had been dreaming. I was leaning against a tree in the playground area at the campground. My feet were straight out in front of me. My left sandal was missing. The guy from the aluminum camper was saying something to me, but I couldn't quite understand him.

Chuck 4

8:45 a.m.

Chris stirred a little and opened his eyes into tiny slits. He tried to lift his hands to his face, but they just came up about six inches and dropped.

"Hey, Data, get me a bottled water, and then take my cart over to 51 and see if his girlfriend is around," I ordered.

He was confused for a minute because I don't let nobody drive my golf cart. Just then I didn't care. I didn't want to deal with the girlfriend.

"Okay, Chuck. When you are done, we need to talk about something," he said nervously.

"Fine, let's get this cleaned up first. I'm going to get a few guys to hose that off. We should be able to get it up and runnin' before it gets busy out here," I said.

I radioed and got things movin'.

A work cart pulled up with Patrick and Vaughn. Vaughn was a thirty-something-year-old black man, big, maybe six foot four, and pushing three hundred pounds. Shaved head, short graying beard, wearing the campground uniform of a yellow polo, yellow hat, black cargo shorts. Big white sneakers. He was pretty quiet and did what he was told without sayin' much. They walked over to me.

"Is it bad?" Patrick asked behind his dark sunglasses, noddin' toward the pillow.

"I've seen worse," I said.

Vaughn walked to the side of the clubhouse and came back with a rolled-up hose. He started unrollin' it as he walked toward the pillow.

Chris moved his hands to his face and covered it. A few minutes later, Data pulled up in my golf cart with Candy in the passenger seat.

"I think we're good, Mike, thanks," I said.

He ignored me and crouched down by Chris. "You okay, buddy?" Mike asked softly.

Chris nodded so slightly it was barely seen. He stiffened up a little when he saw Candy and hopped to his feet. He stumbled and caught his balance with one hand beneath him. I was impressed he could pull that off, given that he was mostly dead a few minutes ago.

"Easy, kid," Mike said, grabbing him by the elbow. His face was covered with sweat, the chest hair above the neckline of his T-shirt caked with flecks of puke. He was missing his left sandal.

"Hey, anyone seen his sandal?" I asked. Vaughn was now lightly spraying the jumping pillow while Patrick watched him.

Candy marched angrily toward Chris, carrying a bottled water. Redheads had a reputation for being hot-tempered, and she fit that, her face scrunched up in anger, freckled cheeks all rosy. Her hair was pulled back tight in a ponytail, closer to a brownish color with traces of red; she wasn't one of those gingers with bright-orange hair. She wore a pink tank top, white polka dot pajama bottoms, and flip-flops.

She walked past Chris and over to Vaughn. Droppin' the bottle, she pulled the hose nozzle out of his hands. It stopped sprayin' when he released the trigger. Vaughn just crossed his arms; it didn't seem to bother him.

She turned the hose on Chris and sprayed him in the face from about three feet away. Chris made a sort of yelpin' noise, shivered, and then ducked and brought his hands up to cover his face. She sprayed him in the torso, then the crotch, then the legs. Chris tried to cover each place she aimed at. Finally, she dropped the hose and picked up the water bottle.

"Drink this!" she hissed, uncappin' it and pushin' it into his hands. He took a short pull, belched, and dry-heaved. He paused for a minute and then took another small swig.

"Can you drive him back to the camper?" she asked Data, who was comin' back from the other side of the pillow with Chris's missing brown sandal.

"Sure," Data said, handin' Chris his sandal. In a daze, he just stood there with it. I didn't want him to get in the golf cart drippin' wet, but I needed to get this circus over with. I would dry it off later.

"What time were you supposed to be at work?" she asked

flatly. He didn't respond at first. She snapped her fingers in front of his nose. "Hello? Earth to Chris! Need me to get the hose again?"

"No, Christ. Nine o'clock," he said.

"You have ten minutes. You ain't losing this job. You need to get cleaned up, and I'll drive you in." Chris didn't respond but started limpin' over to the golf cart, still carryin' his sandal.

I was a little surprised at how bossy she was. She hadn't said two words to no one since she'd moved in. She struck me as lazy. Once Chris left for work, it would probably be naptime for her, and then on to the couch for the game shows and soap operas.

"Put your fucking shoe on," she hissed as she started walkin'. Chris climbed in the golf cart gingerly. He leaned down to slip his sandal on as Data climbed behind the wheel. He gave it some gas and then braked at the edge of the playground. Chris lurched forward and hit his head on the dash. Data apologized as they looped around and exited the gate. Candy didn't even look up as they passed by.

Mike 3

9:10 a.m.

That's what I got for venturing out for an early morning walk. Next time I was going to go off site to a park or something. Chris was lucky he didn't die.

I felt the scratching of the papers against my back as I walked and hoped they weren't noticeable or slipping down deeper into my shorts. I walked to my camper, entering and locking the door behind me.

Reaching behind my back, I pulled out the wad of papers. There were five wrinkled pages.

When I came across the unconscious Chris, the papers were scattered around him. One was underneath him and was only revealed when I flipped him on his side. The top corners of several pages had puke or bourbon on them, making them a light-brown color. I mentally noted the need to shower and change clothes after handling them.

I laid the papers out on the table. I also noted to wash the table when I was through.

It was some sort of records summary. I had given the papers a quick look as I picked them up by the jumping pillow and found they weren't Chris's personal papers. The name at the top was Brady Sullivan, along with his social security number and home address.

I only had a quick moment after I discovered them scattered around Chris to decide a course of action. If I was sure they were Chris's, I would have gathered them and returned them when he regained consciousness. But they weren't his.

I tried to decide if he could have legitimately been holding someone else's papers. I figured they could have been a friend's, but that wouldn't explain why Chris would have them in his possession while wandering around the campground in a late-night stupor.

Brady Sullivan. Site 31. The guy who was a victim of Chuck's alcohol theft earlier that morning.

His home address was in Medina, Ohio. I dug in a drawer and found my US road atlas. It was one of those big ones, about fifteen by eleven inches, beaten up and dog-eared from decades of use. I was one of the few people under the age of seventy who still owned an atlas. I flipped it to Ohio. Medina was a small town about thirty miles south of Cleveland.

I reviewed the rest of the pages. There were summaries of his employment history, income tax records, and property records. Sullivan worked for PAF, a federal agency that I recognized. It was the agency that paid me as a soldier and retiree.

He had a master's degree and a few government certifications. As I worked my way through his employment history, I found a common employer, the US Army, from twenty years ago. That was interesting. He served three years. Matching that against his year-by-year income on the tax summary, I found he was making peanuts during those years, so he was likely enlisted. Most people at that salary were below the poverty level, but when the military food and lodging benefits were factored in, it wasn't quite as bad.

Another page had his credit history. Sullivan had a high credit score. There were a few maxed credit cards, but nothing was paid late. A fifteen-year mortgage with about eleven years to go on a $300,000 house. A $27,000 camper that they financed for ten years. It didn't list the RV model.

The summary continued with Marcy Sullivan, maiden name Kovich. She worked at a place that sounded like a medical billing firm. She made substantially less than Brady.

Overall, the Sullivans were clean, nothing that would set off any red flags. As a senior enlisted noncommissioned officer, I had reviewed more than a few financial records summaries of problem soldiers.

There was only one page on Marcy; the rest was missing. The other pages must have blown away between Chris's collapse on the jumping pillow and my finding him several hours later. I wondered if he had been partying with Chuck, who was also destroyed last night and feeling mighty rough that morning, as demonstrated by his garbage can puking incident.

Did I miss some big party last night? Someone forgot to invite me. Then again, Chuck's partying led him to steal drinks from another camper, so how much fun could it have been?

I generally tried to hold off drinking until after lunch, but I found myself making a screwdriver. Vodka and its scentlessness was the universal go-to for morning drinking. And orange juice was most certainly a breakfast drink.

Data 2

9:35 a.m.

I felt my gut churning. When I got back to Grandma's trailer earlier that morning and went through the backpack, I discovered that some of my summary sheets were missing. I still had most of Marcy's, but Brady's were gone.

If I would have slowed down and reviewed the papers before I left the campground, I would have realized some were missing. But with Patrick and Chris out acting like lunatics, I was flustered.

I went back once I noticed they were missing and asked Patrick, but he swore he didn't have the papers. He had no reason to lie; they were of no use to him. I needed to review the security video.

Patrick was difficult to figure out. He was one of the few guys who was nice to me once in a while, but last night he was obnoxiously intoxicated.

Chris may have had them, but I knew he was at work. I biked over to his camper, just in case he decided to call off, but the door was closed. Knocking could trigger his volatile girlfriend, and I wanted no part of that.

I didn't know if Chris was coherent enough to gather my papers, but he was trying to help me pick them up when I dropped them. Both times. I dropped them twice. *Idiot.*

Randy would kill me if I told him. I was the technology guy, the careful guy, and the sober guy. *The details guy.* This would ruin that trust. This may ruin this job, and then I wouldn't have access to any technology at all.

The entire data extraction only took an hour. It took me another half hour to type up the summaries. The other few hours I spent at Trailer Alpha were on the Dark Web. I liked to check out the places I used to go and see if some of the people I used to know were still out there.

I knew all their usernames. A few were still at it, although others were like me and sneaking around using different aliases.

I was careful not to post anything or go anywhere where I may be recognized. I wanted to gloat about being back, but that would be self-destructive. If I got caught again, that would lead to more hard time.

I was a little annoyed with Travis. If he had standards of hiring and the campground wasn't such a haven for thugs and misfits, then none of this would happen. But if the campground was managed on the level and the employees were all Boy Scouts, then Travis wouldn't have hired me, and Randy would have no use for me.

Travis 2

9:45 a.m.

J esus Christ, it was always something. Trying to get this campground a five-star rating with all these lackeys Randy brought in was bad enough. These seasonal randoms like Chris Randolph were just as bad.

I pulled into the campground in my Jeep and stopped at the security gate. No one was there. Of course not. I thought Patrick would be there.

I parked and walked across to the office. Rounding the corner, I saw Vera at the front desk, staring down at her cell phone. Nothing like paying people to fuck around on their phones all day.

"What's new, Vera?" I asked loudly.

She flinched and stood up, sliding the phone into her purse. "Hey, Travis," she said. She was the typical type of office help I was able to get with the low wages I paid. Nineteen years old, slightly overweight, nose ring, red streaks through her dyed-blonde hair that was down to her shoulders. Tattoos almost every place that skin showed, from her knuckles to her forearms to the back of her neck. Always chewing gum. Probably high or planning how she could sneak off and get high. Probably would happen in a cabin with Chuck.

"I have a truck coming in at any time with a load of chains and fenceposts. They are to be dropped off along the back northeast area," I said, knowing she couldn't identify northeast to save her life. She nodded.

"Please have Chuck or Data escort it back there, and have the chains unloaded to the flatbed trailer and stack the poles beside it. It may require a fork truck. Chuck should be able to make that happen."

I found several hundred feet of used nautical chains at an auction, salvaged from a marina in Vermillion. I also bought a bunch of six-foot metal posts, so the plan was to sink the posts and run the chains along the entire shoreline as a decorative fence. It would also serve to keep stupid people from trying to swim in the swampy shore area.

"Did you hear about the wasted guy passing out on the jumping pillow?" she asked, chomping savagely on the piece of gum in her mouth. I nodded.

"Let's not talk about that when customers are wandering around. It isn't exactly the kind of publicity we're looking for," I said, shaking my head.

Chuck was out front, sitting in his golf cart. As I walked toward him, I heard a voice from behind me.

"Hey, Travis!"

I turned and saw Brady Sullivan walking up. He was wearing a green Medina Lacrosse T-shirt and black gym shorts.

"Hey, Mr. Sullivan."

"What's new?"

"We're waiting on a delivery. I bought some large chains to make a fence along the east shore."

"Cool. That will look good. When will that be done?"

"Hopefully sometime this season."

I sighed and looked over at Chuck. He was slouched down in the seat and looked like he was about to fall asleep in his golf cart.

"Or next."

"Can't wait to see it. I need to settle my electricity bill and then get back to work. Talk to you later," he said and went into the office.

I heard the squeal of semi brakes and knew it was probably the delivery truck coming up Nickle Drive.

Viktor 2

10:00 a.m.

I stepped out of the camper and yawned, reaching for my cigarettes. My head ached from the vodka, but it wasn't bad. I had a little more vodka for breakfast, along with *tara paine*, a ham cold cut, and a tomato.

Dressed in the ridiculous Gravity Junction costume, I sat in my lawn chair on the deck and smoked. The sun was getting bright, so I put on my sunglasses.

The campground was still quiet but getting busier. Quiet except for the train that blew the damn horn as it came by, shaking my RV. I needed to balance the level of the RV, there was a *pantă* ... slope down toward the street. The bathroom door would not fully close, but what did I care? I had no visitors.

I had to be at the park at 1100 hours but had an errand to run along the way. The girls had to be checked on. Over a month in the country should be good enough for them to *regla* ... adjust, and they had started the work they were brought in for weeks ago. It wasn't running roller coasters or cooking cheeseburgers, like the other foreign workers.

It was a surprise inspection that I could do because I had keys to the apartments. I finished my cigarette and locked the camper.

I got on my motorcycle and revved it a few times. Pulling out and going up the street, I went very slowly past the crazy shrieking woman's camper. She was not out yet.

I pulled out of the campground and took a left, then a right into the apartment parking lot. Cloverleaf could be an apartment building in Romania. Run down. Dark. Gray. The parking lot was busted blacktop with weeds growing from cracks. The cars were junk.

There were three large buildings. I went to the far one that was most western. I parked and walked up to the building. The girls were on the basement floor, sharing two rooms.

There was an ashtray by the door filled with cigarette butts. I pulled out my keys and unlocked the door.

The hallway carpet was dirty, and it smelled of garbage and cigarettes. I walked down the stairs to the basement rooms. There were two doors on either side of the hall. Romanians lived in three, the other for Mr. Randy's business. I went to the far door and unlocked it.

Daniela 1

10:15 a.m.

There he was, walking up to the building. Scumbag. He was sure to try to help himself to one of the girls. *Pig.*

I made the lazy girls help me clean this dump. I cannot worry about the other room or the boys. If it is not clean, Viktor will have a fit, but that is not my problem.

I had to be at the park at noon, so there was only so long I would have to put up with this visit. From the first day, rule number *unu* was to always go to the day job. If we lost the day job, we lost the visa, and then we are sent home. This was tempting, but I would have music to face at home if I was sent back early with no money.

My shift was eight hours in the park handing paper cups to fat tourists. Standing at the cash box, punching buttons, scanning cards, and handing cups to fat kids so they could draw sodas from the machine. Fat kids drinking sugar and food dye over and over.

The park had a drink plan that let them have a new drink every fifteen minutes. People pouring this garbage down the mouths of kids every fifteen minutes. *Disgusting.* Why not a cup of juice or water?

But that was better than the other job. I wanted to stay in the apartment tonight or go out on the boat. The boat clients were better. The campground was not so good. Sometimes the cabins meant I had to stay all night, which was *îngrozitor* ... awful. Then I had to leave early, before the sun came up. A few hours of sleep and then to the park. Seven days a week at the park all summer.

I heard keys jingling, followed by Viktor jamming a key into a lock. The doors had many bolt locks. No knocking, he just let himself in. He wanted to see if he could bust us doing something wrong. *Asshole.*

After unlocking them, he walked in, closing the door behind him. He pointed to the window.

"Why is the curtain open?" he asked flatly in Romanian.

"Why not? There is nothing wrong with letting sunlight in here," I said, walking over to the small kitchen.

"Privacy. You don't want to draw attention to yourselves. Where are the others?" he asked, walking over and sitting on the couch.

The very small apartment just had a little couch, a chair, a coffee table, and a stand with a small TV on top of it. A few ashtrays sat on top of the coffee table. The carpet was a dirty white color.

"Maria and Andreea are working in the park," I said. "The others are next door and working later."

"The men?" he asked, folding his arms.

"I don't know." I shrugged.

"Get me something to drink," he said, putting his feet on the coffee table.

I opened the cupboard and took out a half-empty bottle of vodka. I poured it into a red plastic cup and gave it to him. He took it and had a small taste like he was *eşantionare* ... sampling something exotic and not cheap vodka in a plastic cup.

"Are the collections up to date?" he asked, staring at me. I hated that stare. I thanked God that he perhaps did not have time to take me in the back room. He looked more pale than usual and sickly. Hungover. Good.

Viktor looked down at his watch. The stupid watch he was so proud of, some *luxos* ... luxury watch fake that he pretended was real. As if some roller coaster park stooge could afford high-cost jewelry. He fooled no one.

"Do you know where you all need to be tonight? And this weekend? Bike week in Sandusky is also very busy. A lot of money to be made," he said as he finished his drink and set it on the table.

"Yes," I said. I did not care to say anything that would anger him or interest him. The less the better. *Just get him out of here.*

"Good," he said. He looked at his watch again.

"Okay. I am getting changed. I will talk to you later," I said, putting the bottle back in the cupboard.

"What time do you work?" he asked.

"Noon," I replied, trying not to sound nervous.

"Plenty of time. What is your rush?" he asked, squaring up

his shoulders. He looked me up and down.

"I must shower and do my hair. I have to get there early."

"Why?"

"We haven't been receiving regular ice deliveries. The machine runs out, and the tourists get angry. I wanted to ask the supervisor," I said, lying. It was true that the machines ran out of ice several times a day, but I did not give a shit. Let the fatties drink warm soda.

Viktor stared at me for a long time. Then he stood up and reached in his pocket for his keys. He left without saying a word. I locked all the locks and shut the curtains.

Sam 1

7:30 p.m.

My shift ended at the bowling alley later than I expected, and I wasn't going to get overtime for going over eight hours. Big picture, my career with Randy wasn't a career where I punched a timeclock and claimed overtime. I couldn't complain about the bowling alley pay because the side jobs Randy tossed my way more than made up for it.

I was hoping to have a few minutes to relax and get my mind right for the job after work, but I needed to get moving if I was going to get it done tonight. Going out the back door, I unlocked my black Chevy Suburban with the fob. Pulling out onto Columbus Road, I headed to the causeway that connected the mainland to the amusement park.

The causeway was manmade, built for traffic to cross from the shore of Sandusky to Gravity Junction. As you drove along, the open water of Lake Erie was to the left and a smaller cove was to the right. The cove was created by the construction of the causeway, with a small canal letting boats in and out beneath the road.

The traffic wasn't as bad as I figured. Earlier it rained for a few minutes, and that might have scared off some of the people. The causeway was a five-lane road with traffic managed by using orange cones to assign the direction of the lane. Three lanes were going in and two going out. When it opened, four lanes were going in, and after it closed, four lanes went out.

The west side of the park became visible, with the big roller coasters seeming to rise out of the water. As the causeway curved to the right, the east side was visible. More steel rides. The Cloud Ride, a cable car ride going north and south, was dead center.

I stayed in the left lane and showed my park pass as I pulled up to the booth. Otherwise, it would cost a ridiculous twenty dollars to park. Randy bought me a season pass that included parking because I did a lot of business in and around the park. I couldn't remember the last time I used my pass to go on a roller coaster ride. That wasn't my preferred type of entertainment.

The main parking lot was directly ahead and appeared to be about half full. After pulling past the booth, I drove down a street going east-west that bordered the lot.

As I pulled even with the first roller coaster, I took a left into an area that had restaurants, a dog kennel, and the marina entrance. I parked in front of the marina, opened the back of the SUV, and took out a large black duffel bag.

I walked along to the dock, which had several rows of boat slips. Most of the boats were expensive, although there were a few junky ones that found their way there, probably rehab projects.

The marina wasn't cheap. The hobby of boating, in general, wasn't cheap, but that place was next-level expensive.

I could afford a modest boat, but they took a lot of time and effort. Those types of toys ended up owning you. The cost of the boat was high enough, but then you added in fuel, insurance, supplies, transportation, repairs, storage fees, and all kinds of other unexpected costs.

I turned right when I reached the third dock offshoot, looking down at the wooden planks so I wouldn't trip. About halfway down, Randy's boat came into sight.

It was a gorgeous fifty-foot Azimut Flybridge, a half-million-dollar boat. The yacht had a full kitchen, two staterooms, two full bathrooms with showers, and a family room with a pullout sleeper. Decked out with state-of-the-art electronics, it included an advanced nav system, a weather station, cameras, fish finders, a digital antenna, and a sound system. It was powered by twin 669-horsepower inboard engines. *Morning Glory, Sandusky, Ohio* was stenciled in fancy lettering along the back.

Morning Glory. These boats all had stupid names. You probably couldn't buy a boat without promising to name it something stupid. That and the need to fly a stupid flag. Maybe you had to pledge to wear a stupid captain's hat too.

A twelve-foot Saturn Dinghy Tender with a thirty-horsepower motor was tied to the back of the yacht. It was the inflatable type, but it was a premium dinghy and durable.

I was nervous about operating it at first. If I damaged it,

Randy would kill me. But I was pretty good at operating vehicles in general. I learned to crew an amphibious attack boat in the Corps, and that was much more technical, plus it had a weapons system.

I unlocked the door to the bridge and went inside. It was perfectly clean inside; nothing was out of place. That was how Randy liked it and demanded it. At least with everything except the bowling alley. For some reason, he was never concerned with tidiness when it came to that place.

When we were out entertaining on the boat, some clients treated it badly. Drunk, sloppy people spilling things, smoking where they weren't supposed to, dropping ashes on the carpet.

People always treated other people's property like crap. Bowling alley customers were the worst. The things people did to the bathroom were disgusting. You wouldn't go into your own bathroom and throw paper towels in the toilet, punch the mirror, wipe a booger on the mirror, or scratch graffiti on the stall walls. Yet people did that all the fucking time at Glory Bowl.

Overall, clients weren't that bad on the boat. Most didn't intentionally wreck things, and most of the damage was from carelessness. If it was a crew member who damaged something, I addressed that carelessness. If it happened twice, I addressed it with some wall-to-wall counseling. If it happened out on the lake, that crew member could end up swimming back to shore.

If it was damage from the client, I politely asked them to cover it. There was usually very little pushback, given the nature of what was happening out on the boat. Johns out on the water who refused to pay would get a gallery of pictures from a high-definition camera in the main cabin that was very persuasive.

I opened a drawer by the console, pulled out a laminated checklist of pre-launch tasks, and got to work.

A man approached, walking up the dock. He was carrying a big red duffel bag. He walked over and stood in front of my dock, then walked to the back and looked at the back of the boat.

He was a big man, probably six foot four, maybe 250 pounds. I guessed he was in his late twenties or early thirties. He had a military look to him, black hair cut close, a guy who spent a fair amount of time in the gym. Tattoos were visible on his neck, forearms, and hands. His face looked battle worn. His nose was flat, like maybe he used to box. His jaw was square and clean shaven.

I was not happy to see him wearing his park uniform. I left instructions not to wear that. He wasn't starting off on the right foot with me.

We made eye contact, and I waved him on board. I glanced at the white rectangular name tag over his pocket. "Alexander" in large black letters. "Romania" in smaller red letters. He opened the door and came in.

"Sam?" he asked, pronouncing my name as *Som* in a thick accent, holding out his hand for me to shake. I ignored it. He stood there awkwardly for a few seconds and then dropped his hand. Standing next to him, I figured he was a few inches taller.

"Didn't Viktor tell you to change clothes before coming here?"

He stood there unmoving. "No, he did not."

"Fucking Viktor. You are walking around with a name tag and then getting on this boat before we do a job. You don't see the problem with that?" I asked, shaking my head.

He stood there silently with a blank expression on his face. "I will know next time."

"Did you bring a change of clothes, or do you want to do the job wearing a Gravity Junction uniform with a name tag?"

"I have clothes," he said quietly.

"Go change and we'll get started, unless you want to keep chewing the fat onshore," I said, looking back at the check sheet.

"Chewing fat?" he asked, looking puzzled.

"Go back there and change. Hopefully, you didn't pack a shirt with your name on it," I said impatiently, pointing to the stairs leading to the lower berth.

Alexander walked past me and down the stairs. When he came back up, he was wearing a jogging outfit. All black, including black running shoes. I was wearing a black tank top, running pants, and gray tennis shoes. This was a lot of black.

"Do you know how to crew a boat?" I asked.

He stared at me blankly. "Crew?" he asked.

"How to work on a boat?" I said. I turned the key, and the

engine roared to life, gurgling steadily in the water.

"No," he said.

I nodded. "Just do what I say. Untie those two ropes from the posts and toss the ropes into the boat," I said. He went out and started untying ropes.

Once I saw we were untied, I backed out slowly. The engine hummed louder as we separated from the dock. After we were out several yards, I spun it around and went forward at a slow pace. I was careful to watch the wake through the marina area. People tended to complain about the slightest wave, even though we had the marina to ourselves.

I continued along until I was beyond the marina and opened it up a little. The engine hummed louder, and a wake began to form. When I gave it some gas, Alexander stumbled a little, and that made me smile. After I was out in the open, I turned it up even more, moving along at about thirty knots.

The sun was setting to the right. It would be dark in about a half hour. I motioned for Alexander to come up to the bridge. "Sit down, I'm going to brief you on what we're going to do, Al," I said.

He sat down. "It is Alexander," he said.

"Do you expect me to blurt out four syllables every time I need your attention? My name is Samuel. *Sam-u-el.* Three syllables. But people just call me Sam. Neither one of us is royalty. Simplify your life, son," I said in an irritated voice. Al didn't react.

"We are paying a visit to a guy named Tom Polk. He has a beach house over at Torch Point. You ever been there?" I asked. He shook his head.

"We'll anchor about a half-mile west, about fifty yards from the shore. We will launch the dinghy and take that the rest of the way. Pulling in with this big monster would surely draw too much attention.

"Tom is a John who booked a date at a cabin a few Saturdays ago over at the campground. He overlooked the fact that he had to pay. For the second time. He enjoys the hookers but not the bill. Randy knows him and let it slide once, but not twice."

It was odd that Randy would let him have a second date at all, since he didn't pay the first time. That was not the way he did business.

"I don't know why a rich guy wouldn't opt for the boat rather than those grimy cabins, maybe he liked to slum. Some do," I said.

"Slum?" Al asked.

"Never mind. We tried to get a hold of him, but this guy has been dodging us. We are gonna visit him and persuade him to pay up." Al nodded.

"Polk is going to pay tonight. How we work that out with him is up to me. You don't do nothin' unless I tell you to. Got it?" I asked. Al continued to nod.

We moved along in silence for a while. Al stared out across the lake, taking in the scenery.

"How far is the target?" he asked.

"It should take us about forty-five minutes."

"Why take the boat? Why not drive?"

"A couple of reasons. One, Tom lives in a gated community. If we drive there, we have to go in and out past security. On a boat, I can pull up and tie off on the community dock. Two, it is hard to identify a dinghy unless you are right next to it. The odds of someone identifying a small boat in the dark are low," I said. He nodded.

"Just so you know, I'm the only one carrying a piece. Your job is to look scary and to help me out if things go sideways," I said.

"I can handle weapons," he said.

"You former military?" I asked.

He nodded. "*Operaţii Speciale* in the Romanian Army," he said.

"I don't know what the fuck that is," I said, although it sounded something like "special" and so probably special forces.

"Were you military?" he asked.

"Yeah, I'm a marine," I said. He nodded again.

The sun had almost set as we approached the Torch Point Bay. There were a lot of lights I could see and a few campfires. It wasn't quite as dark as I'd hoped, but it was dark enough. There wasn't any boat traffic; the rain earlier had kept most boaters off the lake.

We pulled closer to shore, which was an undeveloped stretch of woods. I cut the engine and dropped anchor. I went below and found my gym bag. I took out my Glock 23 and put it in my pocket. I would rather wear a holster, but I didn't want to be obvious and didn't expect to have to pull it. Tom Polk wasn't going to resist. Even if he did, I wouldn't need a gun to handle him, especially with Al as a backup.

I had met Polk at the bowling alley when he went there to chat with Randy about arranging a date. He was in his late fifties and overweight, with thick, graying hair. He reminded me of Judge Smails from the movie *Caddyshack*, played by Ted Knight. Polk was deeply tanned from hours on the golf course all summer. I forgot exactly what he did for a living, beyond the fact that he owned several businesses in Toledo.

This type of guy never did well with the rough stuff. I was not supposed to get too physical with him, per Randy. Nothing to the face. But I was authorized to send him a message. There was no excuse for him not to settle his bills. This guy tipped his caddy more in a week than what he owed Randy. This was disrespect.

I was sure that there were a lot of times Polk got away without paying for shit. Rich pricks always got away with shit because they kept lawyers on speed dial. They paid late or not at all, and when they got cornered, they delayed and obstructed. A lot of times they ended up paying in the end, but they made the people they owed run an expensive gauntlet.

I scanned the bridge to see if I forgot anything and located a medium-sized waterproof black tote in the corner. Damn, I almost forgot that. I carried it out and loaded it onto the dinghy. I took one last look around the yacht. We untied and headed east.

About fifty yards away from the docks, I idled the motor. I leaned forward and opened the tote. Inside was something that looked like a stereo component with a small green digital display. I flicked it on, and the display blinked a few times and showed "ready." I pushed the red button, and the little triangle Wi-Fi light signal blinked, and then a red circle with a line through it appeared on top of it. All Wi-Fi signals were jammed within a few hundred yards. Tom's cameras were dead in the water.

Data found out that Tom's security system wasn't hardwired but connected through a wireless router. We tested the jammer at the campground the week before, and it worked perfectly. I put it in the front seat of the SUV during the test and kept moving it farther and farther away from the router, to almost one hundred yards before a weak signal started streaming.

Since it would knock out most of the neighborhood, Data was worried what the neighbors would do when it was cut off. Since Wi-Fi failed all the time and we wouldn't be there long, we decided to risk it. If someone called the cable company, we would be long gone by the time they sent someone out.

Finding the battery-powered spotlight in my bag, I flipped it on, carefully pointing it at the water's surface. Sweeping it across the docks, I was careful not to light up any of the houses. A fifteen-million-candlepower beam would draw attention. I found an empty guest slip and carefully steered the dinghy in.

Me and Al climbed out of the boat and crossed the docks. They were about half full, with random boats here and there.

We walked toward Polk's house at a steady pace, trying not to move too fast and draw attention. Just seeing us in that neighborhood would draw attention. Two big gorillas dressed in black would stick out like sore thumbs.

We walked up Standard Street, and I started counting houses. Tom's was the third house on the right. I double-checked the house number on my phone, and it was right. There was a short driveway up to a pricey two-story beach house with a lot of brick and stone.

A black BMW M3 was parked in front of a closed garage. There were lights on in the front window and the upstairs room to the left. I walked up to the porch and knocked, with Al standing behind me on the sidewalk leading up to the porch.

There was no answer. I knocked again. I heard movement behind the door, and then it opened. An attractive blonde woman appeared, in her late thirties, wearing a tank top, gym shorts, and short white socks. Tom's trophy wife. He probably threw the first wife away years ago when she was about the age of this woman, so her days as the current Mrs. Polk were probably numbered.

"Hello there. Is Tom around?"

I knew Tom was around. Data patched into the camera feed,

which was stored on a cloud, and confirmed his car was there before we left. If he saw him leave, he would have shot me a text, and we would have aborted.

"Yes. Whom may I tell him is visiting?" she asked nervously, looking us both over.

"Sam," I replied.

"And he is?" she asked, nodding to Al.

"Sam's friend," I said, smiling. She stood there for a minute. Tom came up behind her. He was wearing a blue Toledo Rockets baseball cap, blue swim trunks, a white polo shirt, and flip-flops.

"Hey, Sam!" he said with excitement, as if we were old drinking buddies. He stepped past his wife and shook my hand. He nodded at Al, who nodded back.

"Do you have a minute to chat, Tom?" I asked politely.

Tom stared down at his feet for a moment. His wife walked further into the house but did not move out of sight.

"I was doing a little work for the company before the damn Wi-Fi cut out," he said, not looking up.

"It will just take a minute. Maybe we could go out back by your pool house?" I asked, still smiling. Tom stood there, shrugged, and then nodded.

"Go ahead and go around by the garage. I will meet you back there," he sighed, stepping back and closing the door.

I glanced over at Al, who was stone faced. I should have cut through the house with him to the back door; this gave Tom a chance to pull something. But it was what it was, so I walked around the garage to the back yard, with Al close behind me.

His back yard was perfect. I had no doubt he had a landscaper; the trees, flowers, and bushes were straight out of a *Better Homes and Gardens* magazine. We walked along a lighted stone path past an in-ground pool to a covered bar area. There were several stools at the bar, and Al took one.

"Need a drink?" I asked. Al shook his head. I took down the bottle of Woodford Reserve, found a rocks glass, and filled it about a third of the way.

I searched carefully behind the bar for weapons and didn't

see any. Looking through the cupboards, I found nothing there either. I came back around and sat down one stool over from Al. A few minutes later, Tom came out.

"Helped yourself to the bar, I see," he said, irritated.

"You ought to know about helping yourself," I said flatly. He glared at me for a minute before looking down.

Tom walked around behind the bar. When he turned his back, I didn't see the bulge of a gun at his waistline. I was glad I was able to sweep the bar area for weapons before he came out; it allowed me to relax a little. But not too much.

He took down a bottle of Bombay Sapphire gin. Opening the cupboard, he took out a fancy crystal glass. He pulled out a bottle of tonic water from the fridge and made a very strong drink. A glass of gin on the rocks with a splash of tonic. He gulped down half of it. His face was already red from drinking earlier, I assumed.

"Do I need to explain to you why we're here?"

I took a sip of my drink. I didn't want to get buzzed; I just wanted the taste of bourbon in my mouth. The burning feeling as it washed past my throat and into my stomach kept me alert.

"No," he replied, standing against the bar with his belly halfway lapping above it.

"Good. You got the money on you?"

"I don't owe Randy any money," he said, taking a drink that emptied his glass. He stared at me with a frown. "I didn't get what I paid for."

"You reserved two dates in a cabin, and you stayed two nights," I said.

"We didn't do what I paid to do," he replied, looking around nervously. "Did you do something to my Wi-Fi? None of my cameras are operating."

He nodded to the camera above the bar. I ignored the question.

"The girls said they did what they were supposed to do. These girls are Slavic peasant girls. If you want some around-the-world kink, you need to go out to Vegas or go Asian or something. You knew what you were getting the first time, and yet you came back for more. Pay up."

Tom made himself another drink. He glanced up at his house to make sure the missus wasn't snooping. "Or what?"

"Or a lot of things. I can bring Mrs. Polk into the conversation. Or I can give the signal to Al here, and he can start off by breaking a few of your ribs. How do you think your golf swing is gonna fare with broken ribs?" I asked, finishing my drink. Polk sneaked a nervous glance at Al.

"How much?" he said after a pause.

"Fifteen hundred," I said.

He let out a laugh. "No way, I agreed to five hundred a night," he said in disbelief.

"How much do you think our time is worth, Mr. Polk? For us to take a fuckin' field trip to Polk Manor out here and waste our time going back and forth about a debt you know that you owe," I said, getting angry. "Keep wasting my time, and it goes up to two thousand. Randy gave me permission to negotiate."

"Negotiate? You are robbing me!" he said angrily.

"If I was robbing you, you'd know it. Everyone in that house would know it," I said, nodding to his house. This hushed Polk, who was about to come back with another comment and stopped short.

"I don't have that kind of money in the house," Tom finally said.

"You have a stash here. You have a safe in the house. You have twenty minutes to get fifteen hundred dollars in my hands, or we start considering Plan B." Polk started to say something, but I interrupted. "You are on the clock, sir, tick-fucking-tock," I said angrily. Tom nodded, set his glass down, and walked back up to the house.

"Was it good to let him go alone?" Al asked, leaning against the bar.

"Maybe not. But if he comes out here and raises hell, he will risk his wife hearing the whole thing. She probably knows about his shenanigans, but having details of it rubbed in her face would be bad for him."

"Shenanigans?"

"Polk's banging other women, paying prostitutes, whatever other shit he is involved in."

Fifteen minutes later, he came out with a small blue back-pack. I stood up as he came over. He walked over and pushed it harshly into my hands.

"Is it all here?" I asked as I handed the backpack to Al.

"You don't trust me?" he asked angrily, folding his arms. Al pulled out bills and was counting them out on the bar. The disabled camera also served the purpose of concealing Mr. Polk's cash pay-off from his nosy wife, who would have definitely been in the house watching the feed. After a few minutes, he nodded.

"Al o mie cinci sutelea, one thousand five hundred," he said gruffly.

Polk sneered at him. "So, Al has a voice," he said sarcastically.

Al put the money back in the backpack and zipped it up.

I walked up to Tom and punched him very hard in his swollen stomach. His gut was harder than I expected. My knuckles grazed the bottom of his rib cage, but I didn't think I broke anything. The wind shot out of him, and he fell to his hands and knees. He grabbed his stomach, rolled over on his side, and started gasping.

"Forget we were here and forget about doing any more busi-ness with Randy. No one has time to waste collecting from fucking deadbeats."

I considered kicking him in the stomach but decided not to. Nodding at Al, we started walking back to the dock. I thought I heard Polk throwing up as we made it to the street.

Chris 3

10:00 p.m.

A cool breeze made for a great night to sit by the fire. Candy still wasn't talking to me, so I was sitting out alone. I was drinking warm Pepsi out of a plastic cup. No fucking way was she going to catch me drinking or smoking anything tonight.

It had been one of the longest days of my life. I must have puked five times. The crew found that shit hilarious, but my foreman Vince didn't. I didn't think I would have any more chances if he caught me slacking off, I needed to get my shit together or else find another summer gig.

I didn't want to find another summer gig. The work wasn't that bad, the crew wasn't that bad, and I didn't mind living at the campground. Although, shit, how many people had seen me passed out on the jumping pillow that morning? It was early when it happened, so maybe only a handful.

I looked down into my cup and wished there was something strong to flavor it with. My hangover was finally gone, and a stiff drink sounded good.

I heard the horn blasting as the train approached, lighting up the east side of the campground. Continuing to stare down into my cup of Pepsi, I thought I could see small ripples in it as the train rumbled loudly past.

I tossed another log on the fire. I was dead tired. Surprisingly, sleeping outdoors on a deflated rubber jumping pillow all night was not very restful. But there was the situation with Candy's anger, and I didn't want to go inside the camper yet. Waiting until she fell asleep seemed to be a better strategy than going in and catching shit from her.

She ordered Chinese takeout for dinner but forgot to ask me if I wanted something. I bought a stale bologna-and-cheese sandwich and chips from the campground snack bar. The bitch paid for her food with my credit card, but I let it go.

That could have been my formal mantra in life. *I let it go.* I let everything go. I was a thirty-six-year-old child living in a broken-down RV, working for peanuts, and living with a woman who contributed nothing. Hardly the American fucking dream.

A wave of depression jolted me. My stomach burned; that ulcer I thought had disappeared hadn't gone anywhere.

I needed to escape and start again fresh somewhere. The reality was that no matter where I escaped to, I would still be there, with my dysfunction and bad habits.

The door opened on my camper. Candy came out, carrying a blanket and a sweatshirt. She tossed them on the picnic table.

"What's that for?" I asked.

"It's going to get chilly out here tonight. Make sure you set your phone alarm, in case the sun doesn't wake you up," she said flatly.

She walked back into the camper, slammed the door, and I heard it lock. At least she was talking to me.

I needed to take a piss. I walked over to the shower house and entered through the north door. Standing in front of the mirror was the black guy from across the street who found me passed out that morning. He nodded at me when I walked in. I resisted the urge to do an about-face and sprint out the door in embarrassment.

"You're looking better," he said as he pulled a few paper towels from the dispenser and began drying his hands. I nodded and walked over to the urinal. The man lingered.

"I'm Mike. I own the Airstream camper over at 65. I would shake your hand, but ..." he said, motioning to me and my current state of taking a whiz.

"Hey, Mike," I said as I zipped up. "Chris. Thanks for your help this morning."

Mike nodded. I walked over and washed my hands.

"No problem. You scared me a little this morning. Glad you're okay."

Mike turned and left. I followed behind him and out to the street. "Yeah, it was a rough night. My girlfriend ... isn't very understanding," I said softly.

"Yeah, that kind of shit will definitely land you in the dog-house. But she'll get over it."

"I'm in for a long night. She sorta locked me out," I said, putting my hands in my pockets.

"Sucks. I will be out by my fire for a while. I typically go late. You are more than welcome to hang out. If you want to crash, I could set a bunk up for you in my RV," he said.

I nodded at him. "I appreciate that, but if she came out and I was gone ..." I said, not knowing how to finish the sentence.

"You can come over and have a drink with me. Whatever you want, it doesn't have to be alcohol, if that ..." he trailed off.

"No, no, I'm ... I'm good. I don't have a problem. I just got carried away last night. Drank way more than I should. But that is not an everyday thing," I said, wondering if I sounded convincing. The guy who pulled me out of a puke-drenched stupor in a kiddy area was probably skeptical. He nodded.

"Been there," he said.

"I may try to rest for a little while. If I get antsy, I will drop by."

Brady 4

11:30 p.m.

My legs were sore, but it was a good sore. I didn't have any knee or ankle pain; it was the sort of muscle soreness expected from running when I hadn't run in a while.

I had considered staying sober that evening but then thought better of it. Since I ran four miles that morning, I rationalized that I deserved it. Treat myself.

"Treat yourself" was such a ridiculous mantra, like I was a trained dog that had just done a trick and was waiting for a biscuit as a reward. Either I had a drink or I didn't; what I deserved was irrelevant.

I pulled out the bottle of margarita mix and made a drink. I spent most of my adult life avoiding the sugary "girl drinks," but margaritas were becoming a nightly thing during my exile at the campground. In the military, I had selected the drinks that fit an alpha male image and then acquired the taste for them. Whiskey, bourbon, Jägermeister, Guinness, etc. Over the course of years and countless gallons consumed, these abrasive drinks began to be tolerable and then actually started tasting good.

Margaritas weren't completely lame because of the tequila, but a daiquiri, piña colada, or similarly girly cocktail would be hard to justify. But I wouldn't need to justify it unless I got caught drinking one by someone who would judge me. Red Solo cups revealed no contents and thus told no tales, at least from a distance.

The margarita was damn near toxic with tequila. I bought a fifth of Patrón earlier that evening while grocery shopping and had put a decent dent in it.

After a few drinks, the wheels in my head started slowing. *Thank God.* I negotiated with Marcy earlier to get the kids out at the campground for the weekend. It had been a few weeks since I saw them, and it weighed heavily on me. I managed to get a phone call or Facetime with them several times throughout the week, but that was no substitute for their presence.

The campground was lively. The people over at the gazebo were out drinking, with their packs of kids running and pedaling up and down the street. Small groups of people walked by with drinks. Work carts and golf carts rolled past.

I hadn't seen the Glory Bowl biker yet. I wondered if he had recognized me as a Sandusky Shores camper with an RV on the same street as his. He probably didn't.

I was excited about having the kids visit the campground for a few days. It would mean everything. Living in the camper away from them was rough.

There was a weird dichotomy that I supposed every father experienced. Loving your family and at the same time wanting to be away from them. The daily grind of raising kids made me crave peace and solitude, to get away from the bickering, the neediness, the constant questions posed, and the relentless need to be engaged. But as soon as they were out of my presence for a short time, I felt a deep void in my life and couldn't wait to be with them again.

There were times when I believed that my campground living situation was optimal for me. That I was meant for minimalism, that this RV and its contents were all I needed. If I never had kids, I could contentedly live that lifestyle indefinitely.

But I could also see the danger in it. Out here, I was not accountable, and with that came the danger of excessive drinking. People who weekend camped were often putting away a lot of alcohol because that was what you did while camping, along with building fires and roasting s'mores. That culture was meant to be sampled in small doses during the course of a temporary stay, not continuously throughout an entire season.

It was a perspective born of battle scars from years of being a husband and father. The pre-family version of myself would have found the current situation sad and bizarre.

I took another swig of my drink and put another log on the fire. Checking my watch, it was a little after 2300 hours. A motorcycle rumbled in the distance and was getting louder as it rolled along Starling.

There were still kids out; I saw them in the headlight of the motorcycle as it crept along. As it approached, I saw that another motorcycle was a few feet behind the first.

It was the Eastern European guy in front, followed by the guy with the GLORYB plate from the gated community. About twenty feet behind him was a black Suburban. I watched as the Eastern European parked his bike in his lot at 15 and the other vehicles pulled up to the camper at site 21.

Mike 4

11:15 p.m.

It was clear that Chris had fully recovered from his previous night's drinking debacle. The alcohol he consumed plus whatever other substances he was on last night. Chris put away four bourbons neat in about thirty minutes and was happily glassy-eyed. I had consumed one and started on number two.

As uneasy as his drinking made me, it would be easier to return his papers if he got hammered. If he passed out, I could tuck them into his pocket.

But I didn't want him to pass out on my lot. Chris was a liability. And I didn't want to get on the radar of that intense girlfriend of his.

In the brief amount of time we hung out, I got to learn a little more about him. I was surprised to hear he was an air force vet in a demanding profession. He could also fly planes. What the hell was he doing living in a trashy RV and digging ditches?

Then again, I figured he was in his current situation because of substance abuse. It was a damn shame. You could tell the kid was bright but had issues with self-inflicted wounds. I could also read the deep depression in him that he revealed with his words and mannerisms. There were enough markers for me to consider him a suicide risk. I knew a lot of combat vets who suffered from PTSD, and I had attended an unsettling number of funerals over the years.

Chuck rolled up on his golf cart playing some country song I never heard of. I guess I lost touch with new hillbilly music.

Chuck slowed down, then looped around and parked in the empty lot next to mine. He stepped out cautiously, as if he was concerned about falling, and walked over to us. He carried a big stainless-steel thermos in his hand.

"Good evening, gents," he said, his voice raspy, a cigarette hanging from his mouth.

I nodded. Chris waved.

I pointed toward a folded chair leaning against the front of the camper. Chuck put down his thermos, unfolded the chair, and brought it near the fire. He grabbed the thermos and walked over to the chair. In attempting to sit down, he fell back clumsily and dropped himself hard into the chair, nearly toppling over, barely saving himself with his non-thermos hand.

"Whoa, coming in hot!" he laughed, picking up his thermos and taking a drink. "I thought you'd be in the rack early tonight, Chris."

Chris forced a smile. Chuck put the thermos between his legs and leaned back.

"Well, I've been sort of evicted for the night," he said, drinking from his cup. While I admired his honesty, I wouldn't have been so forthcoming. Publicizing domestic discord was seldom productive.

"Damn, doesn't that camper belong to you?" he asked. I was sure he knew that it did.

"Yeah. I fucked up, so I guess I can spend a night in the doghouse," Chris said, shrugging, staring into the fire.

"You need a place to stay?" Chuck asked.

"I don't know," Chris said as he stared up at the sky. "It doesn't look like rain. I may just sleep under the stars."

Chuck studied him for a few seconds and took another drink. He joined Chris in staring up at the sky. They both appeared to be deep in thought.

"I tell you what, let me take a look. I may have a cabin I can let you use for the night," Chuck said.

"Don't go through any trouble, Chuck," Chris said. Chuck smiled.

"Well, I'm making the rounds, boys. I'll see you later," he said, struggling out of his chair. He flicked a cigarette butt at the fire and missed. He walked past it to the golf cart.

I got up and stomped it out. Chuck looked at me and nodded. I turned around and walked back to my chair. As he sped off, I saw him lifting his phone to his ear.

Chuck 5

11:30 p.m.

"Hey, Randy," I said as I put the phone up to my ear.

"Yeah," Randy said coolly.

"What is your twenty?" I asked. There was a pause.

"Taj," he said.

"You have a minute?" I asked.

"Roger," he said, slightly garbled.

I hung up and drove toward the Taj, taking another deep drink of vodka and tonic. I saw a campfire at their site as I rounded the corner. Sam's SUV was there. That wasn't what I wanted to see. I parked to the side of his SUV and walked over to the fire.

Randy, Sam, and Viktor were by the fire, drinks in hand. They stopped talkin' as I walked up.

"Evening, gents," I said as I walked up.

"What do you need, Chuck?" Randy asked. He was a bit short with me, which made me nervous. I could never read him, and I hated that.

"Maybe we should chat in the camper?" I asked. Randy glared at me. Sam looked annoyed. But he always looked annoyed.

"Okay," he said, gettin' up. We walked in together. He closed and locked the door.

"This place has been swept," Randy said, sitting down. I sat across from him. He pulled the wand out from a drawer and began sweepin' it over me.

"Chris Randolph is in the doghouse. His old lady locked him out for the night. He needs somewhere to stay. Any girls around?"

Randy took this in, thinkin' about it. "I think so. Let's check with Viktor."

"Okay. I just need to get a cabin number and convince him to go party there. He is hittin' it hard again tonight. It won't take much effort."

Brady 5

11:45 p.m.

I watched from my patio table as Chuck walked out of the RV and took off in his golf cart. That guy stayed busy late into the night. Was he still on the clock? He waved at me as he went by, the cherry from the cigarette in his mouth glowing.

I needed to be online no later than 0730 tomorrow. Although I lost count of my drinks, I hadn't overdone it. I could have one more and then pull the plug.

There was a tightness in my legs from running. I stood up and stretched. Refreshing my drink, I went back outside. A short walk sounded good. I locked up the RV and started north.

There were a few figures around the campfire at 21 where Chuck just was, maybe three adults. I was on the opposite side of the street and continued past. I rounded the corner and turned right on Sparrow.

There was a campfire ahead at the Airstream site. As I approached, I saw there were two men there. I recognized one as Chris.

"Hey, Brady!" I heard his voice yell, thick with alcohol. I stopped and turned toward the fire. Chris waved me over.

"Hey, Chris," I said, walking over.

"Hey!" he said again. The other man was getting to his feet. "Hey, Brady, this is …"

"Mike," he said, stepping forward to shake my hand. We shook hands and he stepped back, remaining standing in front of his chair.

Mike was a familiar face, mostly because there were very few black men camping. A lot of mixed kids, but mostly with their white moms and grandparents.

"Nice to meet you," I said, standing there awkwardly. "Just out for a walk, it is a nice night."

"Absolutely," Mike said. "Want to pull up a chair?"

I was torn because I was getting tired. But I hadn't socialized with anyone other than Chuck in a few days. Isolation was comfortable for me, but perhaps not *absolute isolation.* I nodded, and Mike pointed toward an empty chair by the fire.

"So, what's going on in the neighborhood tonight?" I asked, waving off a cloud of campfire smoke that happened to blow right into my face. I adjusted my chair over about a foot to avoid it.

"Nothin," Chris said. "I'm camping tonight."

"Camping? Aren't we all camping tonight?" I asked, smiling.

"I'm doing some real camping, under the stars," Chris laughed, gulping something out of a plastic cup. "What time do you work tomorrow?"

"I start around seven or seven thirty. How come, you need a ride somewhere?" I asked.

"Nah, I don't want to oversleep. If you remember, can you walk out and check on me?" he asked.

"Where are you going to be?" I asked.

"In front of my camper," he said, laughing. I laughed too, without knowing why that was funny.

"Okay, forgive me if this is a stupid question, but why not sleep inside?"

Chris laughed. Mike put another log on the fire.

"I'm in the doghouse. Candy locked me out," he said.

"Out of your own camper?"

"Out of my own camper," he said incredulously.

"Damn," was all I could think to say. I took a drink.

"I offered to let him stay here, but he wouldn't have it," Mike said, shrugging.

I considered offering him the fold-out bed in my RV but decided against it. I didn't want him there and felt guilty about declining to extend an invitation. Chris was pretty drunk, and I didn't want to deal with him in the morning when I was trying to set up for work.

"If you don't want to stay inside one of our campers, you can borrow my tent," I offered.

"Dude, I'm fine. The bugs ain't bad. It ain't supposed to rain. I'm good," he said, polishing off his drink. He stared down into it to make sure it was empty. He looked up expectantly at Mike.

"Need a refill?" he asked flatly. Chris nodded as Mike took his cup.

"So, how long does your sentence in the doghouse usually last?" I said, smiling at him.

He smiled back. "Should be okay by tomorrow. After work, she should be fully thawed out," he said as Mike came out and returned his cup.

Headlights approached from the north. I didn't hear a car engine, so I knew it was a golf cart. Chuck pulled past the camper and into the empty site. He got out, taking a drag from his cigarette.

"Hey, Brady, I didn't know you wandered over here," he said. I nodded at him.

"Good news, Chris! I can sneak you into an empty cabin," Chuck said, smiling.

Chris stared at him blankly. "Dude, I'm okay ..." he trailed off, taking a drink.

Chuck walked up and stood next to him for a moment. "At least ride over there with me and take a look," Chuck said, staring into the fire.

"I know what they look like," Chris replied.

Chuck motioned for him to come over and started walking back to the golf cart. "Come chat with me for a minute, Chris," Chuck said from the side of his golf cart.

Chris didn't move for a moment, then walked over. Chuck spoke softly to him, a contrast from his usual loud voice. Chris appeared to be thinking about it, then nodded. He went around and got into the passenger side. Both waved as they rode off.

I glanced down into my cup, then finished the last swig of it. There was an awkward moment of silence between Mike and me.

"So, it looks like Chuck made him an offer he couldn't refuse," I joked. Mike chuckled, taking a drink. "So how long are you staying at Sandusky Shores?"

"I don't know yet. I'm paying by the week."

"Traveling the country?"

"Parts of it. For the past few years, I've been going back and forth, north and south during the different seasons. I need to get out of my rut and head out west. Need a drink?" he asked, standing up.

I definitely didn't need another. "Sure, what are you drinking?"

"Jim Beam."

"Straight?"

"Yup. I have ice," he said. I nodded.

Drinking more would probably be a mistake. But sometimes when I got started, I struggled to find the kill switch.

A moment later, he returned with a red plastic cup and handed it to me. I nodded and took a swig. The cubes slid up and hit my lips. The burning sensation of the bourbon going down almost caused me to choke, but I managed not to.

"So, you stay out here all summer?" Mike asked.

"It is looking that way," I said, instantly regretting the odd answer. I should have just said yes. Mike didn't respond.

"We are seasonal, here on and off throughout the summer. My kids will be up this weekend," I said. I realized that my answers were painting a picture for him if he was even slightly astute.

"You friends with a lot of other campers out here?" he asked, sipping his bourbon.

"Not really. I know some of the staff like Chuck, and my neighbor Chris, but otherwise we keep to ourselves," I replied, staring into the fire, which was dying down, the orange embers glowing brightly. Mike got up and threw on another log.

"So, what do you suppose convinced Chris to go stay in a cabin instead of at one of our places?" Mike asked. I shrugged. "Are you and Chris tight?"

"No. We've talked a few times. He seems okay," I replied.

"I found him passed out this morning on the jumping pillow," Mike said, taking a drink. I didn't reply. After a moment, I nodded. "Threw up all over, lucky he didn't die."

"You found him?" I asked.

"Yeah. My impression was that he was on something more potent than alcohol," Mike said.

He got out of his chair and walked to the edge of the campsite, looking around as if trying to determine if someone was listening. I looked at my watch; it was after midnight. Mike came back and sat down.

"It's possible," I replied, not knowing how else to respond.

"So, I figure Chuck is setting him up in that cabin to bring him drugs," Mike said.

"Why would he do that?" I asked.

"That's what I'm trying to figure out. I wish I knew which cabin they were going to," he said.

"Was Chuck around this morning when you found Chris?" I asked.

"He was one of the employees who came over to handle it."

"Mind if I ask you a personal question?" I asked and then instantly regretted it. The alcohol had me running my mouth. He shrugged.

"Are you law enforcement?"

"Nah," he said.

"Former military?" I asked.

"Yeah, retired army," he said. I nodded.

"I did three years, back in my youth," I said, taking a drink.

"I know," Mike said.

"Really? I didn't think I still gave off that vibe. I've been out for a long time," I said, laughing.

Mike smiled and didn't say anything for a long moment. Finally, he got out of his chair and went inside the camper. He came back with a flashlight and a handful of papers.

"I could have guessed. I have seen you jogging around here like you've been doing it for a while. But that wouldn't have confirmed anything; civilians run all the time. This is what led me to believe you were in the army from 1989 through 1992," he said, handing the flashlight and papers over.

My breathing hitched for a moment. How did he know what years I served?

I took the sheets and shined the flashlight on them. As I leafed through them, I felt a small sense of dread. "Where did you get this?" I asked, trying to sound calm.

Anger was starting to build inside. Was this some sort of identity-theft scam? Did he steal data from my laptop through a Wi-Fi hack?

"Relax, the black man didn't steal your identity. I barely know how to turn a computer on. These papers were lying around Chris when he was passed out. I collected them, and when I saw they didn't have Chris's name on them, I pocketed them."

I sat staring at the papers for a long moment. Then I turned off the flashlight, reaching over to hand it back to him. Why would Chris have these papers with my information? Was he hacking me?

I sat there for a moment trying to reason through this, despite the high tequila and bourbon content in my blood. The angry side of me wanted to ambush Chris the next time I saw him and get some answers. This was a complication that I didn't need on top of everything else going on in my life.

"I'm gonna hang on to these," I said. Mike nodded slowly.

"By all means. That is your information." Mike said. "Mind if I ask how you are going to handle this?"

"I'll let you know when I figure it out," I replied, finishing my drink.

Chapter 3

Thursday, June 18

Data 3

12:50 a.m.

I pedaled toward the campground, trying to decide how I would approach the problem. I had some valuable information to deliver, but I also potentially needed to do some damage control. What that entailed I had no idea; it could range from pretending that the data loss didn't happen to fully admitting that it happened and throwing myself at Randy's mercy.

I reviewed the video earlier. Unfortunately, parts of the incident happened out of the range of the camera that covered the security booth. I had to make it a priority to see Chris. Patrick swore he didn't take them, so Chris was the only other person who could have taken those papers that night.

I pulled up along the security gate, and Patrick stepped out. He crossed his arms and started laughing. I remembered that I was wearing my helmet.

"Hey, Evel Knievel is here! Safety first on that badass machine, Data!" he said. Wasted again. I ignored him, looped around the booth, and cycled up Starling.

I pedaled up to the Taj, carefully maneuvering over the speed bump in front of the gazebo. Sam's SUV was parked in front, along with Randy's motorcycle. A feeling of dread set in, knowing I would be dealing with Sam. That guy had been hostile toward me since day one, for no apparent reason. I supposed he felt threatened, as he was most certainly Randy's right-hand man, and I was getting a lot of important assignments.

The three were seated around the campfire and stared at me as I pulled up. I parked my bike near the camper, taking off my helmet and hanging it on the handlebars by the straps. I heard the train approaching from the west as I walked over to the fire.

"Data!" Randy said. He was leaning back in his chair with a cup in his hand. Viktor just stared at me. Sam smirked as he stoked the fire with a stick.

"Sir," I said, nodding at Randy.

Randy stood up and stretched. "Let's go on inside and chat," he said, walking up the stairs. The other two stood up and walked in behind him. I was the last one in.

Once in, I closed and locked the door behind me. The noise from the train passing was barely audible from within the trailer.

Randy sat in his usual chair at the table, with his back to the north side of the trailer. Sam was at the fridge, getting a beer. He turned around and nodded at Randy. Randy shook his head and gestured to the cupboard. Sam took out the bottle of Woodford Reserve and poured it into a plastic cup.

"Get yourself what you want, Viktor," Randy said, as Sam walked over and handed him his drink. Viktor took his cup to the cupboard and withdrew a bottle of vodka, filled his cup, and sat at the table. "Anything for you, Henry?"

"No thank you, sir. Do we need to sweep the trailer?" I asked.

"Chuck got it earlier. Sam, can you check Data here?" Randy asked. Sam nodded and walked over to me. I assumed the position with my hands on the counter. He wanded me then searched me roughly like he always did.

"You look a little red in the face. Why don't you grab a water?" Randy said.

I walked over and took a bottled water out of the fridge. I sat down and took a long drink.

"So, what do you have on Mr. Sullivan?" Randy asked.

"Well, Brady O. Sullivan is employed by the federal government, working at the Payroll Accounting and Finance Agency, commonly referenced as PAF. He is a GS-13, which is a midlevel ranking," I said.

"How much does that pay a year?" Randy asked.

"He is at step six, so about $105k," I replied.

"How many years has he been there?" he asked.

"Eleven years."

"So, what does he do there?"

"He is a program analyst. From what I can gather, he works on finance projects. Like on pay systems, I think. He has a top secret security clearance. That kind of clearance in that agency means it is very likely that he has access to military personnel and pay records," I said.

"Anything else of interest in his employment records?" Randy asked.

"He has worked in a factory and served a few years in the military," I said.

"Which branch?" Sam asked.

"Army. Three years," I replied. Sam showed no reaction. I was sure that if Sullivan was a marine, Sam would have been so much more impressed.

"What did he do in the army?" Sam asked. "Any lethal skill sets?"

"He was intelligence. A few schools, but he wasn't Special Forces or anything like that. Jumped out of planes, for what that's worth," I said.

"Any judicial records?" Randy asked.

"No. A few traffic citations, but nothing major. Otherwise, he wouldn't have the high clearance. It has to be renewed every five years, and he has remained clean," I replied.

"So, we have a Boy Scout in the neighborhood. How do his finances look?" Sam asked. Randy glared at him, as though he was growing weary of Sam asking the questions.

"Not bad. He has a mortgage on a 250k house, a 20k home equity loan, a 25k camper loan, two vehicle leases, and about 10k in credit card debt. Pretty average-looking stuff there. His wife works. I think they need that second income," I said.

"How much does she make?" Randy asked.

"About 60k," I said.

"Other relevant facts?" asked Randy.

"Two kids, a boy and a girl, ages ten and eight. Seem to be perfectly normal. They were at the campground at the beginning of the season. They go to public schools," I said.

"Any idea why he is here by himself?" Sam asked.

"No. There aren't any probate records besides their wedding in 2004 and a small estate filing for his wife Marcy's grandfather; she was the executrix. No pending divorce actions," I said.

"Do you have all the records there?" Randy asked, nodding

toward my backpack. I nodded, patting it lightly. "Okay, leave those with me. I want to give them a look, and then you can shred them."

"I also have a summary," I mentioned as I withdrew the stack of papers and handed them to him.

"Does anyone know you are looking into Sullivan?" Randy asked.

"I don't think so," I said nervously.

"You don't *think* so? What the fuck does that mean?" Sam asked.

"No. Nobody knows that I researched him. I did it cleanly," I said. I could feel my face reddening.

"Okay. What do you guys think?" Randy asked, looking at Sam and Viktor.

"What value is this guy to us?" Sam asked, taking a drink. Randy turned to me.

"What value are military records?" Randy asked me.

"They could be very valuable if you find the right buyer. Names, birthdates, social security numbers. A lot of fraud possibilities, especially if you knew deployment statuses. Bigger picture, that data could also be sold to outside entities," I said.

"Foreign governments?" Sam asked.

"Yeah. If a buyer could be arranged, a big data extract could be lucrative. An asset within PAF who could provide continuously updated data sets could be the gift that keeps on giving. As long as he didn't get caught, of course.

"If he has access to certain financial transactions, that may be an even bigger cache of data. If a number of soldiers are drawing hazardous-duty pay in a certain unit, you can infer that they are deployed. The purchase locations of some of those transactions may reveal the theater. A lot of activity can tip you off that something is either happening or is about to happen," I said, shrugging.

"If you got that raw data, could you crunch it and figure out what was happening?" Randy asked.

"Sure," I answered, although I wasn't certain. It sounded intriguing.

The room was quiet. Sam looked like he wanted to say something but thought better of it. *Good.*

"Okay. Let's take the next step. We need to set up a cabin rental for him, sooner rather than later. He could reconcile with his wife at any time, so his bachelor's life at this campground could quickly come to an end," Randy said.

"Is he a drinker?" Sam asked.

"I believe so. I know Chuck had a drink or two with him. I will have to pick his brain later," Randy said. He finished his drink and looked over at Sam, nodding. Sam got up and poured him another one.

"Isn't this sort of a long shot? We are just assuming that we can get him to play ball?" Sam asked.

"It is a long shot. Most of the lucrative things I have done were long shots. Bringing in working girls and thugs from Romania was a long shot. Entertaining Johns at a campground and on a boat was a long shot. Wiping down bar tops and serving drinks at the bowling alley, not a long shot. And not lucrative. Leave the forward thinking to me," Randy said, staring at Sam. Sam stared back for a moment, then looked down at his beer.

"Did I mention I saw him jogging through my neighborhood this morning?" Randy asked. Everyone shook their heads.

"He snuck in the gate?" Sam asked. Randy nodded.

"I tell you what, I will get this rolling. Catching him in my neighborhood trespassing gives me an icebreaker, something for us to chat about," Randy said.

"What can I do to help? I haven't reviewed the Wi-Fi data that may be out there."

"Yeah, do that. What are the odds that he is using the campground Wi-Fi?" Randy asked.

"If he is working from the camper, pretty good. How else is he going to connect? Using a hotspot through his phone all day would be expensive. If he is tech-savvy at all, he is also using our Wi-Fi with his phone," I said.

"Pull that data, and let's talk again tomorrow. I also need you to pull some video." Randy glanced at his watch. "Should be some footage for Cabin D first thing. Can you pull something for me by 8 a.m. tomorrow?" he asked.

I nodded. He nodded back.

"Nice work, Henry," Randy said, taking a drink.

"Viktor, I need your best talent available tomorrow night. I will have Chuck set up Cabin D. Clear her schedule and have her set to arrive at the bowling alley around dinnertime. Drive her over, park around back, and be ready to send her in when Sam messages you," Randy said to Viktor, who nodded.

"If things work out, I will have more video for you to pull Friday morning," he said to me.

"Okay, we are done," Randy said, looking at Viktor and me. I took my backpack and put it on. We filed out of the door.

"Close it behind you," Randy said.

Chuck 6

3:30 a.m.

My phone alarm went off at 3:30 a.m., vibratin' in my shorts pocket. I scrambled to get it before it woke up Sharon. Shutting it off, I laid still until I was sure she was still asleep. Quietly, I got up and slipped out of the room, slidin' the bedroom door shut behind me.

I used the flashlight on my phone to find the bathroom, steppin' over a pile of clothes and other shit left on the floor. Shuttin' the door, I turned the light on.

The bathroom was in bad shape. I needed to spend some time on it. The mirror was broken, there were cracks on the sink and chips in the flooring. All the time I spent makin' the campground better, and my own camper was in rough shape.

There was a layer of grit on everything. You would think that Sharon could get off her ass and clean once in a while.

I took a piss and then looked in the mirror. I looked like hell, big bags under my eyes. My face drooping. My hairline had slowly crept back to the middle of my head over the past few years. So much gray on my head and in my beard. My body was a train wreck, gray and black hair all over mounds of chub. My gut made my arms look too small.

The coughin' began. I tried to muffle it, but it was almost impossible. It felt like there was a pound of phlegm in my throat and lungs. I coughed and spat up a few times into the sink. Two packs a day made mornings a nonstop coughin' fit. I needed to quit.

I found a hair tie, pulled my hair back, and splashed some water on my face. My buzz was still there from partyin', but I didn't feel too bad. Once I dropped Chris off at the cabin, I quit drinkin'.

I walked back out to the main camper area, where I had a shirt, a hat, my wallet, cigarettes, a lighter, and keys laid out. I got dressed, found my flip-flops, and opened the door. The door squeaked loudly; somebody needed to put some WD-40 on the hinges. I opened it slowly, stepped out, and pushed it carefully shut. I locked it and walked over to the golf cart.

I lit up a cigarette as I kept coughing. A few drags and I started to feel a little better.

The idea to put Chris up in the cabin was a good one, and it made me look like I was on top of things to Randy. But it also made the cleanup my responsibility. If I could get the girl back to Cloverleaf and him back to his camper as quickly as possible, I could still get a few more hours before I had to be back at work at seven. Well, seven-ish.

I drove over to Cabin D. I walked up the stairs and onto the porch. The small window to the right of the door had its curtains closed. I listened for any sounds from inside. It was impossible to tell with the train going by, so I stood there another minute until it was gone.

There was no noise comin' from the cabin. I took a drag from my cigarette and threw the butt into the yard. I raised the key and carefully put it into the lock, turnin' it softly to the right. Once it clicked, I slowly pushed the door open.

I took out my cell phone and put on the flashlight. Walkin' in slowly, I closed the door behind me.

The door opened to the open area that was both the dinin' room and livin' room. A bottle of vodka and plastic cups was on the table. One of the cups was used as an ashtray, half full of cigarette butts. Next to that was the pipe I left with him. I looked at it closely to make sure it wasn't lit, tapped the residue out in the cup, and pocketed the pipe.

I turned the flashlight beam to the couch and jumped when I saw Anka sitting there. She was dressed in a tight sweatsuit. She was a knockout, even after turnin' a trick late into the night. Long, dark hair and green eyes. She pointed to the door on the southern side of the cabin, which was the master bedroom. The door was shut. I nodded.

I walked over to the door and stopped to listen but heard nothin'. I pushed it, and it opened.

I shined the light up and found the bed. Chris was sprawled out on top of it, face down and buck naked. Killing the flashlight, I switched to the camera app and took a few pics. I looked up at the ceilin', where the smoke detector was mounted. The video camera was hid pretty good up there. I smiled at it and waved.

I switched on the bedroom lights. He didn't move at all. Chris's clothes were in a pile by the bed. I picked them up and put them on the bed. Walking over, I grabbed him by the shoulder and shook him.

He didn't move at first. I shook him again harder. He groaned, then rolled on his side, exposin' himself to me.

"Dude, get dressed," I said. He sat up and put his feet on the floor. He put his head in his hands.

"Come on, Chris, let's get you back," I said.

Chris coughed a few times. He looked around the room in confusion.

"Dressed. Get dressed," I said more harshly, but still keepin' my voice down.

"How?" Chris grunted, lookin' around.

"Listen, I'm taking the girl back," I said, openin' the door. "You need to be out of here when I get back. Can you get back to your camper?"

Chris sat there, hunched over. I walked over and snapped my fingers in front of his face.

"Dude. Can you make it back to your camper?" I asked. He looked up, glassy-eyed, and nodded. "You are at Cabin D. You go up Pigeon, around the playground, and back to your camper. No nappy on the jumping pillow this time. Just lay out in your lawn chair. Can you do that?"

Chris nodded again. He reached for his clothes.

"I need a verbal, Chris," I said.

"Yeah. I can do it," he finally said.

"Pull the door closed when you leave. I will lock up when I drop her off," I said.

"Her?" Chris asked.

"Your date, bro," I said, laughin'.

I walked out and closed the bedroom door behind me. I waved for the girl to follow me, and we walked out of the cabin.

Brady 6

7:00 a.m.

I slept terribly and was wide awake when the clock struck 0700 hours. I checked Chris's lot a few times throughout the night, in case he returned. The last time was around 0500 hours, when I found him sleeping in a lawn chair, wearing a hoody and partially covered with a blanket. He snored softly as I slipped the papers into his hoody pocket.

I needed him to tell me why he had my personal information. I knew that he worked construction, and Mike mentioned he had an aviation background in the air force. Neither of those professions required the collection of third-party personal information, so I couldn't imagine a legitimate reason why he would have mine.

Peering through the kitchen window, a bit of blue sky was visible through a break in the tree leaves. I dressed in shorts, a T-shirt, and flip-flops. I made a pot of coffee, filled two Styrofoam cups, and carefully put lids on both.

Stepping out of the camper, I put the coffee cups on the patio table and closed the door. There was a layer of dew on the grass that dampened my feet as I walked over to Chris's.

He was sleeping on his side in the lawn chair, with one arm dangling and touching the grass. I placed the coffee cups down on top of his rusty grill.

"Hey, Chris," I said, shaking him softly. He stirred, rolled back in the chair, and sat up. There was a rectangular pattern from the fabric on his face, pink lines on paleness. He groaned as he sat up straighter.

"Hey, Brady," he said quietly as he ran his fingers through his hair.

"It is about ten after seven. You mentioned last night you needed a wakeup. Need a coffee?" I asked.

"Yeah, I remember. Thanks, man. Sure," he said, reaching out to take one of the coffees. He sipped it carefully and winced. "I'm

not much on coffee. Got any energy drinks?" he asked apologetically.

I shook my head. "Sorry, man, I don't drink those," I said.

How we obtained our caffeine was a generational differenti-
ator. Baby Boomers and Gen X were team coffee; Millennials and
younger were into the sugary energy drinks.

As he shifted, he put a hand in his hoody pocket. I heard the
muffled sound of papers rustling. He was confused for a moment,
slowly taking his empty hand out of his pocket and putting it in his
lap.

"Are you going to be able get your work clothes?" I asked,
sitting on the metal stairs leading up to the back door of his camper.

"That is the question of the day, my man," he said quietly,
sipping his coffee and wincing again.

"Need a ride to work or anything?" I asked. Chris didn't answer for a moment. I put the coffee down next to me on the stairs.

"I don't know. Candy drove me yesterday," he said. "Listen, I
appreciate you waking me up and the coffee. I'm going to chat with
her. You may not want to be around for that convo."

"I'm gone. Good luck," I said, nodding at him and returning
to my lot. I paused for a moment before walking back over to
Chris's site. He was staring down at the folded papers.

"Hey, almost forgot this," I said, gesturing to my coffee cup
on the stairs. Chris jumped when he heard my voice. He folded the
papers and shoved them back into his hoody pocket. I grabbed my
coffee and walked back to my site.

I wiped the dew off a damp patio chair with a swipe of the
hand, sat down, and sipped my coffee quietly. Chris knocked faintly
on his camper door. I heard the door open, a murmuring, and then
the door closing.

Chris 4
7:20 a.m.

A s I stepped out of the shower, I struggled to remember the last part of the night. I recalled riding with Chuck to the cabin, smoking with him, and him leaving. Someone else was around, but I wasn't sure who. Chuck mentioned dropping a person off after I woke up. I hadn't given it any thought as I walked back to my camper early in the morning. At least I didn't puke on myself this time. *It was the small victories.*

Candy most likely would have checked on me in the night and saw that I wasn't there. I would tell the truth, that Chuck was kind enough to give me a cabin since she locked me out of my RV.

The difficult part of the puzzle to put together were the papers in my hoody pocket. Brady's papers. I wasn't sure how they got there. Why would I have them? I was lucky that they didn't fall out in front of him.

A memory returned to me. It was of Data dropping some papers a few nights ago. The night I passed out on the jumping pillow. But why would Data have Brady's papers? Maybe Brady was trying to invest in the campground or refinance his camper or something?

I walked out of the shower house and out on Sparrow. I heard a golf cart approaching and saw that it was Chuck. He rolled up beside me.

"Mornin'," Chuck said, putting a cigarette in his mouth and inhaling deeply. He wore a red do-rag and sunglasses, even though the sun was not yet that bright in the sky.

"Good morning, Chuck," I said.

"Long night last night?" he asked, smiling. I tried to smile back and nodded.

"Yeah. Not too restful," was all I could manage.

"Off to work?" he asked, taking a Styrofoam coffee cup from the holder and taking a drink.

"Yup. Hey, is Data working today?" I asked.

"Yeah, he will be in at eight. Why?" he asked.

"I have something for him," I replied.

"If you want to give it to me, I can make sure he gets it," Chuck said, taking another drag.

Brady 7

7:30 a.m.

I positioned myself at the patio table to get a visual angle on Chris's camper. I couldn't quite see his front door, but I could see most of the rest of his lot. Chris went to the shower house like he always did before work.

The sudden blast of the train horn jarred me. Despite having consumed a fair amount of alcohol last night, I felt okay, with a minimal hangover. I was reasonably alert.

Sometimes I couldn't predict how the liquor would hit me. I could drink half of a bottle of vodka and only feel groggy the next day or I could drink a few beers and feel hungover. There were times I felt hungover when I hadn't drunk a drop the night prior. My theory was that it had something to do with my diet as well as occasional sinus and allergy issues. I should have a better grasp of how booze affected me at this point in my life, with decades of drinking experience under my belt.

The clamoring of the train began to subside as it finally passed the campground, sounding its horn again as it continued west.

My laptop was positioned so I could peer over the top of it, hopefully without revealing that I was staring at Chris's lot. There was a glare on the screen, but I didn't reposition it.

Chris returned, walking into my field of view, and disappeared to the left. I heard his camper door open and close. Then I saw Chuck pull up to the side of his lot. He sat in his golf cart and didn't look over in my direction, taking a drag off his cigarette.

I continued to peek above my laptop screen. A moment later, I heard the squeak of Chris's camper door opening, and Chris reappeared. He had a manila envelope and handed it to Chuck. They said a few words, and Chuck drove off.

A moment later, Chris and Candy emerged, walking north on Sparrow to the overflow parking lot beyond the dumpster. I heard his junker starting, struggling at first, and then roaring to life. It was a 1990s-era Pontiac Grand Am, its maroon color faded to a pinkish hue over time. If the train didn't wake up the sleeping campers, that piece of junk surely would.

The car noise got louder as it approached Chris's RV. It passed into my view briefly as it headed south on Sparrow, Chris staring straight ahead in the passenger's seat.

I went inside the camper and brought out my personal laptop. I had to reconnect to the campsite Wi-Fi, since it would drop the connection if it was idle for a few hours.

I navigated to the Erie County property records site. Recalling that Randy's address was 273 Eagle Creek Drive, I entered it in the search box.

The stats of the house appeared. Square footage, amenities, year built, price, etc. I scrolled down to the owners and found it was in the name of Cynthia Gorey. She was the only party listed. I did a screenshot and saved it on my hard drive.

I did a commercial search for the bowling alley. When I searched "Glory Bowl," I scrolled down through the stats. The business was titled in the name of Glory Properties Limited. I took a screenshot of that info as well.

Next, I searched the Ohio State Secretary of State site and found the search area for corporations. A search for "Glory Properties" found one record. I clicked on the link and saw that the company was chartered in 1987. The authorized representative and statutory agent was an attorney with a Toledo address. Another screenshot.

Mike 5

9:00 a.m.

The breakfast offered by the campground wasn't half bad. It resembled an army mess hall breakfast, with scrambled eggs, pancakes, toast, and sausage links. There was coffee, milk, and orange juice to wash it down. Army cooks had a bad reputation, mostly deserved, but they did get breakfast right. The only thing missing was the grits, but those were a rarity in the Midwest.

The drinks were poured into Styrofoam cups and the food placed in a Styrofoam container. I headed back to my campsite.

It was fair out, in the high sixties, but I decided to build a fire anyways. I sat in my fold-out chair and ate, carefully cutting up the pancakes and sausage with a plastic knife and fork.

The coffee was awful. I was an expert on awful coffee; I had consumed thousands of gallons of it during my army service. Like a lot of things that I embraced in the world, I embraced the awful. I drank the awful, and I drank it black.

I did a few maintenance tasks on the camper. The exterior needed a thorough washing. The mayflies were arriving, weird insects that swarmed the coastal region of the Great Lakes in early summer. They arrived in such numbers that the swarms could be seen on weather radar. They clung to every surface. They weren't harmful; they just sat there until it rained or something else forced them off whatever surface they were on. A few found their way onto my camper.

Spraying them directly caused them to splatter, so I modified my technique to spray them at an angle. The metal exterior of my camper seemed to be less attractive to them than the white exteriors of most campers, as I did have fewer than other RVs.

Chuck made an appearance, scooting around on his golf cart. He pulled over when he saw me, just as I was reattaching the main hose to the camper water intake.

"Hey, Mike," he said, puffing on a cigarette.

"Hey. You get the kid home safe last night?" I asked.

"Yeah, he partied a bit, but I got him home," he said, laughing. I wiped the water off from my hands on my threadbare blue gym shorts.

"You guys party together?" I asked, folding my arms.

"About as much as you and Brady did, having drinks around the fire last night," he replied, squinting against the sun.

"I think his problems go well beyond drinking, based on what I saw at the jumping pillow yesterday morning," I said.

Chuck shrugged. "You some kind of expert?"

"I don't think any of us have a graduate degree in substance abuse counseling, right? Maybe you have some personal experience with it all?" I asked, smiling.

Chuck stared at me for a minute. "Nah, I'm just a simple campground worker, boss," he said, throwing his cigarette butt on my lot. He stood there a minute, saluted, and walked over to his cart.

I watched him roll off, and I pondered what sort of lowlife would intentionally litter another man's campsite, especially given he worked at the damned place. I resisted characterizing his disrespect as racial. The asshole likely tossed cigarette butts on other sites throughout the campground.

I checked my watch and figured that 1000 hours was a reasonable time to take a walk around the seasonal block, on the off chance that Brady was out. He'd mentioned that he worked from his RV during the day, so if he happened to be outside, then maybe he had a moment for a chat.

Randy 2

12:00 p.m.

Riding my bike east on Columbus Road toward the campground, I was hoping lunchtime would be the right time to catch Sullivan. I pulled into the campground. One of the old military retirees was at the booth and nodded to me.

Travis kept a few of these vets on the payroll, and I honestly didn't understand why he didn't hire more of them. They all had a good work ethic. They were old and less physically capable, but they came to work on time, and they didn't have these drug and alcohol vices that the younger guys did. If they did have vices, at least they didn't bring them to work with them.

I slowly rolled up Starling, paying closer attention when I approached Sullivan's lot. His truck was there. I saw that the main door was open, but he wasn't outside. I figured he sat at his kitchen table while he worked.

Parking at the Taj, I considered making a drink but decided to wait. I had some business at the bowling alley to tend to later and didn't want to get bogged down with a buzz.

As I walked up to the porch, I saw Chuck riding north on Starling. He pulled up to the site and stopped, puffing on a cigarette.

"I'm glad to see you out here. Usually, when I send you an urgent text, you respond a little quicker," Chuck said, reaching into the back seat of the golf cart.

"You think all your texts are urgent," I said.

Chuck was out of the golf cart, carrying an envelope. I reached for it as he walked up. I opened it and found five or six laser-printed pages inside. I reviewed them and realized what they were.

"Why are you walking around with this?" I asked angrily.

Chuck looked nervous. "Let's go inside and talk," he said, taking a drag off his cigarette.

Brady 8

12:30 p.m.

Looking out my kitchen window, I saw the Glory Bowl biker ride past and park at site 21. Randy Gorey. The guy with several properties listed under different names.

My workday had been less than productive. I was so distracted by the handoff of my papers between Chris and Chuck that I had difficulty focusing.

I wanted to mention it to Marcy when we talked later but thought better of it. She was a chronic worrier, so she would be terrified that we were having our identities stolen, and it would likely be my fault somehow. But I hadn't applied for credit or otherwise done anything that required a background check, so I had no idea why our information was out there.

I decided to make lunch. There were a few remaining pieces of bread in the bag that didn't appear to be moldy. I searched the cupboard and found a jar of peanut butter. It was actually faux peanut butter, made from soy. Katie's nut allergy prevented us from keeping any type of real peanut products around. It looked like real peanut butter; they must have dyed the hell out of it. It also tasted similar.

I added jelly, found a bag of chips, and grabbed a Diet Coke. The weather was nice, so I took it outside. Damn mayflies were accumulating on the side of the camper. I would have to sweep them off later.

Chuck rolled past, not looking over at me. He pulled up to site 21 and parked. He talked to the motorcycle guy from the bowling alley for a moment. Chuck handed him an envelope, which appeared exactly like the one that Chris gave him. It had to be mine.

He looked in the envelope. He looked over at me, as did Chuck. I pretended not to notice, fixing my eyes on my paper plate. When I glanced back over, they were climbing the steps to the RV.

"Hey, Brady," Mike said as he came around my RV from the direction of the shower house. He walked a few feet into the campsite and stopped. I waved him over to an empty chair.

"Sorry to interrupt your lunch," he said.

I put the pointer finger of my left hand up in the universal "give me a moment" sign while I finished chewing a bite of sandwich. I washed it down with a drink of pop. "No problem," I said.

Mike was wearing a blue Braves cap and dark sunglasses, a plain blue t-shirt, and blue gym shorts. "Any new developments?" he asked.

I nodded, looking around to ensure that no one was nearby. "I found Chris sleeping in front of his camper this morning and slipped the papers into his hoody pocket," I said, quieting my voice. I took a few chips and ate them.

Mike nodded. "Didn't wake up?"

I shook my head. "Shortly after, he gave them to Chuck," I said.

Mike cocked his head to the side slightly. "What the fuck would Chuck need with your information?" Mike asked.

I shrugged and nodded toward site 21. "It gets better. I just saw Chuck give the papers to that guy over there at site 21. Do you know the guy who owns that camper?" I asked.

Mike shook his head.

"Biker guy, maybe in his mid-fifties. I was out for a run the other day and ended up running through that gated community west of here. He has an expensive house there. Then I ran up to the bowling alley, and I think he must own it or at least a piece of it. He has a custom plate that matches the business name, Glory Bowl," I said.

"Did you say Glory Bowl?" he asked, scrunching up his face slightly.

"I did," I said, smirking.

"Hell of a name for a business," he said, laughing. "And he owns a camper here. Why own a camper a few miles from your house?"

I shrugged again. "Chuck seems tight with him. And they are running my background information for some unknown reason," I said as I took another bite of my sandwich.

Mike sat there silently.

Randy 3

12:30 p.m.

Fucking Data. I hired the guy because he was discreet and didn't make mistakes. Sure, he was human and had made mistakes in the past. He got busted hacking a few years ago, so he had a rap sheet. But he wasn't like these other degenerates out drinking and doing drugs all night. He was supposed to be my go-to tech guy. How the fuck does he lose the Sullivan papers? What if Sullivan had found his own damned papers?

I guessed it was contained. I had the papers. I considered having Sam deliver a message. I couldn't afford to lose Data, so nothing too serious, some shouting and maybe some slapping around. Data was a soft little computer nerd, and a little taste of the rough stuff would make an impression. If he didn't get the message and tighten up, I didn't know what I would do, since I had no idea how I would replace him.

The next phase of my business expansion was potentially the most profitable one. Once I got the equipment upgrade, I could start data mining the whole campground. Data said I could collect everything that wasn't encrypted from the campers. It could be a goldmine, once we figured out what to collect and how to use it. Data had some ideas.

The amusement park had a vast Wi-Fi system, but he figured they would have more security. But maybe that was something Data could figure out eventually. That had enormous potential. With thousands of people using that network each day, the sky was the limit.

I decided to introduce myself, since Sullivan was sitting outside at his table. As I got closer, I saw he had company. He was sitting with a middle-aged black guy wearing a baseball hat and sunglasses. My first impression of him was that he was forgettable, despite being one of the few blacks at the campground.

I crossed over and approached his lot, waving as I arrived. The conversation stopped, and they looked over at me.

"Afternoon," I said as I approached, stopping a few feet from the table. They both nodded.

"I'm Randy Gorey," I said, reaching out my hand to Sullivan. He stood up and shook it.

"Brady Sullivan," Sullivan said.

"Mike Clemmons," the black guy said as we shook hands. There was an awkward silence.

"I think we met the other day, Brady, when you took a running tour of my neighborhood. Then you ran over to my bowling alley. Now you are camped out in front of my RV. It's like you are touring all of my properties or something," I said with a smile. Brady returned it sheepishly.

"Yeah, my bad. The running routes around here get a little tiresome, so when I saw the gate open, I decided to take a run inside there. Gorgeous houses. Do you live there year-round?" he asked.

"More or less. I also have a condo down south so I can get away a little when winter kicks in heavily. Otherwise, I like to stay close to keep an eye on my business investments," I said, shifting from my left to right foot.

"Have a seat, Randy," Brady said, gesturing to an empty patio chair. I nodded and sat at the head of the table, with Sullivan and Mike on either side.

"Thanks for not having me arrested." Sullivan laughed. I laughed as well. Mike smiled.

"I wouldn't dream of it. It was just curiosity; it wasn't like you were casing the neighborhood. Some neighbors have sticks up their asses, so I would be careful about it in the future," I said.

"My curiosity has been satisfied. I doubt I will chance it again," he replied.

I looked over at Mike. "Are you seasonal? I don't think I've seen you around," I said.

"No, sir, just here for a brief visit and then moving along," he replied.

I gestured toward his cap. "From Atlanta?" I asked.

"Originally. I have moved around a bit. I'm retired. My RV is my home, so I travel around in it, trying to avoid hot southern summers and cold northern winters," he said.

I nodded and laughed. "Sounds like a reasonable retirement plan. How do you like Sandusky?" I asked.

He smiled and nodded. The horn from the train blasted from the distance. "Well, I could live without those fucking trains going by all day and night," he said flatly. Sullivan and I laughed.

"I was born and raised here, so I barely notice them. I don't sleep in the camper very often; the tracks are so close that it shakes the whole damn thing," I said.

There was silence for a minute as we waited for the disruption of the train to end. Its horn blasted a final time, and then it was quiet.

"Are you and Chuck friends?" Sullivan asked.

I considered my reply. "More like a business relationship. He helps me out with some side jobs here and there," I said.

"Do you own a stake in this campground?" Mike asked.

I smiled. "I own a stake in a lot of things around this city. I've been here for a while," I replied.

I waited for a follow-up to see if I could get away with the non-answer. But Mike just nodded. He likely took my answer as confirmation that I was an investor. Not that he could verify it. I didn't have my name anywhere on any legal documents.

"Your family coming up this weekend? I think they are having some sort of theme for the kids, like superhero weekend or something," I asked Sullivan.

"Yeah, I'm getting out of work a little early tomorrow and heading over to pick them up for a long weekend. We'll spend most of the time at the park but will try to do some of the activities around here too," Sullivan replied. "Does anyone want a drink? I'm going to grab a water, and then I need to get back at it."

Both of us shook our heads. Mike stood up. "Actually, I need to move along, I don't want to keep you, Brady," he said. They shook hands, we shook hands, and Mike headed north on Starling. Brady went to the outdoor fridge and took a bottled water out.

"It seems to me that you've been living somewhat of a hermit's existence up here, by yourself and all. Why don't you come by the bowling alley later? We don't have a fancy menu or any-thing, but we make a good burger, the beer is cold, a baseball game will be on TV, and there's some good people-watching with the bowling leagues," I said, leaning back in my chair.

"People-watching?" he asked.

"Yeah, people-watching. All kinds of interesting people there. Serious bowlers, amateurs, tourists, townies; everyone bowls around here; it is a melting pot. Sort of like this campground, I guess. Some people are well dressed, others are tacky as shit, all fun to watch," I said, smiling.

Brady stared down at his water bottle and appeared to be thinking. He looked up. "Yeah, I may come by for a drink. You don't need to treat me to anything. I can't be out too late. I have a lot going on tomorrow," he said.

"Great! Mention my name at the bar, and you'll get better service. I should be around managing, so I'll stop by and say hi. Maybe we can have a bite to eat or something," I said. I instantly regretted the last thing. I was being pushy.

"Sounds good. Maybe I'll see you later, Randy," he said, standing up. We shook hands, and I walked back to my camper.

Sam 2

7:15 p.m.

No Sullivan yet. Randy figured that if he came in at all, he would be in around 1900 hours. The alley was busy with the bowling leagues, but the bar only had a few regulars. I was lucky I didn't depend on tips to pay the bills; it was chump change.

A guy came up and leaned against the bar, waiting for my attention. I was busy cleaning a glass and made him wait thirty seconds before coming over.

He was obviously a tourist. Sandusky was a small town that was invaded each summer by waves of tourists from all over the region. It was easy to spot them. He was in his mid-thirties and dressed for the golf course, somewhat overweight, skin bright pink from the sun. Probably in town to golf with his buddies.

"Hey buddy, can I get a frozen margarita?" he asked, leaning on the bar.

I glared at him. "See a blender back here, bud?" I asked. He was confused at first, then annoyed. "I have the mix. I can make you one on the rocks."

He seemed to be thinking deeply about this counteroffer, then nodded. I walked over to the bottles.

"Do you have Patrón?" he asked.

I shook my head. "Jose or no bueno," I replied. He shrugged and nodded. I made him his drink. I tended to overpour, but I underpoured his a little.

"Five dollars. Run a tab or cash out?" I asked. He handed me a credit card.

"Cash it out," he said.

"Sorry, the credit card machine is down," I said. He looked annoyed. He took out his wallet, pulled out a ten, and handed it to me. I went over to the till, turning my back to him. Slipping the bill into my pocket, I pushed "no sale" on the cash register, took out five one-dollar bills, and set them on the bar in front of him.

My phone vibrated. I reached in my pocket to check it. Randy had arrived and was in his office upstairs.

I walked back over to the side of the bar and saw that the tourist left me a one-dollar tip. I was okay with that. Twenty percent for pouring a weak drink was fine.

I glanced at my watch—1927 hours. I remembered that there were drops to be picked up. A bowling league pogue came up. I poured him a pitcher of beer, and then hustled over to the lockers area in the back corner. I pulled out my keyring and went through the series of lockers.

Three of the lockers had envelopes stuffed in them. Two small envelopes of money and a larger one with papers that Data had left earlier.

I swept back by the bar, refilled a pitcher, and poured a Woodford Reserve on the rocks. Grabbing the bourbon drink and envelopes, I walked upstairs quickly to Randy's office.

I knocked, looking up at the camera above the door. A few seconds later, the door buzzed, and I went inside.

Randy was at his desk, going through some papers. Behind him was a tinted window with a view of the bowling lanes. I put the drink and envelopes on the edge of his desk.

"No sign of Sullivan yet?" he asked. Randy already knew the answer. He had cameras throughout the building and knew that Sullivan wasn't there.

"Not yet."

"When you pick up the drops, you take them right up to me. You don't leave that shit behind the bar and serve drinks. What I have in these envelopes is a lot more valuable than the cash you're skimming."

I didn't have a response. What could I say? I returned to the bar and made more drinks.

"Can I get a Jack and Coke?" a voice said from the left, startling me a little. I had been off in my own world for a minute, staring blankly at a TV, where the Reds were playing the Tigers. A guy in a bowling league was a Reds fan, so I would put their games on if the Indians weren't playing.

I turned around, and Sullivan was sitting at the bar. He wore a gray, dry-fit T-shirt with a gray-and-black American flag and jeans.

His shirt was made by a company that catered to the military. I owned a few with marine graphics.

He wasn't a very impressive-looking guy. He was six foot and about 180 pounds, one of those leaner functional fitness guys. A cardio guy. When I was in the gym, it was to push iron. I was sure Sullivan didn't lift heavy.

I made his drink, giving him a double pour.

"Five dollars. Want to run a tab?" I asked. He nodded, handing me a credit card. I took it over and put it on the edge of the cash register. I walked back over and stood in front of him.

"Nice T-shirt. Did you serve?" I asked, knowing full well that he had served, per Data's research.

"Yeah, army," he said, taking a sip of his drink. When it passed his lips, he winced a little at its strength. His hair was a brownish color, showing some gray here and there, thinning a bit. He kept it short, something close to a military regulation cut.

"I am a marine," I said, trying to say it flatly but knowing I sounded arrogant. It was hard to do otherwise, especially when talking to servicemen from other branches.

He nodded. "How many years?" he asked.

For some reason, that stumped me. I had been out for a long time but still had a hard time talking about my service when someone asked questions. I only did a little over a year. There were times when I kicked myself for talking about it at all to other veterans because a short stint like mine usually meant either a medical retirement or a less-than-honorable discharge.

"A few," I muttered, and walked over to the other side of the bar and grabbed a rag. I wiped up a few sweat rings on the bar.

"May I see a menu?" Sullivan asked. I reached under the counter and grabbed one. It was only two pages, laminated. I wiped it off with the rag and handed it to him. I pulled out my cell phone and sent a text to Randy.

"Okay. I think I'll have the buffalo chicken wrap," he said.

"Fried chicken or grilled?" I asked.

"How about fried, why not live dangerously?" he asked.

I faked a smile. "Fries or pub chips?" I asked.

"I'll do the pub chips," he said, setting the menu down on the bar. He took another sip, leaving his glass a little less than half full. I wrote down his order and put away his menu.

"Let me run this back to the kitchen," I said, coming out from behind the bar and walking through the swinging door at the back corner of the bar area.

Brady 9

8:15 p.m.

The bowling alley was the dump I had imagined it to be. Dingy, smelly, badly lit. The walls and drop ceiling were a yellowish color from the years of secondhand smoke staining them. Ohio had been smoke-free in public establishments for over a decade, but apparently, it wasn't in the budget to slap a fresh coat of paint on the place.

There was a dull roar of bowling noises. Balls rolling down lanes, pins crashing, and people occasionally shouting. After living mostly in solitude for so many weeks, I welcomed the disruptive sounds of the alley.

The buffalo wrap wasn't bad. The pub chips were a little stale. The drinks were excellent, however, with the big marine making them very stiff.

That was why I generally loved dive bars. The drinks were cheap and mixed strong. Go to a trendy bar in downtown Cleveland and you'd pay twelve dollars for a watered-down whiskey drink with an ounce of liquor in it, meticulously measured with a jigger. You would go broke before you got drunk.

I developed a fondness for dive bars while I was in the military. We were poor privates trying to make our poverty-level paychecks stretch as far as possible, so we settled for gritty little blue-collar bars with no cover charge and cheap drinks.

I spotted a jukebox in the corner and decided to check the music options. It was one of those digital ones that you could either play by feeding it cash or through a phone app. It must have been placed there on consignment from a vendor; it looked modern and out of place in the otherwise retro bowling alley environment. I fed it a few dollars.

After searching for bands I liked, I selected several grunge and alt-rock songs. That genre wasn't a crowd-pleaser at a joint like this, with the older bowling leaguers likely more oriented toward classic rock and pop from the 1960s and 1970s.

I returned to my seat and took another drink. Over the course of about forty-five minutes, I consumed four strong drinks, way too many for that short of a duration. I would have one more and leave.

"Hey there, Brady!" a loud voice boomed from behind me. Randy walked over and shook my hand as I stood up. He wore a black Glory Bowl bowling shirt, jeans, and big, dusty motorcycle boots. He carried a dark-brown drink in a small glass.

"Hey, Randy," I said, sitting back down.

He sat down on the stool to the left of me. "How has Sam been treatin' you?" he asked, gesturing toward him. Sam was pouring a pitcher for a bowling leaguer.

"Good. He has been on top of it," I said, holding up my drink and smiling.

"And the food?" he asked, taking a sip of his drink.

"Good," I said, deciding not to embellish. It was adequate at best. But I wasn't here to critique the food. I wasn't sure why I was here. It seemed like a reasonable idea earlier, but once I walked in, I immediately second-guessed my purpose there.

"Great! Just so you know, your money is no good here. Consider this covered," he said.

"You don't need to do that," I responded.

He shrugged. "This is my joint. I know what the food and drinks actually cost. Believe me, you won't drive the bottom line into the red by accepting a chicken wrap and a few drinks," he said, laughing.

I smiled. I took another swig, and the drink was gone.

"Are you up for another?" he asked.

I wasn't. I was ready to leave. But what was I going to do when I left? Build another stupid fire? Get drunk by myself beside the stupid fire? Obsessively think about my absent wife and kids, who I hadn't seen in weeks?

"Sure," I said.

"Sam, how about a round?" Randy said, setting his empty glass on the bar. Sam took our glasses and began refilling them.

Randy 4

9:30 p.m.

When to serve him that special drink was a hard decision. I figured it would be hard to keep him at the bowling alley late, but it turned out feeding him a steady supply of stiff drinks was a good way to keep him around.

Sullivan came across as straight and narrow, but he was former military, and most of those guys were drinkers. Sullivan drank whiskey. Not rum, tequila, gin, or brandy. That said something about him.

He didn't drink craft whiskey; he drank off-the-shelf Jack Daniel's. It was advertised as Tennessee sipping whiskey, but it wasn't sipping whiskey, it was "get me drunk" whiskey. The guy liked his drink.

Data had dropped off his Wi-Fi activity report earlier, and there was a lot of interesting shit going on in Brady's life. His work laptop was encrypted and gave us nothing. But the stuff on his phone and personal laptop were wide open. Despite his carelessness with losing the write-up sheets, Data was an amazing resource.

Most of Sullivan's texting was either short bits of communication between him and his wife or long, wordy, angry arguments between them.

That marriage was done, but he didn't know it yet. I had been there. He needed to know when to walk away.

A divorce was going to be costly, because his wife was damn near a fanatic. She was so overprotective of the kids that it bordered on insanity. The little girl had severe allergies, and based on discussions about EpiPens, it was food allergies. I had to Google what EpiPens did. If the kid ate something she shouldn't, her throat would close up, and she would need a shot of adrenaline from the EpiPen. Scary shit if you were a parent.

The wife always sounded stressed out and frazzled. The texts went back six months, and they were all hysteria and drama. I was sure Sullivan had an ulcer from that type of stress. I understood why he lived by himself at a run-down campground and drank away his problems every night.

The bad news for Sullivan was that it was about to get worse. I felt for a man who was down on his luck. But he was nobody to me. As an asset, though, he had the potential to be a whole lot to me.

I also saw that Sullivan researched me, looking at my property records. Earlier that day, as a matter of fact. I was sure that failing to find my name on anything intrigued him.

I still had more of the information to review. Once Sullivan left, I planned on going back upstairs and doing a deeper dive into his world.

I swiveled around and regarded Sullivan. He was showing the effects from the whiskey. His eyes drooped a little, and his speech was slightly slurred. Sam was serving them up strong. If I could keep him there another hour, then things would go according to plan.

"So, you are heading home to get the kids tomorrow?" I asked, leaning toward him.

He nodded, taking another drink. "Yeah, can't wait. I'm gonna work for a few hours in the morning and go get them," he said.

I raised my glass and leaned it forward, clinking it against his. We both drank.

"I need to get back to the campground after I finish this. Really, Randy, you shouldn't pay for this," he said.

I laughed. "I told you your money is no good here, Sullivan," I said and took a drink. I nodded at Sam. "How about one last drink?"

Sullivan shook his head. He stood up. "I need to hit the latrine and get out of here. I have a lot to do tomorrow," he said. He walked a little unsteadily toward the bathroom. Sam leaned against the bar across from me.

"Make him one more. Make him a special," I said. Sam nodded and went back to where the bottles were.

Another drink was waiting for him when he came back. Sullivan exhaled heavily and shook his head. "Randy, I really didn't want another one," he said.

I shrugged. "Sam is a marine. Sometimes they don't listen so good," I said.

Sullivan laughed politely.

Sam smirked, pointing to his left ear and shrugging like *"this thing doesn't work so good."* Sullivan smiled, shook his head again, and took a drink.

From the side of the bar, a young woman walked up. I recognized her as Anka.

She was the hottest of the Romanian prostitutes, with long dark hair, perfect skin, and a nice body. She wore a tight little blue sundress that showed off all her curves. Her earrings were very big gold hoops. The purse she carried was also huge; it was practically a suitcase, with some designer pattern.

Standing on the other side of Sullivan at the bar, she leaned against it and squinted to read the bottle labels. It was a non-subtle way of showing some cleavage and sticking her ass out.

Sullivan noticed her and did a double take. I didn't blame him; it was difficult not to. He was a married man. Well, sort of. Legally, but there was no physical relationship happening between him and his wife at that point.

She ordered a drink from Sam and sat down, crossing her legs and adjusting her dress, pulling it down mid-thigh. Sam put down a margarita on the rocks in front of her.

I didn't like to have the Romanians come into the bowling alley. This was not the place for people in their twenties generally. Why would a hot young woman come hang out at a bowling alley dive bar by herself? She wouldn't. Unless she was a prostitute.

She leaned over and said something to Sullivan. The music was too loud for me to pick it up. He smiled politely and said something back.

I tapped Sullivan on the shoulder. When he turned around, I could tell his drink additive was starting to hit him hard. It had been five minutes since Sam mixed it.

You could never tell how fast or hard a spiked drink would hit a person; a lot of different factors were at play. Some passed out immediately. Others functioned for a time and then became zom-

bies before passing out. It was going to be about T-minus one minute before Sullivan pulled a *Weekend at Bernie's* act.

I hoped to get a few more minutes of Sullivan chatting with
the hooker on film, but she arrived too late. Sullivan passing out at
my bar was not part of the plan. I leaned closer to him. "Are you
ready to go? I'll have Sam take you home. You drank your share,
buddy," I said, patting him on the back. Sullivan just sat there, staring straight ahead. He robotically took another drink, finishing it.

"Hey, Sam, why don't you pull the vehicle up? I will handle
the bar," I said, walking around behind the bar.

Sam nodded, grabbed a towel, wiped his hands, and walked
around to the other side of the bar. "You ready?" he asked. Sullivan's eyes were starting to close. Sam hustled over and stood beside him, leaning over and pulling Sullivan's right arm up on his
shoulder. The Romanian girl sat quietly, sipping her drink through
a pink straw.

"Let's take a walk out to my vehicle. Are you okay to walk?"
Sam asked. Sullivan didn't respond. His eyes closed. "Stay with me."

Sam lifted him out of the chair and onto his feet, keeping a
hold of his arm. The two started for the side door. I surveyed the
bar area, and luckily no one else was nearby.

The Romanian girl finished her drink with a slurp and stood
up, following them. She scurried around in front of them to open
the back door, and the three of them walked out. I picked up the
empty glasses and put them in the sink, wiping down the bar top.

Chapter 4
Friday, June 19

Brady 10

12:55 p.m.

The train horn pulled me out of my deep sleep. I lay still with my eyes closed. A wave of dizziness swept over me.

I dared not open my eyes. The sun was definitely out because it was attempting to pierce my eyelids. I put my hands up to my face and covered it, sliding them down below my chin.

My head throbbed. My throat was parched; I was dehydrated. I was fairly sure I hadn't drunk water in a long time.

I felt the bed vibrate slightly from the passing train. I finally opened my eyes slightly. A layer of crust had accumulated around the tear ducts. I squinted and wiped it away, which took a few attempts.

I was staring up at a dusty brown faux wood ceiling fan. The master bedroom in my camper did not have a ceiling fan. This jolted my eyes wide open. I looked around and realized I did not know where I was.

It took me a moment to recognize I was in one of the campground cabins. Marcy's parents had stayed in one for the weekend last summer, and we spent some time in theirs on a rainy day. The same plain white curtains that blocked very little sunlight. Fake wood floors and paneled walls. A beat-up wooden nightstand with a black digital alarm clock and a small lamp with a yellowing white lampshade on it. The alarm clock was blinking 4:47 a.m., which was obviously incorrect, due to the bright sunlight.

I glanced down at my watch, but it was dead. The battery power was running low yesterday evening, but I figured I would charge it when I got home. *Except I didn't make it home.*

The air was dusty and stale. I ran my right hand through my hair and found that I was sweating. The room wasn't particularly hot; it was the alcohol seeping out of my pores.

Where was my phone? I reached down to check my pockets and realized I was in bed naked. That was not how I generally slept; I always wore gym shorts to bed.

I leaned over and looked at the floor. My jeans were wadded up with my black belt still wound through the loops. Stretching over, I grabbed them, revealing my shirt underneath them. I could tell by the weight of my pants that there were items in the pockets.

My phone was in the front left pocket. Pressing the button on the right side, I discovered it was dead. I cursed to myself.

My wallet was in the back-right pocket. Everything seemed to be intact. Driver's license. Credit cards. Money. Wait, I was missing my Discover card. I left it at the bar with Sam.

Slipping on my clothes, I went out into the kitchen area. There was no sign of any cohabitants. My keys were on the kitchen table.

Opening the cupboard, I found a drinking glass. I ran the kitchen faucet for a moment until the water was cold, then filled it up. I slowly drank half the glass. Pausing for a moment to see how my stomach handled it, I belched and waited. A wave of nausea hit me.

Recalling that the bathroom was at the opposite end of the cabin, I walked swiftly over. I got to the toilet and threw up. It was all pale-brown liquid. *Ladies and gentlemen, Jack has left the building.* I dry-heaved a few times and then flushed the toilet.

Returning to the kitchen, I took the glass and filled my mouth with water. After swishing it around, I spit it out into the sink. I did it again, and then dared a tiny sip of it. It didn't come back up.

Leaning against the counter for a moment, I risked another small sip. It stayed down. I opened the fridge to see if there were any bottled waters, but it was empty. I stood in front of it for a moment, savoring the cold air that escaped.

I walked over and peeked out the front window. My truck was not parked in front. I prayed that it was still at the bowling alley or at my campsite.

Walking back to my RV seemed like a nightmare, but I couldn't stay in the cabin. *How did I end up in the cabin?* Renting it made no sense, with my own camper a short walk away.

I found my running shoes by the door, with my black cotton socks wadded up and stuffed inside them. I put them on and opened the door. The sun assaulted my vision. I didn't know where my sunglasses were; hopefully, they were in my vehicle. *Wherever my vehicle was.*

I stepped out and looked around. The cabin was along the east side of the campground, separated by a fence from the auto dealership, about two hundred yards from my RV.

Nausea struck me again, and I nearly threw up. I thought of Chris the other morning and how he threw up on himself while sprawled out on the jumping pillow. *Now I was barely a notch above that level of dysfunction.*

I began the journey to my camper. I reached the playground area and headed west. Kids were bouncing on the jumping pillow and playing on the swing sets. *What time was it?* The sun seemed too high in the sky for it to be morning, which made my stomach churn with anxiety.

I cut through between the pool and the clubhouse and angled across to Starling. The tree cover over the street was a godsend. Nausea hit me again as I approached the gazebo. A few people were out and waved at me. There were a few smirks as they watched me walk past.

I remembered the term "walk of shame" from my military and college years. A woman (or man) would engage in a one-night stand and then have to return to her car or dorm wearing the same clothes they had worn the night before, all disheveled and hungover. That was me, minus the one-night stand. But then again, I woke up naked in a random cabin. *And there was a fuzzy memory of a girl at the bar.*

My truck was parked in front of the camper and not at the bowling alley or some back alley chop shop. *Thank God.* I peered into the passenger window and saw it was locked. I walked over to the front door of the camper and pulled out my keys. I fumbled through them, trying to find the correct one, the one with the purple plastic cover at the top. *It was missing.*

Luckily, I had a backup key. I stooped down beside the camper on the right side of the main doorstep, sliding my hand over until I found the little metal box that magnetically attached to a metal reinforcement underneath. I entered the combination and removed the key, letting myself into the camper.

I had left the air conditioning on, and it was cool inside. I opened the fridge, took out a bottled water, and took a drink. My stomach continued to hold the water down. I took my phone out and connected it to the charging cord in the bedroom.

Stripping out of my clothes, I went into the bathroom. My reflection in the mirror startled me. My hair was greasy. There were dark bags under my eyes. My skin was pale and sweaty. I looked terrible. *Death warmed over.* And I'd just paraded in front of the neighbors in that condition. *Why didn't I go up Sparrow and cut through Chris's lot?* There would have been far fewer eyes on me if I approached from that direction.

I ran the shower and got in, washing thoroughly. I almost threw up again but managed not to. As soon as I got out of the shower, I would need to take a few aspirins and log in to my work laptop.

I finished the shower and grabbed my phone, pushing the button on the side to illuminate the screen. My jaw dropped. It read 1309 hours. *That couldn't fucking be true.*

I pulled my work laptop out and opened it. The government common access card was still in the slot, so I pulled it out and reinserted it. I entered my PIN, and it booted up. I glanced down at the clock at the bottom right-hand corner of the screen. It read 1311 hours.

My stomach lurched. I barely made it to the bathroom to throw up again. I heard the phone make a series of dinging noises as the texts and voicemails that queued up while it was dead began to arrive.

Brady's Cell Phone 1

1:12 p.m.

- Text message – Jeff-Boss (0711) - *U there Brady? Need u to cover call @ 0730*
- Text message – Jeff-Boss (0723) – *Don't see you on*
- Text message – Jeff-Boss (0759) – *R U going to make the 8 conference call*
- Text message – Marcy (0854) – *what time r u going to be at my parents?*
- Text message – Rob Mac (0902) – *Are you calling in? Need your update*
- Text message – Jamal Dogg (0937) – *U alive? People are worried*
- Text message – Marcy (0947) – *r u there? Need 2 know when u r picking them up*
- Text message – Jeff-Boss (1003) – *Call me asap*
- Text message – Marty FIL (1015) – *What time picking kids up?*
- Text message – Marcy (1019) - *?????*
- Text message – Marcy (1101) - *?????*
- Text message – Jeff-Boss (1114) – *Call me asap*
- Text message – Marcy (1139) – *Are you ok?*
- Text message – Jamal Dogg (1201) – *Dude call someone*
- Text message – Marcy (1219) – *Parents taking them to lunch n to park. Call me*
- Text message – Marcy (1231) – *We are worried, plz call*
- Text message – Marcy (1259) – *Kids worried, where are you?*
- Voice messages (7)

Mike 6

1:30 p.m.

was more concerned about Brady than I reasonably should have been. After all, I barely knew the guy. Maybe it was just instinctive concern for a fellow veteran.

I expected to see his camper door open early, but it wasn't. His truck was there but no signs of life. He mentioned he was going back to the Cleveland area to get his kids in the late morning. But there his vehicle was.

I hung out by my campfire most of the morning and early afternoon. I drank an average amount the night before and wasn't hungover, but I still consumed a few Bloody Marys.

I drank my way through lunch, took a walk by Brady's, and then walked back to my campsite. Nothing happening over there. I thought about Chris having Brady's private info and the fact that he handed it off to Chuck. What was the point? My strategic thinking wasn't fine-tuned enough to understand why they would want to fuck with a guy like Brady. He seemed so vanilla, just a family guy, upper middle class. He was unlikely to be mistaken for a high roller.

I decided to go for a walk again. There seemed to be more campers arriving than normal, probably since it was a Friday. A lot of kids riding bikes and employees buzzing past in work carts. There was some sort of superhero theme that weekend, and several kids wore capes and masks. Chuck passed me and nodded, and I nodded back.

I passed the shower house and came upon Brady's site. His truck was still there. I slowed as I walked by. His door was cracked slightly. I considered whether I should knock or not. He may be working inside the RV because he didn't want to be bothered. Maybe he got hit with an unexpected work assignment and couldn't go to Cleveland.

I stepped up and knocked softly a few times. After a minute, the door opened and he appeared, wearing just a pair of gray gym shorts. His face was deathly pale. He wore a very grim, intense expression.

"Hey Brady, just dropping by ..." I began, but he interrupted me.

"Come inside," he said urgently. He held open the screen door, and I climbed the stairs.

Data 4

1:45 p.m.

My burner phone vibrated in my left-front pocket. I pulled it out; there was a text message from Randy.

Crunch BS info and pull shots

I was relieved. I was riding along in the work cart with Patrick, collecting the garbage left at the campsites. It was a gross job, and with the weather warming up, getting grosser. Some of the smells made me gag.

People left disgusting things out. Bags broke, spilling out dirty diapers, rotting food, coffee grounds, moldy plastic cups, dog crap, and other unidentifiable debris. When a bag broke, I had to get a replacement bag and pick up whatever spilled.

We pulled up alongside a transient lot. I grabbed the white garbage bag that was placed by the road, brought it to the back of the work cart, and placed it in gently.

Of course, I was always the one to collect the garbage because Patrick always had to drive. The one time I complained, Patrick just smiled and continued driving, so I let it go. I made a mental note to chat with Randy about it. If I was the invaluable tech guy, I needed to be afforded a minimal level of deference.

I was disappointed that I wasn't spending more time in Trailer Alpha working data angles rather than doing manual labor. But I realized I had to keep up appearances. I was a campground employee, and if my probation officer were to drop in, I should be doing campground tasks.

I kept kicking myself over the data loss. Randy mentioned that we needed to talk privately, and I had a feeling it was about the breach. It made my stomach turn just thinking about it.

"After this row, I need to go back to the office," I said to Patrick, who was stoically smoking a cigarette. He had been subdued all day, which led me to conclude that he was hungover. I liked this version of him, rather than the obnoxious, shit-talking one.

"We still have half the campground to collect from, man," he said, irritated.

"Boss's orders," I said.

Patrick shook his head. "Tired of getting stuck with all the shit work," he complained.

Cry me a river.

He dropped me off at the office. I went to the men's room and washed the garbage residue off my hands.

I came out and unlocked my bike chain. Despite the risks, I opted not to wear my helmet, to avoid being teased. I rode toward the campground entrance. Nobody was in the security booth.

Ten minutes later, I was in the control room of Trailer Alpha. I took a moment to view what was happening at all the locations on the bank of monitors.

A large RV was being hauled alongside the security booth. A woman pushed a stroller and walked a dog in front of Cabin F, trailing a little girl dressed like a Disney princess riding a small bike with training wheels. A lonely elderly day drinker was sitting at the bar at Glory Bowl, with a tall draught beer and a shot in front of him.

I started by clicking on the bowling alley image of the bar area. Clicking and sliding the scroll bar along the bottom of the screen to the left, the video began to reverse. The timestamp rolled back, with the display going darker during the hours it was closed, briefly lighting up when the cleaning crew arrived and worked, and then it was back to the "last call for alcohol" warning to the few remaining barflies by Randy. I kept scrolling until I saw the person I wanted. There was Brady Sullivan.

I let it play. He was practically being carried out of the bar by Sam and one of the Romanian girls, Anka. I had viewed a lot of video footage of her over the past few weeks.

Chuck mentioned I could talk to Randy about getting a date with one of the Romanian girls. The thought of it embarrassed me. Especially since the meeting spots were wired for video. *No, thanks.*

I reversed the footage to the point where Sam cleared Sullivan's dinner dishes. Once they were gone, Sam brought him a drink. I rolled back fifteen seconds and started recording it to a different file. I rolled it forward until they walked him out.

I did the same thing with the parking lot footage, rolling it back to when they exited the building. I recorded until they left the parking lot in Sam's Suburban.

Switching over to Cabin D footage, I scrolled back in time until the arrival of Sam's SUV displayed. I recorded until Sam helped Sullivan into the cabin.

I switched to the bedroom footage, scrolling forward until the lights were turned on. Sam walked Brady over to the bed, propping him up on the edge. Brady's eyes were open, but he was non-responsive.

Sam walked out of the bedroom. The girl walked into the bedroom. She began taking her clothes off. Sullivan just sat there. The girl walked over and started taking his shirt off. He was basically a child, lifting his arms reflexively to assist.

I worked for another hour. Randy wanted a compilation of still images pulled from the video that would paint a specific picture.

Once I consolidated the recordings, I began saving screenshots. From start to finish, I saved over forty pictures. I sent them to a color printer. They were high definition, and it took about a minute to print each one.

I opened a drawer and pulled out two jump drives. I saved a set of pictures on each of the drives. The video review for the Sullivan job was creepier than normal. Typically, it was a willing John practically (and sometimes literally) attacking one of the girls. Take Randy's pilot, Bill Norquist. I don't know if you would call him "his pilot" necessarily, but he owned a small plane that he let Randy use from time to time. Norquist averaged a date per week. The footage of that was a garden-variety John-and-hooker interaction. An old, gray-haired, *married* man pouncing on a young, beautiful woman. Blackmailing over that was a piece of cake.

Then there was Travis. He fell into a crude blackmail trap Randy set before I moved to Ohio. They took him out on the boat with a prostitute and got him so drunk that Sam just snapped off pictures of him on his camera phone having sex with her. Travis had a wife and two young daughters at home, so he had been forced to do whatever Randy wanted since. Randy cut him in on some of the action taking place, but from what I knew of Travis, he would much rather just manage the campground and not bother with all of the crooked stuff going on.

Brady Sullivan's footage was of an incoherent zombie being controlled. Nothing sexual even happened, although that would be tough to discern if you just saw the still shot of her straddling him. That was why Randy didn't want a video of it.

The poor guy should have just passed out. Unfortunately for him, his eyes remained open. Sam dosed him perfectly. The big ape did something right. The totality of the pictures out of context painted a very damning picture.

Per the text messages I hacked from his phone, Brady had stepped in it with his wife. He was supposed to be in Cleveland picking up his kids before lunch, not sleeping off a hard night of drinking and hooking up in some random cabin with a prostitute.

It all seemed too easy. Brady didn't strike me as a street-smart guy in general; he gave off a definite white-collar suburban guy vibe. But how did he blindly get led through the entire setup without suspecting anything? Without even resisting? I would have smelled something. Maybe whiskey was Brady's kryptonite. *Whiskey and Rohypnol.*

I gathered the pictures and jump drives. Taking out my burner phone, I texted Randy. I exited Trailer Alpha and biked toward the bowling alley.

Randy 5

2:35 p.m.

I looked out across the lanes. Only two were being used. I glanced over at the monitor, which was split four ways. I clicked on the bar angle. Genie was working. Sam was due to start his shift soon. I tried to time it so Data and Sam arrived at the same time.

I clicked on the monitor again to enlarge the front-door view. Then I checked the back-door and parking-lot views. Sam rolled up in his Suburban.

A few minutes later, there was a knock at my door. I switched to the office-door camera view and saw Sam there. I buzzed him in.

"Hey, boss," he said, walking in with my glass of bourbon. I glanced at my watch—2:40 p.m. It was a time of day that was a gray area for drinking. I put it on the corner of my desk while I thought it over.

I reached down into a desk drawer, took out the bug detector, and wanded him. The detector didn't sound. I set the device on the edge of the desk. It would be more thorough to check for a wire by making him undress, but I didn't. I took a small sip of the bourbon.

There was a knock on the door. I looked at the monitor and saw Data, hunched forward to balance the weight of his backpack. I buzzed him in. Sam walked over and picked up the bug detector.

Without being asked, Data put his backpack down. Sam wanded him and then his backpack. He opened the backpack and rifled through it with the aggressiveness and efficiency of a disgruntled TSA agent.

"You know the routine, down to your tighties," Sam said.

Data stripped down to his underwear and spun around slowly. Sam nodded. He reached down to start getting dressed.

"Stop," I said. Data stopped. He was confused, hunched over, holding his shorts. "Drop those."

He did. I reached in the center desk drawer and took out a

handful of papers. I stood up.

"Do these look familiar, Henry?" I asked, holding them up. He looked terrified, eyes wide, mouth open. He squinted to see them, then nodded. "What are these?"

"That is my Sullivan write-up," he said meekly. He was a pathetic sight, the doughy little nerd standing there in his white underwear and black socks.

"Didn't you tell me you shredded the Sullivan documents?" I asked, leaning against the desk. Data just stood there. Sam watched from a few feet away.

"I did. I shredded the papers I had," Data said.

"So, why do I have these?" I asked, squeezing the papers in my hand. He didn't answer. "Do you know where I found these?"

Data shook his head. He was sweating heavily, even though I kept the temperature in my office in the mid-sixties.

"I got these from Chuck. Do you know where Chuck got these?" Data shook his head. "Chuck got these from Chris Randolph. Drunk-ass, drugged-up Chris. How do you suppose he got these?"

Data stared down at his feet. I sat back down.

"I dropped them," he finally said. "I went to the campground office late the other night, and Chris was out. Another worker knocked me off my bike, and my backpack spilled. I must have lost the papers then."

I nodded at Sam. Sam walked up to him and punched him in the stomach. Data went down hard, wheezing. He began coughing as he rolled to his side.

"What if Sullivan found those? How would we explain that?" I asked angrily. Sam kicked him in the stomach, and he yelped.

"You are the smartest guy I know, Data, but you are also a damned bonehead. That kind of mistake can bring us down, do you understand?" I grabbed the papers and walked over to him. I dropped them next to him.

"Get rid of these. No more spills," I said.

Data rolled over and got to his hands and knees. He nodded weakly.

"Actually, hand 'em back over. I will get rid of them myself.

Who knocked you off your bike?" I asked, returning to my desk.

He picked up the papers and stood up, breathing heavily. "Patrick," he said, handing the papers back.

"The Mexican at the gate?" I asked. He nodded. I turned toward Sam. "Why don't you straighten this out? I don't need the riffraff messing with the talent."

Sam nodded. I took another drink.

"Get dressed. Sam, get him something to drink. Take a few minutes to get your shit together, and then I want to see the new Sullivan stuff."

Sam left. Data began to fumble with his clothes. I took another drink.

"One more thing, Henry. You are smart enough to know that I have backups of the entire setup. I have stuff encrypted and stored. Among that stuff is you on film for hundreds of hours working on computers at Trailer Alpha. In clear violation of your probation terms, never mind all the laws you are violating along the way. You need to tighten it up. If I go down, we all go down," I said, sitting back in my chair.

I gazed out over the bowling alley. It was still mostly empty. I finished my drink. Sam returned with a bottled water, handing it to Data.

"Get me another drink. When you straighten out the Mexican, do it in the Taj. We don't need any eyeballs on what you're doing," I said. "Now, let's take a look at what that naughty boy Brady Sullivan has been up to."

Data brought his backpack over.

Brady 11

5:45 p.m.

I finally gave in. I dropped a few ice cubes into a plastic cup, poured a big shot of Jack, and topped it off with Diet Coke. The fizz poured over the brim and onto the counter. I didn't bother to clean it up.

Marcy had stopped answering my calls. Then she stopped answering my texts. She had her cousin's bachelorette party she could not miss and needed me to take the kids. Her parents were old and overburdened with watching our kids, and she didn't want them babysitting them all weekend. But that is what they were going to do because of me.

There was nothing I could do about it. I could pull an end-around on Marcy tomorrow and appeal to her parents directly, but if they let me take the kids, there would be hell to pay from their daughter. I didn't want to put them in that position.

I was lucky I didn't miss anything too critical at work. Fridays were not the most productive days on the calendars of federal government employees. The few meetings I had were covered. My attendance record was excellent and Jeff, my supervisor, allowed me to take a sick day. No explanation was asked, and I was grateful I didn't have to lie to him.

I struggled to articulate what happened to me when I discussed it with Mike. I may have been drugged, but then again, I did drink a lot. Especially for a guy who was wary about the intentions of the host.

I didn't find any receipts in my pocket, so I had no idea how many drinks I had. I checked my credit card activity online and found nothing from that night.

I took a sip of my drink. After letting it sit in my mouth for a moment, I rolled it across my tongue and then swallowed. It went down okay. It was the proverbial hair of the dog that bit me. I would start to feel better soon.

The throbbing headache that plagued me all day started to

diminish. I would try to call my kids later to apologize for not picking them up. Jason was especially excited about fishing together. Both wanted to spend time at the amusement park. Instead, both were in Cleveland with their grandparents, and I was alone in Sandusky.

My phone rang. I picked it up and glanced at the screen. It was from an unknown number with a Sandusky area code. I decided to answer it.

"Brady here," I said. The line was a little fuzzy.

"Brady! Sam here," the voice crackled. "You know, your favorite bartender!"

I tried to think of a reply, and none came for a moment. How did he get my phone number? I took a sip of my drink, and a few ice cubes sloshed as I did.

"I remember," I said warily.

"Are you drinking again, Brady? I heard a slurp there and some rocks rattling around. You are a damn soldier for sure!" He laughed.

"Yeah, things got a bit fuzzy last night. I'm assuming you got me back here? And my truck?" I asked.

Sam laughed again. "Yeah, I got you out of the bar safely. I couldn't find your camper key, so Randy had me put you up in a cabin. At no charge," he said.

At no charge. Unbelievable. I sighed heavily, resisting the urge to take a drink and have Sam hear it.

"We drove your truck back to the campground and left your keys in the cabin. The bowling alley cleanup crew found a key in the bar area this morning. Is it purple?" he asked.

"Yeah, that's it. I could come by and get it later. I also left my credit card," I said quietly. So, one key accidentally slipped off my ring and it happened to be the camper key? *Not likely.*

"I have your card. I'm going to be out your way later. I will drop it off. You gonna be around?" he asked.

"I suppose," was all I could respond with.

"You doing something with your kids tonight?" he asked.

"No kids," I said. The line was silent for a moment.

"All right, I'll be there later," he said and hung up.

Chris 5

6:05 p.m.

I t was a long day. Construction work was difficult on most days, even when I was well-rested and not hungover. The sun shining in my face all day was brutal. I was able to keep down a burger at lunch, and sharing a joint with a coworker helped.

The construction job was developing a series of sports fields a few miles east of the campground, called Sports Junction. The land had been empty meadows owned by the city before Gravity Junction had taken an interest in it. The company was forward thinking in finding innovative ways to increase tourism.

Creating a dozen sports fields to host baseball, soccer, and lacrosse tournaments was the next step beyond amusement and waterparks. The tournaments would require hotel stays, and while the teams and their families were in town for the event, they would most certainly want to visit the parks. Sports Junction would offer discounted park passes, and the corporate profits would continue to increase.

I had difficulty piecing things together from last night. That was the story of my life. Drinking, getting baked, and losing my grip on things. That included relationships.

There were long stretches when I didn't care what happened with relationships if they didn't involve substance abuse. Now that I was screwing it up, I realized I didn't want to lose Candy.

How long would she stick around with an alcoholic drug addict in a broken-down RV working manual-labor jobs? *I was nothing.* A wave of depression struck me, it almost felt like it hit me physically.

She had stopped nagging me about getting back my former life. Getting back into aviation in some way; if not returning to air traffic control, maybe private piloting. Eventually, I could start flying short routes, build up a reputation, and go from there. It was doable.

I bummed a ride back to the campground and was dropped

off at the entrance. My stomach began to ache. I popped an antacid as I walked past the security booth. I was diagnosed with a bleeding ulcer a few years ago. The symptoms went away for a while, but now it felt like it was bleeding again. There was nothing I could do about it without health insurance. They sold chocolate milk at the office snack bar; I would grab one if it got worse.

An older-model motorhome was parked to the left of the office, checking in for the weekend. Kids were leaving the pool area carrying inflatables and towels. A lot of kids were dressed as superheroes; it was some sort of theme weekend. Iron Man, Spider-Man, and Batman were scampering around the playground area. They would have superhero crafts in the clubhouse all weekend. Families were going on bike rides, and golf carts were zooming back and forth.

Then there was me, slouching along with my shabby construction-worker vibe, unshaven, cheap sunglasses, dirty blue Detroit Tigers baseball cap, a faded Corona Extra beer shirt, threadbare jeans with dirt and oil stains, and brown work boots in tatters. Next season's campground brochure was unlikely to feature me on the cover.

I turned up Sparrow and saw that the Grand Am was parked alongside my camper. I doubted she used it; she parked it there after she dropped me off and stayed in the camper all day. The car was available for me to take to work, but instead, I caught a ride home in the back of a coworker's work truck with a bunch of other debris.

The camper door was closed. I attempted to open it, but it was locked. I knocked softly and there was no response. I walked over to the outdoor fridge and opened it. It was empty. I slammed it shut and cursed to myself.

Sam 3

6:10 p.m.

As I turned into the campground, I saw Chris in the distance, walking toward his dump of an RV. I glanced at my watch—1810 hours. I decided to swing by and chat with him before dealing with Sullivan and Patrick. I rolled down my window as I pulled alongside his camper.

"What's up, Chris?" I yelled. I startled him, since he hadn't seen me roll up.

"Hey, Sam, not much," he said, putting his hands in his pockets.

"Forget your key?" I asked, nodding to the door.

He shrugged.

"Did you get dinner yet?" I asked.

He shook his head. "I figured Candy and I would get something, but I don't think she is around," he said, taking a few steps toward my SUV.

"Hop in. We can take a spin up to the bowling alley. I wanted to chat with you anyway," I said.

He didn't move for a moment. "I don't know, I was hoping to talk to Candy," he said, sounding pathetic.

"Don't she have a cell? Can't you just call her?" I asked, trying not to sound impatient.

"Yeah. Not answering," he said, pushing his hands deeper in his pockets. He stared down at his feet. Then he nodded and walked around the front of my SUV, getting in the passenger side. He put his seatbelt on. "Mind if I smoke?" he asked as I pulled out and started driving up Sparrow.

"Yeah, I do," I said.

He put his hands in his lap, staring out the window.

Randy 6

6:25 p.m.

Scanning my security feed, I saw Sam and Chris enter the bowling alley from the backdoor cam. I wasn't expecting Chris, but I understood what Sam was doing. He was told to push every angle and to keep every iron in the fire as hot as possible. I grabbed my cell phone and texted Sam:

Get him dinner and a few drinks. Propose the job. Send him up if necessary.

Restoring that guy's pilot privileges was a huge risk. But if I could get him making deliveries, it was worth so much money that it was definitely worth the risk.

An hour later, I heard a knock at the door. I verified that it was Sam and buzzed him in.

"You didn't need to have him up, huh?"

"Nah, I dropped him off at the campground."

"So, it went good?"

"Yeah. He is on board. If we set up the flight ops with Norquist, Chris is in," Sam said.

"No threats necessary?"

"Nah. He was skeptical, but he wants to do it."

"Good. Remind Captain Norquist of this arrangement. And the pictures we have of him, if necessary. Get this moving ASAP. I guess we can keep Chris's cabin pics in our back pocket for now."

Mike 7

7:55 p.m.

It was poor planning to keep buying firewood a bundle at a time from the campground office. Five dollars a bundle was steep when I was going through one each day. I needed to see if I could buy a quarter cord someplace if I was going to stay there for a while.

I opened the door and walked into the hallway leading to the office. A big guy was walking along the hall directly in my path on his left side, staring down at a piece of paper and not paying attention to where he was going. I recognized him as the guy who regularly visited site 21 in his big black SUV.

He had a military haircut and a five o'clock shadow, wearing jorts, a red polo shirt with the USMC anchor-and-globe emblem on the pocket, and white tennis shoes. Fixated on his paper, he took another step, and we almost collided. He looked up suddenly, startled.

"Excuse me," I said.

The guy didn't say anything; he just stared at me. I stood there in front of him. He was a good three to four inches taller than me, staring down at me with a blank look on his face.

We both continued to stand there. The door opened behind me, and a couple of kids walked in, one with a Spider-Man mask, the other with plastic Wolverine claws. They went around us and continued to the snack bar.

"I said excuse me," I said.

The guy's face curled up into a little smile. "I heard you there, boss," he said. Neither of us moved.

"You are walking on the wrong side of the hall, boss. You almost ran into me. I said, 'excuse me.' Don't you think you owe me the courtesy of returning the pleasantry?" I asked flatly. His smile got bigger, and he folded his arms.

"Wrong side of the hall? I don't see any signs telling which side to walk on," he said, his voice getting louder.

"We are currently in the Western Hemisphere, right, boss? North America? That means we travel on the right side of the street. And the sidewalk. And the hallway. You pull out on the street out there, and there isn't a sign saying 'drive on the right side of the street, dummy.' We ain't in England, right?" I asked, looking around theatrically. "Hey, can someone tell me if we are currently in fucking Liverpool?"

"I tell you what, bro, I walk on whatever side of the hall I want. And if you don't get out of my way, I'm going to walk over you," he said, putting his hands on his hips.

"So, I'm your bro now?"

"Sam!" A woman's voice sounded from the desk. He didn't turn to look; he just kept staring at me. "We don't need no friction with the campers. You need to just move along!"

A small middle-aged woman came around the corner, wearing a yellow campground polo. She was heavy with short, graying hair, wearing black cargo shorts down past her knees, black socks, and white tennis shoes.

"Is there some sort of problem, guys?" she asked, stopping alongside us as we continued to stare each other down.

"Nope," I said, looking down at her, nodding, and then walking around the bigger guy. "Just need some firewood."

I walked over to the shelf along the wall and grabbed a bundle, six pieces shrink-wrapped in plastic. The office was in the front, and the rest of the complex featured camping supplies, snacks, an ice cream service area, vending machines, and some outdated arcade games.

The big guy was still staring at me. I put the bundle on the counter and stared back at him. The woman was watching him as well.

"Do you need something else, Sam?" she asked. He glared at me for another moment, turned, and left.

"That will be five dollars," she said, ringing it up on the cash register. I handed her a five-dollar bill.

"So, you know that guy?" I asked, grabbing the bundle off the counter.

"Yeah, that's Sam. Just a townie who haunts this campground

here and there," she said.

"Not a fan of brothers?" I asked, smiling.

"Not a fan of anybody."

"Does he have a last name?" I asked.

She thought for a moment. "Henshaw. No, Crenshaw. Crenshaw. Why do you care?"

"I don't, just curious. I figured he was a townie and not a camper. Most people on vacation just aren't that salty," I said.

She laughed and shook her head. "You seemed a little salty walkin' in here yourself. Most people see a big man like Sam walking toward them and give him some clearance," she said, winking at me.

"I have this bad habit of doing things the hard way," I said, winking back.

As I walked toward the exit, I considered that he may be lurking out there, waiting to jump me. I stepped out warily, expecting to see him crouched by the door. He was the type who wouldn't be above delivering a cheap shot. But he wasn't there.

I swept my eyes across the lot from the security booth to the pool, seeing his big silhouette as he walked up Starling. I decided to take a detour in that direction on the way back to my camper.

Brady 12

8:05 p.m.

I sighed when I heard the knock and walked over to the camper door. I peered out, and it was Sam. I opened the screen door, and he walked in, ducking his head to clear the doorframe. He was carrying a large manila envelope.

"How you feelin' today?" he asked, smiling.

"Fine," I said flatly. "Do you have my key and credit card?"

"Sure," he said. He reached into his pocket and pulled out the credit card, laying it on the counter. He reached in again, pulling out my key.

"Bizarre how only my camper key fell off the ring. I'm sure nobody used it to enter my camper when I was away," I said, placing the items in my pocket.

"Now you're sounding paranoid," he said, laughing.

"Well, thanks for bringing my things by and taking care of me last night. I would like to pay. I reviewed my credit card balance online, and there were no charges," I said.

"Mr. Randy's treat. Actually, I had something else I'd like to talk to you about. Something that may require a little privacy. These RVs ain't exactly soundproof," he said, smiling. I awaited his suggestion.

"Randy's camper over there is a little more private. Care to walk over there with me and chat?" he asked.

"Honestly, it's been a rough day, and I'm going to sleep soon. Partying over at the bowling alley has been costly. I never got to pick up my kids," I said.

Sam shook his head. "Yeah, that was unfortunate. But we either talk now or talk later. I'm here now. So, let's talk," he said.

I exhaled loudly. "Fine," I said.

Sam walked out and I followed him, locking the door behind me. Sam started walking north to the camper at 21. I gazed south down Starling and saw Mike, who was approaching the shower house, carrying a bundle of wood on his right shoulder. He nodded at me. I nodded back. Sam didn't look back.

Mike 8

9:05 p.m.

I restrained myself from doing another pass of the RV at site 21. I lost count of how many times I walked past. The last time was about twenty minutes ago.

After putting another piece of wood on the fire, I took a sip of my drink. I didn't plan on hitting the alcohol too hard. I was on edge and didn't want to get too tipsy, although I wasn't sure why it mattered. It wasn't like that Sam character was going to sneak over and jump me. *Hopefully.*

It sounded like someone had spiked Brady's drinks at the bowling alley. They stole his personal data, invited him out for dinner and drinks, and then drugged him. But to what end?

When I was senior enlisted, I had to counsel a number of privates following bad experiences while getting drunk. A lot of them claimed they were roofied. But once you pulled the string a little and the facts came out, it never quite added up. No one ever got roofied at the library or McDonald's, or in any environment where they weren't otherwise shitfaced. The alleged drugging always happened during the course of a hard-drinking incident.

Brady had engaged in some hard drinking last night. I didn't know him well enough to draw conclusions about his tolerance, but he was out drinking fireside each night like most of the campers around there, myself included.

Brady sat at the bar at the bowling alley and was steadily putting drinks away for a few hours. Big Sam was likely making them strong. He could have just legit got drunk. Whiskey was no joke. It happens.

But he blacked out for hours and woke up in a cabin. And he woke up very late. He slept through the timeframe when he should have been working and picking up his kids. Would he do that?

Most vets I knew didn't oversleep. There were always privates rolling in after the bar closed, resting in their bunks for a short time, and then getting up and PT'ing before the sun came up. If you couldn't handle that grind, then you didn't last long; you either slowed down on the drinking or found your way out of the army.

Brady was a married guy and father who was living by himself in a camper. I understood this wasn't his permanent residence, but that was an odd situation. So, he did have some issues. But didn't we all?

"Hey, Mike," a voice said from beyond the fire, startling me. I nearly dropped my drink. I looked over and it was Brady. He was as pale as a ghost.

Chuck 7

9:15 p.m.

Just as Randy figured, Brady went scurrying right over to Mike after the meeting. Having that asshole around was gonna complicate things. Someone was gonna have to persuade him to move along.

Mike Clemmons. Retired soldier. GI Fuckin' Joe. But practically a vagrant at this point. No property, no job, just a washed-up Negro bouncin' from campground to campground. I took a drink from my cup.

Sittin' at the end of Sparrow in my golf cart along the grass line, I was sure that they couldn't see me. But I could see them, with Mike havin' a fire and all.

Starting the golf cart up, I crept down Sparrow with my lights off. Pulling into an empty lot a few over from Mike's, I got out, grabbin' my drink.

"Evenin', gents!" I said loudly as I rounded the camper. They were sittin' about a foot apart, talkin', and they both jumped. They glared at me. "What are you two bachelors up to on this fine Friday night?"

More silence. I walked over to the empty chair.

"Can I help you with something?" Mike asked.

"Nah, not really. Just out makin' the rounds," I said. I walked around and sat in the empty chair.

"Looking for unlocked refrigerators?" Mike asked, stone-faced.

My face turned red. I could feel the heat in my cheeks and neck. I forced myself to smile.

"Nah, Sharon did some shoppin'. I'm good tonight," I replied, holding up my cup. I took a drag off my cigarette.

"So, you're going to drink your own shit tonight, novel idea."

"What do you guys have goin' on this weekend? Any superhero activities?" I asked, takin' another drink. I turned to Mike. "You've been out here for weeks now, aren't you gonna go to the park?"

"No, I don't do roller coasters," Mike said, taking a drink.

"Afraid?" I asked, laughin'. Mike glared at me.

"You ever serve in the military, Chuck?" he asked.

I shook my head. I thought about makin' an excuse but decided not to.

"I was jumping out of planes and helicopters when I was a teenager. I ran combat operations in Iraq and Afghanistan. Do you think a fucking roller coaster is gonna make me piss myself?" he asked.

"Nah, I guess not," I said, tryin' not to sound angry.

It wasn't my call, but I didn't see any way Clemmons was goin' along with a blackmail setup like the one being pulled on Sullivan. There was always a fly in the ointment.

"So, if you don't like amusement parks and you don't know nobody around here, what is the point of stayin' here all summer?" I asked, trying to sound as friendly as possible.

Mike stood up and walked toward me. I thought he was goin' after me, and I scrambled up to my feet. He shifted to the left at the last second, stepped to the side, and reached down for a piece of wood. He slammed it into the fire, sendin' smoke and embers into the air.

"Because I fucking like it here. It is relaxing. Nice people here, right? Friendly people who you can have a drink by the fire with. Maybe share dinner at the local bowling alley, meet girls, and such. You ever met a fine-looking white girl at the bowling alley, Chuck?" he asked as he sat back down.

"Nah, I got a girl here," I said, smiling again.

"Oh, you're a loyal guy, huh? You never test out any of the mattresses back in those cabins? I thought I saw your little buggy parked behind those a few times."

"All on the level. I do work here and have shit to do in those cabins."

"On the level? You are loyal and on the level? Sounds like you're a regular fucking Boy Scout, Chuck."

I continued smilin' and nodded. This black guy who didn't say jack shit to anyone for weeks was all of the sudden rantin' his ass off. He sounded like a drill sergeant. But then, I read his records and knew he was a drill sergeant and a bunch of other army shit that I didn't know much about.

When he was rantin' he looked right through me, like he was readin' my mind. I took a long drag off my cigarette and stood up.

"If you throw that cigarette butt on my lawn, I swear I will come over there and make you eat the fucking thing," Mike growled at me.

I nodded and walked back to my golf cart, clampin' the cigarette tight between my fingers.

Brady 13

9:45 p.m.

I decided I would tell Mike about the pictures. I barely knew him, but there was no one else in my life I could confide in.

My mind had been racing since Sam spread the pictures out in front of me at the kitchen table in that camper. I heard him refer to the RV as the *Taj*. Like the Taj Majal. That was a bit grandiose for a campground trailer.

While the pictures weren't X-rated or anything, they were bad enough. They were enough to wreck my marriage. They were enough to marginalize my relationship with my kids. If Marcy got a hold of those pictures, I would get torched legally. If she showed them to acquaintances, I would get torched socially. She had a vindictive side, and those pictures would be permanent ammunition to use against me. They were a nuclear weapon in any type of "he said/she said" situation.

"Hey, have you gone out anywhere locally since you've been here?" I asked.

He shook his head. "Just hanging out here or out on Milan Road getting supplies," he replied.

"I tell you what, let's go out and get a drink. There is a Mexican place up Columbus Road. We can grab a beer and unlimited chips and salsa."

"Actually, I'm good here. It's getting kind of late," he said apologetically.

I sat up and leaned forward. "Well, it wasn't just a social offer. I was hoping to chat with you without being overheard. I feel like Chuck is lurking around, and you know how thin camper walls are," I said just loud enough for him to hear over the fire. "I would suggest riding around in a vehicle or parking somewhere, but I think there is an element of risk there for two guys who have been drinking to randomly drive around or park together in a backlot somewhere."

"All right, then. Let's let this fire burn down a little and we'll head off," he said.

He insisted on driving, a gesture of kindness based on the hard night I just had. I left my cell in his camper in case it was being used to track me. His cell was an old flip-phone without GPS.

We didn't run into anyone we knew as we drove out of the campground. I was sure someone would notice Mike's truck missing and report that up the chain, but unless they were tailing us, they wouldn't know where we were.

The Mexican place, the Loco Cactus, was fairly busy. There was a thin haze of smoke inside from the nonstop orders of fajitas, and the smell of sizzling meat and vegetables was almost overpowering as we walked in. The lobby was full of people, and there was a wait list, but tables in the bar area were open, so we chose to sit at one of the elevated tables there. Several Hispanic men were sitting at the bar watching a soccer match, as well as a few middle-aged Anglo solo drinkers.

I ordered a frozen margarita, and Mike ordered a tall Modelo draught, the dark version. The waiter, a paunchy little middle-aged guy with thick black hair and a salt-and-pepper mustache, brought out a bowl of chips and salsa with our drinks. He put two menus on the table.

The table location seemed reasonably private, with the dull roar of numerous conversations mixed with the Mexican music piped in through the sound system.

With the loud music and conversations, a discussion there was more private than at the campground. The fact that the cabins were wired for video meant surveillance was possible anywhere.

The waiter brought our drinks, setting them down in front of us on napkins with the restaurant logo, which was a cartoon cactus wearing a huge sombrero. We both declined to order food, and he took the menus.

My drink was green frozen sludge in a monstrous fishbowl, with salt caked around the rim and a bright-pink straw. I hunched down and sipped through the straw, feeling a little embarrassed that I chose that over a more dignified masculine drink like the dark beer that Mike chose.

The margarita was very strong, as I had hoped. The severe

hangover I awoke with earlier that afternoon was a distant memory.

"So, my drink was definitely spiked last night," I said, as low as possible. Mike nodded. I was glad I didn't have to repeat myself. I took a long drink through the straw. I swallowed and felt the icy pain of a brain freeze creeping in and hitting me hard, making me wince.

"You're like a fat kid with a giant slushie!" he laughed as I tried to play it off. I managed an embarrassed grin. The headache spiked and then faded away.

"I mentioned they took me to that cabin. Apparently, it was rigged with video cameras," I said. Mike was taking a sip and then stopped. He set it down and wiped his mouth with the back of his hand.

"They have cameras in the cabin rentals? Are they visible?" he asked.

I shrugged. "I didn't see any cameras, but I was severely groggy and out of it when I woke up. I am assuming the interior ones are concealed in a ceiling fan or smoke detector, based on the camera angles," I said. I took a tortilla chip, dipped it in salsa, and ate it. The salsa was milder than I preferred.

"So, they taped you last night," he stated. I nodded. "Doing what?"

I felt my face flush. I took another drink, slower this time to avoid another round of brain freeze. "Well, there was this girl I vaguely remember from the bowling alley. We chatted briefly at the bar. She must be on the payroll. The pics show us leaving the alley, arriving at the cabin, and going inside. Then there are pics in the bedroom that are problematic," I said.

Mike stared at me for a moment, then looked away. "Damn, Brady. Seriously?" he asked, taking a big chug of his beer. He casually wiped away a bit of the foam from his upper lip that had settled on the salt-and-pepper facial scruff.

"The thing is, I was dead on my feet. Like a zombie. Some of the bar pics show Sam clearly propping me up. I don't think there is any way I did something with the girl. The pics look staged."

"You sure?" he asked, dipping a chip.

I nodded. "Pretty damn sure. I saw still shots, which were selected most likely because I look like I'm awake. I was passed out, but my eyes would occasionally open. Think of people who black out; they sometimes drift between states of consciousness. I bet if I got the raw video footage, it shows me in a motionless stupor. That is why they just printed pictures and didn't show me a video," I said.

Mike appeared to be thinking about it and nodded. "Still pretty damning, though?" he asked.

"Damn right. This is a relationship breaker. If these get back to my wife ..." I said, taking another sip. "I can't let that happen."

"So, what was the point? What do they want? Was there some sort of blackmail threat?" he asked.

"He didn't make one. So, are we thinking the next step is a demand for money?" I asked.

"I'm going to be blunt. You don't seem like a high-dollar-value target. I've seen your finances. I know your salary, what you have saved, and what you own. What is he looking to get from you monetarily that is worth the effort?" he asked. I shrugged. "It has to be something to do with your job. Do you have something of value you can get from work?"

"I don't know. I mean, I have a clearance. But it doesn't give me what I would call access to valuable intelligence. Would someone like Randy be able to use the data I could provide?" I asked.

"I tell you what, I would not underestimate that guy. He has a plan. He orchestrated that setup last night very easily. You were taken down without a fight. Those guys have done this before. I bet you he can use those cabins whenever he needs to," he said.

"So, Travis is in on this. There is no way Randy is secretly rigging shit up without him knowing," I said, taking another sip.

"Have to assume Travis's people are involved. If Chuck is, there are others," he said. I nodded and ate another chip.

"You need me to dig into this for you?" he asked.

I shook my head. "No, I'm not getting you wrapped up in this," I replied.

"I'm already associated with you, bud. I'm sure someone on his crew saw us leaving together tonight. If they have surveillance capabilities, then they know when we come and go," he said.

"I appreciate your willingness to listen and give me your observations. That's all I need. I will work this out," I said.

"I ran into that Sam character in the office. He got in my face, nothing major. I was able to get his last name, Crenshaw."

"Got in your face?"

"We jawed back and forth a little. He definitely has a chip on his shoulder."

"Okay, so we have his last name, that may help."

"Yeah, you mentioned he said he was a marine last night, so you should have background data on him on your work systems, right?"

"Maybe. I have to be careful. I have access to military records, but I have to watch how I pull the data. Everything I do leaves an audit trail. Sometimes I pull batches of records, so if I can pull his records as a part of a larger data query, it may not raise any red flags."

"There may be something useful we can use. He seems like a local who failed to launch, maybe in his forties. You should be able to narrow it down if you are doing a name search."

I nodded, although I doubted I would find anything useful. I wished I had access to civilian records. I was fairly certain Sam had his share of run-ins with law enforcement over the years.

"Listen, Brady. You have a family. You have a career. Somebody is fucking with that right now. You can't sit back and get played. You have to figure out what they are doing and get ahead of it," he said, leaning across the table. I didn't have a response.

"They are going to find a way to sink their claws into you even deeper. You need help. I don't mind helping. Next time they ask to meet, I can hang back and follow you to see what they are up to. That is counter-surveillance. I used to do this shit for a living," he said.

"You didn't come to Sandusky to babysit me. You don't really know me. You don't owe me anything," I said, finishing my drink. I desperately wanted another one but decided not to.

"It ain't about me owing you anything. You are a veteran. People are targeting you. Honestly, this is giving me something to do. I haven't had a purpose in a long time," he said, shrugging. He leaned across and clinked his beer glass with my empty margarita glass.

Chapter 5
Saturday, June 20

Sam 4

3:05 a.m.

I was pacing the hall upstairs, waiting for Randy to arrive. This was going to be ugly. This was a risk that was always out there, but that didn't make it any less scary when it happened.

I heard Randy's motorcycle pull up and the back door open a few minutes later. I deactivated the alarm. Randy climbed the stairs. He would be taking his time; he was slowing down a little and wouldn't want to risk taking a spill.

Randy didn't look at me, walking past me to unlock his door. He looked exhausted. I forgot his age, but he was looking old, with his cheeks sagging and dark-black bags underneath his eyes. He was wearing a Cleveland Browns baseball hat, a gray sweatsuit, and black tennis shoes.

He unlocked it and walked in, not even holding the door for me. It almost shut before I scrambled and stopped it with my hand.

Randy walked over and turned on the lamp on his desk, not bothering with the overhead lights. He rubbed his face, leaning back in the chair.

"Throw on a pot of coffee," he said, yawning. I left, made a pot, poured some into Styrofoam cups, added cream and sugar to his, and went back upstairs. He buzzed me in, and I handed it to him.

"Two creams, two sugars?"

I nodded. I took a sip of my coffee, black as usual. If you liked your coffee with a bunch of crap added to it, you didn't like coffee, you liked the crap. Starbucks made liquid desserts and called it coffee.

Randy took a drink, jerking slightly as he burned his mouth. He blew on the coffee and took another small sip. He sighed loudly, looking up at me.

"Do I need to wand you?" he asked.

I stood up and took my T-shirt off. We all knew there were advanced devices that did not require physical wires to be on me, but he didn't wand me. He nodded. I put my shirt back on and sat down.

"So, let's hear it," he said.

I breathed in deeply. "Al took one of the Romanian girls over to the Island at around 1800 yesterday ..." I said, but Randy interrupted me.

"Cut the military time bullshit. I can barely keep my eyes open here," he growled.

I glared at him for a minute. This was going to be painful. "At 6 p.m. yesterday. Anka. She had a date at the Islander, in one of those duplexes," I said.

"A group party?" he asked.

"Two guys. The rest of the party is coming in tomorrow ... today, I mean. Saturday," I said. It was after 0300 hours and most definitely Saturday morning now. "He dropped her off at the dock, and they were waiting in a golf cart."

"Who are they?" he asked.

"Jack Webster and Will Schultz. Thirty-somethings. Data ran backgrounds on them, they are from Columbus. Financial planners," I said.

"Al left with their full payment and returned to the marina. He dropped the cash in a bowling alley locker. Anka was going to ferry back in the morning. About an hour ago, I got a call on my burner. Webster was in a panic. The girl's dead. He was going into detail, but I cut him off. He was blubbering about his life, his wife, his kids, etc.," I said.

"Where is the body?" he asked.

"In the back bedroom of the duplex," I said.

"Anybody else know about this?" he asked.

"Don't think so," I replied.

Randy took another drink from his coffee. He leaned back in his chair, put his hands behind his head, and stared at the ceiling for a long time. "Okay, well this is going to take some doing to unravel. This Friday night date just got a world more expensive for these clowns. Do they have a burner?" he asked.

"No. But they called from a landline. Any outgoing calls traced will just hit my burner number, which will be a dead-end as soon as I dump it," I said.

"Positive?"

"Yes, Data verified the number as a landline out of the duplex."

"Okay. Dial them up on your burner and give it to me. Make sure you dump that burner later today when this is cleaned up," he said.

I called the duplex. Someone picked up, and I handed the phone to Randy.

"Is this Webster? Yeah. Listen, don't worry what my name is. You need to just listen. Right now, priority one is canceling your other buddies coming out. Can you do that? I know. Okay, I will get you in a different hotel. Lemme make a few calls. No, we can't risk an early arrival. Okay, I'm sending a few guys over later this morning," he said, taking another drink of coffee.

"Just cover her up. Is there any blood? Okay, good. My guys will be there, and you let them in. Don't let nobody else in, you hear me? No maids, no maintenance people, no one. Don't go nowhere. Don't drink any alcohol. Don't go for a walk outside. Nothing. You sit there and watch TV until they get there. Then you cooperate. You do everything they say. Everything. Once they finish with you, you guys will go to the other hotel I'm booking. Then you will forget about it and go about your weekend. Don't sulk and don't run your mouths, unless you want to be calling your wives from a jail cell on the island explaining what happened. There will be a big bill for this. It is costing me a lot of money to clean this shit up. You hear?"

Viktor 3

9:15 a.m.

S ullivan was not happy to see me. Nobody was ever happy to see me. Maybe Elena back in Bucharest. But maybe she pretended because I paid bills.

When I woke up and looked in the mirror, I was not happy to see myself. My face was whiter than normal. I thought because red-faced Americans who lie in the sun are everywhere and that made me look pale. Some cooked their skin with lamps. So stupid. Paying money for the skin cancer.

I left the RV and started walking to the front of the campground. It was sunny, so I put on dark sunglasses. I was driving a big gray Chevy Express van that belonged to Randy.

We could have met at Cloverleaf, but Randy wanted me to pick him up. Our RVs were across the street from each other, but Randy did not want me to show up at Sullivan's camper and have neighbors see us leave together. So, we were to meet at the end of the street. I unlocked the van and got in.

It was a warm, clear day, with a little bit of wind. It would be better for it to be dark and cloudy, to match the work we had to do.

A few minutes later, I saw Sullivan walking down Starling. He walked to the passenger side. I reached over and unlocked the door from my door panel. He got in and closed the door.

"I am Viktor," I said as I backed the vehicle up. He did not say anything. He did not look at me. We pulled past the security booth.

"Where are we going?" he asked.

I ignored him. "Do you have any weapons on you?" I asked.

He shook his head. "So, what am I doing here?" he asked quietly. It was the kind of quiet that angry men have.

"You are running an important errand with me."

Brady 14

9:25 a.m.

I was very close to pulling the plug on this thing. It was on the tip of my tongue a half-dozen times. The concept of being stuck with this goon all day was ridiculous.

I received a call around 0600 hours from Sam. He needed me to do him a favor. I told him to fuck off. He laughed. Then he threatened.

After the call, I wasn't able to fall back to sleep. Since Mike had given me Sam's last name, I decided to do some research. I logged into my work laptop and opened the system where I could search PAF payees.

The name "Sam Crenshaw" was relatively unique. But I wasn't sure whether his full first name was Sam or Samuel. The program was on a mainframe and antiquated, so sometimes it took some creative wild cards in the search criteria to obtain the desired results.

Directly searching would be risky if my activity was audited. I devised a fictional situation where a call was misrouted to me from the PAF customer helpdesk call center. A veteran named Sam Crenshaw received a USMC tax form, even though he had been out of the military for decades. Strange stuff like that happened.

My initial search returned a shortlist of "Samuel Crenshaw" records nationwide with birth years from the period in which Sam would have reasonably been born, from the mid to late 1970s. I assumed he was from Ohio, but adding that constraint narrowed the list down to nothing. There were no Samuel Crenshaws from Ohio in the database.

I used a wildcard for the first name, searching "S*". That returned one Ohio record, a "Simon Crenshaw". Born in February 1977. I clicked on the name and started reviewing the information.

Simon Crenshaw's home of record at enlistment and at discharge was Sandusky. That had to be the Sam I was looking for.

Sam/Simon was a marine all right, but not for very long. Thirteen months served and then an unceremonious dishonorable discharge. I shook my head. This dope was out waving the marine flag 24/7 but had only done a little over a year and got a dishonorable. If he possessed any integrity at all, he wouldn't have mentioned his service to anyone, ever. Yet he flaunted it with his apparel and a USMC bumper sticker on his Suburban.

I logged out and showered. I went outside and drained the gray water. I came back in and lay back down in bed, staring at the ceiling and worrying incessantly.

I should have bit the bullet and took the pictures back to Cleveland. Shown them to Marcy, explain what I thought happened, and hope for the best. Give Randy and Sam/Simon the middle finger and go about trying to piece my life back together.

Then again, the photos would be the straw that broke the camel's back with my marriage. Understanding that the pictures were exponentially bigger than just a straw, that those pictures were more like a steel beam dropping from the top of a skyscraper on top of the camel's back.

Now I was being coerced into doing something else. An "errand." What it was I had no idea. It couldn't be good. But maybe if I just did that for them, they would leave me alone. *Right.*

A few hours later, there I was, trapped with this Euro clown in a work van. Viktor wore a pair of ridiculous convenience store–quality sunglasses. They reminded me of the kind the elderly wear, oversized and wrapping around the side of his face.

I looked into the back of the van. There was a large blue rectangular plastic tote, maybe six feet long by two feet wide. There were also two large tanks, about half as tall as a standard residential water heater, which had hoses and spray nozzles attached at the top, and a large black gym bag. I decided not to ask about any of it.

He drove up Nickle Drive and took a right onto Columbus Road. He turned on the radio and tuned in a local pop station.

"I assume we are going to the park," I said, staring out the window.

"Not inside. We will be taking a ferry to an island," he said with a thick accent.

"Why?" I asked.

"You will find out soon," he said, smiling. He turned onto the causeway.

"How about I find out now?" I asked, blatantly irritated.

He laughed and shook his head. "Today you are the lowly employee, and I am boss. We do an errand, and you are done," he said.

The traffic backed up about halfway to the park, three lanes of slowly moving vehicles.

"Where are you from?" I asked.

"I am from Romania," he said, in a mockingly majestic voice, pushing his chest out with exaggerated pride.

A memory of Thursday night returned. I remembered the girl at the bar spoke with an accent.

"That girl in my pictures from the bar was Romanian. Is she a friend of yours?" I asked. He shrugged. "What was her name? It is a nice racket you guys have going here."

"It is your fault you drank yourself stupid and got burned," he said, shrugging. "You Americans cannot hold your liquor."

"I can hold my liquor just fine. Whatever you guys spiked my drink with is a different story. What was that?" I asked.

He shrugged again. "I have no idea what you are talking about," he said. He looked over at me, pulled down his sunglasses, raised an eyebrow, and actually winked. I gritted my teeth and looked out the side window.

As we approached, the traffic continued to inch forward, and the security booths came into view. We were surrounded by hundreds of cars filled with people who were excited to spend a gorgeous summer day at the amusement park with their friends and families, and I was driving there with this thug on some secret mission.

Two Jet Skis were traveling parallel to us in the cove, gliding across on the calm blue-green water. Large, colorful metal roller coasters rose above the northern skyline. A digital sign above the booths advertised season pass specials.

Viktor pulled up to the booth to the far west, one of five. He reached into his wallet and pulled out an ID card. He showed it to the attendant and drove through.

Viktor took a left and a right, traveling north on the road that passed along the left side of the park. The traffic attendant at the intersection used an orange flag to wave our vehicle through to a small line of vehicles that were waiting along a large pavilion on the western side of a small peninsula. A crowd of people gathered beneath the pavilion. Boulders lined the shore on the north and west sides to protect it from the erosion of the crashing waves.

Viktor pulled up to the end of the line, got out, and spoke with the attendant. He handed her some cash and received a white slip of paper. He got back in and placed it on the dashboard near the window.

There were a variety of different vehicles, including a large motorhome and two motorcycles. Within a few minutes, we could see a large ferry boat approaching in the distance.

I had traveled on one of these last summer to a nearby island from a different launch. The ferry was two stories tall and about one hundred feet long. Vehicles would drive on board at the main level and park, while the passengers without vehicles went to the top, where seating was available. The boats traveled at thirty-five miles per hour, so they could arrive at the most popular island, Put-In-Bay, in about a half hour.

"Are we going to Put-In-Bay?" I asked. He didn't answer for a moment, then nodded. "Why?"

"You keep asking me questions when I have already made it clear I am not answering questions," he said. He pulled a cigarette out and lit it, rolling down the window.

"Are you allowed to smoke in a work vehicle? On a ferry?" I asked, rolling down my window. He just laughed, exhaling a cloud of smoke in my direction.

The ferry arrived and docked. The vehicles disembarked first, and then the pedestrian passengers filed off. The dock attendant waved us forward.

Viktor was still smoking. It was definitely forbidden to smoke on the boat. Instead of putting it out, he placed it in the ashtray and rolled our windows up so he wouldn't be seen. I waved my hand in front of my face to clear the smoke.

"I'm going to smell like a fucking ashtray," I said.

Viktor drove to the front and stopped on a painted red line. The vehicles behind us pulled in and formed a column until the attendant started another row to our left, and then another until there were three full rows.

The pedestrian passengers boarded. It was a mix of young families, elderly tourists, and small groups of young adults. The island featured numerous bars, restaurants, and sightseeing attractions. It evolved (or devolved, depending on one's perspective) into a spring break atmosphere over the years, where droves of college-aged kids would arrive for long weekends of binge drinking and debauchery. It was also a bachelor and bachelorette party destination.

Put-In-Bay Island was only about a square mile of land. While there were no restrictions on vehicles, most tourists traveled around in rented golf carts. I heard it was possible to get a drunk driving citation in one of those, which was probably the island government's reaction to the excessive number of inebriated tourists who recklessly operated golf carts while traveling from bar to bar.

Although thousands stayed on the island during the busy season, there were only about 150 full-time residents. There were hundreds of summer homes, but those were only occupied between May and September. Outside of that window, the daily ferry service ended, the weather turned cold, and few tourists cared to make the trip.

Last year when we visited, we drove past the island's lone schoolhouse on the way to a vineyard. The one school had housed all students from kindergarten through twelfth grade. It was about the size of my kids' elementary school, one of three in our school district. I wondered what life would be like growing up on that island, experiencing the seasonal extremes between complete wintery isolation and the tourist invasion in the summer.

As the ferry approached the shore, more details became noticeable. Most of the shoreline was heavily wooded, with expensive summer homes peppering the coast. There was a dock that was the mirror image of the one at the amusement park, with lines of people and vehicles awaiting the ferry to return to the mainland.

Mike 9

12:15 p.m.

It was odd that I hadn't heard from Brady. I walked up Sparrow and looped around Starling, passing his camper. As I passed the unoccupied gazebo area, a blue Ford Explorer turned the corner. I locked in on the driver and thought it could be Sam. There was a young female in the passenger seat.

I stepped to the left in front of the shower house. Entering through the south door, I crossed to the other side and stood by the window. I peeked through the dusty brown curtain.

The Explorer passed slowly by. I confirmed it was Sam driving. He did not look over toward the shower house, so I assumed he had not seen me on the street before I ducked in.

Sam slowly pulled in front of Brady's truck and forward into his neighbor's site at 33. I craned my neck to see.

The girl got out. She was dressed in a pair of gray yoga pants, flip-flops, and a short tank top showing her flat belly. Her long, dark hair was up in a ponytail. She wore sunglasses that were too big for her face and was wearing too much makeup.

She was easily the most attractive woman I had seen at the campground. The seasonal campers were largely plain people who were not overly concerned about personal appearances. Days at the pool, the beach, or around the campfire didn't call for spending an hour in front of the mirror in advance. This woman had invested a significant amount of time in getting herself dolled up.

She walked onto Brady's lot toward his camper and disappeared from my view. I scrambled to the north door, opened it quietly, exited, and then took a right heading east. I walked out onto Sparrow and passed a few sites until I was even with Chris's lot.

I walked past without looking over at Brady's lot, then walked onto Chris's lot, at such an angle that I could see Brady's front door without being seen from the Ford. I figured Chris's girlfriend was probably inside the RV, but the odds were slim that she would see me in their lot, since the rumor was that her eyes were glued to the

TV set throughout the day.

I pulled a rickety lawn chair over and situated it so I could see Brady's front door. After ten minutes, the door opened, and she came out. She stepped down and locked the door behind her.

I ventured a peek at the Ford, leaning my head over to the left. Sam was holding his cell phone up, pointing it at her. She approached the Ford and got in as he lowered the phone. I eased back out of sight. I heard the SUV take off.

I got out of the chair and fast-walked my way up Sparrow to my lot. The train was approaching, blowing that damned horn. I sat down in my lawn chair by the empty fire pit just as the SUV drove past me. Sam stared over at me as he passed, smirking when he recognized me. The brake lights illuminated as he slowed down. My heart started racing, expecting him to jump out and start some shit with me, but he continued on.

Randy 7

1:05 p.m.

The damned phones were ringing off the hook. I wanted to get outside on my bike. The weather was beautiful, but I had too much going on.

Three phones were spread out in front of me on my desk. I checked the caller ID on the burner in the middle and answered it. "Yeah," I said.

"Took the pics," Sam said.

"Anybody see you?" I asked.

"Don't think so. The gazebo people weren't out," he replied.

I hung up. Combined with the cabin pics, Sullivan's situation got even worse. Slipping up with a one-night stand was one thing. Shacking up in the family camper with an attractive young girl who had her own key was next-level bad. It would look like that bad boy Brady found a replacement for his wife in a hurry. If the Put-In-Bay job went well, that would be the tilting point.

Brady 15

1:25 p.m.

The sun was shining brightly in the blue skies above, but the temperature had dropped a few degrees because of the stronger island winds. As we rode along the main road of the island, we passed a small airport, golf cart rental businesses, and numerous hotels.

From most vantage points on the island, you could see the towering 325-foot monument to a naval battle in the War of 1812. The kids and I had taken an elevator to the top of it when we visited last year; there was a view for hundreds of miles in each direction.

Viktor pulled into a restaurant parking lot a few blocks over from the tower. He walked to the back of the van and opened his bag, pulling out some clothing.

"Time for a clothes change. Step back here," he said, smiling. I unfastened my seatbelt and went to the back.

He handed me a gray jumpsuit. It had a white patch with black lettering and a logo on the pocket: "Sandusky Pest Control." There was a smiling cartoon mouse above the lettering. He took out matching hats as well. He inspected them both carefully and tossed one to me.

"Why am I putting this shit on?" I asked angrily.

Viktor didn't answer as he pulled out his own uniform and started putting it on over his clothes. "You are still asking questions, as if you think I owe you answers. I was given orders and am following orders. My orders did not say to answer your stupid questions," he said with a scowl.

"They aren't stupid questions, idiot. They are totally reasonable questions. I have better things to do than play dress-up with you," I said.

Viktor reached into the bag and grabbed a big cast-iron wrench. Before I could register what he was doing, he swung it and hit me square in the stomach, doubling me over. I fell to my knees, dropping the uniform and clutching my stomach. I groaned. He walked over to me, leaning over.

"Listen, idiot. I have worse weapons than a wrench I can use on you. If you want a beating, I can give you a beating," he said angrily. He drew his leg back as if to kick me, but I scrambled back to my feet.

I sized him up. I was pretty sure I could take him in a fight. There was a sickly appearance to him, the look of a malnourished man who consistently overindulged in drinking and smoking. I was in far better shape; I could run a half-marathon without a problem. I lifted weights and would have bet I could kick his ass without breaking a sweat. But then what? Those pictures would be delivered to Marcy, and then my life would start unraveling.

Maybe it had already unraveled. Maybe it was time to throw in the towel. I could get a hotel room, buy some clothes from the gift shop, rent a golf cart, and just bar hop for a few days. Drink myself into oblivion. Let whatever happened happen and deal with the wreckage when I returned.

Maybe stay a week. Maybe move the damned camper to the island and winter there, freezing my ass off in isolation until everything blew over. Except it wouldn't blow over, it would all be back in my face when I eventually returned.

I put the jumpsuit on. It was a little big on me, but it was wearable. We returned to our seats, and Viktor exited the parking lot.

Viktor 4

1:40 p.m.

It felt good to hurt Sullivan. Sam warned me not to hurt him, but I did anyway. It could not be helped. I hoped Sam and Randy did not find out.

I checked the GPS on my phone and followed it as I pulled out of the restaurant lot. The pickup place, The Islander Resort, was only a few kilometers away. It was time to give orders.

"Listen. We are here to pick something up. Two men are waiting for us. We are taking gear into the house like we are there to spray for the bugs, filling our tote, and leaving. I do all talking. You talk to no one. We leave with the tote and go back to the mainland. Do you understand?" I asked as I drove down past the resorts. I saw the sign for The Islander and turned in.

Sullivan glared at me. "What is this, drugs?" he asked angrily. "Just a pickup from a customer, that is all," I said. I kept going in the direction the GPS showed. Hundreds of plain *duplexuri* ... duplexes, all the same.

Let him think it was drugs we picked up. That was less bad than what it was.

"Why am I involved? You can get anyone to do this. Why me?" he asked, sounding angry. "I have a job. A legitimate job. I don't need a second one."

"I am sure you don't," I said, laughing. "Mr. Randy is doing you a favor and not putting your pictures on the Twitter or something. So, play the ball."

"Play ball," Sullivan said. "The saying is 'play ball.'"

I made a note of it in my mind. "Thank you. Maybe you can give me English lessons some time? Since we are neighbors and coworkers," I said, laughing.

Sullivan did not laugh. "To teach you anything, you would have to be teachable. I don't sense that you are teachable beyond following basic directions. You are a lapdog. Investing effort in your education would be a waste of my time," he said quietly.

I didn't say anything for a while. I did not know what a lapdog was. "Are you saying I'm stupid?" I asked in anger.

"I don't know whether you are or aren't. I know you are a follower, a lackey. 'Yes Mr. Randy, no Mr. Sam.' People bark orders at you, and you just do it. You question nothing, you don't ask why. Do you even know what you are doing here?" he asked, raising his voice.

"I know what I am doing here. And why. You are the one who does not know. So, you are trying to …" I said, struggling for a word. *Manipula* in Romanian. "Manipulate me and cause doubt. This will not work."

We kept following GPS, passing block after block of duplexes. Many had crowds of people on porches and in front yards, playing loud music, playing yard games like corn hole and horseshoes, and cooking out. It was like the campground, but in place of middle-age fat people with kids, there were young fat adults and almost no fat kids. This was like spring break from American colleges, where kids go and drink and act like fools.

I found Building 117. I pulled past and backed close to the building. Each building was one floor with two doors in the center. It could be rented to two parties or one; there were *mijloc* … joining doors between them. A golf cart was parked in the yard.

I took off my hat and set it in my lap. Behind the silly logo was a mini camera Data added. Very small. It would take a close look to see. Sullivan was looking out the window. I pushed the tab to turn it on and put it on my head.

"You will wait here one minute," I said, getting out and walking behind the van. I opened it and took out one of the tanks, slamming the door.

The duplex door on the unit to the left opened, and a man looked through the screen door. He was in his thirties, chubby, very pale, and scared looking. He was wearing a red Ohio State T-shirt, khaki shorts, and flip-flops.

Americans and their flip-flops and Crocs. How was that a proper shoe for a man? What if he got in a fight or an animal attacked him? What if he had to run? Americans never think anything bad will happen to them. When something bad happens, they cannot believe it. They do not see they make their lives hard by their stupid choices.

"Are you Jack?" I asked, opening the screen door and walking in. He nodded. Another man was leaning against an island in the kitchen. He was a taller, skinny man, brown goatee, wearing a Cleveland Cavaliers hat, a blue Columbus Crew football jersey, jorts, and flip-flops.

The place was one long room with a sofa and TV at the front, a kitchen, and dining area at the rear. There was a *alunecare ...* glass door that faced woods at the back and led to a deck. To the left was a hallway to bedrooms and a bathroom. Data sent me the layout on my burner.

The place needed work. The carpet was stained and worn, and the walls needed paint. No one cared because everyone here just wanted to drink watered beer until drunk and drive around in golf carts. Maybe splash around in the dirty hotel pool in the sun until it cooked their skin bright red.

"What is with the tank?" Jack asked.

"It is a tank of chemicals that will wash away your *păcatele*," I said, staring at him. He looked away from my gaze. "What time did she come here yesterday?"

"I think we met around seven at the docks," he said after thinking about it for a minute.

I nodded. "Did anyone see you with her?" I asked.

Jack shook his head. "I don't think so. We have both sides rented out so no one else was here last night. There weren't many people hanging out around this resort. Most people are at the bar around dinnertime," he said.

"What would your friends think if they knew you got here last night and partied with the dead hooker?" I asked, smiling at them. They both had looks of shock on their faces. That made me happy.

"Show me where she is," I said. Jack nodded and walked past me and down the hall to the second door on the right. He pointed at the door.

"Open it."

He frowned. Then he opened the door and stepped aside. I

walked past him into the room, closing the door. There was a double bed to the left and stacked beds to the right. There was a window with light-blue curtains covering it above the single bed.

There was a lump under the sheet of this bed. A small figure. I had thought very little about Anka as dead until then.

She hated me. All the girls hated me. She never had anything nice to say to me. But I did not force her to the USA. She went using her own will. I was doing my job. Still, I was sad to think she was dead because she was Romanian.

I wanted to walk into the hall and start beating these two men. What happened to her? But Randy made it clear to me there is no *interogare*. He would take care of it later. I wanted to be a part of that.

I walked over and grabbed the sheet at the top of the bed and slowly pulled it back. Her dark hair showed, then her forehead, then her face. Anka's green eyes were open. Her mouth was too. I kept pulling the sheet. She was naked.

She was black and blue around the neck, on her breasts, on her legs. She had a beautiful body, so young it was almost a child's. Small breasts, small hips, a small bit of brown pubic hair.

She was popular with the clients. I had made many dates for her in the time she was there. I had taken dates for myself too.

I covered her. I looked around the room, looking for her stuff. There was nothing else in the room. I looked in the closet, nothing, except for pillows and blankets. I opened the bedroom door, and Jack was standing in the hallway, leaning against the wall.

"Where are her clothes?" I asked.

"She brought a bag. I put her clothes in the bag and put it in the front closet," he said nervously.

"Wait here," I said and walked out of the room. I went to the closet and took out her bag. I put it by the front door and went outside.

Sullivan was sitting in the van and staring at the house. Our eyes met, and I waved for him to get out. I took the empty tote out from the back of the van. I slammed the van door shut and walked toward the porch.

"I want you to go in and sit on the couch until I tell you to move," I said. Sullivan gave me an angry look but did not say anything. We went inside.

I pointed toward the couch. Jack and the other man looked up from the baseball game. I waved them to come toward me. They stood up. Sullivan sat down. We went to the bedroom and closed the door.

Brady 16

3:15 p.m.

Exiting the Islander, I started to feel claustrophobic. I rarely felt any sort of anxiety that manifested itself physically. I was having trouble breathing in that van; the interior seemed to be closing in around me.

During some of the more heated arguments with Marcy, I would walk away with my heart hammering in my chest. A glance at my fitness tracker would tell me my heart rate was elevated. Non-activity-based heart rate increases were never good.

I looked at my watch. My heart rate was eighty-one. That wasn't alarmingly high by any means, but for a guy just being driven around, it was twenty beats per minute higher than it should have been.

I didn't know what happened in the bedroom with Viktor and the two golfer guys. I just sat on the couch like a moron while the three of them loaded up the large tote. Then the four of us carried it out and slid it in the back of the van. I guessed it was around one hundred pounds. Was I helping to transport drugs?

"Is this tote getting delivered on the island, or are we taking it back to Sandusky?" I asked. Viktor didn't acknowledge the question for a few moments.

"Sandusky," he finally said.

"What are we transporting?" I asked. He ignored the question and pretended to pay close attention to the road. At a stoplight, he lit another cigarette. "Maybe I should take a look."

"Take a look, I don't care," he said, turning to me and smiling. Those crooked yellow teeth, most likely never troubled by a visit to the dentist. Didn't Gravity Junction offer dental insurance?

As difficult as it was, I resisted looking at my cell phone throughout this excursion. It was silenced in my pocket. I figured if Viktor knew I had it, he would take it.

He drove to a hotel a few miles west of the Islander. He stood up and walked into the back, taking off his jumpsuit.

"Remove your uniform and hat," he ordered casually. He left his hat on. I was going to bring it to his attention but decided not to. It wasn't my job to cover his ass.

I took off the jumpsuit and hat and walked over to him. He took it and stuffed it in his duffel bag.

I took another look at the tote. The top fastened with a gray plastic clasp that could be popped open by pulling up on it. We owned an identical one at home that contained the pieces of our artificial Christmas tree.

I stared at it for another moment. Then I returned to my seat. Viktor climbed back into his seat, taking off his hat and setting it beside him.

Viktor 5

4:05 p.m.

I needed a good camera shot. But I didn't need to deal with a crazy person after. If he knew what was in the box, would he play the ball for the ride back to Sandusky? No way.

A video of Sullivan carrying a tote out of the Islander meant almost nothing without more. But my main mission was to get the tote off the island without getting arrested.

The drive to the ferry and the ride back across the lake went easy. I did not smoke on the ferry, and Sullivan did not get out of the auto. He did not talk or look at me. I know it was on his mind, thinking about the tote. But he had no guts to look.

After the ferry, I drove back south across the causeway. No one was leaving the park on a sunny day, so no traffic. Only one lane was open to go out.

At the end of the causeway, I took a left going east. I passed the road that went to the campground and kept going.

"Jesus, we aren't done?" Sullivan asked in anger, folding his arms.

"Not quite. We drop off the box, and I will drop you off. Then you are done. For today," I said.

Eight kilometers past the campground there was a warehouse area with six large buildings. The train tracks were near to move shipments to and from the warehouses. Randy owned Building 4. I was sure it was not in his name. I heard nothing was in his name. And yet all the money found its way to his pockets.

I pulled up to a garage door at the east end of Building 4. Putting on the hat, I got out and opened the door. I pulled the van in and closed the garage.

The warehouse was dirty, maybe two hundred square meters, with rows of racks and boxes everywhere. There was a small office on the south side and a forklift parked in front of it. I drove the van to a middle row and parked. Lighting a cigarette, I got out and waved for Sullivan to get out.

I went back behind the van. We lifted the box and put it in on the ground. I stopped for a minute, taking off my hat and wiping sweat from my head. I looked down to the hat to be sure the camera was on and put it back on my head.

"Before I move this, can you open it and make sure the cargo has not been damaged?" I asked. He was standing by the pallet, staring at the box.

"Damaged?" he asked, looking at me. I nodded. He didn't move. I stood there a minute, waiting to see what he did.

At last, he walked over to the box and pulled the handles up. I walked around to get a good view for the camera. He bent over and opened the box.

Data 5

6:45 p.m.

For once, I didn't mind being at the campground. Keeping busy with the manual work served to distract me from thinking about the videos I downloaded from Viktor's hat-cam.

I did not sign up for that type of activity. That was way beyond the scope of what I expected. I was okay with some white-collar stuff, the low-level blackmail and extortion. Murder was way, way, way out of scope. Being wound up in that was exponentially worse than the hacking I was convicted for.

Viktor met me at Trailer Alpha earlier. He knocked at the door, and when I opened it, he just stood there staring at me with that horrible, crooked smile. Then he handed me the baseball hat and stepped inside.

"Load this and put it on screen. I want you to pull some stills," he said, drinking something out of a red plastic cup.

I hated that he was in Trailer Alpha with me at all; it felt like a violation. He smelled especially bad, all sweat, cigarette smoke, and vodka. His clothes were grimy and stained.

I fast-forwarded through the video, which was so jumpy at times I almost felt nauseated. The camera jerked back and forth every time he tilted his head, which was often. Viktor sat down next to me, kicking his dirty shoes up on the nearby console.

"Do you mind?" I asked. He laughed and didn't move his feet.

"How do you like my camera work? Do you think I will get the Oscar?" he asked. I ignored him and kept scrolling forward.

Viktor and Sullivan were wearing jumpsuits and posing as exterminators. The video showed them getting in a van, driving by the lake, and passing several golf carts. They pulled into the resort complex, going in and out with a large tote, and rode the ferry back. There wasn't anything unusual going on.

They approached the warehouse, went inside, and unloaded the tote.

"Slow down here. Slowly. Do screen *captură* in a minute. Do you have anything to drink here?" he asked. I shook my head. Viktor sighed heavily with disappointment.

"For future reference, stop chain-smoking if you want clear camera stills. Some of these shots look like a fog machine was nearby," I said.

"Fog machine?" he asked.

"Yes, fog, condensed water vapor that occurs close to the ground," I said. He gave me an angry look.

"I know what fog is, genius. I do not know what a fog machine is. Romanians don't have time for stupid American toys like one that makes a fog," he said angrily.

So, there were no fog machines in Romanian discos? Maybe Viktor didn't get out much in Bucharest.

On the monitor, Sullivan leaned over the tote. He popped it open and gazed down. Viktor moved in with his hat-cam to get the close-up. At first, I thought it was some sort of mannequin or maybe a sex doll. A pale, naked woman with dark hair.

"Pause," Viktor said loudly. I did and looked closely at the image. Then I recognized her as Anka. My jaw dropped. I felt Viktor's eyes on me, but I couldn't look at him. I was sure he was smiling.

"I need some shots of this. It needs to look as if Sullivan is ... how do you say ... *pozare* ... pose, pose him. Position him. So he looks natural. Not in shock. Get him right before he starts the freaking out," he said, crumpling his cup. He let it drop to the floor.

So, I did. I made several copies and put them on jump drives. Viktor left without taking anything. Randy made it clear that he was not to have any of the material in his possession. When I told him that, he appeared ready to argue but then left without another word.

After he left, I sat in the trailer for a long time, feeling stomach pains and trying not to have a panic attack. I went to the toilet and vomited.

Sam 5

7:55 p.m.

"So you never tried alcohol?" Randy asked, looking across at Data. He shook his head.

"Sure. I had a few drinks in college, but I never liked the taste. Can I get a Coke or something?" he asked. Randy nodded and pointed to the fridge. He got up and got one. I took a drink of my Pabst.

"But they have good-tasting drinks. Ever tried a margarita?" Randy asked.

"Yes, they are fine. A lot of drinks taste good, whether they contain alcohol or not. I don't drink because I don't see the point of it. It looks like a big waste of time and money. Half the world is limping around hungover every Saturday and Sunday morning," he said.

"Drinking takes the edge off. I don't see how you function in the same mental state every waking hour. Sometimes you have to let your mind go a little numb to get past the boredom and stress of it all. Hangovers are part of the process. I would argue that your vice is more dangerous than drinking," Randy said.

"My vice?" he asked. Data had a puzzled look on his face.

"Yeah, your tech addiction. You know, the shit that got you put in prison. The reason why you are here in Sandusky hacking trivial data from campers instead of running shit in Silicon Valley," Randy said, taking a drink from a plastic cup.

Data stared down at his Coke and didn't say anything.

"So, what did we get?"

Randy leaned back in the chair, so far that I thought he might take a spill backward for a second. Maybe he had been drinking more than usual. Data sat up straight and looked like he was putting his thoughts together.

"In no particular order. First, Viktor's hat-cam captured a lot of usable footage. As usual, the raw video itself would not be useful. However, I was able to pull some decent stills. You can piece together him carrying the tote, putting it in the van, unloading it, and opening it. Most of the stills of him seeing the girl show him with a look of horror on his face, but there is a brief moment where he is staring at her and not reacting. He sort of froze up before he started freaking out," he said.

"Okay. Anything there that would implicate Viktor?" Randy asked.

"I'm not sure. I wasn't looking at it from that angle," he said.

"Don't worry about that now. I was just curious. And don't print anything yet. Maybe tomorrow I'll have you put together the package," Randy said, taking a drink.

"Beyond that, trying to directly hack his work laptop has been a dead end. I could probably do it eventually, but it would take a significant amount of time, and there are illegal software programs that I would need to obtain to get the data. Each of Sullivan's programs has its own security protocol. The best bet would be to get his cooperation and for us to sit together," Data said, taking a drink from the can.

I was surprised how easily he accepted orders that were more and more disturbing. It had taken almost no effort to get him to do the hacking stuff shortly after we met him, even though it could put him back in prison.

It was easy for him to justify. While he was some tech guy who made bad decisions and got wrapped up with the likes of me, he only did tech things. His crimes were through a keyboard; he didn't physically hurt nobody. But his tech skills made a lot of hands-on crimes possible.

I wondered if he lacked a soul. It didn't bother him that he was in the middle of a blackmail setup involving the dumping of a dead hooker. Although in his defense, we didn't share that the hooker was the cargo during the Put-In-Bay mission.

On top of the other crimes, he was going to quarterback stealing data that could compromise the US military. He was sleepwalking through this, never stopping to ask questions about the events he was triggering with his hacking. Maybe he told himself he was playing Grand Theft Auto or something, like he was in some virtual world where none of this was real.

Data learned a lot about our business in a short amount of time. One slip-up and he could take us all down. I didn't see how it was possible to keep him around long. When the campground closed for the season, he would have to go.

Gravity Junction shut down in late October. The foreigners and the out-of-state college student workforce went home in early September. The rest of the season, the park depended on local high school and college kids. Most of the tourism ended, except at the indoor waterparks. If the prostitution operation was going to happen again next summer, Randy would need a new data guy or go lower tech. No more blackmail shit. But that was just my opinion.

The problem would be destroying the evidence he had been collecting. Nobody knew exactly how he was storing it. *Nobody knew how he was doing most of the shit he did.*

Brady 17

9:45 p.m.

W e pulled out of the campground in Mike's S-10, heading toward downtown Sandusky. We needed to have a conversation away from the campground, so we chose the Mexican place again.

The restaurant was busy and had the same constant background drone of conversations. We were seated in the bar area at a table one over from where we were the night before. *Could it really only have been a night ago?*

We ordered the same drinks; Mike had a tall Modelo draught, and I had a jumbo frozen margarita. Jumbo was barely going to be adequate for the numbness I needed. I would have preferred if they just brought my chair over to the margarita machine and let me tap it directly from the spout.

I was somewhat embarrassed to be drinking the big, green frozen drink again, but I needed the quick tequila numbing effect and couldn't have cared less about my alpha-male creds at that moment. I considered asking for a double but decided against it. When the drinks arrived with the chips and salsa, I took a long pull off mine through the straw, triggering a minor brain freeze and not caring.

Mike took a big drink of his beer, wiping off the thin foam mustache. He dipped a chip and popped it into his mouth. He looked up at a nearby TV. The Rays were beating the Indians.

Mike undoubtedly had a lot of questions but was patient and didn't push me to talk until I was ready. I took another drink and stared down into the large glass, doubting if I would ever be ready. The events of the past few days swirled around in my head. I needed to figure a way out of whatever was happening, but I had the exact same thoughts the last time I was there. And now I was in deeper. Much, much deeper.

I sat back and scanned the room for familiar faces. I knew no one. The room noise was at a high level, so I felt we could talk with a reasonable degree of privacy. I started telling him about my day.

Sam 6

10:10 p.m.

was pulling away from the Taj when I saw Clemmons's truck pulling up to the security booth. Sullivan was in the passenger seat. I hung back a little and started following them.

After almost losing them a few times, I tracked them down at the Loco Cactus. I called Randy, and we put a plan together. He pulled Data over to Trailer Alpha, and he printed some pictures. I swung by, and Data was standing out on the curb in front of the trailer with an envelope.

Having Data working near Trailer Alpha was really handy. I had to give that to Randy.

I pulled into the Mexican place about a half-hour after I first tracked them. Clemmons's S-10 was still parked by the side of the building. I fought the urge to smash a window after I parked a few spots down.

I never understood why people liked those cantina places. The food sucked, the music sucked, and the waiters were all little beaners who couldn't understand you. They probably fucked with the food in the back because they were sick of dealing with the gringo customers every day. The water was probably dirty.

The lobby was full, so I figured they had either just been seated or were on a waiting list. I looked to the right toward the bar area and saw them sitting at a table. Sullivan was leaning across and having a heart-to-heart with Clemmons.

I stood against the wall for a minute, thinking about my next move. Odds were, Sullivan was telling him everything. So, we either had to draft Clemmons into the operation or get rid of him. I had no doubt we needed to get rid of him.

Data did a background check on Clemmons, and he did have a solid set of soldier skills. His personal and financial life were one big ball of nothing. A family that was long gone, no job, no assets. Just a middle-aged black guy who retired and lived off his military pension at different campgrounds throughout the country.

Clemmons had no obvious vices. He was observed drinking but kept to himself. He didn't chase women. It was hard to imagine an angle to get him to come on board with us.

I slipped around to the end of the bar, waving for the bartender. He was a hairy little Mexican guy, who pretended not to see me for a few minutes and then came over. I could tell when they pretended, because I did it all the time at the alley bar. I ordered a shot of tequila and walked over to their table.

Mike 10

10:25 p.m.

"**M**ind if I join you, fellas?" a voice asked from my left. I recognized the voice even before I turned around. It was the big goon, Sam. Neither of us answered him.

Sam stood beside the table, grinning like an idiot. He was wearing a red USMC T-shirt with that anchor-and-globe thing on the front and a pair of blue jeans. He leaned over a bit like he was trying to intimidate us by casting his big shadow on us.

As a big man, I was sure he had gotten a long way in life through intimidation. He was a bully at the campground office. He had probably always been big and always been a bully. Then he joined the marines, and that fed into his bully persona.

I had been in a few scraps in my day, but this guy appeared to be out of my league. I learned a fair amount of hand-to-hand combat skills in the military, but I assumed Sam did as well.

The running joke in the army was that they taught you just enough hand-to-hand to get your ass kicked at a bar downtown. There was an element of truth to it. As a soldier, you mastered weapons. If you found yourself in a fistfight in combat, things had gone horribly wrong.

Sam carried an envelope in one hand and a full shot glass with salt and a bright green lime on the rim in the other. He pulled out a chair and sat down. I took another swig of my Modelo. I wished it was something stronger, but it was better than nothing.

"What do you have there, Brady? That looks like a refreshing cocktail!" he said. Brady glared at him. "Didn't come with one of those little pink umbrellas?"

"Can we help you with something?" I asked flatly, leaning toward him.

Sam removed the lime from the rim, licked the salted rim, tossed the shot back, and then bit into the lime. He winced and then smiled.

"Cheap shit but refreshing. So, what are you guys chatting

about?"

"Private conversation," Brady said.

"Private conversation? No need to try and keep things from me, buddy. We work together now. You might as well be cordial. Let me give that a try."

Sam leaned over and grabbed Brady's drink. He tilted his head back and started gulping it from the rim, finishing the remaining half of it in ten seconds. Why did every dirtbag in Sandusky feel the need to help themselves to Brady's drinks?

He slammed the glass down. I stared at him, waiting for the pained look of brain freeze, but he didn't change expressions.

"Damn, that is pretty good!" Sam said, laughing, letting out a belch that drew a few dirty looks.

"No brain freeze, huh?" I asked.

He shook his head. I burst out laughing. Brady looked at me, and then he started laughing. Sam was confused.

"Again, can we help you with something?" I asked.

Sam smiled at me. "You bet." He held up the envelope, flipped it around in his hand, and put it down. He belched again, drawing more glares from the other tables.

"Excuse the shit out of me!" he said loudly, laughing.

"How long did you serve in the corps?" I asked, nodding toward the logo on his shirt. His eyes blinked as if he was uneasy about answering the question. I found that odd, given that he was wearing a marine shirt. He was inviting questions on the subject.

"Didn't we go over this at the alley? Two years," he said, looking at Brady.

"Two years?" Brady asked. He raised an eyebrow and looked at me with a smirk.

"Two years," Sam said again, a little louder.

"You sure about that?" Brady asked.

"Positive," he replied, staring at Brady with an annoyed look.

"You sure it wasn't thirteen months?" Brady asked. Sam's face went expressionless for a moment, then changed to a look bordering on hostile.

Brady winked at me. I forgot that I gave him Sam's last name. He didn't mention that he looked up Sam in his work systems, but apparently he did.

"Honorable, general, or dishonorable? Don't tell me! Let me think about that one," I said.

I pretended to ponder the question, rubbing my chin and looking up at the ceiling. Sam's forehead began to glisten with sweat.

"If you know what it was, then why ask?" Sam asked angrily.

"I don't know, but I'm going to go with 'dishonorable,' hoss. What rank were you when you got bounced?" I asked.

"E-3," he mumbled.

"Holy shit, Brady, we got ourselves a fucking private here! By the way you go around peacocking, I thought you were the damned Command Sergeant Major of the Marine Corps!"

"There is no Command Sergeant Major of the ..."

"Do you think I give a fuck what they do in the marines?" I growled, simultaneously smiling and snarling.

I was in full drill sergeant mode. Beads of sweat were forming on my forehead as I felt my intensity build. I leaned toward Brady. "What rank were you when you were honorably discharged, Brady?" I asked.

"Corporal, E-4," he said.

"Well shit, I was an E-7, looks like you are the lowest ranking enlisted in this joint, Sam!" I said, smiling widely. Sam's face flushed and he was rolling his envelope into a tube, probably without realizing it.

"You see combat in your ten minutes in the corps, private?" I barked at him, a little louder than I meant to. A middle-aged couple a table over paused their conversation and stared. *Yes, people, the only black dude in the cantina is getting fired up.* Sam didn't respond.

"I can answer that one, Sergeant Clemmons. That is a fucking negative. Private Simon Crenshaw was dishonorably discharged from the Corps for theft. He went on a shopping spree with another marine's credit card," Brady said. Sam stared down at the envelope and continued fiddling with it.

"Holy shit, what did you say this private's name was?"

"Simon Crenshaw."

"Who the fuck names their baby *Simon*? Did your parents hate you? Is that why you're a fuckin' thief because *Simon* is on your pathetic birth certificate? Why, you are lucky you weren't in my unit when you were stealing shit. I would have put you through a world of fuckin' hurt! Do you know ..."

"All right!" Sam yelled, slamming his hand down on the table. Everything on the table leaped up a few inches and then returned loudly, with my empty beer glass tipping over. I reflexively grabbed it and set it upright.

The entire room hushed, with only the Mexican music playing. All eyes were on him. A teenage busboy carrying chips and salsa paused at the kitchen door. The three of us sat quietly until the conversations around us resumed.

"So, what's in the envelope, Simon?" I said, leaning back.

He glared at me. I was sure I could goad him into throwing a punch. Then maybe I could have him arrested. That would be chickenshit, but these people didn't play fair, so I wasn't concerned about playing fair.

Sam stared down at the envelope as though he was surprised it was there. He looked over at Brady.

"Did you guys chat about you and Viktor's field trip today?" Sam asked him.

Brady shook his head. "No."

"I'm just going to leave this with you. If I were you, I wouldn't open it out here in public."

He slid it across in front of Brady, who didn't look down at it. Brady signaled to the waiter for the check. Sam stood up.

"Don't leave on my account. We'll talk later," Sam said.

"Did you pay for that drink already, private? Make sure you use your own goddamned credit card," I said, looking up at him.

I braced myself for a punch. I looked him in the eye but was also mindful of where his hands were. We stared at each other for an uncomfortable ten or fifteen seconds.

"Paid at the bar," he mumbled.

He turned and walked toward the door. I watched him leave, then turned back to Brady. He was also staring at the door, with his arms folded.

"Looks like we may have some more pictures," I said. Brady nodded. The waiter came over with the check.

"Actually, can we order another round?" he asked. The little waiter nodded, taking the check back with him. "I'm going to use the men's room."

Brady picked up the envelope and walked toward the restroom.

Chapter 6
Sunday, June 21

Brady 18

2:15 a.m.

Four jumbo margaritas in one sitting was never a good idea. Never mind that I threw up one of them. Closing a cantina was never a good idea. In Sandusky or Cancun or wherever. *Never advisable.*

Mike was going to drop me off at my camper, but I asked him to take me to his lot. I was hoping Chris would be out, but his RV was dark and quiet. He must have been out of the doghouse because he wasn't sleeping out front. I cut through to my lot.

I let myself into the camper, unsure of what I would find. Per Mike's recounting of the girl entering my RV, I knew they had a key. Even if they didn't have a key, RVs weren't exactly secure.

Last season we happened to lock both sets of keys in the camper. We asked Travis, and an hour later, a locksmith came out with a skeleton key and popped open the camper. So, all one had to do was get a set of those universal keys to get into any camper.

I didn't think Sam needed a skeleton key. I figured when I was drugged, he took my key and made a copy. I needed to get the locks changed.

Nothing appeared out of place. Not that I would notice a minor change, being as drunk as I was at the moment. I slipped the envelope under my mattress, beside the other blackmail envelope. *Come join the blackmail-of-the-day club.* I noted the pathetic lack of cleverness I'd exhibited by hiding the envelopes in the first place that any respectable criminal would search during a toss of my RV. I would figure out a better place tomorrow.

There would be hell to pay in terms of a hangover when I woke up, and I didn't care. I didn't care to the extent that it sounded like a reasonable idea to make another margarita.

I made my drink and went outside. The temperature had dropped substantially. I went back in and grabbed a hoody. I considered making a fire, but that would just attract attention. Possibly company. Viktor's camper was across the street. If that guy made an appearance, I may have tried to kill him.

I heard the damn train horn off in the distance and saw its lights creating shadows. The ground shook as it roared by and then disappeared.

I thought about the pictures. They had been sequenced carefully. The first one was a call girl entering my camper. Staged as hell. The next one was a selfie of her lying back in my bed in the camper. Correction, *our bed*, it was Marcy's too. Soon it would be neither of ours. Divorced couples don't own campers together; it would be sold and the money divided according to a judge's ruling.

The next picture was taken at the Islander duplex. It was a shot of me carrying one end of the blue tote. Only it was a coffin; I just thought it was a tote. It was from the vantage point of the other person carrying the tote. So, Viktor wore some sort of Go Pro–style camera concealed in his hat. That was why he kept fiddling with it.

The final one was a picture of me next to the tote at the warehouse. The tote was open, and there was a clear shot of me beside the dead girl. I was looking down at her with a blank look on my face. It must have been when Viktor first popped the lid open. She was naked, pale, eyes wide open, her hair disheveled.

It was taken before my brain was able to signal the proper expression to my face. The subsequent look on my face was horror. I stumbled backward and started cursing. I started to go after Viktor with fists clenched but stopped when I saw he had a crowbar in his hand. He was smiling his crooked-ass toothy smile, enjoying my reaction.

I turned and walked toward the door. Viktor yelled something at me, but I didn't understand him. I walked out and headed toward the street.

I kept waiting for Viktor to come after me, but he didn't.

The severity of my peril went from a shady marital infidelity episode to being an accessory to murder. Plus, any associated charges for carting a corpse around.

I could have called the cops. And said what, exactly? That I unknowingly helped somebody transport a dead body from an island to a warehouse, where I posed for a picture with it? That was a joke.

I had viewed the pictures in the bathroom stall of the Mexican place. That was a convenient location at that moment because I was able to lean over and throw up. Half of a jumbo margarita came up, and then I dry-heaved a few times. I heard people coming and going outside the stall door, and they probably figured I was some idiot who'd gotten carried away with the margaritas.

I exited the stall and returned to the table with a death grip on the envelope. My whole life would be at risk if I lost that envelope. But those were just pictures printed from digital images. I could go back to Sandusky Shores and toss the envelope into a campfire, and it wouldn't make any difference. Whoever had those files had *me*.

I described the envelope's contents to Mike. He was understandably shocked and disturbed. He kept staring at the envelope, as if he wanted to see them but knew it was a bad idea. Hearsay was one thing, but direct knowledge of a murder cover-up was serious jeopardy for him.

Mike was already getting in deeper by stirring up shit with Sam. He was on their radar big time, and he made an even bigger enemy of Sam with his insults. Sam mentioned that he was familiar with Mike's military background, so they were digging into his past.

Mike didn't appear worried. He considered himself blackmail free for the most part. As long as he didn't suffer a lapse of judgment and find himself getting photographed with a dead hooker.

The most damning fact for me was that the dead girl was the hooker from Friday at the bowling alley and in the cabin, my costar in the original blackmail pictures. I recounted the errands that Viktor and I ran on the island, and it made sense.

The two golfer bros at the Islander nervously hanging out. Something went wrong with those Johns; maybe they played too rough and killed her. Viktor was the cleanup guy. Viktor and me. We were called out to get rid of a body. *Because that was the shit that Randy did.* He dealt in hookers and thugs and likely all kinds of other shady shit.

I regretted the way I handled my original blackmail situation. I should have just gotten ahead of it and let the pictures be revealed. Had I done that, Randy's people would have nothing on me.

Life would have gone on.

The tote pictures were exponentially worse. It wouldn't just crush our marriage; it would crush our lives. My life especially. I would lose my job and be in serious legal trouble.

I was still tossing around the possibility of going to the police. Tell them every detail. Have them pull in Viktor, Randy, and Sam. Have them figure out who the girl was. Give them the duplex number and a description of the two Johns. The resort would have their names. Let the police investigate.

I didn't have any idea what had ultimately happened to the body. They couldn't keep it in the warehouse for long. Viktor must have disposed of her elsewhere. If they got pulled in by the police, they probably had a plan to connect the body to me. They had access to my camper and could have taken personal items that would lead back to me; maybe something of mine was placed near where the body was dumped.

If the police had a body, evidence traceable to me at the scene, pictures of us in the cabin, and pictures of me with the body, it would be extremely damning. There was so much smoke that no one would doubt there was an actual fire.

Confessing would likely be the wrong path, but so too would continuing blindly along the course of doing what they wanted. Would I get a phone call in the morning to go do another bizarre errand for Randy and keep spiraling downward?

I doubted I would be getting more assignments of the Viktor variety. He was a fixer and did the dirty work. That wasn't my skill set. They wanted something bigger from me. It would involve my security clearance and data accesses at work. If I provided them with military data, I was pivoting from solicitation to murder to treason. I needed to cut my losses somehow.

I was exhausted and needed some serious sleep. But I knew I wouldn't be able to sleep. Instead, I took a drink of my extremely strong margarita.

I wanted to talk to Mike some more. There had to be a way out of this. But he was likely prominent on their radar now, after the verbal abuse he heaped on Sam. *Simon*. I laughed out loud as I remembered Mike's tirade in the cantina. It was a burst of broken, hysterical laughter that sounded more like crying to my ears.

Brady 19

10:25 a.m.

"We have to pause our response," I said quietly. I was standing at the edge of Mike's lot, looking up and down the street. It was drizzling slightly, and no one was outside walking around. I saw Chuck's golf cart driving west along the clubhouse.

"You don't have time to sit back on this, Brady. They are moving against you. We need to get ahead of them," Mike said. He was standing a few feet away, staring blankly into the empty fire pit as though he was lamenting the lack of fire there.

"My kids are coming up. The in-laws are dropping them off. Marcy got stuck with an unanticipated business trip and has to go to Pittsburgh for a few days. Her parents had a vacation planned and can't watch them, so she decided to swallow her pride and let me take them. Normally I would be thrilled. Of course, now … but I can't mess this up," I said.

"Then I'm thinking you need to take them somewhere else," he said.

"I agree. She just sprang this on me an hour ago, so I haven't had time to plan things out."

My hangover wasn't nearly as severe as it should have been. I had slept until 10 a.m. and drunk plenty of water, so that helped take the edge off of it.

My cell buzzed in my pocket. I pulled it out and viewed the screen. It was Marty, my father-in-law.

"Sorry, Mike, gotta take this," I said. He nodded, and I answered it as I walked back toward my camper.

I hung up a few minutes later and sighed deeply. The in-laws were departing from Cleveland. They were spending the weekend in the Toledo area, staying at a cabin at Maumee Bay State Park, and visiting a casino. They would be traveling west along the turnpike and within a few miles of Sandusky Shores, so the kids could be conveniently dropped off. I didn't have another plan in mind, so

I agreed.

Once they were dropped off, we had to move somewhere else quickly. Randy and his people couldn't find out they were in the area.

Even taking them to a random hotel somewhere would be preferable. If we holed up, and they watched movies and played video games, the kids would be okay with that. Once Marcy found out, she would hit the roof and demand to know why they didn't stay at the camper. But I would worry about dealing with that when the time came; the safety of the kids was all that mattered at the moment.

Aside from that, I didn't know how I was going to spend a few days pretending my life wasn't going terribly wrong. *Sorry that Dad is a little distracted; it was probably because a crime syndicate took pictures of Dad posing with a dead Romanian hooker yesterday.* It was going to take a world-class acting performance to portray the fun and carefree Dad that they were expecting.

I decided we would spend a few days at a local waterpark. There were several in the area, but the Zulu Waterpark was their favorite. At one time, it was the biggest indoor waterpark in the country, although I thought I read that a new park had surpassed it in square footage. It also featured an outdoor waterpark, a safari area with exotic animals, and a zipline course.

The park had an African theme. There were statues of wild animals everywhere in jungle and savannah settings. Occasionally they would bring in animals to let the kids interact and take pictures with.

I preferred to visit in the winter, even though there were fewer entertainment options with the outdoor area being closed. The main indoor park area was humongous, over 170,000 square feet under a glass ceiling. If the sun was shining, it felt like you were actually outdoors, especially with the African decorations and foliage throughout.

Winters in Ohio were all grayness and gloom, with plenty of drizzle, sleet, ice, and snow. The early onset of nightfall, with the sun setting around 5 p.m. throughout most of the season, added to the dreariness. A few days wearing bathing suits in a temperature-controlled atmosphere surrounded by water attractions was a welcome change of pace.

The park was also a convention center and hotel. The jungle motif extended to the architecture and décor of these areas as well.

Each hotel room had actual African art. The owner traveled to Africa periodically and purchased items to bring back and display.

Once I selected Zulu for our getaway, I had to figure out how to keep our location concealed from Randy. I assumed I was being watched at all times.

I packed a gym bag with everything I would need for a short vacation. I went through my cell phone and listed the numbers I thought I would need over the next few days on a piece of paper. No one memorized phone numbers anymore, since they were stored in cell phones, and seldom dialed from memory. My cell would remain in the RV for the excursion, so I wouldn't be able to look up numbers I may need.

I put my gym bag in a garbage bag. Taking the garbage bag out to the dumpster, I hid it between the back of the dumpster and the section of stockade fence that ran behind it. I hoped a campground employee wouldn't come along and toss it inside.

To avoid detection from Randy's tech guys, I would purchase everything with cash. Mike revealed that he had a fair amount of cash hidden in his RV for emergencies. That generally wasn't the smartest move, but that was how he operated.

I wrote him a check for a thousand dollars, and he counted out the money, putting it in a white kitchen garbage bag. He protested when I insisted on the check and told me he didn't need that as security, but I felt better doing it that way rather than borrowing the money outright.

Returning to my RV, I changed into running clothes. I went out for a run, leaving my cell phone behind. Meanwhile, Mike drove over to the dumpster, parking his truck parallel to partially block the view of the dumpsters from the street. He tossed his bag in, found the garbage bag I left, and put it in his truck.

He drove from the campground to an abandoned post office

at the corner of Palmer and East Shoreway, where I was waiting behind the building. I came out and got in his truck. The bags with borrowed money and my gym bag were in the front seat next to Mike.

Our first stop was a cell phone store in a strip mall near the turnpike, where I bought a couple of burner phones for us. Then we went to a car rental place, where Mike rented a vehicle in his name. We paid cash, renting a blue Ford Taurus that was a few years old.

I called my mother-in-law and told her I lost my cell phone and that I could be reached at my temporary burner phone. I also told her I would meet them at the Route 250 exit on the turnpike at a restaurant the kids liked instead of having them dropped off at the campground. That would save them a fair amount of time since they wouldn't have to travel along several miles of side roads to get to the campground.

They arrived at the restaurant around lunchtime. I had been watching for them from the table I requested by a window. I hopped up and jogged outside when I saw the white Chevy Equinox pull up.

Marty was driving, as always, with Caroline in the passenger seat. I could see the tops of the kids' heads in the back as they pulled into a handicapped spot. Caroline had a bad knee and thus qualified to get the blue-and-white handicapped rearview-mirror hangtag.

I shook Marty's hand. He was honestly one of the nicest people I had ever known. He was somewhat henpecked and excessively good natured, to the point of gullibility at times, but there were worse vices.

He was around five foot eight, with thin, gray hair. He wore glasses, a blue Cleveland Indians T-shirt, a pair of very big khaki cargo shorts, and a white pair of New Balance tennis shoes. He kept himself fit for his age, having a wiry, capable look to him.

I went over and hugged Caroline. She was also a very nice person, if slightly overbearing. Overly cautious to the point of near paralysis at times. There was nothing too trivial to worry excessively about. With her daughter, Marcy, the apple didn't fall far from the tree.

She wore blue capris and some sort of flowery blouse, carrying a gigantic blue purse. Her posture had worsened over the years, and she tended to hunch forward. She had short hair, dyed dark brown.

I went around and opened the rear passenger door to find Katie sitting in her child seat. She was small for her age, a willowy little doll with fine, dishwater-blonde hair down to her shoulders and dark eyebrows. Both of my kids had that same hair, which would turn almost white after a summer of bleaching by the sun. I had it throughout my childhood before it changed to a darker brown in my teen years.

Her face was a little pale, accenting a faint pink Kool-Aid mustache. She was dressed in gray exercise pants with a red Ohio State short-sleeve dry-fit shirt. She liked to dress like her older brother, who wore nothing but athletic apparel. Her dark-green eyes were hidden behind a cheap pair of red sunglasses.

"Dad!" she howled, leaning over to try to hug me without realizing she was still restrained by her seatbelt. I leaned forward and hugged her, kissing her on the cheek.

"Dad!" came Jason's voice from the other side. He was six inches taller and able to travel without a car seat. His hair was cropped shorter than I had ever seen it. It could have passed for a military "high and tight." Jason seemed to have grown a few inches since I had last seen him, which was impossible since it had only been a month. He was about average sized for a ten-year-old and appeared to be filling out a little. He was wearing black Nike sweatpants and a gray Nike dry-fit T-shirt, with a black Michael Jordan Jumpman logo on the pocket.

Jason popped off his seatbelt and leaned forward to join a group hug. I was so shocked at the positive reception by them that I started to get choked up. Marcy led me to believe they were indifferent toward me and barely noticed I was gone.

Marty opened the hatch and took out two gym bags, placing them on the sidewalk. The kids both got out and stood beside him.

"Where is your truck?" he asked.

"Getting an oil change. I have a rental," I lied.

"A dealership around here gives rentals for oil changes? Fantastic!" he said. He was genuinely excited for me.

I picked up the bags and walked over to the Taurus while the four of them stood on the sidewalk. I loaded them in the trunk and walked back over.

"Here is Katie's EpiPen and inhaler," Caroline said, handing me a small black canvas bag. That was the ball and chain forever fastened around Katie's ankle. The EpiPen must be with her at all times. Hopefully, it would save her life if she ingested any sort of nut substance and struggled to breathe. The inhaler was for mild asthma issues.

"Is anyone hungry?" I asked. Both kids shouted "yes," and Katie started jumping up and down. I thanked the grandparents for bringing them, and they left, continuing on to Toledo.

Randy 8

12:55 p.m.

"So where is he?" I asked angrily as I leaned across my desk. Sam was slouched back in the chair across from me, holding a cup of coffee. "I don't know. We saw him go for a run, and he never came back," he said quietly.

"Did you check his camper?" I asked.

"Yeah, it is closed up. Truck parked in front. No sign of him," he said.

"Where is Clemmons?"

"At the campground. He took off for an hour earlier and came back with some groceries. Data checked, and Sullivan's phone is in his camper. Usually, he brings it when he runs," he said.

"So, he is playing some sort of game. He ran somewhere and got a ride. He could be at McDonald's, on a boat, holed up in a motel, or on a bus out of town. Do we know the whereabouts of his wife and kids?"

"We can have Data check," Sam said, shrugging.

"Have him do that. And when he finds Sullivan, I want Alexander to take the lead in sending him a message. It's his turn to show us what he can do."

Brady 20
1:05 p.m.

was unable to register at the Zulu hotel under a false name, since a driver's license was required to check-in. The desk clerk assured me the hotel would not reveal I was a guest.

My hopes of avoiding the use of a credit card were dashed, since they demanded a credit card to reserve the room. I was assured the card wouldn't be charged unless authorized at checkout, and at that point I could settle up with cash.

It would have been smarter to find a cheap motel that didn't require a credit card hold. I was sure I could find one with a pool. But we were in the lobby of Zulu, and the kids were bouncing up and down with excitement. Dragging them out of the region's biggest waterpark to go splash around in a four-foot-deep motel pool would be a disaster. I prayed that the card swipe at check-in would not hit some external database, since nothing was being charged.

We were issued blue wristbands. These not only authorized us to enter the park for three days but were also key cards that would unlock our door. Our room was on the third floor, room 311, with a balcony facing the parking lot.

We took our bags to our room and changed into swimsuits. The room had two queen-size beds with ornately carved headboards and colorfully patterned brown bedspreads. There were two paintings above the beds, one of a rhino's head and another of a lonely baobab tree in an African savannah.

We exited the room and walked down the wide hallway toward the waterpark entrance. The hall was decorated with carved African hardwoods, masks, and fake torches. The floor was covered with thin carpeting with a busy blue-and-black African pattern.

We walked past crowds of families dressed in swimsuits and flip-flops, carrying giant pool bags and towels. Kids occasionally squealed as they ran past, some being chased by parents pushing strollers. Big carts filled with luggage and coolers were being wheeled to and from rooms. Soft drum music played through speakers concealed by plastic foliage, barely heard above the constant din of talking people.

We passed a series of windows on the right that offered a view down into the waterpark. The area nearest the windows provided entertainment for smaller kids, with tiny slides and fountains for preschoolers and babies wearing little lifejackets. Behind that was a large complex of platforms and slides, rising three stories and supporting a huge bucket.

A steady stream of water poured into the bucket from a fountain above it. When the bucket was nearly filled, a bell would sound, and a moment later, it would tip and dump hundreds of gallons of water onto everyone who stood below.

To the left was a giant wave pool that would generate one- to two-foot waves in various depths of water, going as deep as five feet. The waves would last for ten minutes, and then the wave machine would go idle for five. This process recurred throughout the entire day, with lifeguards in red shorts, white T-shirts, and carrying rescue flotation devices posted along the edges, watching closely.

The center of the park had a bar and a restaurant that served park food, including burgers, hot dogs, chicken fingers, and pizza. There were a few salad options prepackaged in clear plastic containers, but those never sold in great numbers.

The main bar was oval shaped, with several televisions mounted throughout that were tuned in to sporting events. A broad selection of liquor and beer was available.

Along the back wall were several slides of differing sizes and intensities, an adults-only whirlpool that offered bar service, and an indoor surfing area that generated waves for surfing and wakeboarding.

Around the periphery of the park was a lazy river, where guests could slowly float around on inflatable rafts. Along the route were artificial African landscapes and stuffed safari animals.

We continued walking, finding the stairs down to the main level. We had to cut through the arcade to get to the waterpark entrance, a shrewd layout design that forced parents to walk their kids past countless colorful and loud machines offering unlimited opportunities to win prize tickets. These tickets could then be exchanged for cheap, crappy prizes. *Pay five dollars for the chance to win a stuffed animal made in China worth fifty cents.*

The layout conspiracy worked, as both of my kids began begging as soon as they entered the area. I cashed in twenty dollars and bought them each a ten-dollar play card. The money lasted about five minutes.

We continued to the waterpark entrance. There were five turnstiles that required a wristband scan to enter. We scanned in and went through double doors to the towel-distribution area. We each grabbed a few of the thin, neatly folded white towels stacked in a plastic bin and headed toward the giant bucket area. Jason wasn't thrilled about this, preferring to ride the bigger waterslides, but Katie wanted to start there.

If I was to maintain any sense of order and my sanity, I needed to keep them together. Allowing them to split up would require me to bounce back and forth between different areas of the park, which was way too much stress.

I let them play for an hour and then ordered a snack. Food for Katie was always challenging, as we had to make sure she was not exposed to any type of nut. Most fast-food and franchise restaurant menus clearly declared allergens, but you always needed to double-check. Peanut oil was a problem, as well as cross-contamination. A particular food may be nut free but situated next to a station that had chopped nuts for salads or desserts. An errant flick of the wrist could launch a peanut onto a nearby "nut-free" plate of food.

The labor dynamics of the foodservice industry made it difficult to order safe food for her with any certainty. Waitstaff and cooks were paid minimum wage or less, and turnover was always high. There were certainly exceptions, but restaurant work didn't always attract the best and the brightest. A lot of conversations with servers went like this:

"My daughter has a nut allergy, do you serve anything with nuts here?"

"No, we are a nut-free restaurant!"

I further review the menu.
"What about this apple-cranberry pecan salad here?"
Crickets.

The kids shared a basket of chicken fingers and fries, along with two slushies. Jason's was a deep blue, Katie's a bright red. Slushies were a magical combination of crushed ice, refined sugar, and food dye. According to Marcy, red food dye caused hyperactivity in children, but a hyper Katie was not a major problem.

The kids were only separated by a few years, but they were two completely different species. Jason was more hyperactive; he had that jittery *I always have to be moving* vibe to him. Katie was more content being still. She was okay with reading or just people-watching; she didn't have to be in motion every waking moment like Jason.

The difference in sexes was one factor, but another could have been her food allergies. We were more protective of her, so she was on a shorter leash and coddled a lot more.

After the snack break, it was back to water rides. They hit one after another. Both were relatively fearless, probably from taking them to Gravity Junction since they were toddlers. Heights and thrills did not scare them.

There were occasions when we allowed them to bring friends to the park, or there were school fundraisers where many of their friends would travel to the park at the same time. Many of the kids (and some adults) were terrified of these rides. I was proud that my kids didn't have these types of phobias. You want your kids to be bold and fearless. *To a point.*

Jason 1

1:55 p.m.

M y stomach was hurting from that slushie, but it was totally worth it. I didn't complain because I wanted another one later.

It was great to be at Zulu with Dad, but being stuck with Katie was a drag. She did most of the rides, but the stupid stuff she was always saying in line was lame.

Plus, she was too short for the Cheetah ride. Dad would usually ride it with me, but he couldn't leave Katie by herself while we were on. It was better to have Mom along for these times, so we could split up.

I wished we could stay forever. I forgot how much fun it was with Dad. *So much less worrying.*

My brain was stuck on the arcade. I was just a few tickets away from getting those jungle binoculars. The spinning wheel machine was the best bet. Last time I hit the max payout and got five hundred tickets on one spin!

My card needed a refresh, and I doubted Dad would give me any more money for that today. Maybe tomorrow. There was no way I wanted to wait until tomorrow.

I looked down at my wristband. It was programmed to get me into our room, but it was also set up for room charges. The last time we came here, Mom and Dad used it to buy food and drinks. It scanned to their room or something.

We were walking over to the lazy river when I had an idea. It was a bad decision to try to pull it off, but exciting to try.

"Can I use the bathroom? I need to take a dump," I said as we walked by the front door. On both sides were men's and women's lockers with bathrooms. The bathrooms had a door to the back that went out to the hall between the outside doors and then to the turnstiles.

"Too much information, Jason. Okay, we'll be right here," he said. Dad couldn't come with me because Katie was there, and he wouldn't leave her alone. I walked fastly in and right to the back door. I peeked out to see if Dad was standing at the end of the hall by the towel cart but didn't see him. So, I ran out and through the door.

I jogged through the hall toward the nearest card machine. Luckily there was no one using it. Pushing the card in, I tapped the "replenish" button on the screen. I pushed "ten dollars." I really wanted more but knew better. Ten dollars might get lost on the hotel sheet, but a bigger amount would be spotted.

It asked for payment, and I pushed the button with the wristband icon. The piece of glass at the middle glowed red, and I put my wristband in front of it. I had to move it around a little, but it finally dinged. The screen said, "thank you," and my card popped out.

I really, really wanted to play the game right away, but playing would get me busted. Dad would come check on me soon. He would take Katie into the bathroom if he had to.

I jogged back to the entrance and scanned my wrist at the turnstile. I dodged through the locker room, leaped over a bench, slipped on a wet spot, nearly wiped out, and went back outside. Dad was standing with Katie. My face was probably red, and I was breathing hard, but I don't think Dad noticed.

Data 6

2:10 p.m.

"Yes, sir. Just got a ping from Sullivan's credit card. His Discover card was used at the Zulu waterpark. A ten-dollar charge. I'm sure. I'm looking at his transaction history right now. The notice was sent about five minutes ago."

I leaned back in the chair, exhaling slowly. It was great to provide value. Hopefully, I was making up for the Sullivan data spill.

I had been stumped until then. Sullivan dropped off the grid. He obviously wanted to disappear but then used his credit card? *Sloppy.*

He had to know we were tracking him. He ditched his phone and vehicle. Clemmons was assisting him; I was sure of it. Why do all of that and just hide out five miles away at a waterpark?

My feeling of accomplishment in finding Sullivan diminished when it dawned on me what I had actually done to him. The guy was at a waterpark with his kids, and I had outed him. Outed him to the same people who set him up to take the fall for a dead prostitute. I was so eager to please that I lost sight of the big picture. *Whenever I followed an order from Randy, people got hurt.*

Alexander 1

3:55 p.m.

I pulled out from the dump apartment on the motorbike. Everyone in the US wanted Harleys. I didn't care about Harley. I couldn't afford Harley. Yamaha was fine. I bought it for two thousand dollars when I came to Sandusky and would sell it after the summer.

I had met with Olivia there. She had the skill with the printer. She made a copy of the *siglă* of Zulu, a black elephant head. She had put it above the left pocket on the brown shirt, so it would be the same as the workers. She also gave me the Zulu name tag. *Chester*. I frowned when I read. I would have a hard time saying "Chester."

"Viktor said to say your name is Chet if you can't pronounce Chester," she said.

I had to wear a black long-sleeve shirt under the Zulu shirt to cover my tattoos and scars. Military, prison, gangs. Bad, clumsy tattoos, many turned gray and *în ceață* … blurry with time.

Having the tattoos almost lost the job with Mr. Randy. Too easy to remember me if people talked to police.

False papers were made that gave me a clean record. If the park knew my real past, I would have never been able to travel to the US.

With my white trainers and brown shorts, I wore the American waterpark uniform. Mates at home would laugh. But most of them were in jail, so who were they to laugh at Alexander?

I was given a blue plastic bag from the Kroger store. I looked inside and shook my head. This was what I was going to use as a weapon? It did not matter, it was what I was told to do, so I would do it. I put the items in a backpack.

I drove to the Trailer Alpha. I heard of this place but had not been there. Letting me go there was a sign of trust. The Data Man was there and going to brief me on Sullivan.

Chris 6

5:10 p.m.

S am dropped me off at the front entrance of the airport and drove off. We had spent several hours together, where he ran me from one place to the next.

First of all, I didn't sign up for a makeover. But I was given a makeover. My hair hadn't been cut that short since the air force. It wasn't a buzz cut, but it was so drastically different from my general sloppy look that it might as well have been.

Next, we went clothes shopping. Randy had a guy at a store off Milan, and I was measured up and tried on clothes for an hour. I walked out wearing the clothes I was currently wearing: black dress pants, a black belt, a light-blue shirt, and a dark-blue blazer. The socks were matched up too, blue with some sort of pattern. I also had a new wallet and shoes. I had another full outfit I took home as well. The rest of the stuff we ordered would be tailored and ready in a few days.

I found it amusing that Randy had a clothing hookup. I never saw him wearing anything fancier than jeans and a dress shirt. Maybe there was a stylish side to him that he decided not to flaunt at the campground or bowling alley.

We went to a fairly decent sit-down restaurant and had burgers and fries for lunch. No alcohol, only pop.

Sam briefed me over lunch. Randy set me up with his pilot to do a ride-along. If the pilot felt comfortable with me, he would possibly let me take the yoke for a few minutes. If I established a good track record, I could get sponsored for my commercial license and start getting routes.

I would start making money, and that would lead to moving somewhere better than a run-down RV at a campground. It sounded promising, although too good to be true.

I entered the airport and walked to the service desk. There was a middle-aged woman on a black corded desk phone. I walked up and she smiled, giving me the *just one moment* gesture with her right pointer finger. She hung up a moment later.

"May I help you, sir?"

"I'm here to see Captain Bill Norquist," I said.

At that moment, I understood the need to clean up and dress up. If I walked in here off the construction site, she would have greeted me much differently.

"Please have a seat, and I will let him know you are here," she said pleasantly.

Randy 9

6:30 p.m.

I was too deep into the bourbon for 6:30 p.m. This was not the way I did business. A drunk boss makes bad decisions, and bad decisions can impair a business. Not that you would find that in a quote book from leaders of industry, but *what-the-fuck-ever.*

Nevertheless, I sipped a little more. Sam was fidgety. He wanted a piece of the latest Sullivan job, but I couldn't allow him to be involved. If Sullivan saw Sam at the waterpark, the whole thing would have to be aborted. Sullivan and Alexander had never crossed paths, so I had to go with the Romanian.

"We need to do something about Clemmons, and soon," I said, sipping again. I looked at Sam closely for a reaction, expecting to see a nod and a grin. He didn't react, which surprised me.

"Is Mike Clemmons beyond the scope of your capabilities, Sam? Afraid of a colored guy?"

An angry look crossed his face and then disappeared. He shook his head. Then he managed a smile that was 100 percent fake.

"Nah, I'm not worried about Clemmons," he lied. Sam easily had fifty pounds more and ten years less on him. *Maybe the illegitimate marine didn't want anything to do with the legit soldier.*

"Give it some thought. We just need to get him to move along, nothing permanent. Clemmons has no real skin in the game; he is a busybody in the wrong place at the wrong time. I don't know why he is buddying up with Sullivan, beyond the fact that they are soldiers," I said.

"You mean *were* soldiers," Sam said flatly.

"Oh, so that 'marine for life' bullshit only applies to you? Army vets aren't 'soldiers for life'?" I asked. He stared down at his hands and didn't have anything to say. "Clemmons spent twenty years in the army before he retired. Saw combat. Sullivan did three years with an honorable discharge. Used the G.I. Bill to go to college. How long were you in, that you deserve the 'marine for life' honor?"

"How long did *you* serve, Randy?" he asked.

I glared at him for a minute, then I threw my glass at him. It bounced off his right shoulder, flew up past his head, landing behind him with a crash on the hardwood floor.

"I'll tell you one thing I didn't do. I didn't disgrace myself by stealing from a fellow serviceman with some two-bit credit card scam. Dishonorable discharge for a few hundred dollars' worth of bullshit. That is a lifetime label you can wear alongside your tired 'marine for life' bullshit you throw in everyone's face. Your ten minutes in the corps didn't earn you that," I growled.

Sam met my gaze for a moment, then looked down at the floor. He wiped the bourbon from his neck and face with his left hand and then rubbed his shoulder.

"Clean that up and get me a fresh drink. Then I want to hear a plan to get Clemmons out of my campground. I want him gone by tomorrow."

Alexander 2

6:35 p.m.

I was not sure if the card would work, but it did. After looking at the park map, I went in the north door. There were cabins across the street and people walking or taking shuttles to the park. I did not think there would be employees near the north door.

That was what I was to avoid. Employees. Especially supervisors. I parked my motorbike near the back of the lot and walked to the door. It was card-access only, where a swipe makes the door unlock. I did and it worked.

Data Man had a swipe card machine at the Trailer Alpha and boxes of blank cards of many colors. The guests used wristbands, but the employees used cards. I had five cards of different colors. Once I saw what cards the employees used, I would use that color.

He said he could make cards for any hotel with electric locks. The cards he made would open any door at Zulu.

I had the two clear plastic tubes in the pocket of my shorts along the right leg. The inside of the tubes had brown settled at the bottom. When I shook them, the tube became blurry. Those were my weapons.

It would be hard to find Sullivan; there were many places to go. I would check the outdoors first.

So many people. The Sullivans did not look unique. A forty-year-old white man and two kids did not stand out. I saw pictures Data Man had stolen from Sullivan's phone. I would know them when I saw them.

There were hundreds of outdoor chairs, but most of them were empty, with towels or clothes on them. I could not understand this. People could not use chairs because someone put a towel down, so they would go unused most of the day. At the same time, others were trying to find chairs or put their things in the grass.

People were flying above on ziplines, standing in line for

slides, and sitting at tables and bar stools at outdoor cafes. No Sul-livans.

I walked fast with a purpose, as I was told. If I was slow or idle, that would look odd. I had to be a busy park worker.

When I passed other park workers, I smiled a little and nod-ded, then kept walking. I could not talk to them, because questions would reveal me as a fake. Hundreds worked there, so not every-one would *recunoaşte* ... recognize everyone. The workers I passed did not stop me or give two looks.

I passed the outdoor whirlpool and went indoors. I passed the kid pool, the big bucket, the bar, the snack bar, and many rides. No Sullivans.

Along the back southern wall was a ride that had four slides together in a row, and people would lay on mats and race. Not there. Adult whirlpool and bar area, not there. I went back outside and along the building where there was privacy. I took out the burner phone and called Data Man.

"Yes?"

"Do you have any activity?" I asked. A minute went by.

"No. They swiped into their room at 311 at check-in. No other data footprint," he said. I hung up.

I went back in the building and looked in the game room. I looked in the lobby and the gift store.

I found them at a restaurant by the lobby called the Safari Bar. I was walking through and saw them in a booth in the bar area. They only had drinks on the table, no food, or empty plates. I *de-dusa* ... deduced they had not yet ordered and would be there for some time. I walked to the restroom.

I stood alone for two minutes and walked out. I did not look at the Sullivans, but down at the top of their table. Still just drinks. Two kid cups with straws and a tall beer, dark red.

I did not look at any of the workers, and they did not look at me. I left and walked to the lift at a fast pace.

Sam 7

6:35 p.m.

was driving from the marina to the bowling alley when my burner phone buzzed. It was Alexander. I answered.

"I am in the room," he said in a quiet voice. I sat up straighter.

"Okay. Did they bring food?" I asked. There was a pause.

"Yes. Cereal, bags of chips. Box of *gogoși* ... donuts still in the package."

"Take a look in the fridge," I said. Another pause.

"Six-pack of beer, missing two. A box of milk. Juice boxes. Yogurts. Bottled waters."

"Is the milk open?"

"Yes. It is a paper box. Opened."

"How much is gone?"

"Maybe a half-liter."

"I don't know what the fuck a half-liter is. How much, as far as how much left. A quarter? Half?

"It is a half-gallon box, three-fourths full," he said.

"Perfect. Dump a splash of the milk in the sink. Run the water to get rid of the traces. Pour in one of the tubes. Make sure there is no residue ... no stuff that can be seen. Take a Kleenex and wipe the spout of the box if you need to. Take the dirty tissue with you. Close the top of the carton and give it a good shake. Put it back. Then you are done."

"Yes," he said. I broke the connection.

Chapter 7
Monday, June 22

Data 7

9:30 a.m.

"Yes, sir. An ambulance was called to Zulu at 8:35 a.m. Katie Sullivan was checked in at Firelands Hospital at 9:19," I said, viewing the screen.

Hanging up, I reflected on the high degree of technical prowess it took to carry out that mission. But it was nothing to be proud of. I used my talents to harm a kid, and I was in denial about what I was doing until after it was over.

It was just one of many unfortunate events I had enabled over the past few weeks while serving as mission control of a busy criminal enterprise. I winced when I thought about the blackmail, extortion, prostitution, fraud, and racketeering.

I winced even harder when I thought about Katie Sullivan. Alexander had drained the liquid from the top of two natural peanut butter jars into plastic vials at Trailer Alpha. I knew his intentions but didn't say a word.

I had helped cover up the murder of a dead prostitute. I was ramping up a digital extraction system to pull data from all the campground devices connected to Wi-Fi. I was researching how to do that at Gravity Junction as well. I was game-planning how to take Sullivan's defense agency data and find a market for it, which looked a lot like treason.

Where would it end? I was so entangled in it that I couldn't envision a withdrawal strategy that didn't involve me either dead, in jail, or in the Witness Protection Program.

Mike 11

9:45 a.m.

"Hello? Wait, slow down, you are where?" I asked, sitting up straight in my lawn chair. I had received a call from Brady on my burner phone.

Brady was frantic, talking so fast that it sounded like gibberish. His daughter was in the hospital, but it wasn't clear why.

"Which hospital?" I asked. "Okay, on my way."

My campfire still had a log burning, but I didn't stop to extinguish it. The sky was dark, and it was drizzling on and off. The forecast called for showers, so I wasn't concerned about the fire.

I went into the trailer and grabbed my keys and gym bag, which was prepacked with a few items. Survivalists called it a "go bag," but to me, that was just a civilian twist on an army rucksack. It contained my Beretta, ammo, a flashlight, two military Meals Ready to Eat, a change of clothes, matches, a compass, a hunting knife, some cash, and a first-aid kit. I locked the camper and took off in my truck.

Firelands Regional Medical Center was a little south of downtown Sandusky. I followed the signs along Milan, getting a visual of the building from the road as I approached the entrance about ten minutes after I left.

It was a generic-looking modern hospital, medium sized, maybe four or five stories tall with a lot of glass. I flashed back to an earlier time in my life when I drove up to a similar-looking hospital to check on a young girl in trouble. That was at the Womack Army Medical Center at Fort Bragg to visit my daughter Sadie as she lay dying. Hopefully, Brady's daughter's prospects were better.

If anyone was to blame for what happened to my own daughter, it was the US Army. I returned from my final deployment in Afghanistan feeling well. I went through a general medical screening and was given a clean bill of health, so I was discharged from quarantine and reunited with my family.

Within a few days, I started to feel off. I developed a fever and a weird, raspy cough. I went to the doctor, and it was diagnosed as the seasonal flu.

Several soldiers in my squad developed similar symptoms. The army did some additional testing and discovered we had *Coxiella burnetii*, also known as the Q Fever. The army didn't screen for the disease because it was rare, with only a handful of soldiers getting infected during the campaign.

The Q Fever is contracted through contact with livestock. Our squad split off from the platoon on a side mission for a few days and killed a couple sheep we came across. Gutting and eating the sheep had spread the disease to four of us.

Once home, it spread to my family. It knocked us all down hard. We were bedridden for days. They pumped us all full of antibiotics, and three of us recovered okay. Sadie did not. She had preexisting respiratory issues and was having trouble breathing. She ended up in an ambulance. Three days later, she passed away in the hospital.

That began my descent into numbness. Now Brady was in a similar place.

I followed the signs to the emergency room area, parked, and went in. I stopped at the front desk.

"Mike!" Brady shouted from behind me. This earned him a dirty look from the desk nurse, a thin, twenty-something-year-old Hispanic woman dressed in blue scrubs and wearing thick glasses with black frames, her hair pulled back tight.

Brady stood up from where he was sitting with his son in the back corner of the otherwise-empty waiting room. Both appeared rattled, and the boy looked like he had been crying. His eyes were swollen, and his complexion was blotchy. I walked over and shook Brady's hand.

It looked like they had dressed in the dark. Brady was wearing a ragged maroon pair of gym shorts, flip-flops, and a faded black Cleveland Browns T-shirt. Jason was wearing red swim trunks, blue tennis shoes without socks, and a black Darth Vader pajama top.

"Mike, this is Jason," he said. I leaned over and shook his hand. He looked up at me and attempted a smile. I positioned myself in a chair on the other side of Brady.

"What happened?" I asked in a hushed voice. Brady leaned over, put his head in his hands for a minute, and then pushed them up across his forehead and through the front of his short hair.

"Katie had an anaphylactic reaction to an allergen. Her throat started closing up. As this was happening, she also started throwing up. This happened in the hotel room. I grabbed her EpiPen and gave her an injection as soon as the reaction started happening. I was so terrified that I froze for a moment, fumbling around with her Ep-iPen bag forever before I finally got it out. I wasn't nearly as good under pressure as I assumed I would be in that type of situation. But I managed to do it and then called an ambulance."

"What is happening with her now?" I asked. I glanced over at Jason, who was staring down sadly at his hands.

"She is in intensive care, sleeping. Luckily, she did not lapse into a coma. The doctors think throwing up may have saved her."

"What was she eating when this happened?"

"A bowl of cereal. It was a brand she has been eating for years, allergen-free. With two-percent milk straight out of the carton. There was nothing iffy about it. It was all in our hotel room, so it wasn't like something she ate or drank could have been cross-contaminated in a restaurant."

"Could she have been exposed to something last night and it just had a lag? Maybe some sort of incidental contact, getting peanut butter on her clothing, and then touching it the next morning?"

"We came back to the room when the park closed at 2200 hours. The kids showered and put on their pajamas. Everything she wore yesterday was in a pile in the corner."

"Is your wife here?" I asked.

His face dropped. "Not yet. She is on her way from Pittsburgh. My in-laws should be here soon from Toledo. Both cut their trips short," he said.

He looked over at Jason, then back at me. I took that to mean he didn't want to talk in any greater detail in front of the kid.

"Are you allowed to visit her?" I asked.

"Should be soon. The doctor should be out to speak with us at any time."

"Okay, brother. Listen, let me know what I can do to help."

"Nothing right now, thanks. It is going to get … uncomfortable here when Marcy and her family arrive. I have so much explaining to do. Not having my cell and not mentioning the waterpark trip has created a record level of hostility toward me."

"Got it. I'm assuming you didn't have a chance to return your rental car or check out of the hotel."

"No, I drove the rental here, following the ambulance. Zulu is just a few miles down Milan."

"How about I go over and retrieve your stuff? I can come back and return your rental car and take a cab back to get my truck," I said. Brady stared down at his hands while he considered it, then nodded.

"That would be great. Sorry, we left the hotel room in a pretty chaotic state. Katie threw up and all. Just do what you can. Don't worry about checking us out. I will call and settle the bill up later. I think I will hold onto the rental; we can worry about returning it later."

"You got a minute to step out with me?" I asked.

He looked at Jason. "Sure. You good if we talk out front for a few minutes, Jason?"

Jason nodded, then returned to staring off at nothing.

We got up and walked through the automatic doors out to the sidewalk. It was drizzling slightly. Brady positioned himself so he could look through the window and see Jason from where we were standing.

"Was this a legit accident?" I asked.

Brady looked at me blankly. It was as if I said something to him in a foreign language.

"Well, yeah. Are you saying someone exposed her on purpose?" he asked in a whisper, even though there was no one else within earshot.

"You've been managing her allergies the right way her whole life. You brought your own shit from the outside to feed her for breakfast. Nothing she ate should have harmed her. And yet she had a huge reaction. You have to take into account your recent issues at the campground."

"So, someone poisoned her? I don't see how that is possible.

We bought the groceries at Kroger on the way here. They were locked in our room. We hung a 'Do not disturb' sign on the door, so no cleaning people were in our room."

"But you were out of that room for long stretches. What floor is your room on?"

"Third floor. Room 311. It faces the exterior, so if someone Spider-Man'd it up there he would have been spotted by people in front of the building. The balcony door was locked, I'm sure. The kids went out there when we arrived, and I locked it afterward."

"I'm going to take a look around while I'm there. In the meantime, you need anything before I leave? You got cash?" I asked. He nodded.

Brady reached down to the blue band on his left wrist, slipped two fingers beneath the band, and pulled. It broke at the thinner interior section, and he handed it to me.

"This is the room key."

We shook hands. I tapped on the hospital window as I walked away. Jason looked up at me, and I waved. He gave a halfhearted return wave.

Chuck 8

10:25 a.m.

Well, Clemmons sure left in a hurry. It was about time. I had been buzzin' around the campground, waitin' for him to go all morning. Dude was a homebody, just sittin' in front of his campfire.

He left in such a hurry that he didn't put out his campfire. That was very un-Mike-like, being the Boy Scout he was and all. I parked my golf cart up Sparrow and dialed up Sam.

"It's me. Clemmons is away. Yeah, he left a few minutes ago. In a hurry, I'm guessin' up to the hospital. He left his fire goin'. Yeah. Yeah, he did. Okay. There is a camper to his left at 64. Uh, his south. I think south. Okay. Huh? Uh, okay. I will. Yeah, I can text it to Travis later. Copy Data? Got it."

I pulled up slowly along Sparrow toward Mike's camper. I stopped and opened the camera app. Liftin' it like I was textin', I snapped pics of the fire pit, makin' sure I got his camper in the background. To people nearby who could have seen me there, I looked like I was usin' my phone to text.

Alexander 3

11:15 a.m.

How How does a man dress like "campground trash"? These kinds of vague orders annoy me. I put on my swimsuit. It was an American suit, big blue shorts that came down to my knees. American men wear ridiculous swimsuits. Men in Europe wear small swimsuits so you can really swim in them.

I put on a Gravity Junction tourist T-shirt and a blue Cleveland Indians hat with a big red Indian face on it, grinning. What kind of *mascotă* was that?

Cheap sunglasses and silly flip-flops. I brought a big red, white, and blue American flag towel, stuffed in a blue pool bag. It was free. I took it from lost and found at the Gravity Junction waterpark last week.

I also had a backpack. Inside was a small piece of wood, a newspaper, a lighter, and two plastic bags filled with campfire starter bricks I soaked in lighter fluid. The bags were sealed, but I could still smell the fluid.

Viktor drove the van and dropped off a bike in front of the apartment. Light rain was falling. He was leaning against the van with a dumb smile on his face when I walked out. He held up his cell and took a picture. He looked at the screen and laughed.

I walked over and punched him hard in the stomach. He *icni* … gasped, dropped the phone, hunched over.

"Erase that picture or you'll be having that phone surgically removed from the inside of your body," I said in Romanian. Viktor bent over, with his hands on both knees. I only gave the punch at half the force. Full would have put him in the hospital.

He stood up with anger on his face. I did not care. He played games with the other Romanians. I would not be played.

"You should not have done that. Randy won't like that you assaulted me out in public," he whined in Romanian.

"Then go cry to Randy, bitch. I don't care. You're taking photographs of me, and that is a security threat. What if you get picked up with that phone and they ask you to identify me? Do you want to bring this operation down? Randy would have you killed in prison, you idiot."

Viktor picked up the phone and erased the photo.

"Do you have the job information, or did you come here to clown around, boy?" I asked.

He glared at me for a minute. "The RV is in lot 65. It is an Airstream, all-metal exterior. No one is there now, but you need to get there quickly. Try not to be seen. Ride the bike back to the abandoned post office at Palmer and East Shoreway after the job, and I'll be waiting to pick you up," he said in Romanian.

"Once you arrive at the campground, park your bike near the front office. There will be a bag of garbage placed in front. Take it and walk up Sparrow to the end and throw the garbage in the dumpster. On the way back, cut through lot 50 south of his camper and torch it. Torch the backpack as well. Walk away slowly. Loop back to the office and ride your bike out and around to the post office. Any questions?"

"Won't it look strange that I'm dressed for the pool when it has been raining?"

"Not really. They never close the pool for rain, and it is warm, so there will still be a few people swimming," he said.

I nodded. I walked over and got on the bicycle.

"Wait," he said, opening the passenger door of the van. He took out a small, light-gray plastic square and tossed it at me. It was a gray poncho.

"It isn't raining that hard," I said with annoyance.

"This is to cover your ridiculous tattoos. You should not be chosen for these types of jobs. You are a walking piece of fucking graffiti that everyone will remember," he said.

I let that go. I put on the poncho and got on the bike.

"Do you know how to ride one of those?" Viktor asked as he walked around to the side of his vehicle.

"Yes, it is no more difficult than riding your fat peasant mother," I said. He glared at me and then got in the van.

Chris 7

11:55 a.m.

The construction site was down because of some permit issue, and I was inside the RV watching a *Law & Order* marathon. The intermittent drizzling outside would have made for a long day on the job, so I felt fortunate to be loafing around in the camper. But I wasn't making any money.

Candy was at a laundromat off Milan. She hated the laundry room on site; she said the machines made the clothes smell musty.

As soon as she pulled away in the car, I lit one up. She wouldn't have been happy, but she was never happy, so no big loss. She knew I was a burnout when we met, so expecting me to suddenly change into a choirboy was silly. I had never hidden the habit from her; she just woke up one day and decided it wasn't okay anymore. *Fuck that.*

The air conditioning was not functioning. It was just blowing warm air in from outside, so I had the windows open and fans on. A bit of rain was coming in, but nothing major.

The open windows also helped with the smoke from my joint. She would smell it regardless, but at that point, I would be too baked to give a shit.

I detected the scent of lighter fluid. It was faint at first, but then grew stronger, as if it was right outside my RV. That wasn't uncommon, some of these assholes couldn't be bothered with starting a campfire from paper and kindling, they had to dump a gallon of accelerant on it and create an inferno to roast marshmallows in.

I heard a crackling noise like a fire burned nearby. Then I heard people shouting. I looked out and saw Mike's metal RV had flames shooting out of the windows! *Holy shit.*

I took another long toke and went outside. The guy at lot 50 had detached the hose from his camper and was spraying it at the flames. It didn't appear to be helping much.

Patrick hooked a hose up at site 66 to hit it from that side.

Mike's truck was gone, so I wasn't concerned that he was trapped inside his RV.

I stood out front with my arms crossed, along with a small crowd of people. I heard sirens off in the distance.

Patrick 2

12:05 p.m.

I did not need this shit. *Not one bit.*

I was hooking the hose up, but I could barely lift with my left arm, so I was maneuvering everything with my right. The entire left side of my torso was wrecked. *Freakin' Sam.*

Sam came by the campground last night. I saw him walking down Starling toward the office, but instead of veering left, he continued straight up to the booth. He leaned in, smiling at me like he was my best buddy.

He asked me if I could follow him back to the Taj RV and chat with him about something. I was excited, I knew some of the inside guys like Data and Chuck got to go in there.

"What about security?" I asked.

"I suppose they could manage without you for a short time. This place ain't exactly a hotbed of criminal activity," he said, smiling. I grabbed the walkie-talkie and came out of the booth.

Sam made some small talk on the way, something about the weather. Sam's black SUV with the marine bumper sticker was parked at an angle in front of the Taj.

He unlocked the RV and motioned me in. As I stepped in, I felt a hard blow to the middle of my back, forcing me forward. I lost my balance as I crashed to the floor, sprawling out on my stomach. The walkie-talkie flew out of my hand and slid across the floor.

Then I felt another blow, a kick, to my left side, and I swear I heard bones crack. I yelled out and curled to the side, grabbing my ribs. I looked up, and Sam was standing over me, red-faced and smiling.

"Any idea what that was for, Patricio?" he asked, hunching over with a hand on each knee. His brown eyes were dead, almost like he was in a trance.

I inhaled and groaned at the pain. "No ... no ..." I gasped. His foot shot out again, connecting with the lower part of my ribs. This time I howled in agony.

"No use yelling. This place is soundproof. I want you to just lay still and think for a minute, and then I'm going to ask you again."

I squirmed over and managed to sit up, still grasping my left side. Every breath caused extreme pain. I wondered how many ribs were broken.

I didn't know why this was happening, but I had to figure it out quick before he came at me again. Fighting back never crossed my mind. Even if my ribs were fine, he was a foot taller and a lot of pounds heavier, and there was no way I would beat that guy in a fight.

Sam walked over to the fridge, got out a can of Pabst, opened it, and took a long drink. He belched loudly. "Figure it out, yet?" he asked, wiping his mouth.

I shook my head. "Honest, Sam ... what did I do?" I asked, pleading.

He stepped forward to kick me, and I quickly rolled to my side to avoid it, aggravating my ribs and causing me to cry out. Instead of kicking, he just started laughing.

He grabbed me by the shoulders and pulled me to my feet. I found my balance and stood up straight, wincing in pain.

"Sit down," he said, pointing to a chair at the table. I went over and sat, exhaling hard as I did. I broke a few ribs playing back-yard football three years ago, so I knew I was going to be in nonstop pain for weeks. There was no treatment. Even if I wanted to see a doctor, I didn't have insurance.

"This is about Henry. Data," he said. I understood the name, but it took me a minute to process it. I nodded as he sat down across from me.

"Mr. Randy has a fondness for Data. He does some work for him that is very valuable. He ain't some minimum-wage deadbeat just collecting trash around here. There was an incident the other night when Data was out here handling some important papers. You hit him, and it caused him to lose some of those papers. Mr. Randy is not fucking happy. We took a look at the video and saw you do it."

I nodded again. Damn it, there was no talking my way out of this.

"That can never happen again. You got that?" he asked, finishing his beer. I nodded again. "Let me hear you say it."

"It will never happen again," I said, almost whispering it.

"Good. Okay, we are done here. Back to work you go," he said, standing up.

Mike 12

12:35 p.m.

I finished loading the Sullivans' hotel stuff into my truck. I was parked near a reception area at the back of the resort.

When I arrived, I grabbed a luggage cart from the lobby. I wasn't sure how much there was, but my memories of family vacations led me to believe they didn't travel light.

I felt a pang of regret about never taking my kids to a place like Zulu. Sadie was gone, but Mike Jr. would have loved it. Instead, I chose to walk away from him because I couldn't cope with my grief.

Weaving my way through the halls, I found an elevator, taking it to the third floor. Fighting a wobbly front wheel, I continued to push the cart until I found 311. There was a "Do Not Disturb" sign hanging on the doorknob, so hopefully housekeeping hadn't been in. I removed Brady's wristband from my pocket and scanned myself into the room, dragging the cart in behind me.

The smell of vomit was strong when I entered. It looked like a small tornado had swept through the room; they had left in such a hurry following Katie's horrible episode. Stuff was scattered throughout, including toiletries, wet towels, and wet swimsuits.

Brady had bought a box of white kitchen garbage bags, and I began filling them with dirty clothes. I took one of the used hotel towels from the bathroom floor, ran it under hot water, and did my best with the vomit stain.

A few shirts were hanging in the closet. I took them off the hangers and placed them in the duffel bags they were using for suitcases. I began loading the items onto the cart.

The balcony door was closed and locked. I opened it and walked out. There was no way someone would try to scale up there. However, a person renting an adjoining room could climb over onto the neighboring balcony. But it was summer, and the sun set late, so the opportunity for doing that without being seen while the Sullivans were out was very small. I left the balcony door open to let the room air out a little.

The shelf by the refrigerator had cereal, donuts, and other unrefrigerated food. I took one of the garbage bags and put everything from the shelf into it.

Opening the fridge, I took out the sealed items and put them in the bag. The only unsealed item was a carton of milk. I took it out and examined the exterior of the carton, finding nothing unusual. I opened it and smelled it. It had an odd odor that I couldn't identify; it smelled nothing like fresh milk.

I checked the date. It still had ten days before it expired.

I found a small glass by the sink and filled it halfway with the milk. Tampering with something that could be evidence made me uneasy, but the probability of this milk being examined by law enforcement was very small.

If we could establish that the milk had been poisoned, so what? How would they find who did it, fingerprint the box? Was an allergen a deadly weapon? *Could you reasonably prosecute for that?*

I had doubts. Maybe we should have involved the police. But if the evidence pointed toward Randy's crew, Brady's blackmail pictures could come into play. So, no police.

I examined the milk in the glass. There was a greasy film on top and the color was slightly darker than white milk was supposed to be. Brady needed to see this. I wanted to taste it, but what if it was actually poison and not just an allergen?

I smelled the glass again and detected something. It was a faint hint of peanuts. Dumping the glass out in the sink, I ran the faucet and rinsed it out. I sealed the milk carton and put it in the garbage bag.

I sat on the edge of one of the beds for a moment and breathed in deeply. So, someone was sent there to spike Katie's milk with peanut residue. Based on her extreme reaction and hospitalization, that was an assassination attempt. The stakes had been raised exponentially.

I put myself in Brady's shoes and tried to predict how I would react. Having lost a child to an illness that was no one's direct fault, I could empathize. *But Brady's situation was not fully relatable.*

When I lost Sadie, I was mad at God, the world, the army, the medical profession, and myself. I didn't have an actual perpetrator to reasonably lash out against, so I internalized everything and punished myself. If there had been someone to directly hold accountable, I would have focused my anguish hard in that direction.

The story would have likely ended with the death of the guilty party. I had never met Brady's daughter, but I felt my anger rising, like that was *my daughter* in the hospital.

I exited the room, taking the "Do Not Disturb" sign off and dropping it on the floor of the room before I left. Pushing the full cart out to the parking lot, I loaded everything into the back of my truck.

Ten minutes later, I pulled up to the hospital, parking in the same spot as before. I did not want to intrude on Brady's family again, but I had to give him the milk carton information. I decided to call him on my burner and see if he wanted to meet me out in the parking lot instead of having me come into the waiting room.

"Hey, it's me. I'm in the parking lot," I said.

"I'm up in Katie's room. Marcy is here, so I'm not able to come down anytime soon," he said. He sounded exhausted and stressed. His voice had a raspy quality to it.

"How is she?" I asked.

"Better. Marcy is considering transporting her to Cleveland, maybe sometime later today."

"Excellent. Okay, listen, I think I found the poison," I said. There was a pause.

"Go on," he said.

"I think some peanut residue was added to the milk carton in the fridge. It smelled odd. I poured a little into a glass, and there was a tiny bit of film at the surface. You know when you open a fresh jar of natural peanut butter, that oily liquid on top? It reminded me of that. I have the carton."

"She added the milk directly to her cereal, so it would have been hard to notice a strange residue or smell. But how could someone spike it? I bought the carton at Kroger yesterday; I opened it in the hotel room. No one else had access," Brady said.

"Given some of the tech stuff these guys have pulled off, I

don't think it would be beyond their capabilities to gain entry to your room. Either they stole an all-access card from an employee or burned their own. I checked the balcony, it was locked. But of course, an intruder could have locked it after the fact."

Brady paused for a moment. There were some voices in the background. He made a muffled reply to someone and then returned. "Okay. Do me a favor and take that carton back to your RV and refrigerate it. I don't know what we can do with it, there is nothing the police are going to do. There was a chain-of-custody breach with it being removed from the room. You didn't do anything wrong; if the carton was still sitting in the hotel fridge, I don't think I could involve the police. If it leads back to Randy's crew, then they bring out the pictures of me," he said.

"Yeah, I agree with all of that," I said.

"I gotta go, but let me ask you: are you carrying? Because you know you aren't safe. If they are going after kids, you are fair game," he said.

"Not on my person, but I brought a go-bag with a weapon," I said.

"Okay, good. I have something in the camper. I have a concealed-carry license but generally don't carry. Maybe I need to rethink it based on the current situation."

"Agreed. I'm heading to the campground; I will put the stuff I gathered from the hotel in my RV. Anything else?" I asked.

"Not that I can think of. Marcy will take Jason back if they transport Katie. I am not going with them. I was ripped apart by Marcy and her mother; the allergen exposure was totally blamed on me. Marcy is working to prevent me from seeing the kids. A temporary restraining order was mentioned."

"Sorry to hear that," was all I could think of to say.

"They don't think I'm being honest with the doctors. Like I reversed eight years of being extremely careful with Katie and arbitrarily decided to feed her a peanut butter sandwich or something. I'm going to take the doctor aside after we hang up and inform him of the peanut-residue exposure, in case that will make a difference with her treatment. Not sure how I message that. If Marcy hears, things will get really bad."

"Good luck with that. Keep me informed," I said.

"Will do. I just popped the locks on the Taurus with my fob from the window up here. If you could throw the clothing bags in the trunk, I would appreciate it. The rest I can pick up later."

We hung up. I transferred Brady's stuff to his car and headed toward the campground.

Brady 21

3:30 p.m.

I stood in the parking lot of the hospital and watched the ambulance pull out onto Milan Road. It was raining lightly.

Marcy was permitted to ride along inside the ambulance with Katie. Following behind it was my father-in-law's Equinox with Jason inside. Following behind Marty was Marcy's silver Chevy Traverse, driven by my mother-in-law. It was unusual to see Caroline driving, especially on a trip that was almost entirely on the busy turnpike, but she had volunteered rather than leaving the vehicle in the hospital parking lot. I was frozen out of participating at all. I turned and walked over to my rented Taurus.

It took a lot of effort to talk them out of returning to Cleveland. They would be heading west on the turnpike instead of east, heading to Toledo. Once there, they would check Katie in under a false name. Marcy was meeting a college friend there who would use her credit card to rent hotel rooms for Marcy and Jason and the in-laws. I insisted that they use cash for all other expenses, so Marty and I stopped at an ATM and had each withdrawn the five hundred dollars daily max.

It was miraculous that I was able to convince them to abide by my recommendations, given that I didn't provide a solid rationale for it. It was a combination of Katie's condition, my state of deep concern, and the good reputation of the hospital that eventually tilted them in favor of going to Toledo for a week. With an explanation from me to come later. *That would be tricky.*

That had been the darkest day of my life. *So far.* Every day since Mike handed me the wrinkled copies of my financial profile he found at the campground jumping pillow had been progressively darker. *Tomorrow didn't look any more promising.*

I headed east on Columbus Road toward the campground. About a mile into the drive, my burner phone rang.

"Yes, Mike," I said wearily.

"Where are you?" he asked flatly. His voice sounded odd;

there was a hollow quality to it.

"Just left the hospital, heading to the campground," I said. I was at the traffic light at the amusement park causeway and Columbus Road.

"I need you to meet me at the King's Inn Motel," he said. "Do you have your regular cell on you?"

"Wait, where are you?"

"Brady. Do you have your regular cell on you?" he repeated.

"No, it is still in the RV," I replied.

"Good. Room 251, King's Inn Motel. I'm on the north side of the building, the side facing away from the street," he said.

"Listen, I need to drop by my camper and ..."

"They torched my RV," he interrupted.

I pulled past the green light, taking a left into the parking lot of the Tropic Breeze waterpark, and found a spot to park. I didn't feel that I could multitask driving and talking at the moment. "Wait, what?" I asked.

"My RV is toast, a total loss. It was smoldering when I pulled up. Travis was there and in my face for leaving an unattended campfire; he showed me a picture someone took. There is no way that the fire escaped the pit and got to the RV, especially with it raining on and off. One of Randy's guys must have seen the opportunity to burn me out and took it," he said coolly.

I was impressed by the unemotional way he went about describing the disaster. "My God, you couldn't salvage anything?" I asked.

"Nope. Not that I owned a lot. Luckily a lot of my critical items were in my truck. Some cash, my bank books, and financial papers. I did have some cash stashed in the RV that went up in smoke, but not much. They found a quick way to get me out of the picture," he said.

"Damn. Okay, I'm on my way," I said.

"Are you still driving the rental?" he asked.

"Affirmative," I replied.

"Good," he said and hung up.

Mike 13

3:40 p.m.

I was peeking down at the parking lot through the heavy, dingy white polyester-blend curtains. The dusty window hadn't been washed in a while. There were only four cars in the lot.

The King's Inn was a motel about three miles west of the campground, off Columbus Road on the opposite side of the causeway. A series of cheap motels were built in the area in the 1950s and '60s, when the US culture was more enamored with motels.

Motels were associated with freedom and mobility back then, but over the past few decades, they seemed to be perceived as shady. A place to hole up and do drugs or entertain a hooker. Maybe commit serial killings during an interstate crime spree.

Were there any premium motel chains? None came to mind. Most were just cheap and sad. The King's Inn was a dilapidated dump, hardly a palace fit for a king, a faded dinosaur from a different era of Gravity Junction tourism.

The carpet was shabby, with worn patches everywhere. The walls had a yellowish hue from years of secondhand smoke. There was a small TV, an antique model with a deep picture tube, situated on top of a scratched-up bureau.

There were two double beds, separated by a nightstand with a digital alarm clock and a phone on it. The front window had a rectangular heating and cooling unit beneath it, where you could flip up a panel and select "hot/cool" and "fan: hi/lo." I had the air on, but it wasn't noticeably cooling the room.

I saw Brady's Taurus pull up and park along the back section of the lot. He got out, grabbed a white trash bag from the trunk, and walked toward the building. He scanned the motel doors for numbers as he crossed the parking lot, speed walking through the pouring rain.

Brady disappeared from my view at the west stairwell. A moment later, there was a knock at the door. I peered through the peephole and verified it was him. I unchained the door and opened it.

He nodded and stepped in, and I immediately relocked the door. He handed me the trash bag of the unspent money he borrowed.

"Thanks again. I will get you the rest when I have a moment to hit the ATM," he said.

"No rush. Need something to drink?" I asked.

He shrugged. "What do you have?" he asked.

I pointed to the fifth of Jim Beam on the dresser. He nodded. I unwrapped one of the clear plastic hotel cups, placing it on the edge of the scratched-up faux wood dresser. I opened the mini-fridge and took out the bowl of ice I filled at the vending area by the stairs. I put the cup down and motioned for him to make a drink.

"The milk carton is in here, if you want to take a look," I said.

"Thanks. I will check it out in a minute."

I sat on the bed in front of the TV, which was tuned to the news on a local station. My RV fire wasn't reported. There wasn't significant property destruction or loss of life, so it wasn't newsworthy.

Brady sat on the edge of the other bed, taking a sip of his drink. He looked haggard, wearing a wrinkled pair of black cargo shorts, a dry-fit gray "Akron Zips" T-shirt, and a pair of running shoes.

"So, how long before Randy finds you here?" Brady asked.

"I don't think he will anytime soon. The room was paid in cash. I don't have a GPS-enabled device. I checked my truck for a tracker and didn't find one," I said.

"I took the same measures, or at least similar measures, and he found me at Zulu," he said.

"You slipped up somewhere. Did you use a credit card at all?" I asked.

"Just to hold the room. Charges weren't supposed to hit until we checked out," he said.

"Did you check out yet?" I asked.

"No."

"When you do, take a look at the statement and see if something hit that card," I said.

I stood up and went over to the windows, parting the curtains slightly to look out. The rain continued to fall.

"Did you ever discuss your daughter's allergies at the campground?"

"I don't think so. We never trusted anything they served at the campground snack bar, so I don't think we would have discussed it," he said, shaking his head.

"Randy must have been tapping your communications and discovered you have a kid with nut allergies. Something gave you away yesterday, and they found you at the waterpark. He had his tech guy find your room number at the hotel, obtain access to the key system, and sent a guy over to poison the milk. Meanwhile, he torched my RV in broad daylight. Nobody saw anything. Pretty productive day for Randy and his crew, I would say," I said, taking a drink of bourbon.

"Randy plays chess while we play checkers. Actually, while we play nothing, we just trade opinions and jerk off. He has been two or three steps ahead of us. That is sad, given our military backgrounds. Shouldn't we be dropping some *Art of War* types of tactics on them in this conflict?" he asked.

"In our defense, this has been a series of ambushes over a few days. Do you expect an all-out attack while convalescing at some Podunk campground? You should be focusing on getting a margarita buzz and making s'mores with your kids around a campfire, not defending yourself from getting roofied, blackmailed with a dead hooker, or your kid poisoned. This was Pearl Harbor. We've taken some huge hits; now we need to pivot and hit back. Hit back immediately and hit back hard," I said, taking a drink.

The TV played a commercial for the General Motors dealership located east of the campground. I started to make another drink but opted for a glass of water instead.

"This all revolves around tech. The background checks, the surveillance, the tracking, the hacking into hotels, the collection of info from phones. He has a dedicated tech staff. None of those clowns like Chuck, Sam, or Viktor could program the clocks on their microwaves, let alone pull off some of this sophisticated shit," Brady said.

"So, we need to isolate and question one of them. Who is the weak link?" I asked.

"I think it would be Chris, but Chris doesn't appear to be an insider. I think he was getting blackmailed along with me. That free night at the cabin courtesy of Chuck makes zero sense. They probably pulled him in, got a Romanian girl involved, and are blackmailing him too," Brady said, taking another drink. He was staring blankly at the TV broadcast of a lottery show, where a blonde model was pulling numbered ping-pong balls out of a draw machine.

"So, Chris may be a waste of time. I'm thinking either Chuck or Viktor," I said.

"So, pick one," he said.

"I'm thinking Chuck. He seems more pliable. Some of those Eastern European guys have a high pain tolerance. We would pick up guys when I was in Kosovo, and they took a lot of work to get any useful intel. Most of the quality intel came from bribes, not interrogations," I said.

"Okay, that is a starting point," he said. He finished his drink and set the cup down on the dresser.

"Infiltration is easy. You live there. Chuck putts around on his golf cart after dark, ordinarily in an impaired state. There are all kinds of places to have an in-depth conversation with him. The woods are nearby. Lake Erie is nearby. We could find out if Chuck floats or sinks," I said, smiling.

I got up and walked over to the nightstand. There was a pen and a small pad of paper there. I opened the drawer and took out the Gideon Bible. I sat back against the headboard, put the pad on top of the bible, uncapped the pen, and started writing. "First thing we need to do is make a supply run," I said.

"Are we doing this tonight?" Brady asked with a look of concern.

"Yeah. Do you feel comfortable sleeping at the campground tonight after your daughter was poisoned and my RV was torched? We can't afford to wait another minute; the next escalation is going to result in either one of us or someone in your family in a body bag."

Mike 14

8:20 p.m.

Getting on site unnoticed was a piece of cake. I took my campground parking pass out of my truck and put it in the rental van's front window in the lower-left-hand corner. I rented the van for ninety-five dollars cash at the same place that we rented Brady's Taurus. It was a large, white Chevy Express van with over 150,000 miles on it, and it had seen better days. I don't think I would have trusted it for a voyage outside of the county. I verified before I left the lot that the thirty-one-gallon tank was filled to capacity.

I drove slowly down Nickle until I was almost perpendicular to the entrance. I rolled down the passenger window, leaning over and gazing carefully at the security booth. It appeared empty.

I had planned a few different ways to get on site if the security booth was manned, but it appeared as though I could just drive right in unnoticed. I turned into the entrance, with my black baseball hat pulled down low as I approached the booth. The falling rain would also help obscure my identity if anyone was out. As one of the few black guys camping there (or formerly camping there), my presence would be memorable. But I didn't see anyone out.

I was completely dressed in black. I bought some water-repellent gear, including the baseball hat, running pants, running jacket, and Gore-Tex hiking boots. It went against my military training to break in brand-new gear on a mission, but with my entire wardrobe going up in smoke when my RV was burned to the ground, I had no choice.

I drove down Seagull Drive, scanning the grounds, squinting as the windshield wipers kept clearing the light rain. I made my way to the back along the tent lots and found a series of empty campsites. I parked the rental in front of one.

It took some restraint not to drive by my charred RV, which Travis said would be towed to the southeast side of the grounds along the stockade fence by the dealership. The police had created an incident report that I needed to get a copy of. I had no idea what Travis told them. If I was found to be negligent, it could be a problem with the insurance company.

Travis threatened to charge me with the cost of covering the fire damage to the site utilities. Fat fucking chance. I would sit in jail before I reimbursed him for the damage caused by Randy's crew torching my property. Not that I figured Travis did it directly, but he was turning a blind eye to criminal activity in his own backyard.

I used the burner phone to call the campground office and reported a water leak at the east shower house. I was betting Chuck would respond, but if it was someone else, I could adapt. Whether Chuck, the Mexican kid, or the tech guy responded didn't matter to me. I was eager to ruin the night of the unlucky son of a bitch who showed up.

I got out and closed the door softly. Opening the left-rear door, I grunted as I lifted my large, black duffel bag. I slung the carrying strap over my shoulder and walked over to the east shower house. The steadily falling rain was illuminated by the streetlamp directly west of the building.

I entered the building through the squeaky screen door on the right. The door to the left was to the ladies' facilities. Unlike the main shower house, there was only one entrance for each bathroom.

I passed the urinals and the bathroom stalls, stopping at the first of three shower stalls. The flooring was grimy, salmon-colored ceramic tiles. The bathroom stalls had a one-foot gap at the bottom where you could see underneath, but the shower stalls extended to the floor.

The openings to the shower stalls were covered by thick, gray plastic curtains. Each had a small changing room with a wooden bench, separated from the shower area by another gray plastic curtain. I put my bag on the floor of the stall's changing area.

Digging into the bag, I took out a large pair of channel locks. I went to the sink nearest to the door and clamped the wrench on the pipe elbow beneath it, twisting it counterclockwise until water began to run onto the floor. I gave it a soft turn to the right, and the steady stream became a trickle.

I returned the channel locks to the bag, taking out a plastic "Out of Order" sign. I found the small container of putty, broke off a few pieces, rolled them into tiny balls, and placed them on the corners of the sign.

Since the weather was warm, the heavier storm door was propped open, touching the interior wall. I centered the sign at eye level and pressed it against the door. No one entering the building would see the sign while the door was propped open.

I peered through the screen door. A person was walking up the street toward the building, a Hispanic teenager wearing red gym shorts and a plain white T-shirt underneath a clear plastic poncho. I ducked back inside and went into the shower stall, sliding the curtain shut. I listened as the kid took a piss, flushed, and walked out. I waited a moment and then exited the stall, returning to the screen door to monitor the street.

Five minutes later, I saw the headlights of a golf cart moving alongside the playground, taking a left onto Dove. *It had to be Chuck.* I returned to the shower stall and slid the curtain shut.

Chuck 9

8:40 p.m.

The light rain was keepin' most folks in their campers, or at least under their camper awnings. I was on until 6 a.m., so I was doin' my usual circuit. I was almost to the shower house goin' north on Starling when a dark Ford van with a taxi sign on top passed slowly by, tryin' to go softly over the speed bump. It was too dark to see who was inside.

It passed me and then swung over to the right in front of site 31. The passenger door opened, and Sullivan got out. He went around to the back of the van. A guy who looked Indian got out and met him there. Not Indian as in *cowboys and Indians*, but an India Indian. Curry and goats Indian.

He opened the back doors and handed Sullivan several gym bags. Sullivan brought them inside his camper. He came back and got another gym bag and a few garbage bags. Sullivan handed the Indian some cash, and he left.

I pulled up slowly alongside site 31, but Sullivan was already inside his camper with the door closed. I sent a text to Randy and Sam letting them know Sullivan was back and then continued up Starling.

I intended to slow down on the booze during my shift, but it was a little chillier than normal and rainin', so I needed a belly warmer. I texted Viktor to make me a drink and leave it on his deck table. That meant Viktor would pour cheap, warm vodka in a plastic cup. But beggars couldn't be choosers.

I did a big loop of the park and passed by Viktor's. I pulled to the side and walked up to his camper. There was a red cup on his table. I took it and hustled back to my golf cart to get out of the rain. What passed for "hustled" with me, anyways.

I smelled the cup, and it was pure vodka, four or five shots. *Attaboy.* I took a deep drink. Cheap vodka mixed with just a splash of acid rain from above. He didn't disappoint. Maybe Viktor wasn't so bad after all.

I wished I had a cabin to hide out in, but there was none available. Tourists and Johns. Business was good for everyone. I figured I needed a bigger cut for keepin' this racket runnin' so smoothly.

"Hey Chuck, you there?" the walkie-talkie squawked, joltin' me. I had been rollin' alongside the cabins backin' up to Nickle, just sort of daydreamin'. Or evenin' dreamin', I guess.

"Chuck here, over," I said into the walkie-talkie.

"Patrick here. Got a call about a water leak in the far shower house," he said.

Dammit. "A call? Nobody came in and reported it?" I asked.

"Nope, a phone call to the office. You got it?" he asked.

"I guess. What is your twenty?"

"In the office," he said. Of course, he was, schmoozing with the desk girls. On light duty with broken ribs, fuckin' Sam. He ought to be out in the rain fixin' the leak.

But bein' responsible for the leak was partly my fault. I took Travis aside earlier and told him I should be doin' more of the skilled work and less of the trash pickup shit. Plumbing was skilled work, so it was gonna be me. *Shot myself in the foot there.*

"Go in the back room and get the toolbox. Also, grab me a Hawaiian Punch from the vending machine. I'll pay you back. Bring the stuff out front. I'm comin' by now," I said.

"Roger," he said.

I pulled up, and he set the toolbox in the back and gave me my drink. I mixed the Hawaiian Punch with the vodka and had a much tastier cocktail.

Fifteen minutes later, I pulled up and parked in front of the shower house and got out, grabbin' the toolbox from the back seat. It was heavy, and I felt my body leanin' to the right as I walked up to the screen door.

I turned around and squinted to take another look at the white van I passed on the way over. It was parked in front of an empty tent lot. That was odd because nobody was rentin' those. It did have a campground hangtag in the window, but why park there? It was away from everything. After fixin' the leak, I would have to go take a closer look.

Nobody was in the shower house, which was good. I saw the

leakin' sink as soon as I went in. Should be an easy fix.

I set the toolbox down. I lit a cigarette, opened the box, and got out a set of channel locks. I thought about goin' out to get my drink from the golf cart but figured I wouldn't be there long. Bendin' over, I clamped the wrench on the pipe. I slowly started pullin' clockwise, tightenin' it.

Suddenly, something slammed underneath my chin from behind. My head was jerked back, liftin' me to my feet, and then my feet were off the floor. I started to gag. I couldn't breathe. My wrench fell and clanged on the floor loudly. The cigarette dropped from my mouth. I tried to claw at the arm around my neck. A pain shot through my left shoulder.

I looked up at the mirror above the sink and saw it was Clemmons behind me. *That black son of a bitch.* He was snarling with the effort, his face shiny with sweat, leanin' back, pullin' on my neck tighter and tighter.

I was seein' stars. My throat was gurgling as I tried to yell out. The room was goin' black.

Mike 15

9:00 p.m.

I was gasping for air as I lowered Chuck's dead weight to the ground. Dude was heavier and feistier than I expected. I was glad he dropped that wrench; it could have been a problem if he would have swung that back at me.

His neck was pretty damned fat. I was starting to doubt if I had the strength to squeeze his jugular. I walked quickly over and shut the storm door, bolting it.

I rolled Chuck to his side, putting him in the rescue position. He was out cold, breathing heavily, a thick, wet sound. He coughed a few times and moaned. Chuck's lit cigarette had landed on a dry spot on the floor, and I stomped it out.

I reached into my pocket and took out a black zip tie. Rolling him on his stomach, I fastened his hands together tightly, like I had done dozens of times to prisoners when I was deployed. I never had one of those prisoners break free from a botched handcuffing, and this fucking guy was not going to be the first.

After I double-checked his wrists, I rolled him on his side. His clothes were soaked from sweat and the water puddles on the floor.

I went over to the front window and looked out. It was dark and quiet, with a light rain still falling.

I examined Chuck closely, lowering down to listen to his breathing. The strong smell of vodka and cigarettes on his breath made me wince. His breathing was deep, as though he was just taking a power nap. I decided to wait on the gag.

Frisking him, I found two cell phones, a wallet, a pack of cigarettes, a small baggy of what appeared to be marijuana, a lighter, and a pocketknife. I assumed Chuck left his golf cart key in the ignition. I peeked outside again and unlocked the door.

It was steadily drizzling as I walked over to his cart. The key was in the ignition on a ring with several other keys. I retrieved my bag and threw it into the back of the golf cart. I put Chuck's channel locks in his toolbox and loaded it in the cart.

After checking my surroundings one more time, I dragged Chuck out by putting my hands under his armpits and pulling him backward. It wasn't too difficult on the wet tile floor, but more of an effort on the cement.

With a grunt, I managed a fireman's-carry lift and plopped him in the passenger seat. I put his seatbelt on, which was a lap belt without a shoulder harness, and leaned him toward the center.

I went back to the shower house and removed the sign, putting it in my bag. I started the golf cart and put it in reverse, backing out. Shifting it to forward, I rode alongside the shower house, driving across the wet grass until I found the dirt trail. Luckily the trail wasn't too saturated with water from the rain, and I was able to maneuver okay.

I didn't use the headlights. The streetlights beside the shower house and the basketball courts were enough to light the path. I followed the trail up until it veered west and went along the swampy coast area.

Data 8

9:10 p.m.

My stomach dropped as I ended the call. Sam told me to meet Sullivan at his camper and start documenting his government datasets. Since it was after hours, we wouldn't log into his work systems, but I could start mapping out the architectures and look at some of the existing data extracts that he saved. So, I was progressing toward something that looked awfully similar to treason.

I asked Patrick to cover the security booth, and he didn't complain, which was surprising. I never understood why anyone complained about sitting idly in a booth. Chuck had been called to fix a water leak at the east shower house, so it was on Patrick to cover security.

I winced when I imagined Chuck trying to repair a complex plumbing issue. My guess was he was making it worse. Maybe he got trapped inside the shower house and drowned after it flooded. *That would be tragic.*

I put on my Sandusky Shores yellow poncho in case it started raining harder. I went outside and got into one of the yellow work carts, sweeping the puddle of rain from the seat with the edge of my hand. It was a short walk over to Brady's RV, but it was drizzling and made more sense to drive.

The rain suppressed most activity across the campground. I was riding through a ghost town. My walkie-talkie crackled, and a voice came across.

"Data. You there, Data?"

"Roger, is that you, Chuck?" I asked. There was a long pause as I pulled up to the west shower house, a few lots down from Sullivan's. I guided it under the narrow awning, which partially shielded the work cart from the rain.

"Yeah ... listen, I need you to meet me up at the east shower house. I ... I ... need a hand," he said, sounding raspy and labored. I couldn't tell if it was a bad signal or he was having some sort of medical episode.

"No can do. I have been ordered elsewhere by management," I said.

There was another long pause. The radio crackled again. "I ...
I will explain to management that you were delayed by me, it ... it
will be okay," he said.

I sighed. As I figured, Chuck had probably screwed things up
and was in deep trouble with that leak. I had no plumbing expertise
whatsoever, but I was sure it was a common-sense issue and there
was something I could do to help. We needed to get a plumber involved if it was getting worse, but that would be Chuck's call. At
worst, we could shut off the building's water main and close it overnight; the west shower house and the main office facilities were
still functioning. I started the work cart and headed up Starling,
driving past Sullivan's camper.

Brady 22

9:20 p.m.

Peering out the small bedroom window of my RV, I saw the yellow work cart drive past my lot. It was difficult to see who was on it, but it had to be the guy who I was supposed to brief on my government technology assets.

The little fat guy with glasses. That was who Sam told me to look for. I recalled a man fitting that description riding around in a work cart, picking up trash. We had never had a conversation, just exchanging nods when we crossed paths.

I hit redial on the burner phone. A second later, Mike answered.

"The IT guy is heading your way, from what I can gather," I said, closing the blinds.

"Good. In five minutes, get your rain gear on. Cut through your back yard to Sparrow. Walk up to the trail and follow it about thirty meters. Chuck's golf cart is about halfway down, south of the path. Chuck is hogtied and gagged in the back. I'm going to have this Data guy join him, and all four of us can have a chat."

"Roger all that," I said and hung up. I went back into the bedroom and put on a pair of black running sweats and dry-fit socks. I opened the closet and pulled out my biometric safe. Swiping my right pointer finger a few times on the fingerprint sensor, it activated with a click, and the compression gas strut popped the door slowly open.

I took out the Glock, slapped a full clip in, and put the other full clip in my pocket. I removed the holster and placed it on the bed.

Digging in a drawer, I found my black leather work belt. I put it around my waist, slid the holster on, and tightened the belt around my hips. I put the gun in the holster.

I was still surprised that Randy hadn't taken the gun safe. I think they were so concerned about getting their hooks in my IT stuff that they overlooked it. Even though I was army, I didn't come across as a weapons guy. They had underestimated me over and over, with good reason, but maybe overlooking my gun was going to cost them.

I put on a long-sleeve blue running shirt, a black Columbus Blue Jackets windbreaker, and a dark-blue Cleveland Indians baseball hat. I didn't have any waterproof footgear, so my gray running shoes would have to do.

I exited through the exterior bathroom door at the back of the camper, locking it behind me. I figured if I used the back door, then maybe I was less likely to be surveilled from Starling.

I cut through Chris's lot and went north on Sparrow. Passing Mike's old site, only scorch marks on the cement and grass remained to suggest that he had ever camped there. I continued past the dumpster up to the trail. With the steady drizzle, no one was outside, so there was almost no risk of being seen.

It was very dark within the woods, especially with the cloud cover blocking the moonlight. A flashlight would have been helpful, but it would have given away my position.

I saw Chuck's golf cart off to the side and walked cautiously toward it. The figure of Chuck appeared in the back seat as I drew closer, and my eyes continued to adjust to the darkness. I walked alongside the golf cart.

He didn't react when I walked up. Chuck's face was very pale, a contrast to its usual ruddiness. His hands were behind his back, and I assumed they were bound. I could see the metal buckle of the seatbelt over his large belly, holding him in.

He was leaning back against the seat awkwardly, with his long hair hanging down into his face, wet and stringy from the rain. The baseball cap he always wore was lying on the floorboard. He was completely motionless.

Glancing east down the trail, I saw two figures walking in the distance. I moved to the side to conceal myself in the trees beside the trail.

The person in front was short and heavy, wearing a big yellow poncho. The guy that Sam called "Data" when he informed me that I was to meet with him tonight. *So he could steal my classified government information.*

Mike was behind him, marching him up the trail. He appeared to be going willingly; there was no apparent resistance.

As they got closer, I could see that the tech guy was wearing glasses and a yellow hat. His mouth was gagged with a black bandanna.

Mike walked him over, guiding him into the back seat of the golf cart beside Chuck. He cooperated, scooting in and sitting up straight. He bent over a little awkwardly to accommodate his bound hands behind his back. Chuck moved slightly with the tilting of the cart, almost a reflexive adjusting of his position. He continued to stare down at his feet.

"This is Henry, the data guy," Mike said to me in a voice slightly louder than a whisper.

"I have seen him around. He is one of the less-talkative ones. I don't think we've met," I said.

"Well, we are going to get to know Mr. Henry Data. He is going to become a lot more talkative. Any of you guys ever hear of the Army Long Range Surveillance Leaders Course? I would expect not. Among the various skills I learned was enhanced interrogation. For you civilians, 'enhanced interrogation' is a politically correct way to describe 'torture.'"

Mike's demeanor had changed completely. People always claim "I don't see colors" racially, which was bullshit, unless you had some medical condition with your eyesight. But in Mike's case, that had been close to true. Culturally, he didn't act or speak any differently than any of the white guys I hung out with. He spoke with a bit of a twang, but I attributed that to his southern roots.

His eyes were wide and burning, with the water dripping down from his hat and face giving him an unhinged look. He was in full-on angry drill sergeant mode, similar to his demeanor with Sam in the Mexican place, but without the need to be subdued in a busy restaurant. Not just drill sergeant mode, but *black drill sergeant mode*.

I had a black drill in basic training, and it was terrifying when he was in my face and focusing his full attention on me. Especially if you were a sheltered white guy from the suburbs, like I was, and like I assumed Data was.

Chuck was still motionless. Data looked at him a few times, trying to make eye contact, but Chuck didn't move. Data shifted from side to side, trying to relieve the discomfort of having his hands bound behind him, and then sat still. The rain picked up a little, beating down through the leaves above.

"Then I spent some time in the desert, and I got to practically apply my enhanced interrogation skills. On people much harder and more committed than you sorry sacks. By the time I was finished with them, they always spilled their guts. They gave me every bit of intel that I demanded. So, I'm going to pose a series of questions and give you the chance to give me truthful answers. If you refuse to answer or you lie to me, I'm going to introduce you to a level of pain that you've never felt before in your miserable lives."

Mike grabbed his gym bag from the floor of the front seat and put it on the seat. He unzipped it.

"These woods, that swamp over there, and the items in this bag provide a lot of options to persuade you to spill your guts. If you are smart, that is exactly what you'll do right out of the gate here in the comfort of this golf cart. Can I get a word, Brady?"

I nodded. Mike took a step closer to Data and leaned close to him.

"No talking while I'm gone. Not a sound. I'm not going far."

We walked about twenty yards east. We could partially see the basketball courts and the shower house through the trees.

"Chuck is dead," he said softly. My head jerked.

"What the fuck," was all I could manage.

"I guess the stress of my extraction from the shower house was too much. I got him up here and he was able to have a scripted walkie-talkie chat with Data to lure him over to the shower house. But he expired right before I went down to collect Data. There was nothing I could do to help him; he was already gone."

I frowned. Suddenly he grabbed hold of my windbreaker below the collar and pulled me closer to him.

"Don't get emotional on me, Brady. You like getting drugged? You like having your picture taken with dead hookers? You like having your daughter poisoned? Do you think I like having what little I own in this world incinerated in an arson job? God knows what else they are doing to other people around here," he hissed.

I stared down at my shoes as the rain was dripping down from my baseball hat brim. Then I nodded.

"Got it. I'm good, I will follow your lead," I said.

"Chuck's death was unexpected, but we can also use it to our advantage."

Mike walked over to Henry and pulled off his gag. He coughed and wheezed, then spit to the side, breathing heavily. Mike pulled a hunting knife out of a sheath on his side.

"You are in neck-deep with this crooked little squad here that is all about attacking children, burning down RVs, and trying to force patriots like Brady here into committing treason. If you make any noise, I won't think twice about gutting you. And I won't lose a minute's sleep over it. Do you understand that?" he asked. Data nodded vigorously.

"You may have noticed ole Chuck here has been exceptionally quiet. I bet that is the longest he has kept his mouth shut since you've known him, right?" Mike asked. Data nodded, almost robotically, water dripping from the edges of his glasses.

"Chuck didn't fare too well under interrogation. I'm sure his loved ones will be mourning the loss of this pillar of the community for years. I'm guessing you won't miss him much. I'm thinking that working with him was a continuous pain in the ass," he said.

Data jerked his head over and looked at Chuck, with his body drooped back against his seat. His facial expression was one of shock, rather than anger or sadness.

"You are younger and probably more resilient than Chuck, although like Chuck, you are in no danger of succumbing to anorexia. We need a lot of answers in a very short amount of time. I'm just holding this knife here to the side as a reminder. I'm a country boy; I've gutted deer and all kinds of critters growing up in Georgia. I know my way with a knife around skin, muscle, and bone," Mike said, laying down his southern drawl a little heavier.

"We can start with your full name," Mike said. Data's glasses were beaded with water, and a layer of steam was making it difficult to see his eyes.

"H-Henry Hallux," he said softly.

"Good. Now I want you to give me a summary of where you are from, what you are doing here, and how you came to be employed as a criminal here at this campground. Not your entire life story, give me the *Reader's Digest* version," Mike said.

I doubted the reference meant anything to a guy his age, but Henry began talking.

Chris 8

9:50 p.m.

I was sitting at the kitchen table in my RV, staring down at my airport ID card. It had my information and picture (with my fancy new haircut) on the front and a barcode on the back. It was laminated and fastened to a blue lanyard. It was an all-access pass to the airport, categorizing me as a pilot.

Just like that, with the snap of Randy's fingers, I was in. It made no sense; nothing moved that fast in the world of aviation. Unless Randy had this scheme cooking for a while.

It appeared that my checkered slate in the aviation business was wiped clean. Not that it was that sullied before. I was dead to the air-traffic control world, but not necessarily private aviation.

Candy was thrilled. Okay, not visibly excited at all, but she was nice to me for the first time since the jumping pillow incident. Maybe not quite "nice," but she gave me something resembling a smile.

It was wonderful to be fully welcome back inside my own RV again. Especially since it was raining. Candy was sleeping in the back, and I was sitting at the kitchen table in the dark drinking a beer, my mind racing. The adage about things being "too good to be true" kept infringing upon my mood.

I wanted to smoke a joint to slow down my thinking but knew it was a bad idea. I needed to stick to a reasonable amount of social drinking and show up to the airport tomorrow level-headed.

There was a soft knock at the door. So soft that I thought it was some random outdoor noise at first. Then another knock. I was just wearing a pair of gray Adidas gym shorts and socks, so I stood up, went toward the bathroom, and picked up a black Toledo Mud Hens T-shirt that was balled up on the floor. I put it on and went to the front door, unlocking it and opening it just a crack.

It was Brady. He was wearing a black windbreaker and a blue cap. He looked waterlogged, like he may have been out in the rain for a while.

"Hey man, I'm in for the night, can we talk tomorrow?" I whispered. Brady motioned for me to come out.

"I need your help. Get a windbreaker and your car keys," he said in a low voice.

I sighed. I stepped out on the metal stairs and closed the door quietly behind me.

"It's Candy's car, and she is sleeping. I have work early tomorrow. Now is a bad time," I said.

He stepped closer. "I really need your help. It should only take an hour," he said softly.

"Brady ... no, I ..."

Suddenly he grabbed me by the shirt and pulled me closer, making me stumble down the stairs onto the wet grass. He leaned in until the bill of his cap touched my forehead. "Listen, Chris. I really, *really* need your help," he almost growled.

"Dude, I trust you, you can borrow her car, maybe put a few dollars of gas in it," I said.

"I need you and the car. One hour. You are involved in something. They have dirt on you," he whispered.

"They? What are you talking about?"

"Randy and his crew. That free night in the cabin. There was more to it than just Chuck's kindness," he whispered.

I frowned. "Dude, I'm not ..." I started to say, but he interrupted me.

"Listen, there are cameras in those cabins. They have you on tape. Do you want to stand out here and have a convo about video cameras and hookers while your girlfriend is in earshot?" he asked, raising his voice a little.

"Okay, okay ... give me five minutes," I whispered, exhaling slowly.

"Bring the keys to your construction trailer."

Mike 16

10:10 p.m.

I figured the complacency of the campground workers would work in our favor, as well as the weather. If I kept Data replying to radio calls and returning texts, there was a good chance no one would miss Chuck or Henry for a few hours.

The only other worker on site was Patrick, the Mexican guy. He didn't strike me as a go-getter. I pictured him hiding out in the office, security booth, or one of the cabins all evening. Chuck was the guy who liked to patrol, so with him out, maybe no one would be out creeping around until morning.

We needed to get all of the players to gather in Randy's RV. Create an urgent situation they would all respond to. They needed to be there no later than 0100 hours.

They called it the Taj, which had to be some sort of inside joke. It had appeared unoccupied earlier. We weren't lucky enough for them to all be on site at the RV for a prearranged get-together.

It hadn't taken me long to get the name of the guy who poisoned Brady's kid from Data. Alexander. A Romanian, like Viktor and the dead prostitute. He was one of Randy's fixer guys, and he would definitely have to be at the party as well.

This was an all-in game of high-stakes poker for Brady and me. If we didn't resolve this by morning, the retaliation would be swift and harsh. Our element of surprise had a narrow window, and we had to execute.

I was leaning against the golf cart when the burner phone buzzed in my pocket. Henry was still bound and sitting still in the back seat. Chuck was still slumped forward. I took the vibrating burner phone out and saw Brady's burner phone number on the display.

"Go ahead," I said. "Yeah, there are no hooks for the chains on site here. Have Chris get hooks from the construction site. Yeah, there should be crane hooks. Get four. And get at least ten two-by-fours, all around four feet long. He should be able to find a saw there and cut them. There was a handsaw in Chuck's toolbox, but I would rather not be sawing wood out here tonight. Also, we need a crowbar. I'm going to continue chatting with Data. You want to hold on?"

I walked over to the passenger side, putting the phone on speaker. I held it in front of Data.

He looked like a drowned rat. A sad, scared, fat drowned rat. He gave me a look of anger, then realized it was a bad idea and softened it.

"Tell us about the chains at the campground here. Brady mentioned that they were delivered the other day," I said.

"A couple hundred feet of chain, industrial grade. They were originally used for nautical purposes by the Coast Guard. Travis bought them and has them on a flatbed trailer. He is going to run a decorative fence along the east coastline. We sank a few poles, but that's about it," he said.

I switched the phone off speaker and put it to my ear.

"Anything else? Get back here ASAP so I can recon the chains. No, there has been no walkie-talkie traffic. Nobody is missing these clowns yet. Okay, out."

Brady 23

10:15 p.m.

"**H**ooks. Crane hooks. You guys have big hooks at the site, right?" I asked.

Chris nodded. We were driving along Columbus Road toward the construction site. There was barely any traffic out on the road.

Chris was wearing a pair of dark-gray shorts and a black, short-sleeve White Zombie concert T-shirt under a clear poncho. That was as close as he could come to decking himself out in black. He was wearing a blue Adidas baseball cap and his small spectacles.

"Yeah, but I can't steal those. I will get fired," he said.

He looked tired and stressed. It was hard to get used to his new, clean-cut look. He lit a cigarette, and I decided not to object, since it wasn't my car. I cracked the window a few inches and endured some of the drizzle coming in to get some fresh air.

"We aren't stealing them. We can return them before anyone misses them," I said, knowing that was a lie. If it all worked out according to Mike's plan, collecting those hooks later would be the last thing on our minds.

"You guys are going to get me in hot water with Randy and Sam. I need you to start talking about the cameras at the cabins," he said quietly.

"Some of those cabins at the campground are wired for video. They took videos of you the night you got a courtesy cabin from Chuck. They bring in these foreign-exchange girls here for the summer working at Gravity Junction, and they use them as prostitutes."

I thought he was going to drive off the road. He veered a little onto the outer white line, then straightened.

"I wasn't with any prostitute," he said angrily.

"Neither was I. Sam drugged me at the bowling alley, took me to a cabin while I was in a stupor, and videotaped me in a compromising position with a woman. They pulled stills that made it look like we were having sex. Data acknowledged that he was involved in setting me up, and he mentioned your name too," I said.

Chris 9

10:30 p.m.

My mind reeled. They took blackmail pictures of me? That made no sense. I had never given them any problems. They asked me to work with them, and I agreed.

Brady placed the last of the metal hooks in my trunk. They had a D-ring clamp at the bottom to fasten to a cable or chain.

"They showed you your pictures?" I asked.

"Yes. I was drugged and don't remember them being taken," he said. I cringed at the memory of waking up hungover in that cabin with a long period of my memory lost in a blackout.

"Which cabin?" I asked.

"Think it was D," he replied. Same cabin.

"Well, if they have pics of me, they haven't shown them to me," I said.

"They probably haven't needed them yet. What have they asked you to do for them?" he asked.

"Not much. I have an aviation background, so they hooked me up with a pilot at Griffing Airport," I said.

"For what purpose?" he asked.

"I don't really know," I admitted, embarrassed.

"I hate to state the obvious, but that is something you may want to find out. These people are criminals; you have to know that. If they are having you transport cargo, it isn't going to be toys for orphans or boxes of puppies. The cargo will likely be drugs. Or worse," he said.

"You said they took pics of you multiple times," I said.

He frowned. "The second incident was a lot worse, believe it or not. I don't think you want to know the details," he said.

I closed the trunk. We got into the car, and I backed out.

Patrick 3

11:05 p.m.

My cell phone playlist needed a refresh. Music was all I had to get me through the boredom of those night shifts. Music and alcohol. Sometimes weed.

Chuck had told me to watch for Sullivan or Clemmons coming or going. So, I spent more time in the security booth than I normally would. I hadn't seen him or anyone else outside. A rainy night at a campground was pretty quiet.

I thought about checking in with Chuck, but why bother? My ribs were killing me; just breathing was painful. Chuck didn't care. If I showed up to check on him, he would pawn the job off on me, broken ribs or not. With any luck, that plumbing issue would keep him out for a while.

I heard a loud muffler and then saw a set of headlights coming up Nickle Drive, turning into the campground. I stood up and leaned against the booth window. As it got closer, I saw it was Chris in his beat-up Pontiac. It was weird seeing him drive; usually his girlfriend was behind the wheel.

"Hey, Chris," I said as he stopped.

"Hey, Patrick," he said, looking up at me and then in his rearview mirror. He looked back at me, nodded, and drove slowly across the speedbump.

Mike 17

11:15 p.m.

Data received a text that had me concerned. Someone was checking on him.

"Who is this text from?" I asked.

Data looked at the screen. "Sam."

"How long were you supposed to meet with Brady?" I asked. Data didn't look up, shrugging. "That ain't specific enough, how long?"

Data had grown despondent. He appeared to be sleeping, his head bowed low, making it appear as though he had a few more chins.

I had removed Chuck from the golf cart and dragged his body five feet to the south, so he was not visible from the trail. Chris could not discover he was dead; the fewer people who knew, the better.

Data had looked on in horror as I unfastened Chuck and he leaned over, spilling from the golf cart with a sick, wet thud. Once I had removed him from his sight, Data seemed to be less agitated.

I glanced at my watch. 2320 hours. It was reasonable that Data and Brady were still meeting together in his RV. Randy and Sam were not on the premises, as far as I knew. Viktor was across the street and could be sent over to check, which was a risk.

"What is an appropriate response to this text?" I asked.

"A couple of words. Maybe 'still meeting.' I'm not wordy," he said.

I entered the message and sent it. There was no response.

My burner phone lit up. I looked down and saw a text from Brady. They were back at the campground. Looping in Chris to this mission was a risk, but his access to the construction site and his girlfriend's piece-of-shit car were critical to the operation. I was hoping Brady had compelled him to cooperate and Randy didn't have his hooks too deep into him.

Walking east about five yards, I gazed down the trail, keeping

Data in my peripheral vision. I didn't think he had the stones to pull something, but I didn't feel comfortable losing sight of him.

Two shadows appeared from the east, walking toward me. I backed up a step to lean against a nearby tree. I recognized Brady and Chris and moved back out onto the trail.

"Anyone see you coming or going?" I whispered.

Brady shook his head. "On the way out, no one was in the booth. On the way back in, the security guy only saw Chris, I crouched down on the back floorboards, buried in the pile of his fast-food wrappers and empty pop bottles. That damn car is loud as hell, but I don't think any of Randy's guys except Viktor are on site. His motorcycle is out front under a plastic cover. We transferred everything to the work cart in front of the east shower house," he said.

I nodded and turned to Chris. "Thanks for the help, Chris. Are you able to help us out for a bit longer?" I asked.

He didn't respond, looking nervously at Data. "I don't have anything against this guy or any of Randy's guys," he said. I motioned for him to follow me and walked over beside the cart.

"Where is Chuck? He isn't one to loan his wheels out," Chris said.

I ignored him. "Henry, you want to explain some of the stuff you guys have on Chris here?" I asked.

He looked at me blankly for a moment before he started talking. I saw the lights and heard the train horn, feeling a slight rumbling as it approached.

Sam 8

11:40 p.m.

The bowling alley had been busy because of the rain. People who traveled to Sandusky to visit the amusement park needed other recreation when it rained, so business always picked up. I didn't mind being busy. I was making money, and it made the time pass.

Genie was helping out, which put a damper on my cash skimming. She was getting on in age and not as sharp as she used to be, but if she caught me, she would let me know, loud and clear.

One of my burner phones vibrated in my pocket. I set a pitcher of beer and a stack of plastic cups on the bar in front of a middle-aged Oriental guy wearing a Panama Jack hat and what looked like a blue romper. *Just when you thought you'd seen it all.* I gave him his change and pulled out the phone. It was a text from Data:

Need to meet ASAP. Boss and Romeo males V&A. Chuck will b there. 0100

That sounded bad. I looked at the clock—11:45 p.m. The alley was open until one. Randy texted back to the group:

Taj?

Twenty seconds later, the response was:

Yes

"Boss and Romeo males V&A" was Randy, Viktor, and Alexander. It wasn't just Viktor; he wanted Alexander there too. Alexander was looking like Randy's new main Romanian fix-it guy, I was waiting for him to throw Viktor out of the camper and move Alexander in. Was the meeting a problem with some of his recent work, either at the waterpark or torching Clemmons's camper?

Viktor 6

11:50 p.m.

I was ordered not to drive drunk, so I would not offer to get Alexander. Plus, I just had a motorbike, and it was raining. In Romania, I could drive blind drunk and never get in police trouble, even if I ran off the road. Here I could be put in jail for driving after three drinks.

Alexander would have to find his way over from the park. Even though it closed because of rain, he was working late. There was always work to do at the park. I told him to be at the Taj by 12:45.

He would not be late. He was by the book. A pain in my ass. He could put more money in his pocket if he would relax, but he did not like twisting the rules. Who needed a thug that followed all the silly little rules so close?

I looked out my window at Brady's camper. He was inside all night. After my first few vodkas, I wanted to walk over and bang on his door to scare him, but I could get in trouble with Randy.

So, I sat on the couch and watched stupid American television. *The Office. Seinfeld. Friends.* None of them made me laugh once. I passed out I was so bored. Then I got a text about a meeting.

I thought I should drink some water to get my head clear but drank another vodka. What did I care? I was in no trouble. Alexander may be, but I did not know why, and it did not matter to me.

Chapter 8
Tuesday, June 23

Mike 18

12:05 a.m.

I had about an hour to get the last phase of the plan together. I retrieved Chuck's rain-soaked body, dragging it back up to the golf cart, and hoisted him into the back. Driving down the trail, I passed the shower house and parked behind my rental van.

I opened the back doors, looking around carefully. It was dead quiet outside. A soft drizzle began again. I heaved Chuck's body out, fireman-carried it over to the back of the van, and dumped him in.

I drove his golf cart back to the shower house and parked beside Data's yellow work cart. Brady and Chris had loaded it with the crane hooks, a hammer, a box of nails, and a stack of two-by-fours. There was also a cast-iron crank handle, used to lower and raise the scissor jacks that were standard on most RVs, as well as a few other miscellaneous items they put in a large black garbage bag. It looked like they found everything I asked for.

I took my gym bag from the golf cart and transferred it to the bed of the work cart. I opened the bag and dug around until I found a red beach towel.

I drove the golf cart back up the trail, positioning it off to the side by a big tree about halfway down. I considered pushing the golf cart into the water or deeper into the woods but doubted anyone would find it on the trail until well after sunrise. At that point, it wouldn't matter.

I took the towel and thoroughly wiped the interior of the golf cart down. I walked back to the shower house, tossing the towel in the work cart passenger seat.

Starting up the work cart, I headed for the east side of the campground, searching for the flatbed trailer. The rain picked up a little.

The work cart had a hitch that was mostly used to pull five or six little passenger cars around the campground, like a mini train. The cars were loaded with kids and their overweight parents. If it could tow a few tons of people, it had more than enough towing capacity to pull a flatbed trailer loaded with large chains.

I needed to execute the next phase of the plan without assistance. I had to trust that Brady could get the other stuff done on his own. Data appeared to be playing ball, but that could easily change.

I rounded the street parallel to the shore and found the flatbed trailer. Several rolls of chains were stacked on it. I drove the work cart around and backed up to the trailer.

It was a two-wheel, single-axle trailer, with a five-by-ten-foot wooden bed with side rails and a ramp gate that folded down. I dug in my bag and found a pair of heavy-duty work gloves. The rain was coming down a little harder, so everything was slippery. I folded down the gate and climbed up onto the trailer.

It took a while to sort through them, but I managed to find two of the chains I thought would be optimal lengths. The rest I pushed off into the grass and dragged a few feet away from the trailer.

I took the hooks from Chris's worksite and fastened one on each end of the chain. Closing the gate, I kicked the flatbed's wheel chocks to the side. I lifted the hitch and pulled it forward, setting the hitch coupler on top of the hitch ball and clamped it.

I made my way to the western part of the campground, driving down the unlit street that ran parallel to the trail. The work cart handled the trailer well.

It was a risk pulling the trailer through the campground. Any witnesses who saw me driving by would remember me later, as hauling a trailer around after midnight was unusual. I was hoping the rainy weather had meant early bedtimes across the campground. The trail would have provided better cover, but it was too wet from the rain and it wouldn't take much to get the trailer stuck.

I had to get the chains as close as I could to the Taj without being seen. If I was too far away, I would need to drag them closer by hand, and the rattling could draw attention.

I pulled up to the garbage dumpster at the end of Sparrow. It was the most logical place to unload, since it was only three lots down from the Taj. If I made any noise, hopefully people would think it was someone out throwing away garbage.

I unhooked the trailer. Opening the gate, I grabbed an end of both chains and started walking. It was heavy and awkward, but I was able to slowly pull them. It took a lot more effort than I expected. The grass allowed them to slide easier, but it was also more difficult to get traction. A few times, I had to spin around and pull, leaning as I walked backward to get more leverage.

After I reached the other side of the fishing pond, I stopped to catch my breath. Surveying the campground, everything was quiet. I continued to walk across the grass and up the hill toward the train tracks.

Brady 24

12:20 a.m.

We had no further need of Chris, so we let him go. Before we did, Mike had put a scare into him. He didn't exactly threaten his life, but he made it very clear that if anything about our activity that evening was shared with outsiders, there would be repercussions.

Chris never asked what the plan was or why we needed those supplies. By morning it would be evident.

I marched Data, still bound, to the edge of the trail. Once we turned south, we would be more exposed as we traveled the downward grade south toward the dumpster. It was the most precarious part of our journey across the campground, with the best opportunity for Data to draw attention. It would be extremely difficult to explain why I was marching an employee who was bound and gagged across the campground.

We had to make it past the dumpster to the back fence, climb over the fence, and enter Trailer Alpha. Mike asked Data during the interrogation why it was called Alpha. Were there *Bravo* and *Charlie* trailers? Data only knew of the one.

Mike would be heading to the same area soon, and there was a possibility that we would cross paths at the dumpster. I was starting to question the karmic wisdom of executing risky plans oriented around a garbage dumpster.

I looked at Data, who was pale and scared. He was dripping wet and shivering slightly. I barely noticed the rain, even though my feet were thoroughly soaked. I had a single-minded focus that I hadn't experienced since the military.

"Listen, when we reach the fence, you are climbing over first. One leg up, over, and then the next. Then you sit down until I tell you to move. We're in no hurry, so we are prioritizing efficiency and quietness. Don't try to run or yell. If you don't think I'm capable of shooting you, try me," I said, pulling up my shirt and rotating to the side so he could see my Glock.

Chris 10

12:25 a.m.

When I returned to my RV, I found it had been cleaned out. Not *cleaned up*, as in Candy actually cleaned it, but *cleaned out*, as in her shit was gone. Along with her car. No farewell letter, nothing.

I guessed the final straw was disappearing with Brady. Chris vanishing yet again. Her reaction was to pack and leave. Not that it would take long; she didn't have much.

I was only gone a few hours. She must have had an exit plan. The next time I disappeared, she was out the door. She was probably on her way back to Cleveland to stay with Mom and Dad.

The ironic part was that I didn't disappear because I was out partying. Brady didn't give me a choice; he would not take *no* for an answer. I would have much rather stayed in the RV.

My heart was pounding. I needed a drink. I needed more than a drink, but a drink would be a good start. I went to the cupboard under the sink, opened it, and found my nearly full half-gallon of Mohawk vodka was still there. Unscrewing the cap, I took a deep swig. The burn felt good, despite the pain shooting from my ulcer.

I considered the pictures that had supposedly been taken of me in the cabin. They didn't matter anymore. They could show them to whoever the fuck they wanted to. *What difference did it make to me anymore?*

I got up and went to the door to double-check that it was locked. After this odd night, I didn't feel safe at all. I wanted to get away from the campground. But I had no vehicle.

I looked at the clock on the microwave. It was 12:31 a.m. I was supposed to fly with Randy's pilot at 7:30 a.m.

Captain Norquist, the retired pilot. He looked like a stereotypical commercial airline pilot—thick white hair, white mustache, blue eyes, strong jawline, capable of getting everyone on board an aircraft back on the ground safely, no matter what the situation was. I couldn't figure out before why he was involved with Randy and me, taking me on ride-alongs. Now it all made sense. *He was being blackmailed.* Captain Norquist had a hooker habit, and Randy was leveraging that.

I paced the short length of the trailer a few times. How was I going to return all that stuff we took from the construction site? Would they call the police? I was definitely fired if I didn't return those hooks. But with the permit issues, I had a few days.

Hopefully, the piloting thing would be a real gig, or else I wouldn't have a damn thing going on. No job, no girlfriend, no life.

I felt so tired. If I could have laid down and died, I would have. *Just close my eyes and sleep endlessly.* The prospect of flying was all I had at that moment in my life.

Randy 10

12:30 a.m.

"Have your vehicle out back and ready to go in ten," I said to Sam, hanging up my burner phone. I was tempted to call Data to see what this meeting was all about but decided not to. If he was making progress with Sullivan, I didn't want to interrupt. We could talk at the Taj.

Sam thought the Romanian boys may have stepped in something, since Data asked them to be there. Alexander had seemed to get away unscathed from the Zulu job and burning Clemmons's RV, but maybe things hadn't gone as smoothly as he led us to believe.

I took a drink of bourbon and tried to stand up. My legs and back were stiff and fought me, so I used the corner of the desk to steady myself.

I went downstairs and out the back door. The Suburban was parked alongside the building, with Sam behind the wheel. He was wearing a red marines long-sleeve T-shirt and jeans. I went around and climbed in.

I caught movement from the corner of my eye and turned to the back. Alexander was sitting there. He was wearing an all-black jumpsuit and a black baseball hat. His backpack was in the seat next to him. He nodded at me.

"I found a straggler out back waiting for us," Sam said.
I nodded and motioned for him to take off.

Patrick 4

12:50 a.m.

think I must have dozed for a half-hour. I barely slept the night before; my ribs were on fire. *Fucking Sam. Fucking Data.*

The lights from the vehicle turning into the lot must have woke me up. I looked up and saw a big, black SUV pulling in. It would have been bad to get caught sleeping by that crew. I looked at my watch. 12:55 a.m.

I sat up straighter as the SUV pulled up to the window. Sam was driving, with Randy in the passenger seat. Sam glared at me. I nodded. Randy nodded. He leaned over toward the booth.

"Anything happening tonight?" he asked.

I shook my head. "No, sir, not a lot of traffic tonight. Chris Randolph came in a few hours ago. Then his girlfriend left," I said.

"She didn't come back?" he asked.

"Not yet, sir."

"Seen Chuck?"

"No, sir. There was a plumbing issue out at the east shower house a few hours ago. He went out to take care of it, and I haven't seen him since," I said.

Randy nodded, looked at Sam, and shrugged. They pulled up over the speed bump and took a left onto Starling.

Chuck was gone a long time, even for him. I would try to reach him on the walkie-talkie again, and then I would go out looking for him.

Viktor 7

12:54 a.m.

I was sitting on the porch of the Taj when I saw headlights. That had to be them. I did not see Chuck. Not even driving by in his stupid little cart. I took a drag from my cigarette and threw it in the yard.

It was warm with a little rain. Rain did not bother me. I took another sip of vodka and stood up. The big SUV parked in front of the RV. The back door on the driver's side opened, and Alexander got out.

How did he set up a ride with Mr. Randy? It was a sign he was now favored by him after the waterpark job and the RV burn job. That could not be good for me.

Sam opened his door and looked at me. I nodded to him, but he did not nod. Randy got out and walked up on the Taj porch. He took out the keys and unlocked the door. We all walked in behind.

Sam closed the door. He got out the wand and checked us. Randy took it and checked Sam. No beeps.

We got drinks. I poured a vodka, Sam and Randy poured bourbon, and Alexander took a bottled water. We sat at the table.

"Where is Chuck? Where is Data?" Randy asked. No one responded.

"It is 0100 hours," Sam said.

"Yeah, I have a fucking watch," Randy said. I heard the sound of the damn train horn.

Dintr-odată ... suddenly there was a loud banging sound outside. It sounded like a very loud knock. Then it stopped. Then it started again. *BANG BANG BANG BANG!* We jumped out of our chairs.

Randy walked fast over to a drawer by the dishwasher and pulled out a pistol. Alexander opened his backpack and took out his. Sam's gun was in his hand. I did not see where it came from. I did not have a gun on me.

The banging stopped. Then it began at the back door. *BANG*

BANG BANG BANG! Sam waved his arm toward Alexander, pointing at him to open the front door. Alexander nodded.

He crouched forward and moved by the door. He reached down, unlocked the door, and pulled the handle back at the same time, pushing his left shoulder forward. His gun was at his waist and ready to fire. But the door did not move. He pushed harder and it still did not move.

Alexander pointed toward his leg and made a kicking motion, nodding toward Randy. He shook his head no. Alexander could have kicked the door open. I did not know why Randy said no. Maybe he feared guns shooting into the trailer.

Randy nodded at Sam and pointed to the back door. Sam walked over, unlocked it, and pushed. It didn't open.

"Viktor, look out the window," Randy said, pointing to the small window above the sink.

Why don't you look out the window and risk getting your head shot off, Mr. Randy? I walked over to the window anyway. I pointed at the light switch by the front door, and Alexander turned them off. I pulled the curtain over and looked out. I saw no one outside.

Mike 19

1:01 a.m.

I hammered the last two-by-fours to the back door of the RV, then spun around and ran down the stairs. Earlier I had removed the wheel chocks and clamped the chains onto the front metal bars behind the towing hitch. I went to the electric lift and lowered the RV until there was no front elevation. Next, I lifted the plastic propane tank housing, twisted the tank's valves off on both of them, removed them, and tossed them to the side.

Running around to the back, I dropped the hammer into the black garbage bag. I took out the crank handle and manually lowered the scissor-jacks on both sides until they fully retracted from the cinder blocks that supported them. Picking up the cinder blocks, I moved them to the back of the lot. I went to the south side of the trailer and pulled the electrical cord from the plug on the RV's side panel.

At the back of the lot, I grabbed the garbage bag and made my way north along the fence. I passed the fishing pond and jogged up the hill to the tracks, continuing to run parallel to the chains that I had prearranged.

Dropping the bag, I looked east and saw the lights of the train approaching as the horn blew. It would be slowing down once the engine passed through the campground and approached the first traffic intersection.

I picked up the two ends of the chains, each with a crane hook fastened. Moving within ten feet of the tracks, I crouched as the light from the train nearly blinded me. The engine passed and the train cars started whizzing by, towering over me, loud, clacking violently on the track. I squinted to see the end of the train, the last car, scanning for the break that would reveal the eastern shoreline.

Another minute passed, and I saw shoreline and water unobstructed by the train. I heard the horn blow again as the train reached the first intersection by the causeway. As it slowed, the rushing motion became less frantic, and I could see more bits of shore and landscape between the rail cars. The last car approached.

I stood up straight, moving as close to the train as I dared. I began jogging beside it, then running, almost keeping pace. The last car passed alongside me, and as it did, I veered to the right, extending the hooks and lurching forward.

The last car wasn't a traditional caboose but was a modified cargo car. It had an additional structure of metal bars added at the bottom, with a small rectangular white electronic device attached. The device collected metrics like location and speed, but I wasn't sure what else it did beyond that.

I clanged the left hook around the outside metal bar and then the right, with the hook clips popping shut to ensure it didn't unhook. Sprinting for a few more seconds, I jumped off to the right to avoid contact with the chains.

My airborne training from twenty years prior popped back into my head. Standard army parachutes were not engineered for soft landings and often dropped you down hard, depending on the wind conditions. The parachute risers allowed you to steer, but throughout the hundreds of jumps I had in my career with the garden-variety T-10C chutes, the force of my hands pulling on the riser handles never noticeably changed my direction or slowed my descent.

To compensate, we were taught how to perform a safer landing. That aspect of the training took up a full week of Airborne School; it was five days of falling and landing properly, over and over.

Before my feet touched the ground, my arms were cradling an imaginary backup parachute fastened in front of my stomach, back hunched over, head down, feet extended, knees slightly bent, all while trying to stay loose. The key was to have the side of your boots become the second point of contact with the ground after your feet hit, initiating a rolling motion, leveraging the momentum of your fall to have the force of impact distributed evenly along the entire side of your body as you rolled, and then flip over on your back.

The jump from the tracks was at a weird angle, not the slower descent trajectory experienced from being pushed by the wind while descending with a parachute. I still managed to execute the form pretty well, except I tumbled forward after I hit, flipping over a few times until I finally rolled to a stop.

I heard the chains slide as the train pulled them along until the slack ended. There was a huge groan at the moment that the chain was fully extended and the physics of the stationary RV resisting the moving train occurred. I wondered for a moment if the metal bars on the back of the train car were going to just rip free, but then I heard the rumbling from across the tracks as the trailer rolled loose and lurched forward.

The RV rotated and then chased the chains, getting pulled through the clearing, behind the fishing hole, and up the hill. It was bouncing madly, angling to the left, going up on two wheels, settling, and finally aligning behind the train for a moment. It looked like an absurd bouncing railcar, wildly veering from side to side on the tracks. Then it skidded and tipped over on its left side with a crash, the doors now facing down, making escape through them impossible. Sparks began to fly as the siding separated from the metal panels as it slid along the tracks.

I grabbed the garbage bag with the tools and ran over to the work cart. I started it and drove swiftly up the hill. I turned onto the tracks and chased the train, trying to avoid the debris that was falling off the RV as it was ruthlessly dragged along.

Data 9

1:10 a.m.

I gasped as I watched the Taj launch from its lot. I forgot it was mobile with wheels beneath it; the trailer was so big that it appeared to be a fixed structure. Randy had customized it with reinforced metal walls, floor, and ceiling like Trailer Alpha, to withstand a firearms attack. A conventional trailer would have collapsed quickly if it was towed so roughly, but this one was essentially a big metal safe that would not break apart easily.

Sullivan and I were watching from the back window as the Taj launched. He had taken my gag off and let me take off the wet poncho, but then he bound me again. It felt a little looser than Clemmons's cuffs, but I wasn't going to try to free myself.

The RV fell over as it careened up to the train tracks, being dragged violently after falling on its side. We could see sparks from the RV's contact with the tracks farther west for a moment before it was out of sight.

"Holy shit," Sullivan mumbled. I looked at him, and he was as shocked as I was, his mouth agape.

I was speechless. Four guys were in that RV. I personally didn't like any of them, especially Sam and Viktor. But I didn't wish death on them. Under other circumstances, I could have been inside that RV.

"You realize it was my call not to have you in that RV tonight," he said, as if he read my mind. I had no response. "All right, snap out of it. We need to get into the control room back there."

"And then what?" I asked.

"We are destroying everything. All of the data and then all of the hardware, a complete cleansing. We need to start moving," he said.

"Then what happens to me?" I asked.

"You leave. You forget everything you saw tonight. You are a simple campground worker and have no idea what Randy and his crew were truly up to," he said.

I thought about it. If I purged it all cleanly, we had plausible deniability. We could discreetly remove the cameras. I could finish out the summer there and then move along. It was doable.

One thing gave me pause; Randy mentioned he had backups of the data stored somewhere. He threatened to release videos of me using technology, in violation of my probation terms. *But if Randy was dead, how would that work?* I decided not to mention it, hoping Randy didn't have a contingency plan in place to have one of his minions recover the data and weaponize it.

"Okay, you have the keys," I said. Sullivan reached in his pocket, pulling out the key ring Clemmons had removed from me.

"Can you unbind me? I can't feel my fingers," I said.

"Not yet. Be a good boy and we'll see. Which key is it?"

Randy 11

1:10 a.m.

The RV bounced and went airborne, jolting me as I hit the wall above flush with my shoulder and the left side of my face, causing my ear to ring. I could see bits of the night sky through the side window, which was now a skylight. Otherwise, the inside was blackness.

We were moving fast. I felt the groan of the floor, which was once the wall to the south, scraping along the ground. Someone outside hitched us to a tow truck or something and it was pulling us down the street. How long could this go on before the police got involved? A camper being towed along the street on its side had to be drawing attention.

I felt blood gushing down into my eyes. Something gashed my forehead as we bounced around. It also felt like my right leg was broken; it smashed against something.

A gunshot rang out within, so near and so loud that my right ear rang. The flash lit up the inside for a moment. Sam was a foot away, holding the gun he'd just fired. It was all chaos, with bouncing debris churning around like a nightmare washing machine. In the flash, I thought I saw Viktor lying face down by the cove where the fridge once was.

"Get your hand off the trigger!" I screamed, but it was lost in the continuing screech of the RV being dragged. It was like being trapped in a tornado full of hard and sharp objects, with everything inside bouncing and tumbling together.

A loud smashing sound boomed from the front-left section, and the RV came to a sudden halt. My body went airborne and crashed hard into what was probably the stereo components, with plastic loudly crunching. Something hard hit me square in the back, knocking the wind out of me.

My left arm felt broken at the elbow. I could barely lift it. I rolled over slightly, lifting my right hip, and reached into my pocket. Somehow my cell phone was still there. I pushed a button, and it lit up.

The screen was smashed, with spider-web cracks covering it. My hands were slippery from blood. I wiped my hand on my pants and managed to type in the pin and scroll through to find the flashlight app button.

The RV looked like a bomb went off inside it. Everything was shattered, a wasteland of destruction. I saw the back of Viktor's head about a foot away. I reached over and touched it. It rolled back and I saw that his eyes were open. I looked down and saw there was a knife stuck in the side of his neck, sunk so deep that only the black plastic handle was showing, with blood trickling down to his shirt collar. When the drawers spilled the silverware must have been flying around, and a steak knife found its way into his neck. But I also heard rumors of friction between Viktor and Alexander. Could Alexander have … there was no time to worry about that.

I had gravely miscalculated Sullivan. Going after his daughter was a world-class blunder. It was supposed to smash him into submission, punishment for dropping off the grid without my permission, but instead, it provoked a response that was going to end with me in the hospital or the morgue.

Sam cursed on the other side of the RV, and I shined the light over. He was staring at me with one eye; the other was swollen shut. His nose was crushed, with a stream of blood flowing down to his upper lip.

"We … we need to get the fuck out of here," I croaked.

I sat up, feeling severe pain throughout my body. I was having trouble catching my breath. My heart was pounding; I couldn't get it to slow down. The alcohol from the broken liquor bottles was overpowering, making my eyes water.

"How we gonna do that, boss? The doors are underneath us," Sam said.

"The rear cabin has a big window. The bunk area also has a window we could possibly escape through. They are reinforced but can be snapped out from the inside. We need to pick one and try to pop it out. Do you smell any propane?"

"Nah, just liquor," he said. I returned the flashlight beam to

Viktor's body.

"Viktor's dead. You with us Alexander?"

"*Da*, right arm is broke. Picking glass from my face. Still have the gun," he said, his voice coming from the bathroom area.

"Anyone else got their phones?" I asked.

Both said no. I switched to the phone app, looked through recent calls, and dialed Chuck's burner.

"Damn, Chuck and Data are all we got. The fact they ain't in here with us probably ain't good news for us," I growled as the phone rang.

Patrick 5

1:15 a.m.

"Hey!" the guy screamed in the booth, almost giving me a heart attack. I had fallen asleep with my earbuds in. I shot up straight and nearly fell out of the chair. When I jerked over to catch my balance, my ribs screamed, and I winced.

"Hey what, buddy?" I mumbled.

I recognized him as one of the gazebo families, from site 11 or 12. Middle-aged white guy, military haircut, big gut, red face, Notre Dame hat, Cleveland Browns T-shirt, jorts, and flip-flops.

"Randy's RV disappeared!" he shouted, pointing in that direction.

I looked at him closely. Drunk? High? *Drunk and high*?

"That is a permanent trailer, sir, it would take some work to steal that. Where did it go?" I asked.

But I didn't know if it was a permanent trailer. It was seasonal and never moved, so I just assumed.

"Listen, go take a look. You may want to call the police, buddy," he said, then started jogging back to his camper. It was funny watching people try to move fast who aren't accustomed to moving fast; he kind of waddled like a penguin being chased by a polar bear or something.

I left the booth and walked over toward Starling. Site 21 was too far down to see from there in the dark. I walked back to the booth and got out the walkie-talkie.

"Chuck. Data. You copy?" I asked. No answer. I looked at the office building parking lot. A yellow work cart was still missing. No sign of Chuck's golf cart. I looked up at the sky and saw that it was still cloudy, so rain was possible again. I grabbed a flashlight from the booth and started walking toward site 21.

Brady 25

1:25 a.m.

"Chuck. Data. You copy?" came across on the walkie-talkie. I jumped as it interrupted the silence. Data was maneuvering back and forth between several laptops. I saw the different camera angles throughout Randy's little empire on the monitors. The cabins, the bowling alley, and the boat interiors. It was quite an operation.

"Get it all ready, but don't delete anything yet," I said. Data looked over, nodded, and returned to work.

The best option was to ignore the calls, whether on the walkie-talkie or the phone. Chuck's burner phone began ringing.

"Who is this?" I asked, holding the phone in front of Data so he could read the number.

"Randy," he said, after squinting through his thick glasses.

My heart sank. How the hell was he calling Chuck? *He was supposed to be dead?* I paused, then decided to answer it. Mike would not be happy that I violated one of his protocols.

"Hello," I said.

"Chuck?" the voice asked. The voice was raspy, pained, and haggard sounding. It had a gasping quality to it.

"No, not Chuck. Chuck can't come to the phone right now. May I take a message?" I asked.

"Who is ... Sullivan?" he gasped.

"Randy, is that you? You sound like you're having a bad night," I said.

I needed to play it very carefully. If he had a phone, then he could call someone over to my location, if he knew where I was.

I looked over at Data, who had stopped working. I pointed to the monitor, and he continued. He remained a threat, as he could have some sort of digital panic button on one of these systems to signal for help. At worst, if he brought in the cavalry, I was ready to call the police and put an end to the whole damn thing.

"Sullivan ... listen, we need help. We are in rough shape.

What did you do? Some of us are going to die if we don't get out of this box."

"Funny, I had similar thoughts yesterday when my daughter was asphyxiating after you spiked her milk. I was watching her face as her throat closed up. She was minutes from dying. I bet being trapped in that box is helping you empathize."

"Listen, we can work this out. I'm done with you, I don't need you. I just want out. I will leave you alone. I will leave Clemmons alone."

"Bullshit. If you escape, then I'm a dead man. You'll go after my family again. You'll go after Mike. Speaking of Mike, he should be dropping by to check on you any minute now. He has a few questions concerning his burnt-up RV. In military vernacular, that is known as a mop-up operation. Who else is still alive and kicking in the Taj?"

"You killed Viktor. The rest of us are beat up bad. We need an ambulance."

"Viktor is dead? Was he wearing his hat-cam when it happened? I would love to see the footage. That has to be a big HR loss for you. Who else on the payroll has the skill set to dispose of a dead hooker next time one of your Johns gets carried away? Good luck with that. And good luck with your current situation in general. If any of you are still alive when they peel that RV open and start an investigation, you are going to have some awkward questions to answer. I bet there is a paper trail leading back to that trailer right behind the Taj. Or where the Taj used to be. We have been chatting with Chuck and Henry for hours now. We know where all the bodies are buried, Gorey. All of them.

"You weaponized my own life against me. My family and my job. You were ready to annihilate my family and turn me into a traitor so you could scale up your business. How did you think I was going to react? If I were you, I would lay down in that metal coffin and fucking die, because if you do escape, I'm not going to rest until every last one of you sons of bitches are in the ground."

I hung up, my heart pounding. I looked up and made eye contact with Data, who was staring at me slack-jawed. He quickly averted his gaze.

"Can you cut his cell phone?" I asked.

He looked back at me nervously. "Yeah."

"Cut it. Also, cut the other three, now," I said. I should have thought of that earlier when I learned of Data's extensive tech capabilities during his interrogation.

I texted Mike to let him know that there was still life within the Taj and that they possibly could call the police or reinforcements. The urgency for Mike to engage the trailer increased.

I also admitted that I told them he was coming, which was a major, embarrassing blunder on my part. I got caught up in my anger at what Randy did to Katie and I let it affect my judgment. I hoped it didn't end up impacting Mike.

"Does all of the traced phone traffic flow through here, like texts and voice mails?" I asked.

Data nodded. "Everything. Communications, video, GPS pings," he said.

"What was the exit plan for when this operation got compromised?" I asked.

He didn't answer for a minute, thinking. "Run the delete jobs, torch the place," he said.

"How?"

"There are five gallons of lighter fluid in the shed. There is also a case of bleach. Bleach the surfaces, douse the place with lighter fluid, ignite it," he said flatly.

I was a little surprised at the lack of sophistication. With the heavy investment in technology, I thought there would be something more spectacular, maybe C4 charges underneath wired to detonate.

"Okay, start the data purge. Then we are taking a look inside of these safes."

Mike 20

1:30 a.m.

I heard the crash and saw the shadow of the RV as I approached the Pipe River. The tracks ran parallel to Columbus Road, which was to the south. No more sparks were flying from the metal-on-metal friction.

I deduced what must have happened. There was an iron train bridge spanning across the river that was wider than the train by only a few feet on either side. The RV slid crossways and slammed into it. As I pulled closer, I saw that the last train car won the short tug of war with the RV and yanked the chains and hooks loose from the trailer hitch.

The riverbanks were built up to construct the bridge footings, with a sharp grade on either side. The RV was now partially hanging off on the south bank, which ran steeply down to the river. It was about a thirty-foot drop down to the water. The river itself was about a hundred feet across.

I got a text from Brady that there was an outgoing call from the RV and there were still three survivors. I knew when I planned this the prospect of the train killing all four was improbable, but three surviving was a big fail.

However, the survivors had to be in rough shape, and I needed to change their status from *survivors* to *deceased* before the police arrived. If the RV occupants got out alive, Brady and I would have serious problems.

I parked about twenty feet away, got out, and took my M9 out of the bag. Tucking it in the back of my pants, I grabbed the crowbar and a two-by-four. I walked up to take a closer look, hearing sirens off in the distance.

Patrick 6

1:35 a.m.

Jesus Christ! Randy's RV *was* gone. There was a crowd of about ten people standing around and talking to each other. A few were walking along in the grass by the back fence.

I walked over and shined my flashlight. It looked like the camper had been driven off through the backs of the lots and up toward the train tracks. The grass was torn up in places along its path.

Sam's big SUV was parked in front of the empty site. That made no sense. Who would steal an RV with that big gorilla inside? Unless this was a plan that Randy and Sam put together. Maybe some type of insurance scam?

The RV's power cord was still plugged into the box. The sewer line was gone. Two white propane tanks were lying beside the deck, which was partially destroyed. I walked over and pulled the power cord from the box, wincing at the tug on my ribs. I lifted the walkie-talkie to my mouth.

"Chuck, Data. Yo," I said.

No response. I had to call this in to Travis and the police. He would kill me if I called the police first, so I called Travis. Police traffic was a bad situation at the campground, and he always wanted to try to take care of problems in house. My call went right to his voicemail.

"Travis, we have an RV theft. Call me back, stat."

I walked back up to the group of people. They were huddled together and talking loudly. A few had drinks. The gazebo people started a campfire.

"Listen, it is late, and there is nothing to be done tonight. I called the campground manager, and he is on his way to take a look," I announced loudly to the group.

Nobody moved. I stood to the side with my arms crossed. Then I heard sirens. Someone called the police. Now Travis was going to be pissed.

Mike 21

1:40 a.m.

A gunshot rang out as I got closer. I instinctively stopped and crouched. One of the geniuses within was firing a weapon inside of that metal box, risking a ricochet. *Probably Sam.*

The RV was beat to hell, but the steel reinforcements were still intact. It had fallen on the port side, blocking both doors and trapping them inside.

The two-by-fours I'd nailed over the doors must have held. I was a little surprised because if one of the big guys in there repeatedly kicked the door, it would have eventually dislodged the boards. Maybe cutting the power was enough of a distraction during the critical time between nailing the boards and the train's arrival.

There were windows at either end large enough for them to climb out of. The bigger back window would open over that embankment, with a nice tumble down the hill and into the river once free.

The smaller window at the front was angled toward the tracks. That was the only reasonable exit for them and why they were trying to shoot their way out of it. I could wait and pop them when they made it out, but I wasn't sure how much time I had. The sirens were getting louder from the west, the direction of the downtown police station.

The police could have been called because someone saw the RV launch through the campground or because it was being dragged by a train through a traffic intersection. If they were going to investigate the tracks, I had to wrap it up fast. I couldn't be found loitering there with my pistol sighted on the back window.

I heard a thump and then another gunshot. A second thump and gunshot. The window spider-webbed. The plastic interior window latches must have been stuck and prevented it from opening. I shifted over to the left a few additional feet in case a bullet escaped.

I walked to the side of the window in a crouch and pushed against the trailer. It was balanced precariously against the embankment. More of the trailer was on solid ground than was hanging off the side, but not much more.

I jogged back and hopped into the work cart as another shot rang out. Throwing my bag off to the side, I grabbed a two-by-four and set it across my lap.

I got the work cart going full speed, maybe thirty miles per hour. I wedged the board against the gas pedal, shoving it violently into place, with the other end against my seat at waist level. About ten feet from impact, I rolled off to the left, pulling my airborne landing crouch again, but bouncing harder this time. I hadn't jumped out of an actual plane in years, but there I was, pulling off an airborne landing twice in one night, albeit from low altitude. I was going to be a mass of aches and pains for weeks after this.

The work cart continued and slammed into the edge of the RV solidly, pushing the camper about two feet. That was all it took. The whole thing teetered and then started sliding, with the front end lifting up into the air and disappearing as it slid down the bank. The metal screeched as it slid against the dirt and rocks. I heard a big splash as it plunged into the water.

The work cart rolled to its side and followed the RV down the bank, thudding as it skipped and hit the water with a splash. I jogged over to the bridge.

The river was flowing slowly, and the camper seemed to just float in place, completely upside down, a big rectangular bobber. It flipped over as its heavier underbelly pulled it down. I could see a piece of the black sewer hose still attached before the bottom half disappeared. The RV wasn't watertight; there certainly had to be multiple breaches, with the small ventilation ports along the roof taking in water as it bobbed.

It was very dark, with the sky full of big gray clouds, and all I could see by the distant glow of the streetlights on Columbus Road were the tops of the RV's air vents and the white air-conditioning unit. It floated slowly under the bridge, and by the time it crossed to the other side, there was no trace of it.

I swept the area for debris, throwing any parts of the camper

I found down into the water. I also threw the wrench, boards, boxes of nails, and hammers into the water.

Picking up my bag, I started jogging back toward the campground. It was the first time I was going to run a significant distance since leaving the army. The rental van needed to be moved out of the campground before the police locked it down.

Brady 26

2:45 a.m.

I double, triple, and quadruple checked. I thought he deleted everything. But this operation was way beyond my level of technical knowledge. It was entirely possible he could have an alternate storage area I was unaware of.

But why would Henry play games? According to his story, he would go to prison if he was caught using technology. It would be a big risk to save anything.

Henry opened the big safes, and we sifted through the contents. One contained several envelopes full of blackmail material on people I didn't know, as well as various data-storage devices. One was full of weapons, ranging from handguns to an AR-15. The last was filled with ammo. I decided to leave the doors open on the safes and dispose of them when we disposed of the trailer.

I looked at the sad, benign man hunched over the keyboard, and reflected on how he was the one who enabled Randy's entire operation. None of the rest of his crew could probably set up a Wi-Fi router, let alone choreograph the web of high-tech equipment that was the backbone of his operation. Pre-technology, his gang would be all muscle, with maybe a crooked lawyer or accountant to tidy things up. Henry was proof that crime continuously evolves and that a soulless little nerd could wreak as much havoc as a thug with a machine gun could fifty years ago.

"What now?" Data asked, nervously looking at the dead monitors.

"We are going to get rid of this place," I replied.

He frowned. "This is more than two hundred thousand dollars' worth of equipment. Isn't it a little crazy to just torch it all?" he asked.

"What do you think we should do with it?" I asked.

He stood there, staring at the floor, rocking back and forth from foot to foot. "I could take some of it. The high-end stuff," he said quietly.

"What kind of stuff? The hacking software you used to pull up my life's history? The video-editing software you used to blackmail me? The GPS phone-tracking software you used to follow me? The scan-card maker you used to make a duplicate key so some thug could enter my hotel room and try to kill my daughter? What tech shit precisely do you want to take home as a souvenir, Data?" I asked angrily.

"Nothing. Let's get rid of it all. Sorry," he mumbled, adjusting his glasses.

"All right. Let's get that shit from the shed and bring it inside. Stand by, I need to make a call," I said.

"Okay. And please, stop calling me Data. It's Henry."

Mike 22

2:50 a.m.

My head jerked as I caught myself dozing off again. I was parked at the Cloverleaf apartment building lot, along the east side where I could see the campground entrance. So far two police cars went in.

No one was at the security booth when I exited. I figured the Mexican kid must have been down at the Taj lot, trying to figure out where the RV disappeared to. My mind kept returning to the activities of the night and wondering if I omitted any details.

I exhaled heavily. The plan was bizarre and improbable. An ordinary RV would have disintegrated after a hundred feet of being dragged behind a train. I saw an accident on the highway a few years ago where a thirty-six-foot RV had run off the road and essentially just collapsed. They were built light for traveling and not for impact durability.

The idea for my plan originated from a lecture I recalled from an army school over a decade earlier, concerning the USSR's approach to establishing airborne units before World War Two. The US meticulously developed their doctrine by trial and error, using crash-test dummies instead of soldiers, and thereby creating as few casualties as possible. Different altitudes, speeds, parachute types, and aircraft types were tested for years to create the safest and most effective airborne operations possible.

The Russians did things differently. Instead of utilizing sandbags and dummies to simulate the impact of landing, they tested in real situations using actual soldiers as guinea pigs. Want to know what happens if you roll a tank full of Russians off the back of a cargo plane at five thousand feet? Then do just that. And when they pried open the tank after it landed and found a half-dozen mangled Russian soldiers inside, they tweaked the process. Their soldiers were just cattle, and no one minded sacrificing them to develop the doctrine as rapidly as possible.

When Data detailed the reinforced Taj RV under interrogation, I immediately associated it with a Russian tank. There was no way we were going to take it out with handguns; we had to turn its armor against it. I figured riding a few miles inside of a bouncing RV being dragging behind a train traveling at fifty miles per hour would be conceptually similar to a Soviet soldier riding in the interior of a parachuting Russian T-24 tank back in the day. Soft human flesh and bones pinballing around inside of a hard metal box.

The Taj survivors had all surely taken a severe beating, hopefully involving broken bones and concussions. That would make it more difficult to survive when the RV submerged in the river. *I hoped.*

My burner buzzed, and I glanced down. There was a text message from Brady.

Alpha staged. Exiting in 5

I texted him back:

Don't forget the liquor

A moment later, he texted back:

Lush

That made me smile. It was time to pull the final stunt of this insane mission. I had to improvise a little because I never intended for Chuck to die. I almost forgotten that he was in the back of the van, it creeped me out that I was dozing off with a corpse that close.

While it was my fault that he was dead, I didn't kill him on purpose. I failed to understand how poor his health was, and that was on me. It was more manslaughter than murder. *But dead is dead.*

At 0315 hours, a car appeared from the north, driving south on Nickle Drive. As it passed under the nearest streetlight, I saw it was a rusty blue Buick Skylark, a model from the 1980s. The light reflected off Data's glasses briefly as they turned into the apartment parking lot and parked beside me.

I got out of the van and quietly closed the door, pushing it shut lightly instead of slamming it. I went around to the back of the van and opened the left door.

Data and Brady got out of the car, with Data going to the back and opening the trunk. Brady walked over and took the keys from him and put them in his pocket. He motioned me over.

I reached into the trunk of the Skylark and took out a gas can, a butane lighter, and a fifth of vodka. I put the items on the floor between the front seats of the van.

I moved my duffel bag and the garbage bag into the car's trunk. Brady pointed to the Buick's passenger seat, and Data got in and sat down, closing the door slowly until the dome light went out.

I motioned for Brady to get in the van. Once inside, I took a look at his face. He was dead tired and stressed, with black bags under his eyes. The past few days had aged him, a lifetime of stress crammed into a short period. It reminded me of young soldiers who got their first taste of combat. The stress aged a person in dog years.

Brady gazed into the back of the van at Chuck's body. His face was blank, there were no accusations or anger. I hoped he believed it was an accident.

"Any trouble with the car?" I asked. Brady broke from his trance.

"Nah. He uses it to run errands for his grandma a few times a month. It started fine. It was an unexpected resource for us. Any additional police activity?" he asked.

"No, just the two cars that are still there," I said, trying to stifle a yawn. I needed a coffee; the fact that I was caffeine deficient was poor planning on my part.

"Okay, you and Data are going to drive up to the abandoned post office at Palmer and East Shoreway. You get out and start walking toward the campground, as close as possible to the shore. There are going to be some serious fireworks when Trailer Alpha blows up; the cops on site are going to rush over there, and no one is going to be watching the campground. You should be able to slip back to your campsite unnoticed."

Brady nodded. He looked across to the car. Data was sitting there, staring down at his feet, in his own world.

"Data will need to have the car running and facing west, ready to go. After I take care of the trailer, I will be double-timing to meet him. We exit the area via East Shoreway and head to the bowling alley."

For a moment, I thought about bringing Data into the van to talk to him directly, but seeing Chuck's body again would probably disturb him. I trusted Brady to brief him.

"Data has access to everything at Glory Bowl. He knows the door code to Randy's office and the safe combo. He gets everything out of there. The cameras are dead, and it is too early for anyone to be at the alley. Data drops me off at the motel afterward, returns to his trailer, and goes to bed. When he is questioned later, he felt ill and left work late last night, turning his walkie-talkie off. Out of character for him, but par for the course for a campground employee who makes next to nothing in wages."

"What about his work cart at the bottom of the river?" I asked.

"He plays dumb. Says he left it in the proper parking spot. There is no video footage anymore, right? The cameras aren't transmitting?"

"Nope. All video was erased. The cameras are currently just decorations, recording nothing."

"Good. Because the cops will try pulling video soon, if they haven't tried already," I said.

"Getting away with this could hinge on Data convincing them he was not involved at all. His long disappearing act is suspicious," he said, frowning.

"I don't think they are going to focus on Data for anything, initially. If they run his background and find out he is a felon, they will have some questions for him. But it was for white-collar tech crimes, nothing violent, and nothing that would put him on their radar for demolishing the Taj."

"Even when it washes up in the cove with four bodies inside?" he asked.

I shrugged. "I think that campground will be on lockdown big time when that happens. But worst-case scenario, if they find the RV at sunup, there will be a high degree of confusion. Just stick to your alibis. You guys were both in your respective trailers all night. I'm not sure if the police would have knocked on your camper door during the course of canvassing the neighborhood. Just play dumb. They have nothing on you."

"I guess if Alpha is taken care of, the only problem is residual blackmail material," Brady said. "Does Randy have any of my pics stored at home? Data swore that Randy was careful with everything he gave him. I guess we have to trust him, we don't have a choice." He looked out the window at Trailer Alpha. Another cop car pulled slowly up the street, turning into the campground.

"It isn't in Data's best interest to have blackmail pictures around either, because that makes him vulnerable. I think if he knew of any other locations, he would have divulged that. We just have to control what we can," I said. "We can talk again later, but now we need to move ASAP."

Brady nodded. He leaned across and shook my hand. "Good luck, Mike. I can never repay you for all you've put on the line tonight," he said.

I put my left hand over both of our hands. "You owe me nothing, brother. Just execute this, and make sure Data is ready to roll," I said.

He nodded and got out. As he did, Data exited the car and walked around to the driver's side. Both men got in, and Data backed out, leaving his lights off. He pulled forward, taking a left, heading north on Nickle Drive.

I started the van and pulled out with my headlights off, turning north. I stopped four trailers down from Alpha along the curb, leaving the van running.

Standing, I crouched beneath the ceiling and walked to the back. I dragged Chuck up to the front, hoisting him into the driver's seat and fastening his seatbelt. He slumped forward. I leaned over him and adjusted his seat, tilting it backward and then pulling him by his legs until his back rested against it.

It was grim being that close to him, his pale, bloated face inches from mine. I had closed his eyelids earlier when I put him in the back of the van, which reduced the creepiness of his presence somewhat.

The smell of mustiness and vodka were radiating from him. I was sure he had drunk his share earlier. *Just another night on the job for Chuck.*

I found his hat and put it on him. He appeared to be sleeping, with his jaw hanging down. I could almost believe I heard a soft snore coming from him.

I returned to the back and got a two-by-four, bringing it to the front and setting it between the seats. Swinging open the two back doors, I posted them each open with a click of the hinge.

Hopping out, I grabbed the gas can and set it on the sidewalk. Returning to the van, I entered through the back doors and poured about half the bottle of vodka on Chuck's face and shirt. I took a swig of it and wedged the bottle between his legs.

I shifted the van into drive and jammed the two-by-four down, the tires spinning on the wet pavement briefly before it lurched forward. I was pulling off that improvable move that you would only see on hokey 1980s action shows like *The A-Team* or *MacGyver* twice in one night. *I love it when a plan comes together.*

Guiding it down the street, I hooked it to the left as it reached Trailer Alpha. Then I turned it hard to the right. I steered the van toward the trailer and let go of the wheel, spun myself around, and ran toward the back of the van. As the van hopped the curb, the force of the front wheels slamming into it caused both of the back doors to slam shut, timing almost perfectly with my attempt to dive out. The possibility that the door braces wouldn't hold them open when rolling over the curb never entered my calculations.

I hadn't even extended my arms yet to pull a Superman pose as I jumped, so I slammed headfirst into the right door, directly beneath the window. My neck jammed violently back into my body as I drove forward, and I heard a grotesque crunching of bones. I bounced back and landed flat on my stomach.

The van slammed into the trailer forcefully. My body hurled

to the front, with my legs striking the stereo and air-conditioning controls, bending and breaking like twigs. But I felt nothing.

The van struck the trailer flush, dead center, with a huge crashing noise, metal on metal. Glass sprayed everywhere as the windshield shattered. The momentum carried the van forward, bending the trailer walls in and then ripping through, breaching it with about half of the van ending up inside. The trailer's reinforced metal interior was built to repel bullets, but not necessarily a six-ton battering ram propelling forward at forty miles per hour.

I couldn't move. *I literally couldn't move.* I couldn't feel my arms and legs. I couldn't turn my head, which was positioned with a view of the slumping body of Chuck and the broken windshield in front of him. Smoke started pouring out of the hood, and then I heard the whooshing noise of a fire igniting.

I love it when a plan comes together my ass. I guess I was no Colonel John "Hannibal" Smith after all.

Closing my eyes, I thought of my ex-wife Kelly, my son Mike Jr., and sweet daughter Sadie, who had been dead for over a decade. I also thought of Brady, his son Jason, and his daughter I never met.

I was fine with dying for Brady's family. *But I should have been willing to die to save my own family.*

I swallowed down a sob. I wasn't going to go out crying, I had been through way too much to have it all end with a one-man pity party.

A thought occurred to me, and I let out a laugh, which sounded more like a gasp. I imagined the police trying to piece together what the two barbequed assholes in the van had been up to when they crashed their van into a trailer and burned to death. The van-rental company would have some questions as well.

I had left the gas can out on the sidewalk. The plan was to run up and douse the interior of the van with it after it crashed. It was a loose end and a clue to what may have happened.

I hoped that Brady had the sense to blame everything on the black guy if it came down to it. The deaths of Randy, Sam, and the Romanians. I should be the sole fall guy for the entire fiasco. I should have made that clear to Brady, but I hadn't expected to be a casualty in the final phase of a mission where all of the enemy combatants were eliminated hours ago.

The smell of gas and smoke was overpowering, with the fire consuming the entire front of the van. Hot smoke was filling my lungs, making me cough uncontrollably. Thirty gallons of gas in the tank would make for quite the fireworks show. Then fire ripped through the van as an explosion sounded.

Chris 11

5:15 a.m.

I took another pull from the bottle, this one even deeper, chugging for six or seven seconds before I gasped and started coughing. My ulcer burned in protest. My hand shook as I put the bottle down.

I started shivering again. The campground had become a fucking warzone. The Taj was missing. The trailer behind it exploded. The RVs along the fence had been evacuated. This shit was all Mike and Brady. Mike, Brady, and fucking me. *Me.*

It had been the most bizarre night of my life. Around 1:30 a.m., I spent a half-hour milling around on Starling with the others, trying to figure out what happened to the Taj. I inspected the RV tracks and noted how they intersected with the train tracks. Those crazy bastards used the hooks from my worksite to drag the RV behind the 1 a.m. train. The people inside that RV had to be totally wrecked.

Talking to the police was an option. *But wasn't I involved, having stolen the supplies?* I figured I was some sort of accomplice.

I went back to my camper and took another drink. I passed out for a while and then was awakened by a huge boom. The explosion was so loud it felt like the earth moved. I stumbled onto my feet from where I was slumped on the bench seat at the kitchen table, banging my knees so hard I unmoored the table and it crashed to the floor.

The bottle of vodka tumbled to the floor and started emptying. I scrambled over and set it upright, finding the lid and sealing it.

I was still dressed in shorts and a T-shirt. Finding my flip-flops, I stepped outside.

The outdoors was lit up like daytime. I could feel the heat radiating from the direction of Starling.

I cut through Brady's site and walked to the street, staring at the inferno that was the trailer directly behind the Taj site. The flames were easily twenty feet high. The fire had spread to the small shed out back.

People were gathering out on the street. A moment later, two cop cars moved slowly down the street, their blue lights on but not their sirens. They parked along the street in front of the gazebo and the Romanian's place, close to where Sam's SUV was parked.

"What is happening here?" a voice asked from behind. It was Brady. I stared at him for a moment, then looked back at the fire. An orchestra of sirens was blaring from the direction of downtown Sandusky, getting louder.

"Everything okay, Chris?" he asked. I didn't look at him.

"Was this part of the plan too?" I asked softly, turning to glare at him. His face hardened.

"I don't know what you're talking about. Any theoretical plan tonight would be *our plan.* Couldn't have done it without *you,*" he said, staring back at the burning trailer. Fire trucks arrived on Nickle Drive and zoomed over to the trailer lot.

"We'll talk later. Until then, keep your mouth shut," he said.

"Where are Chuck and Data at?" I asked.

"How the fuck would I know?" he asked with a shrug. He turned and walked back toward his site.

I walked back to my camper. I drank more vodka in an attempt to turn my mind off, and it mostly worked. I passed out, woke up, and drank a little more. My ulcer was burning, but I ignored it.

I wanted to fly. *I needed to.* Randy had set it up, but he was likely dead. *But how many people knew that?* Nobody at the airport would.

The train horn sounded, and I flinched. Every time I heard that sound, I would imagine the trailer launching and being dragged up to the tracks. *What kind of people did that?*

I went to the closet and drawers and took out the outfit Sam told me to wear to the airport. Business casual. Light gray pants, light blue shirt, brown belt, blue socks, brown shoes. There was also a navy-blue sports coat. I put that back; it seemed to be overkill. Putting the outfit aside, I grabbed a towel and my toiletries bag and went to the east shower house. The west one was too close to the

Taj and the burnt trailer; I didn't want to even look in that direction.

I brainstormed how I would get to the airport. I had no car and doubted the police would let anyone come and go from the campground. *Where the hell did the Taj go?* Once they found that trailer, the campground would become a crime scene. Was anyone inside that other trailer when it blew up?

I shaved and showered. On the way back to my trailer, I looked over to Chuck's RV. His golf cart hadn't been there all night. The last time I saw it was on the trail.

I returned to my camper. I found a clear poncho and started walking toward the trail.

It was getting brighter out. The sky still had plenty of gray clouds; more rain was possible. It felt like it was in the low sixties.

The trail was muddy, so I was careful to walk on the grassy part along the left side, to avoid ruining my dress shoes. My stomach dropped as I saw the golf cart about thirty yards ahead. Chuck was either kidnapped or dead. There was no way he would leave his cart up on the trail overnight; it was his baby.

I looked around. Nobody was out on the trail; it was too early and too wet. I used my hand to sweep some of the moisture off the seat and got in. According to the gauge, it still had half a charge. I turned the key and steered it onto the trail. If the golf cart had died last night, that would have explained Chuck leaving it there. But that wasn't the case.

I left the trail and headed toward the campground entrance. There was always the chance that nobody was there, and I could slip out.

But as I traveled up Seagull, I saw Travis in front of the booth, talking to a uniformed Sandusky police officer. Did I really want to explain why I was trying to leave with Chuck's golf cart? I took a right on Dove, heading north.

Suddenly, I just broke down sobbing. So hard I could barely see through the tears. I pulled to the side, slumping over the steering wheel and covered my face with my hands. *Get it together.*

The tears wouldn't stop. *What was I doing?* My gig at the airport was dead. Why bother with another fly-along? I wiped my eyes and headed back to my camper.

I took a big chug off the vodka bottle. I needed a wardrobe change.

Taking off my business-casual clothes, I dropped them in a pile on the floor. I dug into the back of my closet and found my blue air force service dress uniform.

It wasn't in bad shape, maybe a little dusty and wrinkled. There were tech sergeant patches on the upper sleeves, a white star in the middle of five white stripes. A respectable number of ribbons were pinned above the left pocket.

I took another big chug off the vodka bottle. I removed the uniform from the hanger and put it on. Even the stupid clip-on tie. I was always teased about it, especially in basic training, but I never gave in and learned to tie a real one.

The uniform was a little snug but wearable. I lost the shoes that went with it. My new dress shoes didn't match, but I put them on anyway.

I looked in the bathroom mirror. With my fresh haircut, I could pull off the appearance of an active-duty airman. I looked myself in the eye for a long moment, then fired off a crisp salute. The loser in the mirror returned it.

I walked outside, realizing I should be wearing an air force cap at all times outdoors. But I lost the cap, and who was going to correct me? Even if I had my cap on, carrying a bottle of vodka around in uniform was against regulations. I flipped off no one and took another drink.

I got back in Chuck's golf cart and headed north, driving around the pond and up the embankment leading to the train tracks. I fought back another sobbing fit as I headed east on the tracks.

I continued out on the train bridge that extended out over the lake parallel to the shore. It wasn't a traditional bridge; the tracks were suspended above the water, constructed on cement footers anchored to the bottom of the lake.

The tracks were too wide for the wheelbase of the golf cart to fit over both rails, so I straddled the left westbound track. The tracks were positioned above rows of parallel wooden slats, fastened to either cement or metal braces below, I assumed. No structures extended above the tracks, so if I veered too far to the side, I could easily drive right off the edge.

I stopped where the tracks turned southeast. I had a clear view of the little campground peninsula. I wasn't sure what time it was; I guessed maybe 6:45 a.m. I still had about a quarter of the vodka bottle left, so I took another drink.

Taking a deep breath, I tried to look at the sky, but the ceiling of Chuck's golf cart blocked my vision. I leaned over and saw a small plane gaining altitude after taking off from the airport and smiled.

It was surreal to be sitting out on a train bridge in Chuck's golf cart. Chuck was dead. He had to be dead. How did Mike kill him, with his bare hands? *Did he snap his neck?*

I looked down at the murky lake; it was almost a greenish color that near to the shore. It was probably ten feet deep. I could safely jump in without hitting the bottom.

I heard the train horn, closer, and felt the rumblings of it as it approached. It was probably going fifty or sixty miles per hour. The engineer would not be watching ahead very closely since he was about to travel onto a bridge with no possibility of colliding with a vehicle or a pedestrian. *Usually.*

I looked down at my uniform. The name tag was on the right side. *Randolph.* It was upside down to me. *Like everything in my life.*

The horn blasted again, and I saw the train. The entire bridge was vibrating. I clenched my teeth and felt them rattle.

It was a flying gray juggernaut, unstoppable, a rolling missile aimed at me. It promised violence and pain, but only for a moment, and then it would deliver darkness. *It would deliver peace.*

I could smell the exhaust of it, the engine, the grease, the rust, everything. The engineer must have spotted me. The horn started blaring, long, continuous blasts, over and over. I heard the screech as he engaged the brakes.

But he was going too fast. He could slow the train down, but he wasn't going to stop it.

I could see the large rusty boxcars being pulled behind the engine, two stories high, most of them covered with colorful spray-painted graffiti. I had no idea what they contained and didn't really give a shit.

I gave it some gas. Might as well go swiftly into the eye of the storm.

The horn was so loud, he was laying on it hard, and combined with the screeching of the wheels locking up, it made an awful, glorious symphony. The friction of metal on metal produced a strong smell similar to sulfur.

This was going out hard while going out easy. I closed my eyes and smiled as I felt the grand collision.

Acknowledgments

I was inspired to write Sandusky Burning while camping alone in my RV in that area several years ago. Our air conditioner needed to be repaired, so I drove the sixty miles from the suburbs of Cleveland and worked from the camper while awaiting the repairman.

I had rarely spent a moment alone there, and I looked at my surroundings from a different perspective. The transient, wide open nature of campgrounds provided a fertile environment for shady activities. I envisioned an underworld that preyed on resort town tourism, and let my imagination run wild from there.

I want to thank all of my friends who took the time to read my book in advance. The two beta readers I couldn't enlist were my parents, Bonnie and Larry, who passed away prior to publishing Sandusky Burning. I lost my mother in 2015 and my father died only a few months before my book was released. I had imagined surprising him with a copy for Christmas. I owe them both for instilling in me the love of reading and writing.

The Story Continues!

BRYAN W. CONWAY

SANDUSKY RECKONING

SANDUSKY DARKNESS
BOOK TWO

His friend is on life support. He's about to be next. As an RV campground becomes a war zone, will he be the next victim in a body bag?

Brady Sullivan won't go down without a fight. Hours after retaliating against the savage gang that attacked him and his family, he struggles to stay one step ahead of a corrupt sheriff pushing for his arrest. But he's forced to flee to another hideout when a vicious crime lord paints a target on his back...

Going dark in a motel room, Brady vows to balance the scales as cruelly staged photos surface endangering his floundering marriage and career. But with competing factions intent on setting him up for the fall, he fears any attempt to engage could end up dead on arrival.

Can he win a brutal power struggle before he takes a fatal bullet?

ABOUT THE AUTHOR

Bryan W. Conway was born and raised in Flint, Michigan. He has been an author, soldier, factory worker, lawyer, project manager, and personal fitness trainer. His hobbies include writing, reading, fitness, scuba diving, and chess. He currently resides in the suburbs of Cleveland, Ohio.

For more information, please visit:
www.bryanwconwayauthor.substack.com